UNDER THE RAVEN'S MOON

She stared up at him and bit her teeth slightly into her lower lip. "Will you take me as a pledge for my brother?" she asked. "I am the outlaw Simon hunts. He will be pleased with you for that."

Rowan drew a deep breath and let it out slow, stirring the dark, silky tendrils near her forehead. "If I decide to take down the Lincraig Rider, lass," he said softly, "I will do so when I please. On the highway or on the moor. Or in your own house. But you will not know when."

She watched him as a fledgling might watch a hawk, still and helpless, while innocence changed to awareness. "And then?" Her voice was a faint whisper.

He lowered his head until his forehead nearly touched hers. "And then we shall see what shall be done with the Lincraig Rider," he whispered.

The Raven's Moon

Susan King

A TOPAZ BOOK

TOPAZ
Published by the Penguin Group
Penguin Books USA Inc., 375 Hudson Street,
New York, New York 10014, U.S.A.
Penguin Books Ltd, 27 Wrights Lane,
London W8 5TZ, England
Penguin Books Australia Ltd,
Ringwood, Victoria Australia
Penguin Books Canada Ltd, 10 Alcorn Avenue,
Toronto, Ontario, Canada M4V 3B2
Penguin Books (N.Z.) Ltd, 182-190 Wairau Road,
Auckland 10, New Zealand

Penguin Books Ltd, Registered Offices:
Harmondsworth, Middlesex, England

First published by Topaz, an imprint of Dutton Signet,
a division of Penguin Books USA Inc.

First printing, February, 1997
10   9   8   7   6   5   4   3   2   1

For my sons
Joshua, Jeremy, and Sean
each one a joy and a privilege
and each one a hero

ACKNOWLEDGMENTS

Thanks go to Mary and Ed Furgol, for a rousing Burns Supper among other Scottish inspirations; to Ted Wells-Green, M.D., for diagnosing and suggesting treatment for fictional injuries; and most especially to Jo-Ann Power and Eileen Charbonneau for understanding so much, and for always being there, regardless of geography.

Chapter One

~

Scotland, the Borderlands
October 1588

The wind whirled around her like a living curse, cold and strong as a demon's breath. A sudden gust of rain made a billowing sail of her black cloak. She kept her horse steady beneath her and waited, focusing her gaze upon the dark road below.

Her body trembled in the next blast of wind and her knees quivered with fear. But Mhairi Macrae stayed still, tightening her grip on the reins and stiffening her spine. She refused to surrender to a sudden, intense impulse to flee.

She had to ride out again. Too much depended on the depth of her courage and the strength of her will, here and now. Her brother Iain, imprisoned and condemned, had no other champion.

Blinking the rain from her eyelashes, she looked down the slope of the hill and across the boggy moor. In the distance, the muddy road looked like a bit of unraveled brown ribbon. Three times now, in the past few weeks, she had waited on this hilltop for the council's messengers to ride along that road.

Those nights had been moonlit or misty, unlike the twilight storm that drenched her now. The rain, though, gave her and her companion, who had not yet arrived, the advantage of surprise. Anyone who rode past this place

would not expect to see other riders out on the moor in
such weather.

She grew more certain with each passing moment that
the messenger would come, sent by King James's privy
council to deliver documents to the warden of the Scottish
Middle March, whose tower lay not far from this place.
She sensed the rider's imminent approach deep in her gut,
a compelling foreboding.

Although she did not share the gift of Sight that her
twin Iain possessed through their mother, Mhairi had
often experienced keen twinges of dread or happiness. As
a child in the Highlands, she had learned to listen to those
mute inner urges.

Waiting on the hill, she felt a distinct heaviness in the
air, a frightening restlessness. At first, she had attributed
that to the shifting, turbulent weather. But now certainty
crackled along her skin like lightning.

A man would ride through here within an hour or two.
She would take this one down too, with her companion's
help. Without this intervention, Iain would forfeit his life,
wrongly accused and deeply mourned. Mhairi could not
allow that to happen.

Turning, she glanced at the ruined keep that crested
another hill a mere bowshot from where she sat. The high
corner tower rose gray and jagged in the rain, and the
crumbling outer walls looked cold, forbidding, and deserted. Inside, she knew, lay only broken stone and empty
passageways.

But Lincraig Castle was rumored to be haunted. For
decades, the local Scottish Borderers had skirted a wide
path around its walls. Rarely had anyone ventured inside.
Recently, the people of this March had begun to whisper
that the ghosts of Lincraig rode once again.

Wild and elemental, the wind shoved at her again, tugging at her cloak, loosening the dark braid that spilled
over her shoulder. Heavy summer rain pounded against
her hooded head. Such discomforts could be ignored,
though she found it less easy to dismiss the fear that battered her will.

Clutching the leather reins, she murmured soothingly
as her black mare sidestepped nervously. Drawing a

breath, Mhairi endeavored to find calm herself, and to be patient. To wait, however long it took.

Hunching her shoulders against the pelting rain, she looked toward Lincraig again. Devil's Christie Armstrong would arrive soon, and they would ride together, as before, to startle the messenger in the darkness. They would stun him if necessary, rob him of his pouch, and take the papers he carried, tossing coins and sundry aside. Then they would disappear into the murk, leaving the man to gallop off in haste; he would be terrified, as the other messengers had been, that the ghosts of the old keep rode out to take his very soul.

The reputation of the old ruin had served Mhairi and Devil's Christie well. But still they had not found what they sought. Perhaps this night they would finally capture the writ of execution that the March warden expected from the king's council. That, only that, was what Mhairi wanted. She had no interest in coin or valuables.

Watching the mucky, deserted length of road, Mhairi shifted her shoulders warily. A delicate prickling rose along her spine. Danger seemed to swirl around her in the whine of the wind, in the chill of the rain. Power seemed to sweep through the air. She knew that if she stood in its path, she would be forever changed. And yet she felt that she had no choice.

"Find your courage, Mhairi girl, and hold to it," she whispered, lifting her chin. "You must do this for Iain." And for his wife and new babe, who waited for him in a small stone house not far away.

She closed her eyes, and felt the cool rain on her cheeks, far cooler than the tears she would not shed, and thought of Iain, and thought of all that she had lost. And she remembered the warning that Iain had given her on the last night he had ridden out.

Far too late, now, to avoid the danger that he had foreseen. She drew in a deep breath, and with it came the memory of another twilight, only weeks ago.

Mhairi, Iain had said. *Mhairi, I had a vision.*

A tiny pool gleamed in the sunset like a fiery piece of sky fallen to earth. Mhairi lifted her skirt and stepped over the water. Turning on her bare feet in the long grass, she looked up at her brother.

"Tell me what you saw," she said.

Iain opened his mouth, then closed it, shaking his head. "I will," he said. "Later. I need to think about what it means."

She watched him, frowning. "I have had no visions, but I have a strong feeling," she said. "Alec Scott is a wild rogue. He will bring you trouble someday, Iain Macrae. Promise me you will not ride out with him this night."

"I must, *leth*," he answered her in Gaelic. "I only mean to help him gain back the cattle that reivers stole from him. Alec did the same for me when my own beasts were snatched by reivers."

"But, Iain"—she glanced at the darkening sky as she spoke—"do you not feel the unease here?"

"*Ach*, Mhairi. Unease rises with the moon in the Borders. There is no harm in riding in the moonlight with the wind at my back, and good Border friends at my side."

"And a sack of booty on your saddle, and beasts that are not yours herded before your horse, and the warden's men on your tail," she said. "You learned a taste for that when we left the Highlands to foster here with our Kerr cousins."

Iain grinned as if to admit the truth of her words, his gray eyes twinkling. The wind riffled his golden hair, and he shoved it back carelessly, looking so handsome, so familiar and dear to her, that Mhairi smiled too, in spite of her trepidation. She had ever been quieter, darker, more somber than her *leth-aoin*, her twin.

Leth, they had always called each other: half. Iain had the golden sparkle of their mother, Elspeth Fraser, turned to handsomeness and confidence. Mhairi was like their father, Duncan Macrae, dark and well-made, with a tendency toward seriousness. More patient and practical than Iain, Mhairi had always depended on his assured, easy manner.

They had fostered together in the same Kerr household in the Borderlands, surrounded by carefree reivers who had taught them to speak English, and to understand southern customs. And to reive swiftly, like the wind stealing the clouds that sail past the moon.

"Ride out reiving if you like, but not with Alec Scott," she said. "One day that one will call great trouble on his head."

"Do you worry because the March warden has dismissed him as a sergeant? I trust Alec more than I do Simon Kerr." He smiled gently. "I pay rent for my house to his grandfather, the Auld Laird, and I owe fealty to them for the privilege. The Blackdrummond Scotts have befriended me, now that I'm wed and settled here, though I am a Highlander in their midst."

She scowled. "None of the Scott family can be our friends," she said. "They are outlaws and murderers."

Iain sighed. "Will your heart never heal?"

"How can it?" She lifted her chin stubbornly. "Scotts killed my betrothed. I will not forget that." Shivering, Mhairi folded her arms. "Do you not feel the danger coming?" She glanced up at the rapidly scudding clouds.

"Just another summer storm approaching. We have had many this season," Iain said. She thought his tone overly reassuring. "Be calm, Mhairi. I will be back before dawn. Watch over my Jennet for me. She is restless at night as her time draws closer. You did come here to help Jennet with her babe."

"And to urge you to move back into the Highlands where you belong," Mhairi said petulantly.

Iain watched the wild sky. "I know you do not like it here in the Borderlands, Mhairi."

"And you love it here. But you have Jennet," she said softly. "And two years past, I did want to be here, where Johnny Kerr was. But he is in the ground now." A familiar, wrenching grief coiled inside her. "After he was killed, I meant never to return here."

"You came to see my child born, and I thank you for it."

"Thank our parents. They urged me to come."

"*Ach,* you did not want to sail with them over the cold sea to Denmark," Iain said, teasing her. "Or did you think you needed to look after me?"

"Let Jennet look after you," she retorted. "But I would not want to see you taken down in the moonlight. Stay here this night, Iain," she urged somberly.

"All will be well," he said. But Mhairi heard the doubt

in his voice. He looked past her, and she suddenly heard distant hoofbeats on the soft turf, but did not turn. She knew the approaching rider was Alec Scott.

"Tell me your vision, Iain," she said quickly. "Tell me."

He toed the long grass, shaking tiny seeds into the small, shining pool between their feet. Then he nodded. "I looked into a pool, no larger than this one, and the vision came to me then."

"When was this?"

"I was herding the sheep in the hills a few days past, and I knelt to have a drink. I saw a rainstorm reflected in the water. A demon of a storm, with black clouds and thunder and lightning. The sky was sunny and blue that day, but the whole surface of the pool had gone dark as night. I watched the pool, and saw lightning breaking white over the dark hills. And I saw a rider in the midst of the storm."

"Who was he?"

"I do not know. He galloped on a horse in the black of night, through heavy rain. When the lightning flashed again, I saw the gleam of his weapons. He looked like a soldier, or a Border rider. A tall man, dark. He was deter- mined, even desperate somehow. Danger lay ahead of him, and behind him. And I knew that he rode through this wild storm to find someone. There was not much time left to him.

"I saw him ride up a hill, screaming out a name over and over. Turning around, calling out desperately." He stopped.

A cold, delicate chill slipped along her spine. "What name did he call?"

"Your own, Mhairi," he said.

Fear stole her breath for an instant. "Where was this man riding? And what does he have to do with us?"

"He was here in the Borderlands, I think. And he rode through that storm looking for you."

"But why? Who is he?"

Iain shook his head. "I do not know. But I felt that he had to find you before I—" He paused. "Before I died," he finished quietly.

She gasped, touching her fingers to her lips.

"The image faded after that," Iain said. "Who this man

is, or why he will ride through that storm, I do not know. But danger surrounds him somehow. And I felt something else, Mhairi. His deep need to find you."

"I do not understand," she whispered. She wanted him to stop talking of this disturbing vision. Shivery bumps raised along her arms, bringing a sense of dread and power—and truth.

"He was frightened for you, Mhairi. I felt his fear, his need to find you. His powerful love for you."

"Love!"

He nodded. "As if he were a man who would take any risk, lay out his very life for the woman he loved. For you."

"There is no love in this, only danger," she said. "Iain, what of you? Why was your life threatened in this vision?"

"I do not know," he answered somberly.

She frowned, crossing her arms tightly over her chest, fear rolling through her. "The vision you saw must be related to the unease that I have been feeling. Iain, please do not ride out."

"Mhairi, what I saw—the rider, the storm—might not be a true vision."

She shot him a doubtful glance. "True or not, it is a warning of some kind. He is likely a demon of a man who will bring only disaster and death. How could such a man feel love for me?" She huffed a bitter laugh. "That part must be wrong. But the rest—Iain, please stay here."

"I cannot hide in my house because of a vision."

"What if that stormy night is this one?"

He paused. "Then what will be, will be."

Her gaze fastened to his, gray mirroring gray. Then Iain looked past her, and Mhairi turned.

Shadowed black against the twilight sky, Alec Scott sat on his horse at the edge of the yard. His steel helmet caught a glint of red from the streaked sky. He lifted a hand silently.

Iain grabbed Mhairi in a quick, fierce hug. "Watch after Jennet for me," he said gruffly.

"You know I will," she whispered. Iain strode across the darkening yard to untether his waiting horse, then mounted to join Alec Scott.

Mhairi turned away abruptly, unwilling to watch him ride away. She feared that he might never return, although she had not had any vision of disaster. She only felt it: a cold, heavy, hard burden.

The hoofbeats faded into the wind. Mhairi lifted her gaze to the brilliant sky, where black clouds scudded ominously toward the rising moon.

She wrapped her arms around herself against the sudden chill. And wondered about the man who would ride through a wild storm to bring a threat to Iain and to her. She could not accept what Iain had said about the man's feelings for her.

Only danger approached, as surely as that overhead storm.

Cold, wet trickles ran along her brow and cheeks. Mhairi tilted her head inside the shelter of her wide hood and opened her eyes, sucking in a deep breath, stirring herself out of her thoughts.

She glanced again at the muddied, empty strand of road below the hill. Though she saw nothing, the messenger's approach pounded in her gut and in her heart, as forceful and real as the raindrops that struck her.

A flood of anticipation went through her, a crackling tension, as if an instant of lightning streaked through her veins. The feeling was as alarming as it was exhilarating.

She peered through the downpour at the heavy sky, and wondered again, as she had so often during rainfall, if this storm would bring the man whom Iain had foreseen.

If he came this night, she would be waiting.

Chapter Two

~

"Trust yow no Scott."

—Andrew Boorde, in a letter to
Thomas Cromwell, 1536

Black clouds moved across the sky as if they were the devil's own galleons, buoyed on the strength and flow of the wind. Rowan Scott leaned his shoulder against the doorframe of the inn and looked upward. *Rain will sweep in before dark,* he thought. He ignored a shouted demand, which came from someone inside the inn, to shut the door. Sipping ale from a pewter flagon, he studied the violent sky.

He had heard it said that the breath of Jehovah had produced the frequent and heavy storms that had buffeted Scotland all this year. The weather had been equally severe in England, where he had heard it claimed that the Almighty had sent powerful winds and waves into the English Channel to help defeat the Spanish Armada just two months earlier.

The breath of God had continued to huff at the fleeing Spanish ships as they had headed north to sail around Scotland and return home. But the treacherous northern waters and relentless storms had swallowed several galleons, many of which were overloaded with treasure and cannon.

Rowan had seen the jagged remains of one galleon that had washed up on a Scottish beach several weeks ago. The hull and mast had lain along the strand like the stripped bones of some monstrous water beast. He had walked among the debris, and as a Border officer sent to

the site by the Scottish privy council, had helped to super-
vise the gathering of salvaged gold.

Remembering it now, he sighed. That Spanish wreck
had entrapped him in this dilemma. Had he never walked
upon that beach, he would not be standing here now,
about to ride home to Blackdrummond Tower again. He
would not have the council's orders to find his rogue of a
brother—long before Rowan felt prepared to face him.

He peered out into the wind and darkness, yet no one
rode toward the inn. He had waited here for Geordie Bell
for over two hours. Uttering a sigh as if it were a curse,
Rowan turned away from the doorway and strode back to
his seat in the corner near the hearth. Someone got up and
slammed the door shut against the wind.

Rowan sat with his back to the wall, angled so that he
could see the wild, darkening sky through a small
window. He felt the warmth of the hearth fire heating his
left side, from the top of his head to the square toe of his
long boot, as he relaxed against the wall. When the innkeeper passed nearby, carrying a large crockery jug, he
motioned for another fill of threepenny ale.

"Wicked night," the man muttered, shaking his balding
head. Rowan nodded and slid a few coins across the table.
"Storm's coming in from the west. Ye'll be wanting a
bed, then?"

Taking a quick sip of the thin stuff, swallowing, Rowan
shook his head. "I'll ride out soon enough. I trust that my
horse is as well fed as I am."

"Och, ye ride the fine bay stallion? He's well cared
for—my own son tends the stable. Stay here and travel on
the morrow, man. The de'il himself wouldna ride out on
such a night."

"That may be," Rowan said. "But I'll leave shortly."

The innkeeper narrowed his eyes. "Ye're a familiar
face. One o' the Scotts, I think, hey?"

He nodded, a little surprised. "Rowan Scott o' Blackdrummond."

The man grinned. "Hey now, Blackdrummond himself!
Welcome, man. Ye've been gone a while from the Middle
March, I think."

"Three years," Rowan said softly.

The innkeeper leaned closer, his breath heavy with

meat and a stronger ale than what he had served Rowan. "I was well puzzled when the English March warden named the Black Laird o' Blackdrummond a thief and a murderer those years back," he said. "All o' us here knew ye for a fine and notorious Scottish reiver, and nae petty brigand."

"Notorious I was, but 'tis changed now," Rowan said evenly.

"Och, time spent in an English prison willna stop a Blackdrummond Scott. That lot is born to reiving and riding," the innkeeper said. "Yer brother Alec is another one, hey?"

Rowan sipped his ale without replying.

"Hardly a riding family on either side o' the border has more outlaws to its credit than the Blackdrummond Scotts." The man grinned again. "My own kin have ridden out wi' kin o' yers. Armstrongs, we are."

"Ah. Fine riding companions, your kinsmen," Rowan said.

"And ye'll ride again wi' us, now that ye're back, hey."

"I dinna think 'twould be wise," Rowan said. "I've been named a deputy here in the Middle March."

"Aye?" The man chuckled. "Well, there's naught more common in the Borderlands than a reiver named an officer." He scratched at his bald head, a bemused grin on his face. "A Blackdrummond Scott is deputy to Simon Kerr now, hey. I like that, I do. The king's council has a way wi' a jest. Here, man, I willna take yer coin. Drink as much as ye will, and welcome to it." He pushed the coins toward Rowan, and, still chuckling, picked up the ale jug and walked away.

Smiling faintly, a little bitterly, Rowan eased his shoulders against the wall again and stretched out his long legs, in high black boots, beneath the table. Word of reiving forays, arrests, and newly appointed officers traveled fast in the Middle March. He was certain that the innkeeper would spread the word about Rowan Scott's new position. Well enough, for it would save him the trouble of establishing his authority in the March.

Doubtless word had already preceded him concerning his equally notorious brother, Alec Scott. Another rogue from Blackdrummond Tower, Rowan thought wryly. He

wondered what the innkeeper would have said if he had
known why the Scottish council had sent the Black Laird
back here again.

Sighing, he picked up the silver coins and dropped
them into the leather pouch that hung from his belt. He
withdrew a small gold medallion and held it in his fingers,
turning it in the firelight.

Elaborately engraved, the center of the golden oval
contained the tiny figure of a saint in delicate relief. Tiny
letters spelled out a prayer in Spanish on the reverse side.

Closing his hand over it, Rowan glanced around the
crowded, noisy room. None of the other men seemed to
notice him, absorbed as they were in drinking ale, gambling, and teasing the redhaired serving lass who laughed
along with them. He watched them, wondering if any of
them knew the information that he sought, or knew anything about missing Spanish gold.

He turned the medallion thoughtfully between two fingers, then dropped it back into his pouch. The piece had
washed ashore after the wreck of the Spanish galleon,
along with a few coins and a polished stone mirror that he
had picked up and kept. Rowan had not bothered to seek
out English officials to give them items of such scant
value, despite his orders.

Bright pieces of gold and silver, coughed out of the sea,
had disappeared into the pockets of Scottish fishermen.
Rowan had not begrudged them their profit, although he
had been told to collect any scavenged items for English
authorities.

Queen Elizabeth's advisers had regarded the salvage as
victor's spoils following the defeat of the Armada. They
were furious now that two large sacks of the salvaged
stuff had been stolen from that Scottish beach. In part,
Rowan mused, that theft had drawn him here on this
demon of a night.

He glanced out the window again. Trees whipped in the
rising wind. He frowned, concerned that Geordie Bell had
not arrived. The English March deputy, both a friend and
a reiving companion from years earlier, had arranged to
meet him here before set of sun, claiming that he had
some information concerning the missing gold.

Rowan had not intended to wait here so long. He was

anxious to travel on to Blackdrummond Tower, since he
had already sent word to his grandparents that he would
arrive that night. His home was only an hour's ride from
the inn, but the storm, if it hit full force, would slow him
considerably, and he did not want Anna and Jock Scott to
worry over him.

Still, he decided to wait a few more minutes. Settling
back, he slipped his hand inside his sleeveless leather
jack, which he wore over a woolen doublet and shirt. He
withdrew a round, flat object nearly as wide as his palm,
wrapped in linen.

Uncovered, the smooth, polished black stone winked at
him like a dark star, just as it had the day he had found it
washed ashore on the beach. He ran a finger slowly over
its convex surface and the surrounding wooden frame.
Clearly the plain piece, lacking fine materials, had little
value, but he thought it a curious thing, and a serviceable
mirror. He planned to give it to his grandmother, along
with the little medallion, though his grandfather would
think that a silly papist gewgaw.

The carved wooden frame, gilded and cracked, had
empty niches where semiprecious stones might once have
been set. The frame circled a slick stone which looked
like onyx, though its thickness was smokier, slightly
translucent.

The surface, as he angled it one way and another,
reflected first the firelight in the wide hearth, then the
stormy sky beyond the window. Rowan wondered if the
stone had been made as a hand mirror, for it was too large
to be jewelry. Tilting it again, he saw a clear reflection of
his face.

He had not often seen his own image: a lean, dark
man who appeared younger than he felt. He looked tired
and hard-edged after a short night's sleep. He could
see, too, the traces of deeper fatigue from a long prison
confinement.

His features were strong, stubborn, and well-balanced,
much like his father had been. Like his father, too, his
hair and beard stubble were as black as the stone he held.
But his mouth resembled his late mother's, and his black-
fringed eyes were hers; even in the firelight, they were as
green and deep as the northern sea.

Suddenly his image dissolved and faded, replaced by the turbulent sky. Tipping the mirror, he found a face again. But it belonged to a young woman.

Startled, Rowan glanced up, but the serving lass was nowhere to be seen. He looked back at the mirror. The girl was there still, like a ghostly, misty dream image. He saw wide, calm gray eyes, a delicate chin, a graceful cascade of dark hair. Her serene face seemed to float, perfect and eternal, somewhere inside the stone.

Rowan tilted the mirror, and the image disappeared. He turned it over, certain that a portrait had been cleverly painted on the back to give the illusion of a vision through the stone. But the thick wooden backing of the frame revealed nothing. He examined it from the side, and saw only smoky translucency, with no hint of soft blushing color, no exquisitely modeled face. She had dissolved like a dream, and he could not recapture her.

His own face was there again—keen eyes, a frown, long hair in need of trimming. He rubbed the slick surface with the sleeve of his doublet, and peered again: only his face, and a few brilliant points of firelight. The woman must have been some sort of strange waking dream. Perhaps he was greatly in need of some rest; perhaps the threepenny had been far stronger than he had thought.

He rewrapped the mirror and slipped it inside his jack. Then he picked up his sloped-brim helmet from the bench, settled it on his head, and stood. Fastening his dark brown cloak, he left the inn with a brief wave to the innkeeper.

He was disappointed to have missed Geordie Bell, but if his former comrade wanted to find him, the Englishman would just have to send word to Blackdrummond Tower. For now, Rowan wanted to ride out before the storm grew worse and he changed his mind about traveling on such a devil's night.

He opened the door of the inn and stepped out, shutting it firmly behind him. Ducking his head against the force of the wind, he crossed the length of the innyard toward the stable, intent on fetching his horse and weapons.

The howl of the approaching storm masked the sound of footsteps behind him until too late. Laying his hand on the hilt of his dirk, he began to turn. Someone grabbed both of his arms from behind, jerking him backward so that he momentarily lost his footing.

A large, powerful arm circled his chest, and the sharp edge of a dirk pressed against his throat with enough insistence that Rowan ceased to struggle. He craned his head sideways, but the slanted brim of his helmet blocked his view of his attacker.

He stood still, gripping his fist tightly. He would have slammed that fist into the man's face, or his elbow into the substantial gut behind him, if he had been able to move his arm.

"Give over what you've got," a rough, low voice said. Equally as tall as Rowan, the man was a good deal heavier, judging by the leaden weight of the arm that squeezed his chest.

"Give you what?" he gasped. The man jerked back on Rowan's chest, causing him to exhale faster than he cared to do. The keen knife edge cut, very slightly, into his skin. He felt the sting, and the first drop of blood.

If he moved forward, he would slice his own throat. But if he moved backward or grabbed for his sword, he would invite the attack of the blade. The slash of the knife would be swifter than any movement he could make.

"The moon," the man growled. "Do you have it?"

Rowan shot his gaze sideways, but saw, past his helmet brim, only a broad neck and a whiskered jaw. Another man, tall and bulky, stood in front of him, wearing a sleeveless jack of frayed, quilted leather. His broad face was covered by a thick brown beard, and a conical shaped helmet shadowed his eyes.

"Moon? What the devil do you mean?" Rowan rasped out. Perhaps these were not thieves, as he had first thought, but mad vagabond soldiers. Crazed, and asking for the moon.

"The raven's moon," the bearded man said. "We know you were there on that beach where the Spaniard ship wrecked. We're thinking you have something that we want. The raven's moon."

"I have naught o' value," Rowan said.

"Check his pouch," barked the man with the knife.

The bearded man tore open Rowan's leather pouch and

reached inside. "Coins, and a wee papist thing," he growled, snatching the medallion. "Nae stone."

"Look again," the first man said. The other one thrust his hand back into Rowan's pouch and fumbled around again.

Rowan wondered if they sought the black stone mirror, but he dismissed that. These ruffians would not covet such an unpretty thing, lacking gold or jewels to give it worth. The men clearly had jumped him to steal gold, and Spanish gold in particular.

He sensed a slight relaxation in the hand that held the blade to his throat. Rowan tipped his head backward suddenly and slammed his helmet against the nose behind him. Then he jutted his elbow into the man's solid belly and kicked his foot into his knee. His captor howled and began to fall. The knife blade fell away, and the restraining arm loosened.

Breaking free, Rowan kicked at the second man and caught him in the knee as well. Then he slammed the edge of his hand into the man's broad throat. As the brigand stumbled backward and fell beside his comrade, Rowan drew his dirk.

An explosive sound ripped through the howl of the wind. Something zipped past his helmet, sounding like a fast bee. As Rowan glanced around to see who had fired the gun, his attackers scrambled to their feet and barreled into him, knocking him off balance. The larger man grabbed him around the legs and slammed him down to the damp ground.

Another shot sounded. Both attackers stumbled hastily over Rowan and ran past, less like thieves than like opponents in a football match who had just grabbed the ball.

Catching his breath as he got to his feet, Rowan launched forward in pursuit as the men ran out of the yard. Even if they got away, he would find them. He had not seen their faces clearly, nor did they have distinguishing armor. Both wore leather jacks, sloping helmets, and long boots, the common gear of many Bordermen. But he would know their sturdy, big builds and each man's manner of running—the larger one moved like a mummer's trained bear—if he ever saw them again.

He heard a shout, and glanced back. A wide-shouldered

redhaired man, grinning and waving two smoking pistols, ran toward him. Rowan waved at Geordie Bell and raced ahead.

Within seconds, Rowan had covered the length of the yard, tearing past the stable and out onto the moor, where he had seen the two men disappear over a hill. Geordie caught up with him, breathing heavily, and together they crested a grassy slope.

Rowan ran along the hilltop and watched as two horses galloped across the moorland with riders hunkered low on their backs. He swore loudly and turned.

"At least you're unharmed," Geordie panted, shoving the pistols into his belt. "I was riding toward the inn when I saw them take you down. I was too far away to save you."

"Godamercy, man. You might have put a lead ball in my brain if you'd been closer," Rowan growled. He took off his helmet, shoved his fingers through his hair, and drew a deep breath.

"What did those rogues want from you?" Geordie asked.

Rowan shrugged. "They took a few bits o' gold from my pouch. And they demanded something called a raven's moon. I thought they were crazed at first."

"Raven's moon? Sounds like a night for witches."

"They mentioned a stone of some kind. I dinna know who those two ruffians are, but I wouldna doubt that they are tied to that missing Spanish salvage. They knew I had been on that beach, and they wanted this thing from me—and seemed willing to slice my throat to get it."

" 'Tis possible they've been looking for you since you left the beach two weeks past and went to Edinburgh. Rowan—did you pick up aught from that Spanish wreck? Something of value?"

Rowan lifted a brow slowly. "Would I do that?"

Geordie grinned, so engagingly that Rowan laughed too, a hollow, unaccustomed sound at first that soon grew. "Well, I found a nice garnet and a gold brooch when I was on that shore," Geordie said. "I gave it to my wife. I thought Queen Elizabeth would not miss one brooch, after all."

"Ah, you're a reiver to the heart—for an Englishman."

Geordie chuckled. "I once rode with the best, the Blackdrummond Scotts. Tell me what you found on that beach," he added in a more serious tone.

"Only a small gold medallion and a few coins, which they took. And I found this," Rowan said. He drew the dark mirror out of his jack and loosened its wrapping. "It washed ashore after the English officers had packed up and gone home. So I kept it."

"That? Hardly looks as if it has any worth." Geordie peered at the black stone. "Hey! An ugly thing, too."

" 'Tis just the reflection o' your face," Rowan said wryly as he dropped the mirror inside his leather pouch.

"Could that be the raven's moon?"

"Why would they want to snatch this thing? They obviously thought I had something valuable from that wreck."

"True. Raven's moon. Hmm. Perhaps 'tis a black pearl," Geordie mused. "Queen Elizabeth would covet such a thing highly. I heard she has raised hellfire with her council over fetching every bit of coin and fancy gewgaw that washed ashore." He scratched his bristly chin. "Spies would do much to gain a valuable prize wanted by the English queen."

"If those rogues were the men that the Scottish privy council mentioned to me, then your queen wants them found."

"Aye, Scottish agents working for Spain would be a dangerous threat to her. I hear Spain pays highly for the services of spies willing to help Spain invade England. And Elizabeth fears such efforts will get her assassinated. Of course she wants them found, and fast. So the council explained this to you?"

"They did." Rowan looked at him evenly. "Your English government doesna trust me, but the Scottish council has some faith in me still."

"You're a rogue and a reiver, Rowan Scott," Geordie said, "but I'd ride with you to the gates of hell."

Rowan huffed a flat laugh. "My thanks, man. May it never come to that. The council has appointed me to the post of deputy in the Middle March. I'm to pursue these men and find out what I can about the missing gold. But I didna expect the scoundrels to jump me as soon as I set foot outside the inn."

Geordie nodded. "I just learned about your post. 'Tis why I wanted to meet you here. And I've heard something of the rest of your assignment," he added grimly.

Rowan watched the sky, where the clouds ran fast and dark. "They say Alec has taken up with Spanish agents. He and another reiver were caught carrying Spanish gold. His comrade was arrested, but Alec got away."

"And you're to find him."

"Hey, the best man for the task," Rowan said, a false lift in his intonation. "But the council doesna know that I willna ride out after my brother for king or warden, or anyone else."

"I understand your loyalty—"

" 'Tisna loyalty," Rowan said flatly. He did not utter his next thought: *If I see Alec, I may kill him.*

Geordie watched him for a moment. "Is it Maggie?" he asked softly. "Or is it because of your prison term?"

"Maggie is dead," Rowan reminded him bluntly. "And as for the time I spent in English confinement, 'tis past too. But I willna ride out, either to save him or to hang him."

"Brother or not, you'd best find these spies, or you'll be the one to hang."

Rowan turned, his senses sharpened by the edge in Geordie's tone. "What do you mean?"

" 'Tis why I wanted to meet you here," Geordie said. "The English officers have sent word to Queen Elizabeth's advisers that the notorious Rowan Scott knows where the gold has gone. They mean to accuse you officially if the Spanish gold is not found soon."

"On what basis?"

"They reason that you were there on that beach, and that you are a reiver and a usurper of authority."

"A known thief and rebel, and the likeliest suspect," Rowan said. He repeated the phrase from memory. The English had used just such logic to condemn him, three years back. He scowled as he looked up at the wind-driven storm clouds. "So I will receive another valentine from the English."

"An arrest warrant? Very likely, unless the gold is found."

"Easy enough to find spies in the Border," Rowan said

sarcastically. "Two Scotsmen in jacks and steel helmets. There must be five thousand like them."

"What do you mean to do?"

"What choice do I have? I'll find these spies. If I run, I will be named an outlaw wi' my brother."

Geordie offered his hand, and Rowan grasped it firmly. "Take care, then," Geordie said. "Watch that rogue's neck of yours, my friend. 'Tis worth a ransom in Spanish gold."

Chapter Three

~

There came a wind out o' the north,
A sharp wind and a snell,
And a deep sleep came o'er me
And frae my horse I fell.

—*"Tam Lin"*

The horse shifted restlessly in the driving rain, hooves pawing the muddy ground. Mhairi leaned forward and patted the broad black neck, slick with moisture. "Steady now, Peg, my friend," she murmured in Gaelic. "Steady, girl. Soon we will ride fast and far, and take this messenger down. And then we will find you a warm, dry place and something to eat."

She heard the soft nicker of a horse behind her, and turned. A man rode toward her, cloaked and hooded against the drenching rain. Christopher Armstrong lifted a hand in greeting as he drew his horse to a halt beside her.

"The storm is worsening, Mhairi," he said. His youthful voice was reedy, in keeping with his long, lanky, adolescent body. "You've waited here a long while. No one will travel the Lincraig road in this weather. Come home now, back to Jennet's house. She has a hot meal ready."

"The messenger comes this way," Mhairi said stubbornly.

"Aye, tomorrow perhaps. Surely by now he's taken shelter at some inn or a croft on the moor."

"He is close," she said. "We would likely see him already in the distance if the rains werena so heavy."

"Mhairi—"

"I will stay."

Christie shoved back a strand of his damp blond hair

and sighed in resignation. "Well, stay, if you will be wet
as a fish. But we mustna ride after this man. My kinsmen
told me that this messenger would ride through here, but
they warned me to leave him be."

She shook her head. "I canna do that."

"He isna like the others, Mhairi. This one willna be
frightened o' Lincraig's haunts. 'Tis too great a risk. Let
him pass."

"I canna."

"This man is dangerous, they told me," Christie said.
"They had heard word in Edinburgh that the council
would send him."

Her grip tightened on the reins, a swift reaction to his
ominous words. "What did they hear of him?" she asked.

"He's a notorious reiver. 'Tis all they said."

Mhairi smiled a little, knowing that the Border hills
were full of notorious reivers. She had learned that many
of them were sound and good men, though overbold in
moonlight forays against their enemies.

"As notorious as you will be someday, Devil's Christie?" she teased gently, using the riding name given him
by his reiving kinsmen.

He grinned. "Almost," he replied, then frowned. "I
mean it, Mhairi. Let this one pass if you treasure your
life."

"I treasure my brother's life," she said firmly. "As do
you, for Iain is your sister's husband. I would not be out
here otherwise. I would not be in the Borderlands at all,
but home in the Highlands."

Christie was silent as he watched the sweep of rainy
moor and road. "Look there," he said sharply, after a few
moments. Mhairi peered through the dismal blur of rain.

A fair distance away yet, a man rode a bay horse at a
slow, steady canter. Tall and wide-shouldered beneath his
soaked hood and cloak, the rider sat straight, his head
bowed only slightly.

Watching the manner in which he rode his horse
through the rain, Mhairi sensed the messenger's weari-
ness as well as his determination. Despite sheeting
rain and failing light, he had not taken shelter for the
night. She knew, suddenly, that this messenger would not
give up.

Neither would she.

"Aye, here he comes," she said. "Alone and wet to the skin. He rides as slow and careful as an old woman." She gathered the reins. "The ghosts of Lincraig Castle will have his papers from him quicklike, and say—*Boo*! And he'll ride off in fright like the others. He doesna look dangerous to me."

"More than you know," Christie muttered.

"If you dinna want to do this, I will take him down myself," she said, more boldly than she felt. Urging Peg forward a little, she watched through rain and murk as the messenger rode steadily closer along the narrow ribbon of highway.

A sudden chill went through her. The foreboding that she had felt earlier returned tenfold. Destiny, she thought suddenly. Destiny and purpose rode with this man. She shivered, but the chill was not from cold.

Perhaps this man is the one. But she shook her head as soon as the thought came. He could not be the man Iain had predicted would ride through storm and danger to find her, only her. This messenger rode toward the March warden's tower, as he had been ordered. He did not know that she and Christie waited on the crest of the hill.

She shivered again. Chill and fatigue, she told herself, from being out in the cold and the wet too long. Dismissing the rest of her thoughts as folly and nonsense, she drew a breath and watched the approaching rider.

She did not care if the man was dangerous, as Christie had warned, or as slow-witted as the other messengers. Mhairi only wanted to know if he carried a warrant that could harm Iain. He must not be allowed to give it to the warden.

Her heart beat rapidly, and her hands flexed and tightened on the reins. A sensation spooled down her back, a lightning surge that tingled and spread through her body. The rain beat all around her and the wind tore at her cloak, but Mhairi did not take her gaze from the man who rode relentlessly closer.

Rowan sneezed. Hurtling through wind, rain, and increasing darkness, he muttered a curse as he shifted the reins and bent his head inside his hood. Sharp, slanting

raindrops beat over his shoulders as he rode toward
Blackdrummond Tower.

Rain drenched his cloak and hair and ran in miserably
cold rivulets down his cheeks into his stubbled beard.
His leather jack and the rest of his clothing were nearly
soaked in places, and his feet squished uncomfortably
inside his long boots.

Earlier, he had removed his helmet because the pattering rain against its steel surface and brim had produced
a maddening, tedious noise. Pulling at the hood of his
sodden woolen cloak, he peered through twilight and
dense rain.

The earthen roadway had turned to muck, and the
grassy fields to mire. Murky light made the twisting route
even more hazardous. As the road slanted upward, Rowan
slowed the horse to a walk, not wanting the bay to break a
leg, or to plunge over the side of a steep hill.

He was familiar with the slopes and curves of these
hills and moors, for he had ridden this way many times in
weather as fierce as this. But he had not been through here
for years. At this slow pace, he doubted he would make it
home before complete darkness swallowed up every
detail of the landscape.

He swore, and then, because it felt good, swore again,
crude and loud. That vented some of his frustration at
being delayed, but did not relieve the wet, the chill, or the
fatigue.

At least the weather would be sufficient insurance
against reivers along the road, he thought. On bonny
moonlit nights, clandestine traffic often crisscrossed these
moors—stealthy riders, both Scottish and English, and
their stolen cattle and sheep. He had ridden on many such
raids himself, as had generations of Blackdrummond
Scotts. But he had no desire to meet a group of reivers out
here alone, on a slippery road.

On a dry night, with men at his back, he would relish
such an encounter. The letter tucked inside his boot to
keep it safe from road thieves—hopefully the ink had not
blurred into an indecipherable mess—guaranteed that he
would ride here both in moonlight and daylight, as deputy
warden in the Middle March.

He knew this wide expanse of territory well, and knew

most of the lairds, tenant farmers, and herdsmen who inhabited it. A good proportion of them were Border reivers as well: cattle and sheep thieves, many of them honest men, some of them scoundrels, rogues, and rascals. He had been raised in their midst.

Rowan considered, as he traveled along the muddy road, the unknown Scotsmen who had forged a spy link with the Spanish crown. Borderers tended to be fiercely loyal to kin and companion, and less so to their sovereign. The greater rascals among such a lot might be tempted by the glitter of Spanish gold. He intended to find them if they were hiding in this area.

He had accepted the council's assignment with one private reservation. Until he had spoken with Geordie Bell, he had been unwilling to pursue his own brother, not out of loyalty, but out of a desire never to see Alec again. When he had heard about the English accusations, he had realized that he would have to find Alec in order to save his own life.

Simon Kerr, the March warden, had sent word to the council that he fully intended to find Alec Scott, who had fled into the hills the night his comrade had been arrested. Kerr stated that Alec and his friend had carried Spanish gold from England into Scotland. The warden had requested that the council allow him to give his prisoner into English custody for trial and punishment.

The Scottish council had been aware that Rowan's younger brother was suspected in the matter when they had appointed Rowan to the task of finding the spies. Most Scottish Border officers were related to reivers, or were reivers themselves. King James and his advisers believed that such men could best discipline the wild Borderers. Despite the thievery, feuds, and favoritism that continued among many of the officers, the plan was moderately successful.

Smiling grimly as he rode through the soaking rain, Rowan decided that the post suited him well after all. The notorious Black Laird of Blackdrummond was now deputy to a Kerr. He enjoyed that irony, especially where it concerned a Kerr; that family had feuded with the Scotts for generations.

Rowan halted his horse to scan the dreary rain-soaked

blur of rounded hills and low, gloomy clouds. In the distance, he recognized the ancient ruin of Lincraig Castle, a pile of broken stone and cobwebbed passages that had been built by an ancestor of his own branch of the Scotts.

Blackdrummond Tower lay fewer than two miles north, past the broad hill that stretched beyond the old ruin. Darkness would arrive before he did, but he would be home soon.

The bay horse whickered softly and pricked his black-tipped ears forward, clearly uneasy.

"What is it, Valentine?" Rowan asked. "Do you sense the ghosts in that old keep? Settle, lad. They willna harm us." The horse stepped restively to the side. Rowan stilled him and sneezed again, a loud, ripping snort that startled his horse. Patting the bay's neck reassuringly, he urged him forward, but the stallion shifted sideways and whickered.

"Ho, Valentine," Rowan said softly. "Phantoms, hey? I doubt you'll see any reivers in this rain." But he felt a prickling sense at the back of his neck, as if someone watched him. Narrowing his eyes, he turned slowly.

Silhouetted on a hill not far from Lincraig, a single horseman sat stone still. Rowan could make out a wind-blown black cloak and hood and a black horse, but rain and distance obscured other detail. He saw no glint of helmet, breastplate, or lance. After a moment, he glimpsed another rider behind the first.

Through misty sheets of rain, the horsemen cantered down the slope and headed across the moor. Snapping the reins, Rowan leaned forward. Valentine obliged him with a galloping stride.

Wind tore the hood from his head as Rowan looked around, half expecting to see riders converging from other directions, an old reiver's trick. But no one else was there.

Border reivers would not bother with a lone horseman on a highway unless they hunted a specific man for a blood feud. And most of the reivers he had ever known would have stayed home on such a wet evening. Even those who might hunt members of the Scott family.

Despite the increasing rain, he urged Valentine to a faster pace, wary of the slippery road. The deep thunder of the bay's hoofbeats mingled with the steady beat of the rain. Rowan risked another backward glance.

The huge black, with its mysterious rider, had reached the highway and now galloped after Rowan in rapid, pounding pursuit, ahead of his companion. Rowan glimpsed a face, pale and ghostly, swathed in a black hood before he turned to guide Valentine.

Scraps of tales from his childhood tumbled through his mind—phantom riders in the dead of night, ghosts eight feet tall, specters who waylaid travelers. One man, a tale went, had been frightened to death when a ghostly Scott had loomed up along the Lincraig road a long time ago.

Rowan wondered briefly if the haunts of Lincraig rode behind him. But since his ancestors had not found cause to harass him before this, he doubted that they would begin now.

This rider was only a flesh and blood highway robber, one foolish enough to ride out in a heavy storm to steal a purse. Border reivers would not stoop to such demeaning activity. He doubted that even a ghost would bother with the trouble of it.

He looked back again. The rider came on, never faltering, never slowing, his black cloak filling out eerily behind him. Rowan noticed that the second rider, another dark blur of speed, followed steadily.

Leaning low, his senses alert to the dangers behind him as well as in front of him, Rowan let the bay gallop at a reckless pace. The road sloped down, dipping left. Valentine hurtled ahead, veering with the incline, through the steady downpour.

In the next instant, Rowan saw that the nearby bog had spread, filling the dip in the road. He pulled on the reins, but could not prevent the horse from sinking to its knees in the deep muck. As Valentine stumbled further and lowered his head, Rowan was thrown loose. He landed on his side in ooze, like a sausage flung into porridge, and rose sputtering to his feet.

Spinning in the cloying stuff to grab the reins, he guided the struggling, whinnying stallion to stand. As Rowan stepped back onto a patch of solid ground, he heard the snort of another horse close behind him.

Dropping the reins, he grasped his sword hilt and began

to draw the blade, turning as if in the slow grip of a night-
mare. The black-cloaked rider loomed just behind him,
his companion, a blond fellow, nearby. Rowan raised his
sword.

The blond man's horse surged forward. Rowan saw the
sudden gleam of a blade in his hand as the man angled an
ax-headed lance at him. Reaching up as he swung his own
sword, an awkward position, Rowan managed to knock
the long staff aside briefly.

As he drew back to thrust, he shifted his weight. The
earth sucked at his heels, and the bog gave way. He
stumbled, taking a precious second to glance down and
regain his stance.

From the edge of his vision, he saw the lance arc again.
He lifted his sword blade and swiped upward. Then the
first rider, who had been circling Rowan and the blond
horseman, yanked a pistol out of a saddle loop.

Rowan stepped sideways in the slippery muck, twisting
to avoid the wicked point of the blond man's staff. When
Rowan turned, the other rider advanced, leaned forward,
and swung his arm.

The pistol butt slammed into Rowan's brow, wrenching
his head sharply backward. Flashing brightness exploded
into searing pain. The bog seemed to whirl around him,
and the strength drained from his upheld arm. His knees
slumped under him.

As he went down, the highway rider bent over the
saddle. A gloved hand stretched outward. The wide hood
slipped back.

Glancing up into the rider's face, Rowan felt an odd
sense of surprise as he fell. Time and urgency disappeared, and he became suspended in the wonder and awe
that filled him.

She had a tranquil, innocent beauty.

And as the light faded curiously around him, he tried to
remember where he had seen her before.

Chapter Four

❧

"Ye are the sleepiest young man," she said,
"That ever my twa een did see;
Ye've lain a' nicht into my arms,
I'm sure it is a shame to be!"

— "Clerk Saunders"

"Oof," Mhairi said. "*Ach.* He's heavier than he looks. Here, Christie, take his legs. We got him this far. We can surely get him down the steps." She slipped her arms under the unconscious man's armpits and lifted. His dark, wet head lolled on her shoulder. Behind her, the wind shoved at her back as she stood at the top of an exposed staircase.

The tower walls in this corner of Lincraig Castle were collapsed and broken beyond repair, but the steps leading down into the dungeon were still sound. While Christie took hold of the man's legs, she listened to the heavy rhythms of the rain that pounded on the fallen stones in the courtyard, and on the earth and grass between. A lonely, deserted sound. Yet she had never felt any fear of this place.

As Christie angled toward the stairs, Mhairi glanced once more at the man's face. His eyes were closed, lashes black against ghastly pale cheeks. But the gentle rise and fall of his chest reassured her that he was breathing still.

The messenger's total collapse, just after she had hit him with her brother's pistol, had frightened her deeply. She had jumped down from her horse to step into the bog after him, lifting his head out of the muck and slapping his cold, muddied cheeks anxiously. The messenger had not even groaned.

Christie backed down the stairs, while Mhairi followed with the heavy burden of the head and torso. They maneuvered slowly down the cracked stone steps to a corridor at the lowest landing. Two stout doors were tucked at the end of the small, dark space.

Together they shifted and bumped their way through the narrow corridor, and entered one of the dark cells.

Mhairi grunted as she eased the man's head onto the bare stone floor. "Like carrying a side of beef," she muttered.

Christie chuckled. "He will need some beef and broth," he said, "and warm blankets as well. I'll ride back to Jennet's house to fetch them."

"Aye. And bandages and healing ointments too. But before you go, help me with him, please. We'll need a light," Mhairi said. Murmuring in agreement, Christie rummaged in the folds of his cloak until he withdrew a thick candle and a piece of flint. Once the candle flamed, he set it in a pool of its wax drippings on the floor.

"Borrowed a dozen o' these from an English household a few weeks back," he said with a sly grin. "Good rolled beeswax, they are, and English make."

"Borrowed?" She laughed and shook her head. "You and your Armstrong kinsmen reived them in the dark o' the night."

"Well, my sister Jennet was muckle glad to have them. I'll bring another when I come back wi' the food and such."

Mhairi nodded, and reached out to brush back the damp waves of black hair that fell over the unconscious messenger's high, cool brow. "He's chilled, and this wound on his brow looks poorly." Blood seeped from the cut, staining her fingertips. "May I have your dirk, please?"

Christie handed her the thin blade. She cut a long strip of linen from the tail of the shirt she wore, which belonged to Iain. She wore, too, Iain's quilted black doublet, his best breeches and cloak, and a pair of high boots that their parents had sent Iain from Denmark. Though too large for her, the garments, which her brother had previously worn to kirk meetings and funerals, had been useful for riding the highway at night.

She held the folded piece of linen to the man's injured

brow and pressed down to discourage the bleeding. Lifting one of his eyelids, she saw no response in the shadowed, gray-green iris. Beneath her hand, his cheek was lean and cool, and his stubbled black beard felt harsh. But his breath stirred soft and warm over her fingers.

"I wonder if we will even be able to lock him in here," Christie said, looking around. "I doubt the door will hold. This place is crumbling apart."

" 'Twill hold," she said. She wrapped another torn strip of linen around his head to hold the folded cloth in place, and tied it securely. "I checked the lock myself not long ago. And there's a strong door bar."

"Ah. You'll keep this man for ransom, then," Christie said.

She looked at him in surprise. "Ransom? I willna do that."

"But ransoming is the custom o' the Borderlands, Mhairi. What d'you guess his kin will pay for him?" Christie looked speculatively at the messenger.

"I am a Macrae of the Highlands. I willna ask coin for a man's life. When he is recovered, we'll let him go."

"Let him go? You willna need to. By the look o' him, we willna be able to keep him here. He's a braw, tall man. As soon as he can move, I trow he'll twist that latch and pull the door loose, and come after you and me both. If you mean to keep him here, then we should at least chain him, and enjoy a ransom fee for our trouble."

She shot him a disgusted look. "We dinna even know who he is. Are you foolish enough to ransom the king's council for their messenger? We'll keep him here for now, and let him go when we judge it safe. Lincraig may be falling to pieces, but this dungeon is still stout enough for a prisoner. And secret. 'Tis said no one has been here for forty or fifty years."

"But for phantoms." Christie glanced around anxiously.

"That threat keeps others away. I've seen naught here. And haunts wouldna frighten me nearly as much as reivers and wardens would."

"I shouldna leave you here alone. This man is a real enough threat. Your brother would want me to protect you."

Mhairi smiled. "And you've done that well. But you go

on to Jennet's house. I'll be safe here. This one will sleep a long while." She gently touched the man's forehead, avoiding the swollen purple bruise above his left eyebrow. "And pray that he does wake, or we'll be guilty of murder. But before you go, Christie, help me search for his papers." He nodded and leaned forward to undo the clasp of the messenger's wet cloak.

Mhairi untied the thongs that attached a leather pouch to the man's belt. Opening the flap and shoving her hand inside, she rummaged around and pulled out a small circular black stone surrounded by a wooden frame. She frowned at it, tilting it, barely glancing into its polished surface before shoving it back into the bag. A moment later, she tossed the pouch away. It jingled as it fell.

"Only coins, and a little mirror," she muttered with disinterest, and began to pinch the hem of his cloak. "Naught is stitched inside here."

"Perhaps he lost his papers in the bog," Christie suggested. "Or he may have carried them in his saddle. I can check his mount when I go up."

"Be sure to lead his horse back with you, and tend to it in Jennet's barn. No one will find it there—unless the reivers come again. But the new lock on the stable should keep them out for a while." She frowned, turning her thoughts back to the messenger who lay so still beside her. "He must be carrying some papers. Your kinsmen sent word that he brought orders from the privy council. He wouldna lose those in a bog, or leave them in his saddle to be lost or stolen."

"My kinsmen also warned me that this man was dangerous."

"Did they tell you who he is, or why the council sent him?"

He shook his head. "When I saw my cousins at the inn at Kelso two days ago, 'twas only briefly. All they said was, look well to the life of Jennet's husband, and leave the council's messenger be."

"Are you sure they dinna know that we rode down the other messengers?"

"I dinna think they do. And even if they did, they wouldna care. They consider Jennet's husband their own

kin now. They meant to warn me that Iain would be in
danger once the messenger reached the warden."

"You didna ask the messenger's name?"

"They wouldna say, only laughed. Notorious, they said,
and no man to cross, day or night. Then they patted me on
the head, as if I were a wee lad, and said I would know
him soon enough. And they left me to pay the bill for their
ale. Lucky I had the coin," he added in a low mutter.

Christie knelt to roll the man sideways, and Mhairi
tugged the unconscious man's cloak out from under him.
The thick black wool was saturated and heavy. Feeling
quickly for papers hidden in the lining, she found none,
and laid the cloak aside.

"Well, your cousins were wrong," she said. "This one
was easier to ride down than the others. He rode straight
into the bog. And he isna dangerous just now—he looks
quite peaceful, sleeping there." She scraped gently at the
mud caked on the side of his chin. His beard rasped
beneath her fingernail. She tilted her head. "He has a fine,
handsome face, beneath that dirt."

"Dinna be swept away by a bonny face." Christie
frowned as he looked at the stranger. "I swear I've seen
him before. Well, whatever his name, he's a strong, tall
man. We should tie his hands and feet tightly before he
wakes."

"We hardly need to hurry, by the look of him. Now
help me find that message." Christie nodded and tugged at
one of the man's long boots, while Mhairi patted her
hands over the man's sleeveless jack.

Faced with dark leather stitched in a diamond pattern,
the jack gained its thickness and armorlike protection
from inner layers of quilted linen sewn around thin iron
plates. Molded over his broad chest and tapering to his
lean waist, the jack flared slightly over the loosely cut
wool of his breeches.

Mhairi undid the numerous metal hooks that closed the
garment tightly from his waist to his neck, feeling the stiff
iron plates beneath her hands. She pulled the heavy garment open, revealing a brown serge doublet and linen
shirt.

Leaning a hand on his hip to balance herself, Mhairi
discovered that the fullness in the cut of his breeches

came not from fashionable horsehair stuffing, but from the gathers in the thick woolen cloth. She knew because his hipbone was lean and hard beneath her palm.

Blushing, she moved her hand quickly and laid it on his chest. Through the doublet, the firm, slow beat of his heart under her fingertips was full of vital strength, and vastly reassuring. She was guilty of highway robbery and abduction only. Not murder.

"There's naught here so far," she said, and unhooked the doublet.

"Nor in here," Christie said, holding one long black boot upside down. Water dripped onto the stone floor.

"Ach," Mhairi whispered. "Where have you put the order, messenger?" Shoving open the doublet, she tugged at his damp shirt, then slid her hand inside the drawstring waistband of his breeches.

Warm, firm skin, tight with muscle and softened by thick hair, met her grazing touch. His abdomen rose and fell beneath her hand. A curious tingling sensation swirled in her own belly. Mhairi withdrew her fingers suddenly, as if she had been burned.

"Without a doubt, he's a strong man," she said. "Be sure to bring some stout rope from Jennet's house."

"Aye," Christie grunted, yanking at the other boot. The messenger's dark head lolled awkwardly with the motion.

"Go careful, Devil's Christie," she said. "He's injured." Shifting around, she sat cross-legged and lifted the messenger's head into her lap. He lay still, his beard-shadowed cheeks drained of color, his black hair spread out over her thigh. She felt fresh concern. "And he's chilled to the bone. We must get these wet things off, and get him warmed. You must hurry to Jennet's house."

"I will." He frowned, looking suddenly quite young in the flickering candlelight. "What if he dies, Mhairi?"

"He'll do fine if we help him. If we'd left him in the bog, we'd be guilty of murder."

"Should we leave him here for long? Perhaps we should tell my kinsmen—"

"Ach, dinna do that. The Armstrongs would ransom him for certain. If we think of it, we'll soon know what to do."

Christie began to tug again on the boot, but stopped.

"Mhairi, I heard that the March warden has already told the council that Iain is a thief and a spy. He wants the English to take Iain to trial."

"I dinna understand why Simon Kerr does this to his own cousin," she said. She slowly smoothed the damp folds in the messenger's doublet. "Simon insists Iain is guilty. I can only think 'tis because Iain rode with Alec Scott, and the Kerrs have long feuded with the Scotts."

"Simon Kerr was in the inn the same day that I was there," Christie said. "I heard him say that King James will surely send him a warrant o' execution for Iain. But he didna boast so loud when it was pointed out that he hasna found Alec Scott."

" 'Tis Alec Scott knows the truth of that Spanish gold they say Iain carried." Mhairi sighed. "Mercy of God, I hope the king hasna approved Iain's execution."

"You've heard nae word from your father?"

She shook her head. "This has been a year for storms, and the gales continue. My letter may take months to reach my father in Denmark. I paid well for the posting of it, but I heard that the ship hasna even sailed yet because of the weather. Even when my father receives the letter, he willna be able to sail back here or send a reply in time to help us. His duty is to the king just now."

"King James's marriage negotiations will keep your father and mother in Denmark for the better part of a year," Christie said.

"At least that long. And my other brothers are all away, and canna help us either. We are alone in this for now, Christie."

"Then we must do well for Iain," he answered firmly.

Nodding, Mhairi undid the clasp of her cloak, and swept it over the still man, whose head and shoulders were gently balanced in her lap. She greatly missed her parents and brothers, whose support would have been immediate had they known of Iain's predicament, and her efforts to free him. But some design of fate had left her to take the task on herself, and she would not fail her twin brother.

She tucked the cloak around the messenger. Though damp with rain, the inner side, lined with fur, would soon warm him. "We must get him dry, or he'll be ill," she said. "And we must find that paper."

"Perhaps 'tis inside his shirt," Christie suggested.

Mhairi slid her hand beneath the damp, bunched linen. Her burrowing fingers skimmed over thick, matted hair and warm skin, over the bud of his flat nipple and the hard curving cage of his ribs. His heartbeat was heavy and insistent beneath her palm.

Her fingers felt a piece of metal on a thong around his neck, and she pulled at it. Finding a small metal cylinder, she gently drew the thong from around his neck and handed it to Christie. "What is this?"

" 'Tis a key for winding a wheel-lock pistol," he said, putting it inside the discarded leather pouch. "He has a fine set of pistols carried in his saddle. We are fortunate he didna use them on us."

Mhairi slid Christie a scowl. Then, aware suddenly that she still rested a hand on the messenger's bare, warm chest, she blushed furiously and withdrew her hand.

As he pulled at the messenger's boot, Christie fell back with the effort when it finally loosened, and shook it upside down. Only a little dribble of water came out. "Nae paper, Mhairi," Christie said.

"I see. Well, take off his nether stockings. We need to get his feet dry."

Christie peeled off the woolen hose, and gasped playfully, as if the odor was overwhelming. Mhairi shook her head in wry amusement, but sat upright when a folded paper dropped to the floor. She snatched at it.

"The privy council's seal!" she said, waving the page.

"Read it!" Christie said eagerly.

The folded paper was sealed with glossy red wax. She peeled the edges apart with a flourish. "Didna even have to break the wax," she said. "The parchment is that wet. Ah, good, 'tis written in Scots. I can read it—though the ink is blurred," she added, frowning as she scanned the water-stained words.

"I wish I knew some of the ABCs," Christie said plaintively.

"I will teach you someday," she murmured, studying the letter. "Christie! This says his name is Rowan Scott of Blackdrummond!" She looked up in surprise.

"Blackdrummond!" Christie stared back at her, then looked down at the messenger. "I did think he looked familiar. But I havena seen him since I was a wee lad. The Black Laird, they called Rowan Scott."

"I havena heard the name. Is he kin to Alec Scott, and the Auld Laird o' Blackdrummond Tower?"

"He is Alec Scott's elder brother. And he is the laird."

She frowned in confusion. "But the Auld Laird holds Blackdrummond. Iain pays rent to him."

Christie shook his head. "Auld Jock Scott lives there, but the tower rightfully belongs to Rowan. This man is Blackdrummond himself. The Black Laird has come home."

"You know him?"

"My father rode reiving wi' the Blackdrummond Scotts. The Black Laird was clever and bold, like his brother Alec, and their father before them, and the Auld Laird himself—Jock Scott is near a legend in the Middle March. The Blackdrummond Scotts are a fierce bunch o' rascals." A slow grin spread across Christie's face. "And there'll be many who will be glad to have Rowan Scott back. But Simon Kerr willna be among them." The mischievous grin widened.

"I've never heard of the Black Laird. But I know enough about the Scotts," she added bitterly.

"Och, Mhairi, nae all Scotts are murderers," Christie said softly. "Jennet and I grew up wi' tales o' the Blackdrummond Scotts. Heroes they are, near here."

"But why has he been gone?"

Christie shrugged. "He was imprisoned, I think."

"A Scott he surely is, then," Mhairi said. "With some charm about him, for now he's carrying messages for the council." Mhairi squinted at the paper she held, tilting it toward the feeble candlelight as she tried to decipher the blurred writing. "Listen—this says Rowan Scott has been appointed by the privy council to serve as deputy warden of the Middle March."

"He's the warden's own man?" Christie rolled his blue eyes. "Ho, my kinsmen will enjoy that. Does the writ mention Iain?"

She shook her head. "I dinna see his name here. But I canna read all of it for the wetness. Oh—this word may be 'messenger.' " She looked at Christie in alarm. "Do you think he's been sent to find the Lincraig highway raiders? The council must know by now that their messengers have had trouble along the Lincraig road."

"Either way, when Blackdrummond wakes up and finds out how he was taken, you and I will have a cell near Iain faster than you can say the moon is green cheese." He eyed the unconscious reiver critically. "A stout rope may work for now, while he's hurt, but when he wakes—"

"That rope might serve for our necks when he finds out who we are," Mhairi interrupted. Christie nodded, his blue eyes so wide suddenly that Mhairi was reminded of his young age. " 'Twill be fine, Christie," she added. She folded the damp paper and tucked it inside her doublet. "Why would the king's council send a kinsman of Alec Scott to be a deputy here? I dinna understand."

"My Armstrong kinsmen say that the Scottish council is desperate for Border officers. There are so many feuds and ties of kinship, and so many reivers among the Bordermen that the council canna always find honest men, and so they appoint whoever is willing to act as warden or deputy to the post. I wouldna be a warden, myself. I hear the pay is dreadful."

"As are the risks. For now, we must keep this Rowan Scott here for a while, until he heals." She looked down at his handsome, still head where he rested in her lap. "Help me take his jack off, please. Easy, lad—move him as if he were a bairn." She and Christie removed the heavy sleeveless jack, and the damp doublet and shirt beneath it.

"Give us your own shirt, now, Devil's Christie," she said sweetly.

"Ah, Mhairi," Christie moaned.

"Will you have him die of the chill while you're warm and well? I willna be accused of murder, even of a Scott," she said. Christie growled and muttered while he took off his doublet and shirt. He tossed the shirt to her and dressed again in the doublet, turning his skinny back and shoving back his long blond hair, which fell sleekly over his shoulders.

Mhairi pulled the warm linen folds over Rowan Scott's head and lifted his heavy, limp arms into the sleeves. Then she tucked her outspread cloak up to his chin.

"He willna have my breeks, too," Christie said petulantly.

"He willna," she agreed. "But give me your nether stockings."

With a low growl, Christie sat and pulled off his boots, threw his knitted hose at her, and yanked his boots back on.

"My thanks," she said as Christie knelt to draw the hose, warm with body heat, onto Scott's bare feet. "Go, now, if you will, to Jennet's house, and bring back whatever she will spare."

Christie stood. "Perhaps I should stay wi' this one while you ride out. I can fight him off if he wakes."

"He willna be fighting anyone soon," she said. "Would you send me to deal with your sister's temper, when she learns why we want the supplies? Go charm her. Tell her how beautiful her new son is, and she'll let you have whatever you ask."

"An easy task," Christie said, smiling. "He's a fine laddie. Jennet says he looks like me when I was wee."

She waved at him. "Hurry then. I'll be safe here. This one will dream for a long while yet. And we'll tie his hands and feet secure before he ever wakes."

Christie nodded and left the room, closing the door behind him. She heard his footsteps scrape up the steps and fade. After a moment, all that she heard was the muffled, steady fall of rain outside the walls.

Mhairi sighed and looked down at the man stretched out on the stone floor, his head and shoulders resting against her thigh. Leaning back and shifting her hips until she was more comfortable, she watched him in the flickering light of the candle flame.

His features were lean and well-balanced, a subtle blend of strength and softness. The jaw and chin were firmly angled, the nose bold, the brow high and smooth. But the almost delicate curve of his upper lip lent a vulnerable touch to his strong, masculine features. Looking at him, Mhairi could easily imagine stubborn temper, pride, and keen intelligence as part of his notorious character. But she could sense hurt in those features too, and kindness as well.

Scanning the long, firm length of his body, she

remembered the athletic grace and strength with which he had swung his sword in the bog. If not for the mud and the rain, and the lucky, wild swing of her pistol, she and Christie might be dead now.

But instead, the infamous reiver lay like a babe in her arms. She touched his cool cheek, feeling the rasp of his beard, harsh as she drew her hand one way, soft as she drew it the other. He breathed out a soft, low groan.

Startled, she tensed, and then relaxed when he did not wake. She laid her hand gently on his head. His damp hair curled softly over her fingers like threads of fine black silk.

He was a Scott, and yet, for all the animosity she could stir up against his kin, for all the ill feeling she could certainly bestow upon him and his scoundrel of a brother, she felt only compassion stir through her here and now, in the candlelight and the silence. His injury had come from her hand. She owed him some comfort for that.

He did not look like the notorious reiver of his reputation. She saw the resemblance to his brother Alec, who was a dark, slim, well-favored young man. But Rowan Scott, beneath the mud and the bruising, was more than handsome. The graceful balance of his features and the agile strength of his body had the stunning, powerful beauty of a dark angel.

Notoriousness—harsh and rough, clever and heartless— was surely part of this man. But all she saw now was vulnerability. All she knew was that she must help him.

She stroked his head as if he were a child in her lap, and wished that she could wipe away the pain and the harm that she had caused. She and Christie had done the best they could for him, but he would need warmth and comfort to survive the shock of the blow. The stone chamber was as chilly as a winter morn.

While she regretted bringing an injured man here, she did not know where else she could have brought him. Jennet's house was not to be considered. Mhairi and Christie had tried not to involve Jennet in the scheme that they had created between them, although she was well aware of what they were doing.

Pressed against the bare wall, she shivered, her back and shoulders cold against the stone. She continued to stroke her fingers through the man's hair, slow, peaceful movements. After a while, she began to hum softly in Gaelic. The tune, with its gentle, lilting rhythm, was one her mother had sometimes sung while Mhairi and her brothers had drifted off to sleep.

Lulled by the melody, Mhairi was deeply startled when the man in her lap moved suddenly, lashing out his hand to grip her arm.

Chapter Five

 drawing of a decorative flourish

"O drowsy, drowsy as I was!
Dead sleep upon me fell;
The Queen of Fairies, she was there,
And took me to hersell."

—*"Tam Lin"*

"Who are you?" Rowan asked. Although the woman did not reply, he felt a sudden tension in the press of her fingers on his head. He tried to turn, tried to raise his head, but the agony that slammed through his skull decided him. Closing his eyes again, he kept his grip on the slender wrist in his hand.

After a time—he had no idea how long—he raised his eyelids. Willing them to stay open this time, he looked up. Her face, blurred and shadowed, hovered above him. A single candle flame sliced like a golden blade through the darkness. The brightness hurt his eyes.

The little flame flickered and split into two wavering images. He slid his glance around, unable at first to focus. He was aware of a crushing ache in his skull, and a warm, comfortable cushion beneath his head.

The woman watched him. His shifting vision made two of her, then one again, like images reflected in rippled water. Sighing in exasperation and pain, he drifted his eyes shut. His hand slipped from her arm.

"Rowan. Rowan Scott." The gentle whisper lured him away from the soporific fog that sucked at him. Forcing himself to stay awake, he looked at the vague, soft blur of her form. There was only one of her this time. Her face was pale, and her hair swept over her shoulder like dark, braided silk.

He turned his head. Agony shot through his skull and dulled to a fierce ache. The warm, firm cushion beneath him, he realized, was her thigh. Her body heat felt utterly soothing. Inhaling the sweet, earthy fragrance of woman and rain, and the sharper smell of old, damp stone, he drifted back into a numbing half-sleep.

"Rowan Scott," she said again. "How do you feel?"

He forced his eyes open and lifted his hand to his wound. He wondered how much time had passed since she had last spoken. She pushed his fingers away from his brow, her touch cool and light.

"Who are you?" he asked.

"Mhairi." She pronounced it with a long, nasal "ah": *Mah-re*. The sound was breathy, velvety, Gaelic. Intrigued, he narrowed his eyes to see her more clearly.

A gentle, ethereal Madonna looked down at him. Her oval face and delicate features had the perfect serenity of a marble sculpture, her skin as softly colored as a pale summer rose. With dark hair bronzed in the candlelight, and large eyes of a tranquil gray, she was a restful sight for bleary eyes.

Yet this was surely the same lass who had slammed the ball of a pistol butt against his head with the force of a cannon shot.

Rowan frowned. He had seen that peaceful face somewhere, even before he had glimpsed it above an arcing weapon. But his mind was too fogged to pursue the vague memory.

He grimaced and tried to touch his head again. Her fingers pushed his away. "Dinna touch the wound. You'll make it bleed again," she said.

He accepted that, and slid his glance slowly around the room. Dark corners, stone walls, no furniture, a narrow window slit. One torch on the wall. The place looked suspiciously like a prison. He had seen enough of them to know.

"Where am I?" he asked.

"Safe enough. You'll be well cared for until you're able to leave," she said. He frowned again, trying to place the lilting pattern of her speech, but could not follow the thought through.

He tried to sit up, but his body seemed too heavy to

move. He leaned back against her slim shoulder, dimly and pleasantly aware of the soft slope of her full breasts, swathed in layers of clothing, behind his back.

He swallowed, tasting thick dryness. "How long—"

"Only a little while," she said. "I was concerned about your head wound, and didna want to leave you alone just yet."

"Where am I?" he asked again, glancing at her. The curve of her cheek was blushing cream. She evaded his eyes and did not answer.

Rowan forced himself to sit up and away from her, maneuvering until he leaned against the cold wall. The action swamped him in pain and dizziness.

The blood seemed to rush and throb inside his head, and his stomach lurched. He inhaled against a sudden urge to puke like a babe. Squeezing his eyes shut, he opened them again. The lass, seated on the floor, divided into two hazy images that merged and separated and blended again.

"Stay still. You could injure yourself further," she said.

"You stay still," he muttered. Raising his hand to his aching brow, he touched a soft strip of cloth that was wrapped about his head. He deeply regretted, now, taking off his helmet just because of a little noise of pattering rain.

"Leave it, Rowan Scott," she said. " 'Twill heal. I've tended to it." Her calm voice, far clearer to him than her face, had a magical quality inside the cold, dismal chamber.

He squinted at both of her until she became one. "How do you know my name?"

"There was a paper," she said, "in your—"

"You took it?" He looked down and noticed that his leather jack was gone, and his doublet as well. The shirt he wore was not his, and too small; the sleeves did not reach his wrists. He still wore his damp breeches, but the woolen hose he wore were too tight, and smelled foul. And his boots were gone too.

"Where did you find the paper?" he asked.

She gave him an odd look. "Has your memory gone? You carried it in your boot."

"Ah," he said; *good,* he thought to himself. The

thieving wench had not found the other document that he had been given by the council. "Where is the rest of my gear?"

"Your clothing will be returned when 'tis dry."

"Where is my horse?" he demanded. Valentine was a valuable animal, a worthy prize for any Border reiver. He doubted he would ever see the horse again, and that thought infuriated him.

"Stabled and fed," she answered. "You will have him back."

He sighed gustily, doubting he could trust what she said. "My weapons?" he asked sharply.

She smiled a little, as if he jested. "Would I leave them here for you to use? Your dirk and sword, your pistol and your lance, are safely put away."

"My leather pouch? And coin?"

"Safely put away as well."

Into your pocket, he thought. He scowled, trying to absorb all of this. Obviously the girl and her companion— had he dreamed it, or had two riders chased him in the rain?—had taken him for ransom, a money-making tactic typical among Border reivers. He had been captured and imprisoned before, more than once, and ransomed now and again in his youth. And he and his Scott kinsmen had taken their share of prisoners, collecting coin or cattle in return for a little Blackdrummond hospitality.

He wondered which riding family had taken him. The girl's manner of speech was soft and precise, unlike the broad accent common in the Borders. Frowning, he tried to make sense of his situation, but his head ached and his thoughts were fractured and incomplete. "Who are your family, Mhairi?" he asked.

She hesitated. "My cousins are Kerrs." Her tone, quite suddenly, was edged with ice.

"Godamercy," he said softly, and sighed. The Kerrs in this area had feuded with the Blackdrummond Scotts for years. "I am a hostage then," he said. And physically incapable of doing much about it for the moment, he thought. "I assume I am to be ransomed."

"Ransomed?" She frowned. "Dinna concern yourself with that for now. You willna be here long."

Scowling despite the throbbing pain it caused him,

ignoring his sour stomach, Rowan tried to think. He glanced at the bare walls and the dusty earthen floor. "Where is this dungeon cell?"

"In an old tower," she said.

"Ah," he said, suddenly recognizing the pattern of the stone blocks. This was one of the lower chambers in Lincraig Castle, not far from Blackdrummond. The place belonged to his grandfather. Rowan had not been inside Lincraig for years, but he knew every crumbling stone and shadow in it.

Rowan was thoroughly muddled. Had he heard her correctly? Why would Kerrs confine him on Scott property? If the lass had the letter he had hidden in his boot—and if she could read it—then she surely knew that he was the laird of Blackdrummond.

He briefly considered how much effort would be required to grab this Mhairi, subdue her, and walk out. But even the thought exhausted him. He tilted his head against the stone wall.

"Dinna fret yourself, or try to move," she said. "I will have to tie your hands and feet if you willna be still. Your head is sore hurt."

He cocked a brow at her; the wound throbbed viciously. "My head is hurt because of a bonny wee lass with a great pistol. Why did you hit me?"

"You were attacking my friend," she said.

"Ah." He did not recall that, exactly. He pressed the bandage slightly and winced.

"You will reopen the wound. Leave it be."

He shot her a wry glance and took his hand away.

She stood then. She was not tall, though she was long-legged and slender beneath male clothing that was too large for her. The thick, tousled braid fell over her shoulder, its dark sheen rich in the candlelight.

Her face was sweet, her eyes wide and honest. She puzzled him. He could not reconcile that ingenuous face with her deliberate attack against him, and the theft of his gear.

"What riding family sends a lass to do their work?"

"Kerrs. I have told you that. But your head wound seems to have affected your memory. I am here because I tended to your wound."

"You gave me my wound," he said pointedly. "You chased me like a highway thief. And you took everything but my breeks."

She lifted her chin haughtily, opened her mouth to retort, but seemed to think better of it. "I will come back later, with food and drink," she said, and stepped toward the door.

Ignoring the pain when he moved, Rowan lashed out a hand. Grabbing her ankle, he yanked. She fell to her hands and knees on the stone floor with a smack and a grunt. He seemed to hold two squirming girls, both of whom struggled and reached down to pry his fingers loose. They cried out in one frustrated voice when he tightened his grip further.

"Let go," she gasped. She hit at his arm.

"Tell me why you rode me down like a common highway robber," he growled. Nausea and pain filled his awareness, but he kept hold of her ankle, wrapped in a leather boot. He meant to frighten her as well as mislead her. And he did not want her to know that hanging onto her slender leg took all of his strength.

She did not answer, only smacked at his shoulder.

"Who are you? Answer me true, now." Blinking hard, he was relieved when his wayward vision transformed her back into one pink-cheeked, scowling girl.

"My Border kinsmen will hang you if you harm me!"

"Border kin? You are as much a Border lass as I am," he snapped. His slowed thought processes had finally given him the detail he sought: her soft accent had given her away. "Tell me why a Gaelic-speaking Highlander rides a Lowland road in the night, attacking travelers for their purses!"

She stopped hitting him and stared. A strand of hair slipped across her eyes. She blew at it irritably.

"Highlander?" she asked, as if she had never heard the word before.

"You, my lass, are a Highlander," he said. "And a highway thief. You attacked me and took my pouch, my coin, my weapons and my horse. Why?"

She twisted to pull away from him, but he tightened his grip. Kicked by her free foot, he blocked the blow; four feet came at him, and he hit them all aside.

"Answer me!" he roared. He thought his skull would surely split at the noise.

She glared at him, breathing heavily. "I am no thief."

"You are a thief, and a Highlander," he said. She whipped her leg at him, and kicked again, but he held fast. "You broke my head, but I will break your ankle like a dry twig, or have the truth from you now. Who are you?"

"My cousins are Kerrs," she gasped out. "And my friends are Armstrongs. And you are a dead man for this deed."

"I will more likely be a dead man for the head crack you gave me." He tugged firmly on her leg. "Kerrs or Armstrongs, I suspect that you were born and raised in a Highland clan. Your first wee word was a Gaelic one."

Her chest heaved. "Why do you say that?"

"You speak Scots like a Highlander, softlike, with a lilting rhythm. You said your name was Mhairi"—he said it as she had, *Mah-re,* a gentle, breathy word—"as in Gaelic, not Mary, as is said in English."

She grunted with the effort to twist away, but Rowan did not let go. While Mhairi kicked at him, he dragged her back toward him, and bent her leg back with such force that she flipped over onto her stomach to avoid having the knee cracked.

"Let go," she said. "That hurts."

"Tell me your game," he demanded. She nodded desperately.

He released her. She scrambled away from him and sat against the far wall, rubbing her ankle and her knee, sending him acid little glances from beneath her slender brows.

"I meant to tie your hands and feet, but didna think you would wake so soon," she muttered.

"I am a good deal tougher than you know." He leaned against stone and closed his eyes. He had no desire to see two or four women trying to flay him with their beautiful, disturbing eyes.

His head spun and ached. And he thought, for one horrible moment, that he was going to be violently sick, or black out entirely. He sucked in cool air again and again, willing the feeling to fade.

She was silent, thank God, long enough for him to gain

mastery over the dipping, whirling world around him. He fixed her with what he hoped was a steady and intimidating gaze.

"Well?" he asked again. "Why did you ride into the bog?"

"I wanted something from you," she said.

"I have—or had—twenty pounds Scots silver, a sword with an Irish hilt, two wheel-lock pistols, a lance, a latchbow, and a good steel bonnet. And a Galloway horse as fine as any I will ever see again. You have all of it, Mhairi o' the Highlands."

"You will have them back again," she said.

"I had better," he grunted.

"I dinna want your silver or your gear."

"Then what?" He hoped she would answer. He had no more strength to force her. He hoped, too, that she would leave soon. He would prefer privacy if he was going to get sick and pass out.

"I wanted—to know who you were," she said.

"Why?"

She looked away. The braid whipped over her shoulder, a streak of red fire over deep gloss. Her small chin had a stubborn lift. "I just needed to know."

"You have the writ. Now you know, if you can read. So tell me who ransoms me."

"You willna be ransomed, as I said."

If she was of the Kerrs, then he had no doubt he would be ransomed. Even if the warden of this March was among their kin. "Who is Simon Kerr to you?" he asked. "Are you his daughter?" He doubted it. "His leman, perhaps?"

She lifted her gently shaped chin higher and radiated an icy silence. His wayward vision made two of her again. He blinked. When his vision cleared, she looked fair and pale and proud.

"What is your family name, Mhairi o' the Highlands?"

She fixed him with an even gaze. "Why did the king's council send you here?" she asked. "Are there other papers?"

"Did you find others?" he asked sharply. "What interest do you have in my assignment?"

"What orders did the council give you?"

"You seem to have some quarrel with me, though I have none with you," he said. "Or had none, until you rode after me."

"You and I have more quarrel than you can guess," she said through tightened lips.

"What is that?" he asked softly.

She folded her arms stubbornly and looked away.

His head hurt violently. He wondered how much longer he would be able to continue this polite conversation before he had to lean over and be sick.

"Very well," he said. "Answer me this at least." She looked at him grudgingly. "Are you a Highlander?"

She nodded slowly. "I am that."

"Why does a Highland lass ride a Border road like a common thief?"

She stood. "I willna answer more questions, if you willna answer mine to you." Marching toward the door, she yanked it open and stepped through. The door slammed. Rowan winced at the noise, and heard the sound of the door bar dropping into place.

He sighed. He had made no move to stop her. Any overt motion would have brought on an embarrassing bout of illness.

After a few moments, he heard a muffled male voice. Surprised, he listened, but could make no sense of the low words. But he distinctly heard the irritable tone of Mhairi's reply.

Assuming that the man was one of her Kerr kinsmen, he expected to see the door burst open shortly. He hoped he was wrong. He had neither strength nor stomach to confront an angry Borderman just now.

He was partly right. The door was wrenched open again, but no irate reiver entered. Mhairi's slender black-clad arm tossed in two plaid blankets and a wrapped bundle, which fell open when it hit the floor. Several oat-cakes and a joint of roasted meat rolled out and spun across the floor. A leather flask hit the floor after them. Rowan stopped it deftly with his foot.

"There's food and drink," she said.

"My thanks," he drawled into the silence that followed the slam of the door. He heard the door bar slide into place again. Quick footsteps stomped up the steps.

Though his head spun dangerously and his belly threatened to heave upward, Rowan smiled. Looking around the small, dank chamber, his smile widened in satisfaction.

Lincraig Castle was hardly a severe confinement for a Blackdrummond Scott. There were crannies and passages within the old ruin that he and his brother had discovered as lads. When his head ached less, he would explore the small chamber and soon enough find one way or another out of here.

He sighed and leaned back, wadded the fur-lined cloak Mhairi had left behind into a comfortable pillow, and drew up the plaids for warmth. His head throbbed and the room seemed to sway like a ship each time he moved.

The flask, when he picked it up, was heavy and warm. When he pulled out the cloth-wrapped wooden plug, he discovered that the flask was full of broth. Looking doubtfully at it, preferring something stronger at that particular moment, he took a sip. Beef broth, thick and hot and salty, slipped down his throat. He swallowed more.

Heavy fatigue slid through him, and he closed his eyes. A long, undisturbed nap would go far toward healing his head. He needed a bit more strength to be able to walk out of there.

Relaxing, he wondered idly if this Mhairi o' the Highlands had met the phantom Scotts who lived at Lincraig. And then a last thought drifted through his mind.

Perhaps he should ask the Highland lass if she knew anything about Spanish gold.

Chapter Six

~

"O gin ye winna pay me,
I sall here make a vow,
Before that ye come home again,
Ye sall ha'e cause to rue."

— *"Lamkin"*

Thunder rolled through her dream and became the steady pounding of hoofbeats. Waking quickly, Mhairi sat up. Moonlight threaded between the rafters overhead, illuminating the low pallet bed and slanted rafters of the loft where she slept in Iain's house. She heard her name, and turned to see Jennet's russet curls and pale face peeking over the top of the loft ladder.

"Reivers are here again!" Jennet whispered urgently. "Come down!" She waited, glancing nervously toward the front door of the little house. Mhairi could hear the rumble of horses' hooves and the growl of men's voices in the yard outside. She heard, too, excited barking from Iain's young wolfhound.

Sliding out of bed, Mhairi snatched her linen shift and yanked it over her head, then fumbled in the shadows for her plaid shawl. As she moved, she felt alert, calm, scarcely frightened.

She felt numb. During the weeks following Iain's arrest, she had endured constant threats from reiving raids, and had faced the urgent risks of her own clandestine activities. Some inner, softer part of her had retreated.

She felt, at times, as if she had hardened, as if her intense feelings and deepest fears were encased inside the boldness that had become her armor and her ally. The reivers outside knew only that of her. Rowan Scott had seen only that of her. He had been unconscious, she was certain, when she had softened with compassion toward him. He had not seen all of Mhairi Macrae—nor would he.

"Christie isna here," Jennet said. "We will have to meet these men ourselves."

Mhairi nodded as she snatched up her plaid and threw it around her shoulders. "I'm coming. What of Robin?"

"He's sleeping sound," Jennet said. "But he will wake soon to nurse again. And the dog is useless, of course, happy to see visitors."

"What riding family are these men?"

"Heckie Elliot and his brothers, riding wi' English outlaws."

"They've been here before," Mhairi said, and sighed. "We had best go out, or they'll break down the door." Jennet nodded and climbed quickly down the loft ladder.

Mhairi wrapped the length of plaid over her shoulders and around her waist, over her linen shift. She had no time to properly dress in the woolen gown, with its fitted bodice and lacings, that hung on a wall peg. Shoving back her tousled hair, she went barefoot down the loft ladder.

Her foot, reaching toward the floor, was licked several times. She jerked it away and leaped down. "Stop, Blue-bell," she muttered, shoving the large, silver-haired wolfhound pup out of her way. "*Ach,* when will you learn to respect proper danger? Stay, now. Stay." She pushed the dog gently toward the cradle. "Guard Robin. You're good at that much. If a reiver were to reach for the bairn, you'd sever his hand. But when they ride into your own yard at night—" She gave the dog a look of disgust. All she received in return was a sloppy grin in the moonlight.

Bluebell padded to the hearth and lay down. As Mhairi crossed the main room of the house, she remembered that such raids had terrified her years ago, when she and Iain had first fostered with Hob Kerr and his family, cousins of her father Duncan Macrae.

Sometimes, on those nights, she had lain awake, frightened that reivers would come and burn down the house or even kill them all, just for the reward of cattle or spare clothing, or the mere thrill of the raid. She was older now,

and knew more about raiding and reivers, and had lost
much of those early fears.

The Borderlands had changed her indeed. She wondered, if Johnny Kerr had lived and she had wed him, if
she would have become as dour and hard as some older
Border women she knew, toughened by constant threat
and soured by distress. Deep in the night, she sometimes
lay still on her pallet and trembled with fear, or wept into
her folded arms. Border life had not hardened all of her
yet. But as much as she longed to return to the Highlands,
she had to stay here and help Jennet, and Iain.

Glancing toward the open door, she saw the quick
gleam and jostling shadows of several riders. She ran past
the peat bricks glowing on the hearth, past the scrubbed
oak table and the box bed that belonged to Iain and
Jennet, past the little cradle with its bundled, sleeping
babe and the dog that sat beside it. Pausing in the spill of
moonlight that poured through the open door, she looked
out into the yard.

The wind whipped around the silent riders and their
restive horses. Pale light danced and glimmered on steel
helmets. Lances thrust upward like cruel thorns into the
moonlight sky.

Gripping the edge of the door, Mhairi summoned calm.
She hoped that the Elliots' mission here tonight did not
involve Devil's Christie, who had ridden off hours earlier
to the old ruin to guard the injured laird of Blackdrummond.

Whatever brought the reivers here, she must act bold
and steady. She strode out of the house and shut the door.

Jennet stood barefoot in a simple gown, gripping a
shawl tightly around her. She stared up at the men as
Mhairi approached, her thick red curls blowing back, her
pretty face moon-pale.

"What do you want here, Heckie Elliot?" Jennet asked.

"We were thinking you might want someone to herd
your Highland cattle, Mistress Macrae," Heckie said,
grinning. "Since your man has been in Simon Kerr's dungeon these long weeks. Or would you need someone to
plow your fallow field, perhaps?" Coarse sniggers rippled
through the men who listened. Mhairi sucked in her

breath at the crude insult. Jennet raised her chin and said nothing.

Heckie Elliot had come before in the black of night to speak to Iain. His band of outlawed Bordermen, his own kinsmen and some English outlaws, were known for swift, fierce, and unpredictable night raids. And were equally known for collecting illegal fees to prevent those very raids.

Their mood this night was dangerous. Mhairi could feel the tension of their intent crawling on the back of her neck, could sense their menace in the whine of the wind.

She hoped they would reive quickly, steal whatever cattle or sheep or household goods they wanted, anything, as long as they rode away soon and left them unharmed and the house whole. Two women had little defense against such men.

"Where is Devil's Christie this night?" one man, large and burly, asked. He grinned through a dark beard. "He snaps at our heels like a yard-dog if we come near here. Is he chained inside wi' your silly pup?" Someone behind him laughed.

"My brother will be back soon, Clem Elliot," Jennet answered. "And he'll be riding wi' my Armstrong kinsmen, so you'd best be gone from here." Mhairi watched Heckie steadily while Jennet spoke the lie. Both women knew that Christie had gone to Lincraig. Heckie and his brother Clem gave no reaction. Mhairi felt certain that they had not seen Christie or his prisoner. Her secrets were still safe. "Aye, Heckie Elliot," she said. "The Armstrongs will ride here soon. You'll be caught in a blood feud if Jennet's kinsmen find you here harrassing us."

"Ech, lassie," Heckie said, pouting like a great, ugly child. "We only came to help Mistress Jennet herd her husband's fine Highland cattle, and her black-face sheep too."

"Right over to our own lands," Clem commented.

Dread spiraled through Mhairi. "You dinna have cause to be here. Be gone, now," she called out.

"We've cause to be where we care to be, Mhairi Macrae," Heckie replied somberly.

"You break the king's peace by coming here. The

warden will have arrest warrants made wi' all your names," Jennet said.

"Aye, valentines. We've had those before," Clem said, and turned to grin at his companions.

"We mean nae harm to you this night," Heckie said impatiently. "Iain Macrae wouldna grudge us a few sacks o' meal and some o' his beasts, since we're willing to watch o'er his household while he's gone." He grinned, a fleeting, dark slash in his whiskered face. "For a wee price now and again in grain and hoof, we'll see to your safety, mistress. The Borderlands can be an ill place in the night."

"We willna pay black meal to you," Jennet said defiantly. "You ask criminal rent. We pay our rightful rent to the Auld Laird at Blackdrummond Tower."

Heckie sighed patiently. "Mistress Jennet, your husband struck a bargain wi' me afore he was taken by the warden."

"He didna mention it to me—" Jennet said.

"Perhaps he forgot, when he was taken for a treasonous spy," Clem interjected.

"False charges!" Mhairi said hotly. "Even crossing the border at night is March treason. You're guilty of that crime yourselves."

"We will boast our treasons boldly when it comes to crossing into England," Heckie said. "Most reivers dinna care about such. But this treason charge is different. I hear the council means to let the English decide your brother's guilt." Heckie looked at Jennet. "Mistress, Iain Macrae isna here and you need protection. A beast or two, and a few oats, is all we ask in exchange for the strength o' our lances. Paid each week. Or we can take the goods from you."

Jennet looked at Mhairi. "Godamercy," she whispered. " 'Tis a fair price to buy their departure. But Iain always refused to pay their blackmail. I dinna ken what to do. Iain spoke to them as a man to men, and Heckie would even laugh wi' him. But—"

"You dinna have to do this," Mhairi said in a low voice.

"But what shall we tell Heckie?"

"Simple enough," Mhairi said, and turned. "Go away

from here, Heckie Elliot. I'll soon speak to the warden about your visit if you dinna ride out now."

"Simon Kerr favors this lassie," Clem told his brother. "I warned you he wouldna like it if we came here."

"Simon Kerr canna stop us," Heckie growled.

"Demanding black rent of good folk is wrong," Jennet said, her voice trembling.

Heckie started in mock surprise. "What, are you the kirk minister now? Well, I dinna listen to him, either. Dinna refuse me, mistress. Your man will be hung, and then you will wish you had accepted our help when 'twas offered you."

"Iain will soon be free," Mhairi said. "And then he will come looking for you, with Kerrs and Armstrongs at his back."

"Aye, Scotts too, I wager," Heckie drawled. "You'll pay me, lassies, or lose your cattle and your gear. We wouldna care to hurt you, but it might come to that as well. What d'you choose?"

"Get out of this yard," Mhairi said firmly.

Heckie turned and called out behind him. One of the men rode forward. "This is Thomas Storey," Heckie explained. "We call him the Merchant, since he handles our accounts. He'll help you decide how many beasts you'd care to give us now."

Thomas Storey, whom Mhairi knew was an Englishman in league with Heckie, rode his horse toward Jennet, relentless steps that caused her to move backward until her shoulders pressed against the stone wall of the house. The animal's heavy breath blew at the strands of her hair. Smiling grimly, Thomas drew his sword.

Mhairi's anger flared. Running toward Jennet, she yanked her free, then glared up at Thomas. "Only a lackwit would harm a woman who nurses a newborn bairn!" she cried. His horse whickered and stepped back. Mhairi turned to face Heckie, her breath heaving. "Heckie Elliot, I hear your own handfasted wife has a bairn at her breast. And you know well that the Crown could declare fire and sword on your heads for an unspeakable act if you harm this woman!"

Heckie swore crudely, then motioned Thomas away before gesturing to the rest of the men. Leaping from their

horses, some of them shouldered past Mhairi and roughly
pushed Jennet aside. They entered the house. Mhairi
heard loud thuds and scrapes as furniture was knocked
over and chests and cupboards were thrown open. Bluebell barked in loud agitation, then began to growl and
snarl menacingly, her good temper tested too far.

Two other reivers went to the bairn, a wattle structure
attached to the side of the house, and used their pistol
handles to break the new iron lock off the door. Going
inside, they came back leading two horses.

Heckie, mounted on his horse, turned around, and
looked down at the women. "Stay where you stand. Dinna
move, and nae harm will come to you."

"But my child is inside the house!" Jennet cried.

"Fetch it, then, and come back," Heckie snapped.
Jennet ran into the house.

"You have given us your word we willna be harmed,"
Mhairi said. "And a Borderer's word is his life."

Heckie grunted. "Mhairi Macrae, you have seen my
honor for the last time. The next time I come here, I will
ask payment nicely of you. If you refuse me again, I'll put
a firebrand to your brother's rooftop. And nae nursling
nor its mother, nor any bonny dark-haired lass, will keep
me from doing what I please." He turned the horse and
cantered away.

After what seemed far too long a time, the men
emerged from the house, carrying sacks of grain, cooking
pots, linens, clothing, and kitchen utensils. Packing the
loot onto their horses, they muttered and laughed among
themselves, and patted the dog who circled restlessly in
the yard, even feeding her one of the stolen oatcakes they
had thrown into a sack. Soon they mounted and began to
ride out, leading away two horses, four cows, and nine
bleating, confused sheep.

Watching beside Mhairi, Jennet bit back a sob, holding
her swaddled infant protectively in her arms. The reivers
pounded noisily away. Jennet turned to walk back inside
her ransacked house, cuddling her son, who had begun to
scream, in her arms. Bluebell followed her.

Mhairi ran toward the barn door, closing and locking it
to keep the remaining animals inside. She had not made

an exact count in the dark, but thought that about six cattle and a dozen sheep were left inside. Her own horse was in there as well, and for that she was grateful. But Jennet had lost her sturdy workhorse, and Christie's stallion had been taken.

He would be furious about that. Earlier that day, he had managed to befriend Rowan Scott's sleek bay horse; he had been so proud of that feat that he had ridden the bay to Lincraig Castle.

Climbing the crest of a low hill, Mhairi clutched her plaid around her in the whipping wind, and watched as the reivers faded into the distance and the darkness.

After a while she heard the vibrating thunder of horses behind her. Turning, she saw a shadowed group of riders gallop over the dark moors in pursuit of the reivers.

The lead horseman angled away from the rest, motioning them on. Cantering over to where Mhairi stood on the hill, he halted his horse and looked down at her in the cold moonlight.

"Are you harmed, Mhairi?" he asked.

She shook her head. "I am fine, Simon Kerr," she answered.

Sitting his tall English horse, the warden of the Scottish Middle March looked equally as frightening as the reivers whose horses pounded furiously over the hills. A breastplate of smooth Spanish steel circled the solid girth of his torso, and his coarse features were shadowed beneath the wide rim of his peaked helmet.

"I've been trodding after that band o' scoundrels all this night," he said. "Heckie's Bairns, they call themselves. Elliots and other Scotsmen, wi' English scoundrels too, riding together and taking what they please. Did they harm you or Mistress Jennet?"

"Nay. But they took some of Jennet's best things, and stole cattle and sheep, and two horses."

"They raided Willie Nicksoun's house tonight and stole ten o' his cattle. Burned his byre to the ground when he refused to pay blackmail to them." He looked grimly at her. "Did they ask blackmail from Mistress Jennet?" She nodded. Simon sighed and rubbed at his wide, whiskered jaw. "I swear to you, Mhairi, that I will arrest Heckie Elliot. He deserves to be hanged."

Mhairi scowled up at him. "Not all of your prisoners deserve that," she snapped.

Under the force of her unblinking stare, Simon looked away. "Holding a wardenry isna easy, lass," he said. "Just this night I've chased English reivers back over their own March. And I've been searching for that wild Alec Scott yet again, wi' nae trace of the rascal. Then I had word o' the raid on Willie Nicksoun's place, and we've been trodding after Heckie and his lot since then. We followed them here."

"So many brigands to catch," she said bitterly.

Simon glanced at her. "Will you never like me well, Mhairi? I do my best to keep the law here. And I've kept my eye on your safety here, since my nephew Johnny would have wed you. Tell me what I must do to please you."

"Little chance that you can."

"I'm sorry for Mistress Jennet's troubles, and yours. But I canna help the better part o' them."

"You caused the better part of them," she said coldly. "When you are sorry enough for our troubles to release my brother, then I may like you better."

He grinned. "You're a bold lassie, like a hot pepper spice in my stew. I like that well. We could be a fine match together, eh?"

"In hell," she said between her teeth.

He laughed, a lusty burst, and held up his hand. "Peace then. I dinna forget that you and your brother are kin and fosterlings to my Kerr cousins. And you were betrothed to my nephew. But I canna release Iain Macrae, as I've told you before."

"You can," she insisted. "I dinna understand. Borderers always protect their own. We're cousins to the Kerrs."

"True, but I dinna have a choice. The council and the English wardens are watching me on this. We caught Iain in the red hand that night. He and Alec Scott had crossed into England and were bringing back a herd o' cattle and a sack o' goods. That alone is March treason, as any Borderer kens well."

"Iain isna a Borderman," she said.

"If a Highlandman comes down to wed a Border lass and stays to raise cattle and sheep in the Middle March, he's Borderer enough. And Iain should ken better than to ride wi' Alec Scott. What did it get him? Alec took off for the hills, and your brother was caught. And that Spanish gold we found wi' him proves his link to this spy chain that both governments are looking for."

"I willna believe that," she said.

"I am sorry for you, then." He stared soberly at her.

She tipped up her chin. "Alec Scott is your spy and your scoundrel. He rode off and left Iain to be caught. Capture him before you condemn my brother."

"I'll wager they are both involved. 'Tis a shame your brother took up wi' that lad. Those Blackdrummond Scotts are all scoundrels. They ride wi' the devil, if they ride wi' anyone."

A vivid image of the laird of Blackdrummond flashed through her mind—a dark, lean, handsome man, probably asleep in the dungeon at Lincraig. She had last seen him this morn, when she had checked his bruised brow, which had shown improvement, though it was still swollen. She had roused him and had waited nearby while he had eaten some of Jennet's barley soup. Then he had gone back to sleep, as if he were too weak to keep awake.

Mhairi knew what Simon did not—that the only devil with that particular Blackdrummond Scott was his guard, young Devil's Christie.

"Though we will shortly have more trouble from that quarter," Simon was saying.

She glanced at him in alarm. "What trouble?"

"One of my land sergeants rode in with the news that the privy council has decided to send me a new deputy. Rowan Scott—brother to Alec!" Mhairi started, gripping her shawl as he went on. "I expected him to arrive days ago. Where he is I dinna ken—wenching and swine drunk in some inn, I trow. But when he does arrive, there will be more o' the devil to these nights than you or I have ever seen. The Black Laird, they call him here. He was always the first to ride reiving when the moon was high, from what I have heard."

Mhairi upturned an expression of beatific innocence to him, though her heart pounded heavily. "But he will be a deputy, and so willna ride reiving—"

"Hah," he said simply.

"Will this Rowan Scott help you arrest his own brother?"

"I hear there's ill blood atween them. He'll help me, I'll wager. That family are rufflers and scoundrels, I tell you, from the Auld Laird down to his two grandsons. If you meet this man Rowan Scott, be wary, lass. Come to me if you need help."

She kept her gaze calm, though she burned with curiosity as much as with trepidation. "Why would the council send such a man to be deputy?"

Simon leaned forward. "To catch the highway thieves that ride out near Lincraig," he said in a husky whisper.

She caught a guilty breath in her throat. "Th—thieves?"

"Aye. The Lincraig riders, the ones who've taken down the council's messengers in the last few weeks. You've heard o' them. I wrote to the council regarding the trouble they've caused here. So what does the council do? Sends me another deputy." He spat to mark his disdain. "As if 'twould help. I have a deputy already, and three land sergeants, and a host o' troopers inside my tower walls. Christ himself! I could have used some wheel-lock pistols and powder shot, or a small cannon. But I get another ruffling Scott to watch after." He swore under his breath.

"The council must have their reasons," she said.

"The council are madmen. My cousins the Ferniehurst Kerrs have been feuding for near thirty years wi' these very Scotts. But I hear he's knowledgeable about reivers and laws—hah, and outlaws too—and if he means to do well by the appointment, then I will find a use for him." But he shook his head, muttering.

"Rowan Scott means to go after these highway riders, then?"

"I'll send him out to do that. I canna send him after Alec Scott, ill blood or nae. Alec will scheme a new scheme and win his brother back to him. There's devilish charm in those Blackdrummond rascals."

Mhairi remained silent, grateful for the darkness that kept her face partly in shadow. Clouds had scudded over the moon, and a cool, misty drizzle had begun while they had been talking. The rain reminded her, suddenly, of the downpour the night that she and Christie had taken down Rowan Scott.

An idea, risky and dangerous, had began to form. If this Black Laird, this Rowan Scott, meant to go after the highway riders, then she and Christie would be hunted and caught before long. She faced prison from every angle. She had acted as a highway robber and had taken down the warden's new deputy—and that deputy would make her pay for her crime.

But Christie was seventeen years old, too young to be taken down for a criminal. Mhairi's efforts to help Iain were failing miserably. Forced to find her way through this dilemma without the loving protection of her family, and without Iain's sound advice, she could only follow her instincts and do what she thought best. And she could only hope that her actions would not bring down herself and Christie in the bargain.

Christie was already convinced that Rowan Scott would toss them into a cell as soon as he could walk upright. They would all fry in their own fat, as the saying went. And then her brother would have no hope at all, short of escape or pardon.

No hope at all, unless she tried one last alternative. She knew that she could pledge her life in exchange for her brother's.

As she stood in the darkness and cold drizzle, listening to Simon's mutterings, she decided to offer herself in Iain's place. Simon Kerr was familiar with the rules regarding pledges, and might allow it. If so, Iain could return to his family, and flee into the Highlands for safety, where he would never be found.

Taking a human pledge as a promise of another's good behavior was common practice in Scots law. As a child, she had heard the story of her own father's legal predicament as pledge for the good behavior of the Fraser clan during their feud with the MacDonalds. Duncan Macrae had nearly lost his life that way. But Mhairi, as a woman, would face a lesser risk. She would take the chance that Simon Kerr would not keep her in a dungeon, and might even set her free within a few weeks.

She glanced up at Simon and wrapped her arms tightly around herself, as if to protect her precious, fledgling idea.

The warden was looking at the night sky. "There'll be

rain again," he said. "This has been a bad year for storms
and floods and winds. Jehovah's breath, they say. We
should all beware the wrath behind such omens. A dangerous time, Mhairi." He glanced at her, and his eyes
seemed to glitter like black ice. "Mind you stay in the
safety o' your house at night."

"I will," she said, a touch too brightly.

"Where is that Armstrong lad, Devil's Christie?"

Startled, she gulped. "Oh—he's here. Somewhere."

"Tell him I said he's to stay wi' you and his sister, and
see to your protection. There's more than storms out on
these moors at night." He gathered his reins. "I must find
my men and pursue Heckie Elliot and that gang."

"Simon, wait! Will—will this deputy Rowan Scott
bring word from the council about Iain?" She had tried to
decipher the rain-spoiled page that she had taken from
Scott, but the ink was too blurred to tell her what she most
wanted to know. She had not seen Iain's name written
there, but she was not sure. The paper did not appear to be
the warrant she sought.

"I am awaiting a warrant from Edinburgh," Simon
admitted.

"You havena yet received orders from the council?"
She clutched at the plaid she held at her throat and waited.

"Some messages I have had, but there may be others
that havena made it to me, thanks to those cursed Lincraig
riders," Simon said. "I need a warrant from the council
before the next appointed day o' truce. The English
warden wants Iain handed over when the Scottish and
English wardens meet that day."

"You mean to give Iain into English custody?"

"When I get the warrant."

"Will you let Jennet see him before then? Will you let
me see him?" She was unable to keep a plaintive tremor
out of her voice. "You havena let us speak with him."

"Come to the truce day meeting. I will let you see him
before the English take him away."

Her heart seemed to plummet through her body at his
cold words. Simon had repeatedly refused requests that
she and Jennet be allowed to visit Iain. Impulsively she
touched his sleeve. Damp, cool leather met her fingers, as

if warm flesh did not exist beneath. "Simon, please listen. I want to act as a pledge for him."

Simon stared at her. "Are you daft? Iain will pay for what he's done, nae you."

"Please, Simon," she said. "You must let me do this."

He reached down and laid his hand on the side of her face. His broad fingers felt like cold sausages against her cheek. His touch, though not rough, lacked comfort and warmth. "How far will you go to save him, hey, lass?" he asked in a low voice.

Something prickled along her spine. A heavy, warning dread turned in the pit of her stomach. His hand crept down to caress her shoulder. His palm, resting against her neck, grew warm and damp. Mhairi repressed a shudder.

"Iain is innocent," she said. "He shouldna die for what Alec Scott has done. I will pledge for him. 'Tis simple, and legal."

"You'd serve nice enough as a pledge," he said. "And I am tempted, for I like pepper, as I said. But 'tis nae simple at all, Mhairi." His fingers traced over her cheek. "How much value do you place on your brother's life, hey?" he murmured.

"Priceless." She stepped away, watching him warily. "Let me pledge honorably, Simon."

"I will think on it, lass," Simon said, too softly, as he stared intently at her. Then he lifted the reins. "I've stayed here too long. I must catch up to my troopers." He turned the horse, kneeing it forward.

As the hoofbeats faded into the misty darkness, Mhairi raised her face to the rain. But the cool drops on her face could not rinse away the fear or the bitterness or the disappointment that churned within her.

The ghost of Simon's heavy touch lingered on her face like a sour residue.

Chapter Seven

~

"Thanks for thy kindness, fair my dame,
But I may not stay wi' thee."

—*"Lord Maxwell's Goodnight"*

Shoving his fingers through his hair, Rowan groaned and rose to his feet. When the room spun slightly, he placed a supporting hand on the cold wall. The severe headache had finally eased and he felt stronger and more alert than he had for days, although some dizziness still lingered.

Leaning his shoulder against the wall near the tiny slit window, he glanced around. For the past three days, perhaps more, he had been locked in this small cell at Lincraig. The tower walls above him, he knew, had crumbled long ago. But the rusty iron lock on his door still held fast, and the door bar on the other side was surely in place.

Until last night, he had hardly been able to walk the several steps across and back. But now that his strength was returning, he was determined to find some way out of here.

A silvery wedge of daylight filtered through the window, a narrow, deep aperture in the wall. He stretched his arm into the opening and caught the light full on the tips of his fingers. When he tilted his head, he saw a bank of clouds. Delicate sunshafts poured through that softness to touch the ground.

Blackdrummond Tower lay in that direction, not far from Lincraig. His grandparents would be concerned by now. He had promised to be there days ago. Tilting his head back, he stared up at the stone ceiling, festooned with spiders' webs, and swore. The angry echo resounded with his own frustration.

Sitting on the floor, he picked up half of an oatcake from its cloth wrappings, nibbled at it, and laid it back again without appetite. He swallowed some water from a flask. The lanky blond lad, Christie, had come frequently in the past few days to bring food, hot broth, and plenty of fresh water.

The food was consistently delicious—salty broths and porridges, juicy roasted meats, chewy oatcakes, and apples stewed in honey and spices, but Rowan had eaten little. He rubbed his hand cautiously over his head. The bump on his brow was still tender, but the swelling had reduced. The cool, water-soaked cloths that Mhairi had applied must have helped. As had the enormous amount of sleep he had gotten.

That part of the treatment had not been entirely his choice. The blow to his head had been serious enough to produce, besides an aching pate and spinning vision, a compelling lethargy that had kept him prone. He could not have escaped if Mhairi and her young comrade had held the door open and invited him out.

Unconscious much of the first day, waking only sporadically, he recalled Mhairi's soft touch on his head, and her soothing, dulcet voice. She had lavished gentleness and kindness on him, had even fed him broths, and he had slept like a babe in her arms.

And felt the fool for doing so. He should have summoned the strength to wring her slender neck for putting him here, in this condition, in the first place.

Sighing loudly, he stood again, his increasing strength and energy making him restless. He prowled the chamber, running his fingers deftly over the stone blocks and the joints between that formed the floor and walls. A means of escape was not yet obvious, but he was not overly concerned, knowing he would solve the problem somehow. He crossed the room to try the most obvious solution once again.

Rattling the door ring in his hand, he yanked and twisted. Rust powdered into his hand, and he smelled the sharp odor of old metal, but the lock refused to give. He yanked again, roughly.

"Did you want something?" The lad's reedy voice came to him through the thick, dry oak of the old door.

"Ah, Christie, you are on guard again," Rowan said through a crack in the wood. Hearing the door bar slide free, and the latch rattle as the key was inserted, he stepped back. When the door swung open, Christie stuck his head around the edge.

"Are you well, Master Scott?" he asked. "Mhairi would be angry wi' me if you were taken bad again, and I didna fetch her."

"I'm fine," Rowan said. "Come in."

Christie stepped inside, holding a heavy silver-barreled gun in his hand. Rowan tilted a dubious brow at the weapon.

"Pardon, sir." Christie sounded embarrassed. "Mhairi wouldna let me bind your arms and legs, because o' your crackpate. So I thought this would do. I ken your reputation well. I've heard o' you since I was a bairnie."

"Best to be cautious," Rowan said easily, leaning his shoulder against the wall. "You must have been raised near here, then, to know of the Blackdrummond Scotts." Christie nodded, and Rowan probed further. "Perhaps I know your kin."

Christie nodded again. "They call me Devil's Christie."

Rowan grinned. "You're Devil Davy Armstrong's lad?"

Christie straightened proudly, and Rowan saw the resemblance to the lad's father immediately, in the long face and straight ash-blond hair. But Christie's deep blue eyes, almost feminine in their prettiness, were his mother's. Rowan remembered her as a handsome, strong-willed lass with red hair.

Devil's Christie Armstrong would be a strong, tall man one day, Rowan realized, like his father. And like Devil Davy, handsome enough to make young lassies silly with yearning.

"Your father was a brave, fine man. I was sorry to hear that he died last year. I learned of it at an inn, rather recently."

Christie nodded. "Kerrs took him down one night. My da was proud to ride wi' you and your kin, Blackdrummond. Said it often to my mother, he did."

"And he'd be proud of such a braw lad," Rowan said. "You and the lass are riding bold, indeed, to go out on the highway as you did." He narrowed his eyes. "Do your Armstrong kin ride the road wi' you and Mhairi?"

"Nay, just us alone."

"Ah. And is this Highland Mhairi your cousin?"

"My sister Jennet is wed to Mhairi's brother." Christie hesitated and looked flustered, as if he realized that he had said too much.

Rowan nodded slowly. He could have overpowered the lad easily, but Christie held the weapon, an older match-lock style, quite steadily, and watched Rowan with an expression that approached reverence. Rowan respected both the weapon and the lad's admiration. And he might need that loyalty someday.

"You can put down the pistol, lad," he said. "I willna attack you. I assume this is an honorable confinement for a ransom, based on faith between two Bordermen."

After a cautious look, Christie shoved the gun into his belt. Rowan relaxed more completely. "You're a Border-man, but your friend Mhairi is a Highlander," he said pleasantly. "How is it that the two o' you ride the high-way at night?"

"Christie, you dinna need to answer him," a melodious voice said, as the open door shoved wide. Mhairi entered the room, and Christie spun around to look at her.

Rowan made no outward reaction, only crossed his arms where he leaned against the wall, and watched Mhairi keenly. Her simple gown of blue-gray wool, with a bright plaid wrapped over it, was a pretty change from the first time he had seen her—she had looked then, in funeral-dark doublet and hose far too large for her, like an underweight, ferocious black kitten.

Her gray eyes darted toward him more than once, as if she was surprised to see him standing, strong and alert. A vivid pink blush stained her cheeks. He noticed, though he was not certain why such a detail caught his eye, that her dark hair, braided loosely and hung over one shoulder, had a silky gloss. He watched her without comment.

"I came to tell you that I would stay with the prisoner now," she told Christie. "Go on home to your sister. Reivers visited us last night."

"Heckie's Bairns? Did they harm Jennet or—"

Mhairi gave him a little shove toward the door. "She's fine, as am I. But they took gear, and more animals. And they took your horse."

"By hell! Sneakbait thieves!" he shouted, stomping out of the room and up the steps. "Those leeches will pay wi' their hides for this! That was Devil Davy Armstrong's horse!"

"He sounds like his father," Rowan remarked as the furor and the stomping faded.

Mhairi shut the door. "You knew Davy?"

"Quite well. I recall his bairns too, now that I think on it, a wee blond laddie and a redheaded daughter. Jennet, I think?" He smiled when she nodded. "Is Jennet Armstrong the fine cook I should thank—or is it you?"

"Jennet. You must have been a young lad then, if you knew Davy's bairns."

"I first rode out wi' my kin when I was as young as Christie, I guess. I was sixteen when Davy's wife Jean birthed the lad." He frowned at her. "You said reivers rode on his sister's home last night? Heckie's Bairns, Christie called them?"

"They have ridden on us several times in the past few months. My brother's cattle are nearly gone now, and his sheep as well. We have only one horse left to us. We willna have the proper number of beasts to offer for our Martinmas rent." Her tone was flat with suppressed anger. But he could still detect the soft, musical influence of Gaelic in her Scots.

"Who are these reivers?" he asked.

"Mostly Elliots, and a few English. Their leader told me that the next time they come, they will burn the place—"

"Unless you pay their blackmail price."

"Aye. But we willna."

"Highlanders willna pay," he said, nodding.

"Have you blackmailed many Highlanders?" she asked crisply.

He shot her a wry look. "I meant that Highlanders in my experience are stubborn as stones." He strolled the few steps across the room toward her, and gestured toward her empty hands. "Where's your own weapon? I know you wield the butt piece well, though I canna speak to your skill with the shot. How will you guard your prisoner today?"

Her pink cheeks took on a rosier color as he came closer, but she held her place near the door. "I heard you tell Christie that you regarded this as an honorable confinement. So you willna harm me."

"As a Borderman and a Scott, you have my word on it. I willna harm you." He felt a slight wave of dizziness, and leaned his shoulder against the wall again, a casual pose that provided an essential buttress. And a position of advantage, for Mhairi was only an arm's length from him. If she moved, she would leave the doorway unbarricaded.

He had a pleasant, close view of her translucent skin and shining dark hair, and the soft gray in her eyes. Her beauty was simple and serene, and somehow took his breath away in this dismal, shadowed place.

She was a refreshing medley of color and texture, from her petal-delicate skin to the bright blue-and-red plaid wrapped over her shoulders and hips in the manner of Highland women, and shoved back to reveal her uncovered head. He tipped his head against the wall and looked down at her. She blushed, a pink that flowed up her throat into her cheeks, and looked away.

He wondered, briefly, how warm and creamy the skin of her cheek would feel beneath his hand, and whether the thick plaid that billowed over her breasts had taken on the warmth of her body. The cloth added a little bulk to her form, but he could see the strong, slim line of her torso beneath. Beneath the low, square bodice of her gown, she wore a high-necked white shift of fine, plain lawn, which showed the delicate shadows of her collarbones and breastbone.

A quick stirring ran through his body, and he cleared his throat. "You dinna wear your black doublet and breeks, though you were a fair sight in them," he said in a teasing tone. She looked at him, her eyes flashing like silver.

"I only wear those to ride the road at night," she said.

"Ah. So you dinna plan to take down messengers this day?" He kept his intonation light, but knew his expression was stern.

"You know about the other messengers?"

"Surely. The council had word from Simon Kerr that their messengers had been attacked by rascals and thieves." He watched her keenly. "Why did you attack them? And why did you come after me, lass?"

She gave him a frank look. "For your papers."

"Why would you want my council orders?"

"What I sought is a warrant of execution," she said. Her honesty surprised him. He had expected more evasion.

"Oh? Do you have use for such a warrant?"

She gazed at him silently. Dull shadows fell over her face and shoulders, but her eyes glimmered with thought and feeling. He had an odd impulse to measure those black lace lashes with the tip of his finger.

"Blackdrummond," she said, "you are a Scott and a notorious scoundrel." He tipped his head graciously, as if she had bestowed a great compliment. Casting him a wry look, she continued. "But I have decided to be honest with you. Since you are a deputy in the Middle March, I canna keep you here much longer—"

"If at all," he drawled, "now that I'm awake."

"—and I also know that Simon Kerr wants you to capture the highway riders."

"How do you know that?"

"Simon told me he's expecting your arrival. He rode by with his troopers after the raid on our house last night. He said you were to be the new deputy, and that you would search for the Lincraig riders soon enough." She spread her hands gracefully. "Well, I am the rider you seek."

He tilted a skeptical brow; what did the lass have in mind? "So easy as that?" he asked.

"I propose a bargain, Blackdrummond."

"Why should I bargain with a highway thief?"

"I hear you were a thief yourself."

"I was a reiver, lass," he said sharply. "Thieves rob purses. Reivers trade cattle. A difference in intent."

"I dinna see much difference," she said bluntly. "But I will give myself over to you—if you agree to what I want."

"Give yourself to me?" he asked softly, stepping a little closer. He let his gaze slide over her graceful form and linger on the luscious curves beneath her bodice.

Her telling cheeks brightened considerably. Rowan liked that bonny splash of color in this dismal place, and liked, too, how easy it was to bring it out in her.

"I mean that I will give myself into your custody," she amended. "And I will set you free from this dungeon."

"What is to stop me from taking you here and now, as I please?" he asked in a low growl.

Those cheeks looked hot enough to melt ice. "You gave your word that you willna harm me. A Border promise is as sound as any a Highlander will make."

"It is. But why ask me to take you into custody? Have you had some fit of righteous thinking?"

She pinched her lips together as if she had done just that. "You will take me as a pledge for my brother."

"Ah. And who is this important brother?"

"The warden holds him prisoner at Abermuir Tower."

He frowned. "Simon Kerr holds your brother for reiving?" She nodded almost hesitantly. There was more to this, Rowan realized, than the mere stealing of beasts and gear. "Was there murder involved?" he asked quickly.

"Nay! Iain is accused of a crime he didna commit. Simon intends to give him into English hands at the next truce day. But if I serve as the pledge for my brother, he could go free."

"And what of you, then?"

She shrugged, a small gesture, and looked away.

He stared at her, trying to absorb all of this. "God have mercy," he said slowly, "you will have me ride to Kerr's castle with you, the highway rider, already in my custody? Am I to introduce myself as the new deputy, and demand his prisoner's release in exchange for your wee hide?"

"You could do that," she said. "Simon wants the Lincraig rider taken, and I am the one."

"Are you daft?" He tried not to laugh in disbelief at her ludicrous suggestion. She looked so earnest. "Simon Kerr willna believe a slip of a lassie took me down on the Lincraig moor, or took anyone else for that matter. He'd declare you free before you even got off the horse. Beside that, I dinna have authority to release the warden's prisoners."

"Iain must go free," she said. "He hasna even seen his newborn son. You can help us. I have spent the last few hours thinking on this."

"I see that," he remarked. "This is quite a scheme."

"Iain is one of your own tenants. A laird owes right of protection to his tenants."

"My grandsire has handled the rents in my absence. Ask him to take you on and demand Iain's freedom. He was always a clever man for gaining fat ransom fees."

"You are the deputy. You can do this."

He sent her a skeptical look. "If you have such a wild urge to be a pledge, let Simon Kerr oblige you. Ask him."

"I tried. He said me nay. But I didna tell him that I have been out on the Lincraig road—"

"Ah," Rowan said. "Then he's in for a surprise."

She scowled at him. "If Simon knew, I—I think he might do what he likes with me. None of that will save Iain. But I hoped that you might help me."

He sighed, frowning. The lass was deeply, utterly serious. Perhaps she only needed reassurance. The women-folk of reivers sometimes took the news of their men-folk's imprisonment hard. But this lass reacted in the extreme, ready to sacrifice her own freedom rather than wait for the truce day hearings that would likely free this brother of hers.

"Dinna fret, lass, your brother willna stay imprisoned for long," he said. "Cattle thieving doesna run to hanging as often as you may think. He will be declared clean on truce day, or pay a fine. Unless murder has been done, the English wardens only want the satisfaction of pressing the charge. And the truce day juries are mostly reiving men, who look after their own. He'll go free."

His attempt at comfort was lost on her. She glared at him. "Simon wants to hang my brother. He says he is a spy."

He narrowed his eyes at that. So, the errant brother was Kerr's spy. "And you claim he is innocent," he said softly.

"He only helped Alec Scott bring back some cattle."

"I suppose you know Alec Scott is my brother," he said.

"I do. And 'twas your brother rode off into the hills,

and let mine be put in prison for a treason he didna make." He watched her eyes flash, her slender fists tighten at her sides. "Alec and Iain rode out together that night, but only Iain was captured. Simon told me he found Spanish gold among Iain's booty. But if any man is foul with this deed, your brother knows the truth of it. Perhaps you owe us this favor after all, Blackdrummond, in your brother's place." She folded her arms over her chest as she finished.

"My brother settles his own debts." He looked at her intently. "So this is why you ride the road, and why you seek a warrant of execution. To delay your brother's inevitable death."

She lifted her chin defiantly. But he saw, for an instant, a flicker of fear in her stormy eyes, and a tremor in her soft lower lip.

"You defend your brother heartily, lass. Few men would go to the risks you take on." He leaned toward her.

If honor had its own light, it burned bright in her eyes, he thought, watching her in fascination. If what she told him was as honest as it seemed, then she was capable of a rare loyalty, the finest kind. The kind that did not exist in his own life.

"He has been wronged, and there is no one to right it but me."

"Is he as clean as you think?" He murmured the question, shifting slightly so that he faced her. She backed against the door. "Your brother took up wi' Border reivers, lass. And he took up wi' Alec Scott."

"If Alec were my brother, I would defend him until I knew the truth," she said. "And beyond."

"I dinna doubt that. And if Alec favors spying these days, he'll pay the price for it late or soon. He will be caught." *But not by me,* he thought. An undercurrent of tension ran through him. He knew well his brother's capacity for treachery. Now this lass did too.

"Will you ride out after Alec if Simon orders it?"

He shrugged, and leaned a hand against the wall, over her head. "That I canna say."

She stared up at him, and bit her teeth slightly into her lower lip. "Will you take me as a pledge for Iain?" she asked after a moment. "I am the Lincraig rider Simon hunts. He will be pleased with you for that."

He drew a deep breath and let it out slowly, stirring the dark, silky tendrils near her forehead. "If I decide to take down the Lincraig rider, lass," he said softly, "I will do so when I please. On the highway or on the moor. Or in your own house. But you willna know when."

She watched him like a fledgling might watch a hawk, still and helpless, while innocence changed to awareness. "And then?" Her voice was a faint whisper.

He lowered his head until his forehead nearly touched hers. "And then we shall see what will be done with the Lincraig rider," he whispered.

She watched him, gray eyes shadowed, for the space of a few heartbeats. "You could still take me as a pledge," she offered, a brave tremor in her voice.

Rowan smiled and drew back a little. "Rare stubbornness," he said. "And rare loyalty. But a foolish notion."

She lifted her chin and stood stiffly against the door. "If you dinna take me now, I will ride again, and take down the next messenger. I havena found the warrant yet."

"Stubborn as a stone, as I said," he murmured. "And you may get yourself killed. I am not the only one who will come searching for you, if you spoil travelers again on that road."

"Spare me, then. Take me as a pledge now," she said.

"I dinna make bargains with daft Highland lassies."

She swore in Gaelic, a breathy but vicious sound, and whirled away, stepping on his foot as she yanked at the door latch.

Rowan placed his hand firmly over hers. "If you leave here, you leave with me," he said. "I think I am done with my wee rest." He pulled the door open wider, grabbed her arm, and stepped out into the close, dark corridor with her.

"Let me go!" She pushed at him, but he kept an iron grip on her arm. Mhairi twisted and kicked. "What of honorable confinements? You gave me your word!"

"I said I wouldna harm you. But I didna promise to stay here. Think you I am as daft as you?" he asked, as he drew her, struggling, up the stone steps. "After all, it seems you didna intend to ransom me, so I'm free to go."

"I wouldna take a penny for you!" she yelled.

"Ah, not now, hey. But I had value when I rode past you on the Lincraig road," he remarked, and yanked her up another step.

"I wanted your papers! Ow! Where do you take me?"

"To your horse," he said. "I think you should go home."

"And where are you going?"

"Home," he answered mildly.

"Let go of me!" She spun and wrenched free from his hold. Losing her balance on the edge of the step, she tilted, waving her arms. Rowan caught her deftly around the waist.

"Listen, wild lassie," he growled, "I willna harm you. Trust me for that. But I am leaving here, and so are you. I have matters to attend to."

He made certain that she was balanced on the steep step, and then let go of her. Taking the risers in pairs, he reached the top of the staircase and emerged into the cool air.

He heard her footfalls stomping up behind him. Rowan set off across the courtyard with a long stride, cutting through the deep grasses and ferns that clustered around the old, broken stones. Just inside the crumbling outer wall, a black horse was tethered to a stone.

"You willna have my horse!" Mhairi called out.

"I dinna steal horses," Rowan muttered. He walked past the animal and through the gateless opening.

His rapid stride brought him quickly out into the middle of the moor. The day was bright enough to make him squint, but the cold wind cut through his thin shirt, and the saturated earth seeped through his knitted hose. He found it easy enough to ignore such discomforts when the air was crisp and clean and, most important, unconfined. He ducked his head against the force of the wind and walked on.

Behind him, he soon heard the soft hoofbeats of the horse. He did not turn around.

"Where are you going?" Mhairi called.

"Go home, Mhairi," he said, and walked ahead.

"You dinna have your boots!"

"Then give them back," he answered over his shoulder.

She drew the horse alongside of him. "We will make it clear that I didna steal your things," she said firmly. "I only took them home to dry them by the fire. Your boots may as well have been drowned in the salt sea, and your cloak was dripping wet."

"Then I hope they are dry, for I will soon come to get them from you," he said, marching on, heels sinking in the muck with each footfall.

She rode up beside him again, and something soft and warm descended over his head. He snatched at it. She had thrown him her plaid, still warm from her body. He gathered it to toss it back.

"Keep it," she said. "The wind is cold." He draped it over one shoulder and walked on.

"Take me as a pledge," she said. He sighed gustily, and stopped to look squarely up at her. She halted the horse and returned his gaze. "Please," she said.

"When I take you for riding the highway, lass—and I will, be sure of it," he added in a deliberate, stony voice, "I will take you on my terms as I declare them. Now go home." He turned and resumed walking.

She did not leave. He had not expected that of her, from what he was learning of her willful nature. Her horse kept pace with him. "Will you tell Simon Kerr where you have been?"

He slowed and looked at her. The sun made a halo behind her, shining reddish through her tousled hair, warming her shoulders with brightness. She held her head stiffly, but the tilt of her chin revealed an uncertainty that made Rowan frown.

She was not the virago that she would have him think. And for some reason, she did not want to be taken down by Simon Kerr. He remembered her words earlier. She did not trust the man to mete out justice to her brother, or to her.

"Nay," he said quietly. "I willna tell him." Besides, he wanted to capture her himself. He owed her for the head-banging and the hospitality, after all.

And he would not be so foolish as to tell Kerr that a lassie had clobbered him into unconsciousness and had locked him in an abandoned ruin for three days. He walked ahead of her again.

"Rowan Scott," she called. "I need your help." The words, riding the wind behind him, had a plaintive tone.

"Your brother is a blessed man, to have such loyalty," he said. "Now go home."

"Rowan Scott—"

"Keep my gear and my horse well for me, until I come for them," he called back.

"I might let the reivers have them," she snapped.

"You do, and you'll pay dearly for it."

The wind whistled low around him, and the cold muck sliced through his stockings as he walked on. Though he did not turn again, he knew that Mhairi watched him for a long time.

He could feel her gaze upon his back, as keenly as if she had touched him. And that touch, this time, was not gentle.

Chapter Eight

~

"O when he came to broken brigs,
He bent his bow and swam;
And when he came to grass growing,
Set down his feet and ran."

—"Rob Roy"

Half the way to Blackdrummond, Rowan stopped, yanked off his soggy stockings, and tossed their sorry remains in a small pool. Adjusting the bright Highland plaid around him, he covered the last league rapidly. Climbing craggy hills dotted with rocks and thick with old grass, he crossed a tumbling burn that chilled his bare feet, and finally stopped at the base of a rocky slope.

He stared upward at the home he had not seen for over three years. Blackdrummond Tower rose high and stark as if it emerged out of bare rock, an impenetrable Border tower on an outcrop at the crest of the hill. Built seventy years earlier, when Rowan's grandfather had been a child, the stronghold was brilliantly protected by its remote, forbidding setting. Only single riders could maneuver the steep slope, and the roof offered watchmen a view that extended for miles.

He walked closer. Within the stout barnekin wall, the four-story stone tower thrust upward. Narrow windows pierced the grim facade like suspicious, watchful eyes.

Never daunted by the grim appearance of this place, Rowan smiled. Dark smoke spiraling up from the chimney reminded him of warmth, of pride, of home. He broke into a run.

Farther up the long slope, sheep grazed through the rough grass. The man tending them sat leaning against a boulder, his bonnet tipped low over his face, his snores loud and rhythmic. Rowan climbed toward him, and raised his voice in an eerie wolf's howl.

The shepherd leaped to his feet, startled awake, and drew a long dirk. Rowan, laughing, waved. The man stared, and his mouth dropped open. He shoved the knife back into his belt, worn over a loose, dirty green doublet.

"Master Rowan! Is't you, dressed like a Highland savage?"

Rowan nodded and came forward. "Sandie Scott! Greetings!"

"Ah, the Black Laird's come back at last!" The man grabbed Rowan by the shoulder, his wide grin partly toothless and full of joy. Rowan hugged his distant cousin, once his father's most loyal riding companion, and stood back. Sandie looked older, his beard nearly white, his reddish hair sparsely arrayed over his head. But mischief still twinkled in his brown eyes.

"You look banged about. And you're wanting for gear," Sandie said, frowning at Rowan's appearance.

"A long journey, Sandie."

"Aye, was it? We had thought to see you a few nights past," Sandie said. "The Auld Laird's been waiting for you. And Lady Anna has been ready to ride out searching for you herself."

"I was delayed," Rowan said. "I couldna send word. Are my grandparents well?"

Sandie rubbed his jaw and grimaced. "Well, I've seen 'em better. This business wi' Alec has been a sore fret to Lady Anna and the Auld Laird both. But they're tough as old meat, that pair. Auld Jock is troubled betimes by the bone-ache in his legs, and doesna ride out much on account o' it. But Lady Anna is more spry than I am."

"You've stayed with them all the time I've been gone, Sandie," Rowan said. "I thank you for it."

"Och, I've been wi' the Auld Laird for all these years, I wouldna leave now, when my beard is near as white as his. And where would I go, but to riding again, or livin' in the Debatable Land, where the worst scoundrels nest? I'd be in a dungeon cell again fast enough. Auld Jock keeps me honest, he does."

"Lady Anna keeps you honest," Rowan corrected.

Sandie chuckled. "Aye, true. She's reformed me and Auld Jock, though it's taken her years to do it. And yourself—? What did those years in that English prison do for you?"

Rowan shrugged. "I was kept in fine quarters. I read some excellent books."

Sandie burst out laughing, throwing back his head in delight. "Books! Your young brother should try that remedy, eh, to cure his reiving mischief. Books! I ne'er read one in my life. Canna do it, see. But when I was imprisoned in Carlisle for thinnin' out the English herds, another prisoner taught me the letters in my name. Uh . . . A-L-X . . . er . . . A—" he stopped, scowling, holding up his fingers.

"Anna can show you the letters sometime, I'm sure. Now, tell me about this business with my brother."

Sandie tipped a shaggy red brow. "You've heard some o' that sorry tale? And you ken about Maggie's death in childbed," he added. Rowan nodded brusquely. "If you carry a grudge against Alec, you've a right to it, hey. I told him that myself. 'The Black Laird will take you to account now that he's free, Master Alec,' I says to him, but you didna come back—"

"Sandie, what of this business about spies?"

"—and Alec didna quake wi' fear, though he should've," Sandie continued, unperturbed. Rowan had nearly forgotten his cousin's long-winded penchant for expressing himself. Now he remembered. "Spies. Hmph. That trouble has your grandparents muckle upset. Well, Alec rode out to fetch Iain Macrae, who lives about a league south o' the Lincraig Hill—"

"Iain Macrae?" Rowan asked sharply. "A Highlander?"

"Aye, a young Highlandman who's wed Devil Davy Armstrong's daughter. They live on land that is deeded to her mother. Iain pays rent to you, lad, which your grandsire accepts for you. The man has been a bonny friend to Alec and the Auld Laird, too, come to that, and now Simon Kerr has put him in his dungeon for the deeds o' that night." He scowled expressively. "Well, a few weeks past, Iain Macrae and our Alec rode out after a gang that's been foraying near here. Those tricksters had shifted your own cattle, see, from the hill pastures to the south. Alec rode out after Heckie Elliot—"

"Heckie's Bairns," Rowan said, half to himself.

Sandie looked at him in surprise. "You're muckle well informed for a man just arrived. Who've you seen?"

"I met Mhairi, Iain Macrae's sister," Rowan said. "And a lad called Christie Armstrong."

"Devil's Christie," Sandie said, nodding. "Favors his da, that one. You met Iain Macrae's own sister? Now there's a bonny lass to rest an eye upon." Sandie grinned. "If I were twenty years younger, I'd court her myself. Sweet as honey to make a man's days and nights glad, hey."

"Oh aye," Rowan said dryly, touching his fingers to his head wound. "Tell me about Alec."

"Well, they rode out on a misty night to reclaim the cattle that had been snatched from Blackdrummond land."

"Hot trod?"

Sandie scratched his head. "Well, nae quite a hot trod in the legal manner, wi' a burning peat on a lance, and a troop o' warden's men. Just the two men after the reivers."

"I would have thought a Blackdrummond Scott would have more sense these days. Go on."

"The next day Simon Kerr rode here to say that Iain was taken and Alec had fled, a broken man. An outlaw. Spies, says Kerr, both of 'em." He spat. " 'Tis what I think o' that, and what I think o' Simon Kerr, a braw brute—"

"Sandie," Rowan said patiently. "Alec—?"

"Och aye. Kerr said Iain had Spanish gold among his booty. The English want him, see, to hang him now. And Alec is gone into the hills. And that's what I ken o' the matter," Sandie finished, folding his great arms over his chest.

"What do you think happened?"

"They reived gear off naughty English papist spies, is what I think. They snatched something by mistake. Why else would Iain have a Spanish load on his horse's back? What good would that do him? Cattle and sheep, aye, and steel back-and-breasts, or a wheel-lock or two, all good gear to take. But Spanish gold is poison in Scotland."

"Well, poison pays well when 'tis melted down. And the Scottish council and the English government both are looking for Scottish agents in league wi' Spain." He nodded to Sandie. "My thanks for the news. I'll go on up now."

"Knock loud at the yett. Your grandparents can hear as keen as dogs, but that serving lass o' theirs is a lazy wench."

Green and tenacious, ivy vines climbed the lower part of Blackdrummond's barnekin wall, and sent tendrils down over rocks and turf. Walking toward the entrance, Rowan looked up. The two massive gates, an outer one of crisscrossed iron and an inner door of stout, iron-studded oak, stood wide open.

His grandfather stood in the shadowed entry. He stepped forward as Rowan approached. Sunlight glinted over his thick, silvery hair and over the stubble that whitened his lean, impassive face. Rowan saw immediately that his grandfather had changed little. Perhaps thinner and whiter, but still hard and lithe as a whip.

Jock Scott lifted an eyebrow and looked slowly and calmly at his grandson's bruised, bearded face, at the Highland plaid and ill-fitting shirt, at the bare feet. Without a comment, he turned to gaze out over the hillsides beyond, squinting his keen blue eyes against the bright sun.

"My father built this place," he said in the calm, quiet voice that Rowan remembered so well, a voice that had commanded so much respect, though it had rarely been raised. "High on this hill, so that he could watch out over the glen and the moors. Blackdrummond Tower has always been a stronghold for Scotts."

"And ever will be," Rowan said, scanning the forested hillsides beyond Blackdrummond hill. "I thank you for keeping it for me, sir."

Jock Scott nodded once, brusquely. "My elder brother inherited Blackdrummond from my father. I inherited Lincraig. This tower came to you, Rowan, when my brother and his son died. That was the night my own son Will—your father—also perished. All at the hands o' the Kerrs. A black night for Blackdrummond."

Rowan nodded, knowing well the litany of that terrible night twenty-five years ago, when the deaths of his uncle

and cousin and father left him to inherit Blackdrummond.
"You were but eight years old, and Alec two. Your
mother birthed a wee one a week later, and lost that child,
and then died in her weak, unhappy state," Jock finished
quietly.

Rowan let out a slow breath, sensing the burden of his
grandfather's deep grief, so deep that Jock Scott, called
the Firebrand then, had made a vicious retaliatory raid of
slaughter and burning upon the Kerrs that still echoed in
local memory, and had kept the flames hot in the feud
between the Kerrs and Scotts for years afterward.

" 'Twas long ago, sir," Rowan said. "You and Anna
became our parents, Alec and I. You were fine guardians
for two wee lads."

Jock shrugged. "You were nae trouble to us."

"You have always been the true laird of Blackdrummond," Rowan said, "although 'tis chartered in my
name."

Jock shook his head. "I am laird o' Lincraig Castle, that
hasna been lived in for decades. And laird o' Newhouse,
that burned too. There's never been coin to rebuild either
place."

"That doesna matter. Blackdrummond is your true
home."

"And yours once again." Jock glanced at him. "So
you're here. Your grandmother will want to know if you
got the letters she sent you in England. We heard nae
word from you until a few months ago, when you were
released, and then again a few weeks ago."

"I had a letter from her just after I was confined, that
told me Alec had taken a wife." Rowan paused, and then
went on, his voice flat and low. "And a few others. I
rarely got letters. The posting services were at the discretion of the guards and the warden."

"You know about Maggie, then?"

"Aye, I got that letter." Rowan stared out over the landscape, feeling as gray and hard as the rocks at his feet.

Jock watched the hillside where Sandie whistled after
the sheep. After a while he spoke again. "Sandie will have
told you the latest news o' Alec, then."

"Aye. I had heard word o' that in Edinburgh."

"I will believe Alec went reiving and riding March

treason all over the English border in moonlight. But he is clean o' true treason. He is nae spy. Tell that to the king's council."

Rowan said nothing. He would not support his brother. Neither would he argue his guilt. Frowning, he gazed southward, toward the rounded slope of Lincraig Hill.

Jock turned to tilt a brow toward his grandson, taking in the Highland plaid, the bare feet, and the head wound "That's a handsome bruise."

Rowan shrugged. "Scoundrels abound in these moors and hills, sir. I met the highway riders o' Lincraig."

Jock huffed a low laugh. "Purse shifters. You outran them?"

"A tricky thing in the murk and the rain. My horse slipped in the bog," Rowan answered. "I went down."

"Some say the ghosts o' Lincraig ride that moor now, and nae true thieves." Jock gave him an amused glance. "Lost all your gear, and your horse, I see, to your own ancestors."

"I'll have my gear back within a day," Rowan said.

"A Blackdrummond to the bone," Jock said in a satisfied tone. "Your grandmother will be anxious to coddle you wi' a dram and a hot meal." He laid his hand briefly on Rowan's shoulder, a rare expression of affection that warmed him like no fire or dram could have done. "Come in and bide, then."

Blessed words, and a blessed welcome. Rowan smiled.

" 'Tis no bairnie's drink," Anna insisted.

" 'Tis," Jock said. He settled back in his wide elbow chair. " 'Tis."

His wife handed the pewter flagon she held to Rowan, and looked sternly at her husband. " 'Tis an English recipe from my own mother. Cream, honey, and healing herbs. Look at his pate, man, he's sore injured and needs a posset, not a dram of that Spanish sherry wine to act like another horse-kick to the head."

"A posset and coddling," Jock said. "Only an English-woman would give a braw Scotsman a bairnie's posset o' hot milk and honey." His eyes twinkled as he raised his own flagon to his lips and drank.

Rowan, watching, remembered how much Jock

enjoyed teasing Anna. But he knew that she gave it back often enough.

"Aye so," Anna said, fisting her hands on her hips. "You took me from my English family in the middle of the night fifty years ago. D'you expect me to change my English ways so quick?"

Jock twisted his mouth awry and looked at his grandson. "Nah," he said, "you're still the fiery wee bride I stole on the eve of Arthur Musgrave's own wedding. He will die happy, that auld man."

Anna batted her hand gently at Jock's head. "You'll be the one to die happy, auld man," she said softly, smiling.

"That I will." Jock kept his expression serious, but Rowan saw that a smile, and a little of his heart, too, glimmered in his grandfather's eyes.

Rowan bit back his own grin and lifted the pewter cup to his mouth. He sipped the cloying, creamy stuff slowly.

"There, see you, Anna, he still does as you say," Jock said.

"Hah, and never did, for he was made in your mold," she replied. "Rowan, if you want more of the beef roast, or another bowl of porridge, I'll have Grace fetch some from the kitchen."

He shook his head and pushed away the empty bowl near him. "My thanks, Granna, I am full to bursting." He patted his stomach and glanced up. His use of the child-hood name had pleased her, for a rosy blush seeped from her cheeks into the roots of her white hair, wrapped about her head in thick braids, and her green eyes softened. A moment later she placed her hands on her thin hips and scowled at him as if he were eight years old again.

"You hardly tasted that meal," she said. "And here you come in, as thin as I have ever seen you, with a black, swollen egg on your pate, and dressed as bare and strange as any Highland loon. Where did you get such a plaidie? 'Tis not Lowland make."

Knowing he had much to explain, Rowan sighed, and held out his hand to Jock. Wordlessly, his grandfather handed him the flagon of sherry. Rowan downed a long gulp, and another. His grandmother watched, frowning. Jock refilled the cup.

"I got the plaidie from a Highland lass," Rowan said. "Mhairi Macrae." Jock raised his brows. Anna smiled.

"A pretty lass, and a kind one," she said. "Simon Kerr has taken her brother, and God knows why. But 'tis no surprise to me that she helped you when she saw that you had been robbed and taken down by shifters and thieves."

"Mmm," Rowan said noncommittally, and sipped again.

"Go easy, Rowan," Anna said. " 'Tis drawn from that cask of Jerez wine. You'll surely feel its kick later."

Sipping again before setting the cup down, Rowan turned on the bench and leaned toward the fire in the hearth. In a low voice, he quickly explained to his grandparents the assignment given him by the privy council. He mentioned the Spanish shipwreck briefly, and told them what little the council knew of Alec Scott's involvement. He made no further mention of Mhairi Macrae or the Lincraig riders.

While he spoke, Sandie Scott entered the hall, taking a seat by the fire to listen quietly. When Rowan finished, his cousin chuckled.

"A Blackdrummond Scott made deputy to Simon Kerr?" Sandie grinned. "I like that, I do. The council has humor."

"Or a foolish wish to see the lawmen at each other's throats over an old feud," Anna said.

"The council canna easily find a clean man to take a wardenship, or to ride the law among the Borders now," Jock told Rowan. "Every warden, deputy and land sergeant in Scotland has ridden reiving himself, or feuds wi' a riding family."

" 'Tis said o' Simon Kerr that he turns a blind eye to some o' the night riding that goes on in this March," Sandie said, "if the reivers give him a share o' what they snatch."

"He's the son o' a spoiler and a murderer," Jock said.

"What his father did does not mean the son is corrupt," Anna said.

Jock stared at her. "He took down Iain, and he's after Alec. And he's a Kerr," he said indignantly.

"Do you mean to ride down the highway thieves now that you are deputy?" Sandie asked Rowan, who nodded.

"Luck go wi' you, then, for nae man has seen their faces, nor kens when they will ride out again."

"I will find them," Rowan said.

"They say that the haunts o' Lincraig—" Sandie began.

"Nonsense," Jock muttered.

Anna leaned over and murmured something into her husband's ear. "Aye, Rowan kens that matter," Jock said.

"And the rest?" she asked. Jock shook his head.

Puzzled, Rowan looked from one to the other. "What is it?"

"We had a message from Alec last week," Anna said.

"You know where he is?" Rowan asked sharply.

"Nay. But he sent us a letter," Anna said. "He needs our help."

"He has no right to ask," Rowan growled.

"Oh, he does," Anna said. "For Jamie."

"Who?"

"His son," Anna said. "Alec wants us to fetch him."

"His son?" Rowan felt as if a lead ball had slammed into his gut. "I thought the child died with Maggie," he said slowly.

"Not at all," his grandmother said. "Jamie, he's called. He's over two now. Strong and bonny, dark like his father and lovely as his mother—" Anna stopped. "Pray pardon, Rowan," she said quietly.

Rowan turned a stony glance to the fire.

"Alec has a bastel house nae far from here," Jock said. "He handfasted to a lass several months ago to help raise the bairn. He could see that the laddie was a handful for your grandmother."

"No handful, that wee angel. But Alec chose poorly this time," Anna said. "The lass has a good enough heart, but no head, and no courage."

"Where is the child now?" Rowan asked.

"With Alec," Anna said. "After the night Alec fled, I went to his house and found that the lass and bairn were gone too. She followed Alec into the hills, though he had told her to come here."

"A reiver came to our door in a cold rain last week," Jock said. "Lang Will Croser, he's called. He brought word from Alec. Lang Will said Alec's lass has fled

again, and left Jamie wi' him. And Alec has hidden him,
and wants us to fetch him."

"Sandie meant to go," Anna said. "But now that you are
here, you can do it." She smiled at Rowan.

He sighed. "I canna go off to coddle a bairnie, Granna.
I have duties here as deputy. Alec made this cursed maze
of his life, and he can walk through it himself."

"Alec betrayed you in the lowest way a brother can
do," Jock said. "But he is your blood. And his wee lad is
your own nephew. And my great-grandson. I want the lad
fetched."

"I dinna care to help my brother," Rowan said coldly.
"Let Alec find a nursemaid for him wherever he is."

"Alec isna calling for a nursemaid," Jock growled. "He
sent word that there is danger for the laddie."

Rowan glanced sharply at him. "How so?"

"Alec is a broken man now, an outlaw wi' wardens on
his tail," Jock answered. "The English want him handed
to their custody at the next truce day meeting, just as they
want to take Iain Macrae. Lang Will said that the English
warden is searching for the child in hope of flushing out
the father."

"They might better hunt the father," Rowan said.

"Aye, but he's a Blackdrummond Scott, and willna be
taken easily. They mean to find the bairn and keep him as
a hostage."

"A pledge against Alec's good behavior?" Rowan
asked. "I thought that method was Scots law only."

" 'Tis," Jock answered. "The English willna pledge the
lad, wi' signed papers and agreements. They will take
him, and hold him hostage for Alec's surrender. Or keep
him."

"Aye so," Anna said. "Even if Alec gave himself to the
law to protect his son's welfare, we might not see our
Jamie again. Many times, the English have kept hostages
for years and years."

"We'd have to steal the laddie back," Sandie added.

"Nae Blackdrummond Scott will be raised in England,"
Jock growled. Anna gave her husband a steely look. "You
ken well my meaning, lass," he said. "You taught our lads
your English talk when they could have learned good
broad Scots, and you gave them those clerky skills wi'

letters and books. But they are Scotts and Scotsmen from their hairs to their toes. Alec's laddie will ne'er feel his Scottish blood if an English family raises him."

Anna looked at Rowan. "You'll fetch our Jamie," she said. "The English warden must not find him first. He needs to be with kin who know him and love him."

"I'll ride wi' ye," Sandie said. "We'll give 'em a taste o' Blackdrummond law, hey?"

Rowan felt a heated flush slide up his face. He saw his grandfather sidle a glance at him.

Maggie's child. He stifled an indrawn breath at the thought. Any hope he had cherished of a wife and child in his life had been destroyed when Maggie had wed Alec, soon after Rowan had been taken into English confinement. The shock of that betrayal still lingered in his heart. And here they sat, talking of Maggie's child.

Alec's child. Rowan steeled his jaw and clenched his fist.

Anna chewed her lip fretfully and watched him. Jock's expression was carefully reserved, but the brilliant azure gleam in his eyes revealed how deeply Jock cared about Alec's son.

Rowan sighed. "Where is this bairn?"

"In the Debatable Land," Jock said.

Rowan stared at him. "Jesu," he muttered. "You expect me to ride through that nest of vipers carrying a babe in arms?"

"He's no babe in arms. He can run, and says several words now," Anna said proudly. "And he's taught to the jordan pot."

"What a fine riding comrade," he drawled. "I know naught of bairns, Granna."

"Sandie will go wi' you," Jock said.

"He knows less of bairns than I do."

"But he knows Jamie," Anna said.

Rowan sighed. Then he nodded. "First I need some rest. Then I will have to get my horse and my gear. And I must meet with Simon Kerr."

"You will hasten," Anna said, beaming.

"He's the Black Laird," Sandie said, grinning. "He'll hae his gear back and take down the Lincraig riders in but an hour or twa. He'll yammer whatever Simon Kerr wants to hear most, and be off to the Debatable Land by rise o' sun tomorrow."

"Aye," Jock said, nodding in satisfaction. "He will."

Rowan downed the last of the wine and sighed again.

Chapter Nine

~

*"As for your steed, he shall not want
The best of corn and hay;
But as to yoursel, kind sir,
I've naething for to say."*

—*"The Laird of Knotington"*

Mounted on a dappled horse from Blackdrummond's stable, and wearing an old doublet of his own and boots borrowed from his grandfather, Rowan passed Lincraig Hill at a steady canter. The castle looked lonely and deserted, a ruin of broken stone softened by moss and ivy. Far ahead, he saw the dark and light shapes of grazing cattle and sheep moving slowly along the distant hillsides.

The dale supported many tenant farmers who raised herds and lived in stout bastel houses, the fortified stone and thatch buildings common in the Borders. Most of the farms had been settled generations ago, owned by the Scott lairds of Blackdrummond and Lincraig, and rented by the subsequent heirs of the tenants. Most of those families took their living from cattle and sheep, since the hard, scrubby land yielded few crops.

But the better part of many livings, Rowan knew, came from reiving in the night. Furtive and often violent trading of beasts and goods had long ago become the accepted custom of the Borders. Most of the Blackdrummond tenants engaged in some form of reiving, and defended themselves and their goods against both Scottish and English riders in the dead of night.

As a deputy, he was obligated to discourage such reiving. But as a Blackdrummond Scott, he understood the use and the custom of it, and had ridden night forays himself more times than he could have counted.

Frowning against the sun, Rowan watched tendrils of hearth smoke rise into the sky from the few squat, thatched-roof houses scattered over the hills. He was not out here to chase and harry reivers, but to find the house of his tenant, Iain Macrae, and Macrae's bonny sister. The laird wanted his gear back.

Guiding the dappled horse, he rode across the moorland, which was drier now than the first evening he had ridden through here. His recollection of that night and the days that followed was dim—although his memories of Mhairi were clear enough.

He remembered her serene face, so easy to watch, and the gentle warmth of her hands while she had nursed his wound. Stirring in his saddle, he recalled, too, the sultry softness of her body when he had lain against her. He had spent a good deal of time thinking about her, about her earnestness and her loyalty, about her Madonna's face and her devilish ways, and about what she had asked of him. And about how she had affected him, both intentionally and unintentionally.

She was a blend of contradictions, peacefulness and torment whirled together, like the wild, unpredictable sea, he thought. Stormy or serene by changing moments, always astonishingly beautiful, and equally capable of dealing hurt as well as succor.

Rowan had an uncomfortable feeling that he would never be the same for having met Mhairi Macrae. And he wondered if she would stir the tide in his life again soon.

He would definitely turn the tide in hers. He fully intended to take her down. He only waited for the proper opportunity. If naught else, he thought grimly, he owed her a few nights on a cold stone floor—although he would generously forgo the crack on the head. But he had decided not to take down Devil's Christie Armstrong. The lad's father had been a good riding companion, and Rowan owed this favor to his son.

He had scant interest in allowing Mhairi to act as a pledge for her brother. Turning her over to the authority of a Kerr had no appeal, and the privy council had directed him to apprehend the Scottish spies, not scheme with the locals. Beyond all else, releasing the only suspect in custody would be foolish.

Rowan wondered if Mhairi truly understood the danger she risked each time she rode the Lincraig highway. She had earned a hard lesson, and would be taken down eventually. If Rowan did not teach her the peculiarities of Border custom himself, reivers or Simon Kerr would take on the task, and she would learn the consequences of her highway rides.

He recalled Mhairi's blushing cheeks, remembered her wide gray eyes as she had pleaded with him to help her. Rowan did not want any reiver to touch her. If concern for Iain sent her out on the road at night to rob the king's messengers, then there was an element of honor in what she did. Such loyalty should not suffer punishment.

And if there was no honor to it, if she too was linked with this circle of spies, then he would discover that quick enough. Capturing and holding her at Blackdrummond Tower would give him the chance to determine what she knew about the matter.

When the Lincraig hill was a league and more behind him, he reined in his horse and looked south. A few dark, shaggy cows grazed along a rocky hillside. At the top of the slope, a square stone house sat beside a stand of trees.

In the yard, a fine bay horse, its reddish coat gleaming, nuzzled at the grass. Valentine lifted his head, whickered, and dipped his head again.

Rowan spurred the dappled horse and rode forward.

"Much trouble could come o' this," Jennet said, as she stacked wooden bowls to clear the table after the breakfast meal. "Dinna ride out again, Mhairi, I beg you."

"Trouble, aye, now that you've freed the Black Laird," Christie said ominously. "Here, Jennet, leave that," he said hastily, grabbing an oatcake from a wooden platter.

"Could I stop Rowan Scott when he walked out, and he twice my size?" Mhairi asked irritably. She shifted her infant nephew, a tiny bundle in her arms, and sat on the bench beside Christie. "I didna hold a weapon. And he had given me his word."

"And kept it. He promised nae to harm you," Christie said. "He said naught about staying where we had set him.

Listen close to a Border promise next time." He reached
down to pass a broken bit of oatcake to the gray wolfhound hovering beneath the table. "Gone, and nae even a
coin o' ransom from the Auld Laird."

"Dinna fret so at Mhairi," Jennet said. "The Black
Laird couldna be held for long. And I'm grateful to you
both. You've risked your lives for Iain's safety, and
surely kept him from hanging. Simon has had nae word
from the council this whole month."

"Nae word that we know about," Christie amended, his
mouth full. "Is there any roast mutton left?"

"You ate the last bit," Jennet said. She looked at
Mhairi. " 'Tis an amazement to me that you took down
the Black Laird at all, from what is said about that one."

"He wasna so hard to take down," Christie said, licking
his fingers. "Weak as wee Robin."

"*Ach,* dinna listen to your Uncle Christie," Mhairi said
to the infant tucked in her arms. "You're muckle strong,
and bonny too, and will be a braw man," she cooed,
smoothing the silky tuft of blond hair crowning his small
head. Robin blinked at her with dark blue eyes, his
expression so serious that Mhairi laughed.

"If Rowan Scott was in your dungeon, then he's surely
a bonny, braw man, from what I recall," Jennet said.

Christie made a sound of manly disgust. "Och, what
does bonny matter? The man is riding free now, and he
knows who the Lincraig riders are. He'll soon take us
down and toss us into Simon's dungeon. He has the
authority as laird and as March deputy. If he doesna
snatch us on the road, he'll summon us to appear at the
next truce day meeting. We'll be tried for robbery, and
likely hanged or sent to prison."

"I hoped he would help us free Iain, since his brother is
involved too," Mhairi said. "But he said me nay when I
asked."

"Ask again," Christie said. "He's had time to think
on it."

"I hear there's nae great love between Alec and Rowan
Scott," Jennet said. "That may be why he refused you."

"What happened between them?" Mhairi asked. Robin
squirmed restlessly in her arms, and she shushed him
gently.

Jennet wiped crumbs from the table, her brow furrowed. "Truly I am nae certain," she said. " 'Tis said there was betrayal atween them, over the incident that sent Rowan to an English prison."

"What did Rowan do?" Mhairi asked.

She shrugged. "I know little about it. A reiving crime, March treason I think. I recall some word o' murder."

Mhairi frowned and rubbed Robin's warm little back while he settled against her shoulder, and wondered what had happened between the brothers. She had seen Alec Scott only once or twice, and knew little of him except that he was handsome and was said to be a bold reiver, and that he had led Iain into serious trouble. But she knew his grandparents at Blackdrummond, and thought them kind people.

When she thought about Rowan Scott, she felt a blush rise into her cheeks. He was as complicated a man as Alec, and more disturbing to her than she cared to admit.

"If Blackdrummond isna inclined to help Alec Scott, I canna blame him," Christie said. From beneath the table, the wolfhound laid her head on his thigh and looked up at him with dark, pleading eyes. "Och, Bluebell, you great greedy lass," Christie murmured, slipping a piece of oatcake into her mouth.

"Mhairi, when you spoke wi' Simon the other night, did he say we could see Iain?" Jennet asked.

"He promised we would see him soon," Mhairi answered evasively as she handed the bundled, sleepy infant back to his mother. She did not want to tell Jennet what Simon had said.

"I hope to visit him soon," Jennet said wistfully. "He hasna yet seen Robin." She walked over to the hearth and laid the child in his cradle. Then she picked up a plaid shawl from the bench and draped it over her head and shoulders. "Mhairi, will you watch the bairn for me? He'll sleep for a bit, I think. I want to take the sheep to the far hill to graze."

"I'll come wi' you," Christie said. "Here, Bluebell!"

"Och, leave the dog. She ran the sheep too far the other day," Jennet complained as she accompanied her brother out of the house. "She'll be a better comrade for Mhairi than for us."

Mhairi stood in the open doorway and watched them walk through the yard. Christie stopped for a moment to pat Rowan Scott's bay horse, which was tethered in the sweet grass near the house. Then they headed toward the sheep that grazed in the rough grasses along the west side of the hill.

The sun was warm on Mhairi's uplifted face, and a soft autumn breeze blew gently through her hair. In the distance, the trees edging the hillsides swayed, golden and blazing, beneath the bright sky. Mhairi watched Jennet and Christie until they disappeared over the crest of a distant hill. Then she turned to go inside.

Bluebell, standing beside her, barked abruptly. Mhairi glanced around the deserted yard, then looked east, and caught her breath.

A man on a dappled horse cantered toward the house. The rider's black hair whipped out in the wind. Mhairi knew that raven hair. She had smoothed it with her own hands.

The dog barked again. "Easy, Bluebell," Mhairi murmured, patting her shoulders. "He willna harm us." But suddenly she was not entirely certain of that.

Excitement and dread churned within her as she watched Rowan Scott approach. Her keen intuition seemed to have lost its usual clarity. She did not know why he rode toward her with such calm determination. She hoped he only meant to fetch his gear and his horse. But he might intend to arrest her. Perhaps, she thought hopefully, he had decided to help her brother after all.

Bluebell barked again. Inside the house, Robin awoke, crying out, a piteous cry that Mhairi could not ignore. Glancing anxiously at the approaching rider, she ducked inside. Scooping the child out of his cradle, she went back to the doorway and stepped out into the sunlight.

Rowan Scott halted his horse at the edge of the yard. Somehow his green eyes were as piercing from there as if he stood a handspan away. She drew a deep breath and walked toward him.

He could have watched her endlessly. She moved as easily as a breeze floating through heather, her hips and shoulders swaying in a gentle rhythm, her bare feet sure on the hard, tufted ground. The hem of her skirt swung like a soft bell around her ankles. Sunlight glinted over the dark, thick braid that spilled over one shoulder.

Once again Rowan had the haunting sense that he had seen Mhairi somewhere, not long ago before she had cracked his head out on the Lincraig road. But as before, the time and place eluded him, evasive as a fleeting dream.

Mhairi stopped in the middle of the yard, lifted her bundle to the other shoulder, and stared evenly at him. Her gray eyes had the clarity of silver. The breeze lifted tendrils of her hair and stirred her skirt. Rowan watched her silently.

He wondered if the small, swaddled infant she held was her own, and realized how little he knew about her. A sudden, piercing jealousy went through him at the thought of the unknown father, and the intense wave of displeasure he felt surprised him. Tightening the reins, he cleared his throat.

"Madam," he said formally.

"Master Scott." Coming closer, she seemed to flow toward him, strength and grace and nimble ease in every step.

Walking in the Highlands must have taught her to move like that, Rowan thought, like wind rocking the heather. Then he scowled. He need not dwindle from a deputy to a poet just because a lass swayed like heaven, and made his body go hard as he watched.

"How did you know where to find me?" she asked.

"My family seems well acquainted with you," he said, grateful for a practical question to address. "My cousin Sandie Scott told me your name, and where you lived. And Lady Anna, my grandmother, assumed that you must have showed me generous hospitality when I was set upon by thieves."

She blushed as easily as he remembered, pink spreading through her translucent skin. The scrap inside the swaddling mewled and moved against her, and she patted the tiny back and head. Watching that slender, gentle hand, Rowan remembered how softly she had touched his own head. And then he reminded himself how forcefully that sweet hand, wrapped around a pistol butt, had struck him. However bonny, a lass to beware.

He nodded toward the bairn. "Is that yours, then?"

"He's my brother's bairn," she said. "My sister-in-law has gone to tend the sheep." She lifted her chin. "Have you given thought to what I asked you? Are you here to take me as a pledge for Iain?"

He crossed his hands over his saddle and looked down at her. "When I am ready to take you down," he said softly, "you will know it. I have told you that."

Mhairi watched him, her eyes as gray as rain. He returned her steady gaze, then turned to lift the folded plaid tucked behind his saddle cantle. "I came for my horse and my gear. And to give this back to you." He handed her the cloth.

She took it, balancing the babe as she did so. "I will fetch your things," she said curtly, and turned away.

Rowan dismounted and walked over to Valentine, patting his shoulders and murmuring to him as he looked the horse over. The animal was well brushed and keenly interested, just now, in the damp grasses at his feet. Hearing a dog bark as he turned toward the house, Rowan cautiously approached the door.

A lanky gray wolfhound, all legs and ugly head and bared teeth, faced him over the threshold. Rowan stood still while the dog, on closer glance no more than a pup, took a step toward him.

"Easy, Bluebell." Mhairi's voice came from inside the shadowed interior of the house. "Be still, lass."

The dog relaxed and sniffed at Rowan's breeches, then shoved at his stomach and thrust her nose into his hand. Rowan hesitantly patted the wiry gray head. When the hound begged for more, he rubbed his fingers over her head and neck, murmuring a greeting. A moment later, the dog yelped and jumped up, resting two large feet on Rowan's shoulders, and began licking his cheek.

"Bluebell!" Mhairi called. "Down, lass!"

Rowan, chuckling, shoved gently at the dog. But Bluebell lifted higher on her back legs, standing nearly as tall as Rowan, and barked happily as she continued to slather his face.

"She isna much of a guardian," he commented as he

shoved at her again, harder this time, turning his wet
face away.

Mhairi came forward to push at the dog's shoulders
with one hand, holding the swaddled infant in her other
arm. "She isna much for herding sheep, either. She's
young and big, but she wants for fierceness," she said, as
Bluebell dropped to her four feet and stood gazing raptly
at Rowan.

"Even when reivers come?"

"Aye. She only growls a bit, and barks, and would
make them welcome if she could. Daffin lassie," Mhairi
said, ruffling Bluebell's tufted brow.

The infant suddenly began to wail, and Mhairi jiggled
the bundle in her arms, distracted. Rowan stepped inside,
and Bluebell turned to lick his hand enthusiastically.

"Where is my gear?" he asked, glancing around.

The bairn whimpered loudly. Mhairi glanced at Rowan.
"When I can put this one down, I'll fetch it," she said, and
moved toward the cradle near the hearth.

Rowan looked around the small, simply furnished main
room. The smoke-darkened walls, once whitewashed,
gave the house a dim, cozy atmosphere, enhanced by the
mingled scents of garlic and herbs suspended on ropes
attached to the ceiling rafters. In the shadows at the back
of the main room, he noticed that a large curtain hid one
corner of the chamber, where he guessed a bed was
located. In the other corner, a ladder led up to a dark loft.

The bairn now abandoned whimpering in favor of long,
quivery wails. Mhairi began to sway, murmuring to the
infant, and glanced at Rowan distractedly.

He gestured toward a storage chest beneath the small
front window. "Is my gear in there? I can get it myself."

" 'Tisna there." Mhairi made a cooing noise, rubbing
the child's back.

"What's bothering it?" Rowan asked over the din.

"Hungry, perhaps, but his mother is gone for a bit. He
may be wet." She worked a finger inside the wrappings,
and wrinkled her nose. "Aye."

Turning away, she took a few cloths from a basket and
tossed them over her shoulder. Then she dropped her
folded plaid to the hearthstone and knelt to lay the infant

down on it, murmuring softly to the child as she unwrapped the swaddling cloths.

Rowan stepped forward, waiting silently, watching her
back as she bent over the babe. The sinuous curves of her
hips and waist revealed a lithe, elegantly shaped body
beneath the woolen dress and plaid shawl. Her braid
slipped down, a dark, gleaming rope that he knew would
feel like cool silk.

Rowan flexed his hands, wanting, suddenly, to touch
her hair, to capture its glossy mass in his hands. He imagined, too, so quickly that he could not stop the image, the
path that his hands would take as they traced the sensuous
contours of her hips and breasts. Drawing a deep breath
against his impulsive thoughts, he found it nearly impossible to shift his gaze.

She spoke softly to the infant, and Rowan heard its
mewling response. Mhairi laughed and glanced over her
shoulder at Rowan, her eyes sparkling, her expression
unconsciously sweet, as if she wanted him to share her
joy in whatever the bairn had done.

Something stirred and awoke in him then. He clenched
his fist to still the feeling, but he could not stem its tide. A
lost dream came pouring back, compelling and urgent.
That dream had been destroyed when he had learned of
Maggie's marriage to Alec. The wound left behind had
been probed afresh when he had heard that she had left
Alec a son.

Mhairi laughed, a little trill, and continued to play with
the infant, glancing again at Rowan. Once he had hoped
to watch Maggie smile and coo over a babe, and then turn
to him in just that way, proud and sweet and welcoming.

He nearly walked out of the stone house in that
moment.

But he was unable to take his gaze from the simple,
beautiful sight at the hearth. Such gentleness, such nur-
turing was a rare gift, and did not exist in his world.
Craving that warmth, wanting to stay near it just for this
moment, he stayed. And knew such love would never be
directed at him.

Betrayal and loneliness had rendered his world far
darker than the one he witnessed here. He felt isolated

suddenly, as if he stood outside a firelit, laughter-warm house on a cold night, and longed for an invitation inside.

He forgot, for the moment, the troublesome highway robber, and saw only the woman, and wished she were his. He stepped closer. Then he stopped, feeling awkward and far too vulnerable.

"I'll get my gear, then, from the storage chest," he said.

She shook her head as she adjusted the infant's clothing. "I said 'twasna there. Reivers might snatch it quick, if I had put it there."

He frowned. "Have they come again?"

"Nay, God be thanked." She glanced at him, her eyes like soft smoke in the dim light, the surrounding lashes thick and black. "Only you, Master Reiver."

"Dinna speak to me of snatching gear, lass," he said softly. "I wouldna be here looking for my own boots and jack if you didna have such a fine talent for reiving yourself."

She shot him an irritated glance this time. Rowan felt relieved to be on more familiar ground with her. He scowled at her in return, and she turned her back abruptly.

Bluebell padded over to Mhairi and nosed at her head. Mhairi shifted away. The dog sniffed curiously at the child, who jerked its tiny arms in a startled manner and began to scream again. The wail surprised the dog, who barked loudly.

Rowan laid a firm hand on Bluebell's shoulder and moved her out of the way. Mhairi looked gratefully up at him.

"Thank you. Could you wet this, please?" She flipped a white cloth toward him. Catching it, he dipped it in a bucket of warm water near the hearth, and handed it to her. She applied it deftly and swiftly to the child's bottom, murmuring softly all the while.

Rowan had hardly been this close to an infant before. He leaned closer, peering over Mhairi's back at the pink, tiny, perfectly formed creature, which had ceased its pitiable squalling. Mhairi lifted the miniature legs with one hand, and slid a soft cloth beneath its skinny rump.

Rowan blinked in surprise when he saw the fleshy male artillery displayed there. "Quite a laddie," he remarked.

Mhairi shot him a sidelong glance. "All laddies look

quite overblessed at this age," she said. " 'Twill change as
he grows."

"Ah," he said, nodding. "And how old is this one, then?
I trow he is wee enough to fit in my hand."

"Five weeks," she answered.

A disturbing thought occurred to him. "Will he be
much larger when he is—ah, say, two or so years, then?"

"A good deal larger, and quite sturdy by then."

"That's good to know," he said with relief.

Mhairi laughed and gave him a perplexed look.
"Why?"

Rowan shrugged and stood back. "Just a thought." He
felt his cheeks heating in embarrassment. Though he did
not wish to appear a lackbrain, he truly had scant experience of small bairns. But he would be challenged with the
care of one soon enough, once he fetched Alec's son as
his grandparents wished him to do.

Watching Mhairi tuck the clean cloth in some mysterious manner around the babe, he was relieved that his
grandmother had said Alec's lad was trained to use a
jordan. He had no desire to be untangling soiled cloths
from a squealing bairn inside the boundaries of the worst
nest of thieves in the Borderlands. Such untangling
should be Alec's task, he thought bitterly.

Mhairi finished wrapping the babe and stood. "Here,
take him if you want your gear," she said, pressing the
infant to his chest. "His name is Robert Macrae. Robin."

Rowan's arms came up in surprise, moving instinctively to catch what came toward him. Mhairi laid her
hand over his for a moment to make sure he had a firm
hold of the head. Lightning flashed through his belly, a
deep stab of awareness as she touched his skin.

"Keep hold of his head, and stay still," she said. "You
willna be a threat, I think, Master Reiver, with your arms
so full of a bairnie." Eyes twinkling, she tossed him a
sweet, bright smile, as if pleased to have cleverly and
gently waylaid him. She went to the loft ladder and
climbed up.

Rowan looked down at the infant, who blinked at him.
A frown wrinkled the tiny face, and the miniature chin
was scrunched and wobbly, as if a loud wail was imminent. Rowan was not entirely sure he had the thing

securely, for he could hardly feel the slight weight in his
arms. The head, hardly larger than an apple, bobbled in
his hand.

Robin mewled and squirmed, and a gummy, dimpled
grin blossomed on his little face. Rowan could not help
but laugh. Glancing up, he saw Mhairi's feet and the hem
of her gown at the top of the ladder. Glimpsing a fine,
firm length of lower leg, he strolled closer, holding the
child awkwardly but with better confidence.

Mhairi disappeared into the loft. Waiting, Rowan
walked the perimeter of the room, jiggling the infant.
Bluebell trotted at his side.

A few minutes later, Mhairi came back down the rungs.
From where he stood, Rowan could appreciate the slender, muscular lines of her bare calves. Then he noticed
she grasped his long black boots in one arm. She tossed
them to the floor.

" 'Twill take a few moments to bring down your
things," she explained. "But if you are in a hurry, I can
throw it all down to the floor quick like." She climbed up.

"Nay!" Rowan called, thinking of his undented Spanish
helmet. He looked at the bairn. "Laddie, you must fend
for yourself now," he muttered.

Crossing the room, he bent over the cradle and gently
laid the babe on the soft linens piled inside. While Robin
stared up at him, Rowan tucked a square of wool over the
child's waving legs. Then he set the cradle to rocking
with his foot and looked at the dog, who was chewing
nonchalantly on one of the boots that Mhairi had tossed to
the floor.

"Hey!" he exclaimed. Bluebell looked up. "Here, guard
the lad," Rowan said, pointing. The dog padded over and
sat near the cradle. Rowan raised his eyebrows in mild
surprise at such ready obedience, and climbed the ladder
swiftly.

Chapter Ten

*"But now I've got what lang I sought,
And I may not stay wi' thee."*

— *"Lord Maxwell's Goodnight"*

Thin sunbeams pierced the thatched roof and spilled down into the loft. Kneeling in a dark corner, Mhairi shoved aside the loose floorboard and reached into the shallow space created between the loft floor and the ceiling of the main room. Grasping Rowan's heavy leather jack, she dragged it out and turned to set it down. She jumped slightly when Rowan Scott emerged over the top of the ladder.

He stood upright in the small loft, bumping his head on a sloped rafter and wincing. Mhairi remembered his head wound with a twinge of remorse. Rowan glanced at the low bed, then looked past it to see her in the shadows.

"Where's Robin?" she asked.

"Watching that hound of yours," he said. He came forward tentatively, stooping with the gradual slant of the ceiling. Kneeling beside her, he peered into the hole in the floor, which was crammed full of his gear.

"A canny place to hide valuables," he commented.

"Dinna tell your reiving friends about it," she said, digging her arm inside.

"Think you I am such a scoundrel? I've been muckle courteous this day. I've even tended your bairn."

"My nephew. And you have been courteous," she agreed, glancing at him. Caught by a shaft of light, Rowan's eyes shone a soft, clear green as he looked back at her.

Courteous indeed, she thought, and suddenly wanted

him gone almost as much as she wanted him to stay. This notorious reiver had a strange effect on her, with his eyes as green as moss and his hair like tousled black silk. Her heart seemed to beat unevenly whenever she was near him.

She could not judge whether or not he meant danger for her. When he had first ridden into the yard, she had been afraid, although he seemed intent only on regaining his gear. He had won Bluebell's heart—though that took no great charm, she told herself wryly—and had held Robin so tenderly and awkwardly that her heart had melted to see it.

Still, uncovering his gear had hardened her heart again. He was not only a Scott, but a March deputy, and posed a heavy threat to Iain and Christie—and to her. And he had refused to help her free Iain. She could not forget that so easily.

"Here," she said stiffly, and backhanded his woolen hose toward him. She followed that with his bunched-up linen shirt and his belt. His brown serge doublet landed, sprawling, on his knee. Gathering up the things, he set them beside the jack.

Rowan knelt so close beside her in the cramped corner area, hunching forward to avoid bumping his head on the rafters, that she could feel the warmth of his body. Her bare toes brushed his boot-clad leg.

Drawing his heavy steel helmet out of its hiding place, Mhairi sat back with it on her thighs. The glinting metal surface mirrored Rowan's hands sliding over hers as he silently took it from her.

That warm contact took her breath for an instant. Mhairi bent hastily to grasp the hilt of his sword. Discovering that it was somehow stuck, she uttered a soft, exasperated sound.

"I canna get it free," she said, and yanked, overbalancing herself. Rowan caught her waist firmly, sending another shock through her. She felt as if she had been touched by tangible fire. When he pulled her gently to the side, she glanced at him, certain that her onrush of feeling brimmed in her eyes.

"Let me," he said, and braced an arm on the floor to stretch out full length. As he reached downward to dip his arm into the dark space, his shoulder bumped against her knees.

She watched the strong play of his broad shoulders and long back beneath the leather doublet he wore. His dark hair swung forward, and she remembered how smoothly textured it had felt beneath her fingers, when he had lain injured and unconscious in her lap. She recalled how deeply good he had felt in her arms, strong and solid and real.

An urge to touch him again washed through her. Unable to resist that compelling force, she reached out a hand, her heart fluttering, and rested her fingers lightly on his shoulder. Though he did not look at her, she sensed a subtle relaxation in him, as if he accepted her touch, even welcomed it. An intense warmth flowed through her hand, but she looked calmly into the hiding space as if no wayward thoughts distracted her.

Rowan groped for the scabbard loop, detached it from the nail, and pulled out his sword. Mhairi gripped the basket hilt, her fingers grazing his until he let go. She laid the heavy weapon on the floor, her fingers trembling slightly.

He brought out his dirk, sheathed in leather, and his small latchbow, and rose to his knees beside her. "Where is the rest?"

"On the other side," Mhairi said, and stretched her arm down into the cranny in the other direction. To reach what she sought, she found it necessary to lean over his leg, her knee touching his and her upper body grazing over his thigh.

She heard him draw in his breath sharply. When she felt the gentle weight of his hand on her back, Mhairi nearly forgot what she reached for in the hiding space.

Flustered, she huffed a strand of hair out of her eyes as she groped into the blackness. Her hand grasped the cool brass and wood of his gun. As she lifted the heavy wheellock pistol and straightened, the barrel swung toward him.

"Ho!" He took the gun from her swiftly. "Where is the other pistol, and the key and shot?"

"In here." Again she stretched her torso over his legs. This time she was not so startled when his steadying hand rested on her waist. His touch felt strong and good, hardly the threatening touch of a man determined to destroy her. She could almost forget that she knelt closely, intimately, beside the March deputy assigned to capture the Lincraig highway riders.

When Rowan's hand shifted to her shoulder, a cascade of pure pleasure descended along her spine. She felt heat blossom in her cheeks, and wanted more of the sultry sensation that his touch caused.

Instead, she closed her hand over his other pistol under the floorboards. He grabbed it from her quickly. She picked up a small leather pouch and then sat up. "This is yours as well. I found the pistol key on a string around your neck when you were injured. 'Tis in here," she said, handing him the heavy bag.

"This is the pouch where I keep the powder and lead balls for the guns," he said. "Where is the larger pouch? What else do you have hidden away in there?"

She reached again, supporting herself over his knee, feeling increasingly comfortable with his body pressed to hers and their voices drifting, low and intimate, through the shadows.

"Your quiver," she said, pulling out the slender leather cylinder. Inside rattled a dozen iron-tipped arrows for the latchbow. He took it from her.

"My Jedburgh ax canna be down there, too." He sounded amused.

"It is." She reached down and tugged. Rowan helped her pull out the seven-foot shaft, turning the wickedly curved point away as he laid it down.

"Truly a clever hiding space."

"Iain built it by adding new flooring in the loft to make this place. We can hide valuables from the reivers here." She sat back on her heels and shoved carelessly at her hair. " 'Tis all that's here. Your saddle is in the byre, and you've seen your horse. I'll help you carry the gear down." She shimmied backward, intending to stand.

"Hold." Rowan grabbed her wrist. "My leather pouch is missing yet—the larger one, with my coin. Where is it? And where is the council's letter?"

Wisps of dark hair slipped over her left eye. She tossed her head. "I thought your pouch was here with the rest."

"Did you?" His black brows drew together in a deep scowl.

As clearly as if he had said the words aloud, she knew what he thought. She pulled her arm back, but he held it fast. "I didna steal your coin," she said.

"Or my orders?" he asked softly. Their hands were raised between them. His fingers wrapped around her wrist like iron.

She lowered her eyes. "I only wanted to look at the letter," she said.

"You have it still," he said. "Give it me."

She was silent, looking down. Rowan reached out a hand and brushed the hair away from her eyes. A thousand tiny shivers streamed over her head. He tilted her chin up with one finger.

"Give it me, Mhairi," he said. His touch was steel wrapped in velvet, his voice was quiet and stony. But when he said her name, something inside her belly fluttered.

She sighed and reached her fingers into the neck of her shift beneath her gown, withdrawing a corner of the paper that she had earlier tucked into her bodice for safekeeping.

Holding her gaze securely, Rowan reached out to take the paper from her fingers. The edge tickled her breast, and a startling, wholly pleasant sensation swirled through her lower abdomen. Heat seemed to spin and rise through her. She felt it bloom in her cheeks when she looked up at him.

Rowan flicked open the folded paper, still curved from her body, and glanced at it. She knew what he saw. The first lines, introducing Rowan Scott as the new deputy, were legible enough, but the rest had deteriorated into a mess of blurred strokes where the lampblack ink had run over the wet linen fibers of the paper.

"The words were spoiled in the rain," she said.

He tucked it inside his doublet. "Where is my coin pouch?"

"I thought 'twas in the hiding nook," she said. "But I might have dropped it at Lincraig."

"Pray 'tis still there," he said grimly. He let go of her wrist and rose to his feet, shifting backward until he stood, head bowed under the rooftree. Mhairi crawled out of the corner and stood too, looking up at him.

At his keen downward glance, she felt herself flush again. She could not seem to stop those heated blushes from rising whenever he looked at her like that, as if he saw into the depths of her being, beneath the blood and skin to the marrow of her soul.

Though stern, his gaze was perceptive and intelligent, as if his thoughts spun quickly and cleanly. She sensed no meanness of spirit in his lancelike glances, nor did he seem to criticize her with his sharp gaze.

Still, no matter what he thought of her, there was one question she had to have answered. Boldness of action was what the Borderlands had taught her, and so she tumbled ahead.

"What do your orders say?" she asked him bluntly.

He lifted one black brow. "I presumed you had read the letter yourself," he said curtly. "You can read?"

"Surely I can read," she snapped back. "The words were blurred in the rain, or I wouldna ask. Think you we are savages in the Highlands? My brothers and I were all taught to read and write in English and Latin both."

"You have more than one brother?"

"I have four," she answered. "And if they were here, or if my father werena in Denmark, then I wouldna need your help."

He quirked a brow at her. "Why is your father in Denmark?"

"He is a king's lawyer," she said. "My mother is with him."

"Ah," he said. "Ah."

"And what does that mean?"

"That must be why Simon Kerr needs a council warrant to proceed with the transfer of your brother. The son of a king's lawyer canna be hanged or handed over without permission. Have you asked your father for help, then?"

"Of course I have. He hasna gotten my letter yet or he would be here. With all the storms in the northern sea, the ships willna sail," she said impatiently. "Now if you please, tell me what the council said."

"You have a bold way about you, lass," he said, not

unkindly. A shadow seemed to pass through his green
eyes before he lowered his gaze.

Then, as clearly as if he had spoken, Mhairi knew that
Rowan was fully aware of the council's orders for her
brother. She had ridden out in cold and rain and black of
night, placing her life and Christie's in peril—and Rowan
Scott knew the information that she sought.

But he would not tell her. Iain's life suddenly seemed
to hang in the balance between Rowan's will and her own.

She watched him, her breath heaving softly in her
throat. Rowan turned away to pick up his sleeveless jack,
and shrugged into it. Then he retrieved his belt, attaching
the looped ends of the sword scabbard and dirk sheath
before buckling the whole around his hips. He tucked his
helmet under his arm and lifted his pistols, shoving them
into his belt, and hefting the latchbow in his hand.

Standing to his full height, with his hair touching the
beam, dressed in his armored jack and fitted with
weapons, he seemed to fill the confining space of the
loft with a dominant, intimidating presence that nearly
stopped her breath.

She looked up at him more boldly than she felt. "You
know what the council has ordered for Iain," she said
softly.

"Do I?" he asked, adjusting his belt.

She dreaded the next question, and its answer. "Do you
carry the orders for Iain's death? Do you have them on
you now?"

"Would I tell you if I did?" he murmured.

"I need to know," she said, striving to keep her
voice calm.

"You ride out like a reiver in the night," he said, eyeing
her steadily. "You assault a Border officer, and then beg
to be taken as a pledge to free your brother. Now you
expect me to tell you confidential orders." He cocked a
brow at her. "Apply for assignment as a warden, madam.
Your talents are wasted swaddling bairnies." Sweeping
his lance off the floor, he spun and strode toward the
ladder.

Mhairi snatched up his shirt, doublet, and hose, followed and began to climb down after him. Rowan leaped
to the floor, jammed his helmet on his head, picked up his

long boots, and crossed to the doorway. Reaching the foot of the ladder, Mhairi glanced toward the cradle, saw that Robin slept peacefully, and ran toward the door.

Bluebell blocked the threshold amiably, wagging her short tail and panting. "Move, you daft hound," Rowan muttered. He patted her head and shoved past her to step outside, uttering no word to Mhairi. She followed silently, accompanied by Bluebell, who seemed eager to play.

In the yard, Rowan untethered his horse, paused to gently push the attentive wolfhound away, and led the horse into the small barn attached to the house. When he led the bay out again, fully saddled, Mhairi was waiting, her hand on Bluebell's head. She handed him the bundle of clothing.

Rowan took it and walked past Mhairi with barely a glance. "I thank you for keeping Valentine," he said.

"Valentine?" she asked, momentarily startled. " 'Tis what the reivers call a king's warrant for arrest."

"Exactly," he said.

"Master Reiver, indeed," she murmured.

He glanced back at her. "I'll leave my dappled hobbie in your care."

"Christie will bring him back to you," she said stiffly.

"The reivers have left your byre fair empty. Keep the horse for now."

"Will you ask redress of us if he is snatched in the night?"

He shook his head. "I willna. My word on it."

"I have had the word of the laird o' Blackdrummond before. And the Scotts as well," she added softly, unable to keep the bitterness out of her voice.

His glance was lightning-quick and keen as he shoved his lance through a loop on the saddle. "I know naught of your experience with other Scotts, but Blackdrummond's word is good."

"Alec Scott rode out with my brother and now Iain is in a dungeon," she reminded him pointedly. "And my cousins are Kerrs, and have a blood feud with your kin." She would not tell him the rest, that Scotts had killed her betrothed.

"None of that should change the value of a promise I make."

"Then I wish you would promise to help my brother."

"Stubborn Highland lass," he said softly, as he attached the latchbow and quiver to the saddle.

Mhairi sighed. Despite his notorious reputation, she sensed fairness in him, and had hoped he would help her to free Iain. But he had refused, and showed no sign of altering that decision.

She was reaping the harvest of her attack on him along the Lincraig road. He knew her for a robber and a schemer, and he would not trust her. He still suspected her of stealing his coin pouch, although she truly did not know where it was. There was little she could do or say to redeem herself after all that she had done to him.

Sighing, she watched him shove his pistols into the leather sheaths on either side of the saddle. He would leave in a moment, and she had nowhere else to turn for help. Her inner sense told her that he knew, indeed, what was to become of Iain.

If she was right, Rowan Scott alone could stop it from happening.

She stepped forward as he adjusted the girth straps. He did not look at her, his long fingers nimble with the leather, and gentle where they eased over the horse.

Mhairi remembered, suddenly, how his hands had felt on her, warm and strong. He had made her feel safe. She wanted that man to listen to her, to help her.

"Rowan Scott—" She paused, feeling as if she should coat her words with honey. But she had no knack for false tones. All she had to offer was honesty and earnestness.

She drew a deep breath. "If you mean to deliver to Simon some message concerning my brother's fate, hold back. Wait until your brother is found before you condemn mine."

His glance revealed only mistrust. Silently, with a grim expression, he settled his helmet on his head. The sweeping brim formed a cold, graceful frame around his handsome face. He was armed and jacked like the king's own arsenal, ready to ride out to join the warden. Whatever kindness she had glimpsed in him was lost behind the steel and the leather and the hard frown. In another moment he would ride out of her sight.

She grasped his arm. "Simon Kerr will convince you of Iain's guilt. Dinna listen to him."

"I'll decide for myself," he said. "Let the law tend to its own matters."

Fear and anger, feuling each other, flared in her. She stomped her foot wildly and swore in Gaelic. The dog, startled, yelped, and the bay horse whickered and stepped back.

"This is my matter!" she shouted. "Iain is my brother! Alec Scott put him into this bog! Have you no loyalty to your own brother, at least, to help his friend?" Too late, she remembered what Jennet had told her of Rowan and Alec Scott. No loyalty, indeed. She bit her lip.

His hands slashed upward to grip her wrists hard. "Dinna expect me to help my brother," he said coldly. "Have you thought that perhaps both of our brothers are guilty? Do you defend yours because of blood only, regardless of what he did?"

"He isna guilty!" she said ferociously, between clenched teeth.

He huffed a mirthless chuckle and dropped her hands. "He was with Alec Scott," he said, as if that resolved the matter.

Mhairi took his arms again. Rowan glanced down at her shaking hands, then fixed her with a silent, impenetrable gaze, as green and cool as the sea.

"I willna believe ill of my brother," she said.

"I see that," he said. "Do you believe the moon is made of green cheese, as well? I've heard it said so."

She ignored his sarcastic remark. "Dinna think I ask you because I am fond of Scotts," she said crisply. "As laird o' Blackdrummond, you have an obligation to seek justice for your tenant. Iain has been a friend to your kin. How can you let Simon Kerr punish him without looking into it yourself?"

"Simon Kerr represents King James's justice in the Borderlands. As do I," he replied. "I have no assurance of your brother's innocence, or Alec's. Or yours," he added firmly.

"Take my assurance," she said. "I place my life on it." Her hands still shook as she clutched at his sleeves. She could not seem to stop the trembling. Behind her, the dog whimpered and nuzzled at her waist.

Rowan slid his hands along to grip her elbows. Needing the support in that moment, she leaned into him. "You sound sincere, I will give you that," he said.

"Rowan." His name came naturally to her lips. "Hold back what you know. Dinna give Simon the council's word for Iain until you decide for yourself if he is guilty."

His grip and steady gaze did not lessen. "What makes you think that I know the council's opinion on the matter?"

"You do," she said. "I know it. Somehow I know it. And if you dinna listen to me now, I canna say what I will do." She blurted the last remark in a rush of desperate emotion, her voice as tremulous as her limbs. His hands under her elbows seemed to be all that held her upright.

"I would be a lackwit to trust you after that masterful head crack you gave me. Take heed, lass. If you think to ride out again to force justice for Iain, 'twill go ill for you both."

"I would give my life for Iain."

"Dinna be foolish," he said brusquely.

"He is my twin."

He regarded her thoughtfully. "Ah. Then perhaps such fierce loyalty is understandable." He let go of her arms. "But you have had my warning."

"Warning?" She watched as he mounted the bay.

His gaze pinioned her own. "If you ride out again, Mhairi Macrae," he said, "be assured that I will take you down."

"I will do what I must," she answered.

"Then God keep you, madam." He snapped the reins, and the bay launched forward.

Bluebell ran after him for a short distance, barking. But Mhairi stood as if rooted in the yard, watching Rowan Scott. Sunlight glinted over his steel helmet and weapons, and his back and shoulders were proudly balanced. And she knew that the Black Laird would never bend his will to hers.

Nor would she bend to his.

Chapter Eleven

~

He was a hedge about his friends,
A heckle to his foes, lady . . .

—*"Rob Roy"*

Rowan dismounted in the barnekin yard of Lincraig Castle and tethered Valentine. His boots crunched over crumbling stone as he walked toward the corner tower and descended the stairs.

A quick scan of the empty, familiar cell in which he had spent three days showed him just what he had expected. The leather pouch was not there. Nor was it in the corridor, or inside the second cell, a dismal twin to the first. If Mhairi had indeed dropped it, then it lay elsewhere.

Sighing in exasperation, he went back up the stairs and crossed the sunlit yard again, scanning the ground as he went. If he found the pouch here, accidentally dropped, then he could believe Mhairi's claim that she had not stolen from him. And he realized that he wanted to believe her.

He recalled her face as she had looked up at him outside her brother's house, her serene features crumpled in fear, her slender fingers trembling on his arms. Rowan had sensed true anguish in her then, and had been tempted to help her. But he did not trust her, and regarded caution as his best course.

As he walked, he searched among the fallen stones and the tall grasses and bracken that had overtaken the barnekin yard. Clarity and grace had once existed in the castle design, but the whole had become wild and elemental, as if the Lincraig haunts had transformed the place to suit their own needs. Glancing around the yard, he neared the roofless chapel.

Lincraig's chapel, along with the rest of the castle, had been destroyed more than forty years earlier by English soldiers, when King Henry had ordered his army to ride ruthlessly through the Lowlands. But the English attempt to convince the Scots that their infant queen, Mary Stewart, should wed Henry's son Edward failed. The Scots had resisted, and the marriage had never taken place.

But Lincraig, along with several other Scottish castles, had not been rebuilt. Rumors of phantoms had discouraged laborers from agreeing to the work, and a lack of funds had convinced Jock Scott to abandon the expensive task. Instead, he had built a pele tower elsewhere on Lincraig land, calling it Newhouse, where he and Anna had raised their sons.

But on the same night that Rowan's father and uncle had been killed, Newhouse Tower had been burned by Kerrs. Jock and Anna had barely escaped, coming to Blackdrummond Tower to live.

Rowan sighed now as he gazed at the graceful skeleton of the Lincraig chapel. He wished once again, as he often had before, that he had the funds himself to rebuild Lincraig, and Newhouse as well. Jock Scott deserved to be laird over more than a lonely heap of ancient stone and weed, and the burned-out shell of a fine pele tower.

Turning, Rowan caught sight of a dark shape near a pile of collapsed stone. His leather pouch was caught in a thick cluster of bracken. He picked it up and opened it. A quick survey told him nothing was missing. Twenty bright Scots coins, some of his pay as a Border deputy, glinted inside. The black stone mirror in its broken gilt frame, which he had also salvaged on the beach weeks ago, was in the pouch as well, wrapped in a white linen handkerchief. He had planned to give the thing to his grandmother.

He opened the linen and held the dark stone, with its broken gilt frame, in the palm of his hand, tilting it back and forth. He frowned slightly as he remembered what he had seen that day he had waited at the inn for his friend

Geordie Bell. A woman's face, serene and ethereal, with a sheen of dark hair and soft gray eyes—

Jesu. His fingers grasped the frame convulsively. He had seen Mhairi's face that day. He was certain of it. And that was why, when he had turned to see her as she took him down with the butt of her pistol, she had looked so oddly familiar to him, like a half-forgotten dream image.

He peered at the mirror now, and saw only his own face reflected in the slick black surface: intense green eyes, stubbled cheeks. Nothing so extraordinary as the face of a woman he had not yet met. But he was sure that it had happened.

Turning the stone speculatively, he remembered the Scotsmen who had attacked him outside the inn.

They had demanded a raven's moon from him, and he had thought them mad. But now, as he gazed at the stone, he wondered again if they had sought this mirror. He tilted it back and forth. Round and reflective, and dark as a raven's soul. He frowned and held it toward the light.

Nothing unusual appeared. He saw his reflection, and the stone-littered yard of Lincraig behind him. Although the explanation had little appeal to him, he decided that he may have experienced some kind of supernatural moment that day at the inn. He knew that some people had prophetic powers; the Sight, it was called. But he knew no one like that, and refused to believe that he was capable of such things. Perhaps the stone had some ancient charm about it. Old stories, which he had heard as a lad, spoke of such charm stones.

But why would it be carried on a Spanish ship—and why would spies attack him to retrieve it? And why would Mhairi Macrae's face appear to him in the thing?

Frowning, unable to answer his own questions, he wrapped the stone mirror in the linen and dropped it back into his pouch.

Then he took out his dagger from its sheath on his belt, and slit the dark silk lining inside the pouch, cutting into the leather behind the silk. He did not slice through the pouch leather itself, for this was a false backing. Behind it was tucked a parchment sheet, its red wax privy seal still intact.

Rowan nodded in satisfaction, seeing that the document

was still there. He closed the pouch and threaded it onto his belt. Mhairi had told the truth, then. She had not taken his coin or valuables, or even the stone mirror.

And she had not found the council's warrant regarding Iain.

The document hidden in the pouch gave permission to Simon Kerr to hand his prisoner over to the custody of the English warden, who would then decide his fate. But the English would not be sympathetic to a Scotsman accused of spying. The document, in essence, was Iain Macrae's death warrant.

Mhairi's persistent defense of her brother had begun to raise doubts in his mind regarding Iain's guilt. He intended to investigate the matter as thoroughly as he could.

Somehow she had guessed that Rowan had the warrant that she had sought to capture. But he could not oblige her request to keep the document from Simon Kerr. The writ must be delivered, and the council must receive a statement, signed by Kerr and sealed with Rowan's own signet, that the letter had indeed been received. If this did not occur within two weeks, Rowan himself could be arrested for obstruction. And he would need the Crown's support if the English laid charges against him concerning the missing Spanish gold, as Geordie Bell had warned him they would do.

He walked toward Valentine, who nuzzled at stray grasses near the old chapel. Rowan turned and saw a small, distinct bootprint on the first cracked step. Frowning, moving quickly beneath the overhead arch, he entered the nave, a jumble of sun and shadow and stone.

Pointed and roofless, the walls soared toward the blue sky, their torn stone edges softened by lacy clumps of moss and ivy. Rowan walked down the central aisle, where grasses grew between the broken floor stones, and followed the small footprints.

On the collapsed altar slab, a mark on the surface caught his attention. He stepped closer and saw the imprint of a small hand pressed into the undisturbed grime of decades.

Frowning, Rowan went to a narrow doorway at the back of the apse. The door itself no longer existed, and

the short corridor beyond was totally dark. Again he saw
the mark of those slender fingers on the doorjamb. He
knew, with immediate certainty, to whom they belonged.

Rowan passed through the darkened doorway, his boots
scraping softly in the silence. He was familiar with the
recesses in the chapel. Although he had not been here for
a long time, he had visited here often as a lad. Once, many
years ago, he and Alec had sheltered in the chapel during
a heavy storm.

A curving set of stairs led down into a blackness as
dense as a moonless night. Rowan cautiously descended.
Below, he knew, lay the Lincraig crypt. On that stormy
day long ago, he and Alec had stirred up enough courage
to venture down these steps. Rowan smiled, remembering
how his younger brother's skinny legs had frozen in panic
on the bottom step as a burst of lightning had illuminated
the tombs in the crypt. Even gentle coaxing from Rowan
had not convinced Alec to step down.

His own eleven-year-old heart had pounded fiercely,
but Rowan had summoned enough bravery to walk
through the dark chamber, past the carved stone tombs
and the engraved memorial brasses. Alec, only five, had
emitted a dry scream and had fled up the stairs.

When another crack of lightning had illuminated the
carved faces on the tombs, Rowan had decided that he had
shown enough courage. He too ran, and caught Alec's
hand to drag him out of the chapel into the driving rain.
They had hidden in one of the dungeon cells until the rain
had ceased. Alec had calmed down only after Rowan had
repeatedly reassured him that there was nothing to fear.

But the next day, and the next, Rowan had returned
alone, at first because he demanded courage from himself.
Later he came because he wanted to be there. Each day
his fears diminished, until the Lincraig crypt became a
private refuge for him.

Knowing that no one, not even his grandfather, was
willing to spend time in that crypt had given him an exhilarating sense of triumph and bravery. But beyond that,
Rowan had found a strange, wonderful peace in the silent
tomb, a balm for his youthful loneliness as well as his
tumultuous feelings. Later, he had brought Maggie here,
but she had not liked the place and had refused to enter.

She had felt only her own fear, and not the serenity that he knew was there.

Now, as he descended the steps, he felt that familiar tranquil silence surround him. Tucking his helmet under his arm, he walked into the crypt chamber, his head nearly touching the low, vaulted stone ceiling.

Dusty shafts of light seeped through the masonry. The center space of the room contained three large stone coffins with carved figures resting on their lids. In the shadows, other tombs topped with flat engraved brasses lined the walls. Rowan hardly glanced at those.

He looked down at the carved effigy of a knight dressed in chain mail, legs crossed, hands joined in prayer: James Scott, laird of Lincraig more than three hundred years ago.

Beside the knight, with a narrow aisle of space between, lay the demure figure of the laird's wife. Lady Isobel's hands were clasped over her breast, and her long, carefully chiseled skirts draped gracefully over her feet. Her toes rested against a small dog, the symbol of her fidelity and devotion to her husband.

Rowan bowed to Isobel Scott as he had often done, and brushed some of the dust from her delicately shaped face. The veil that surrounded her head, though formed of stone, seemed to flow like silk. He moved past, his hand lingering over her cold stone fingers.

The third tomb featured a small, sensitively carved figure in skirts and delicate veil. Beatrice, the daughter of Isobel and James Scott, read the letters carved into her flat stone pillow. Rowan translated the Latin inscription in his mind: Bringer of joy, dead at the age of three years.

When Rowan had been much younger, this ancient Scott laird and his family had provided a kind of peaceful, mute support. During the years when Rowan had experienced confusing adolescent emotions, he had found privacy and solitude, even a sense of welcome, here in their crypt.

He smiled wistfully in the shadows, and patted Beatrice's tiny clasped hands. Then, because his eyes had adjusted to the dim light, he saw the clear imprint of four fingers by the effigy's small feet.

Mhairi Macrae had been here in this crypt, where no one but Rowan Scott had set foot for decades. He spun in the room, looking around. Footprints, smaller than his own, disturbed the dust on the floor. He circled the chamber and scanned the dark corners, but saw nothing else unusual.

He turned to leave, his arm brushing against Isobel as he went past. He felt an odd, slight tug, as if she had touched his sleeve. Frowning, he turned and glanced at her peaceful face.

His knee bumped against something soft where only stone should be. Bending, he saw a cloth-wrapped bundle tucked deep in the shadows, behind the freestanding miniature pillars that decorated the side of the lady's tomb. He drew out the packet and laid it on Isobel's knees, in a shaft of thin light.

Inside the cloth, he found a few folded papers. The topmost page was marked with the seal of the privy council. Frowning, he scanned the contents. Dated nearly six weeks earlier, the letter ordered Simon Kerr to interrogate the suspected spy and send word of his findings. But the paper had never reached Kerr. A highway thief had taken it from a messenger.

As he lifted the next page, a broken bit of a stick, painted red, clattered to the floor. He picked it up, and recognized part of a red wand carried by the messengers at arms, who were appointed by the Lord Lyon, King of Arms, to serve the crown. He knew that the wands were broken by the messengers themselves if the secrecy of their packets was compromised.

Scowling deeply, Rowan glanced quickly through the other papers. He found another letter from the council, similar to the first but dated two weeks later.

The last two pages were written in a cramped hand in what he thought, at first, was Latin or French. Peering more closely, he realized that the words were Spanish. The papers were a letter of some kind, perhaps a long document.

He swore out loud.

Wrapping the papers and the broken wand in the cloth, he shoved the whole packet inside his doublet. Turning, he took the steps in pairs, his boots ringing an angry echo as he rose toward the sunlit chapel.

He had been wrong. Mhairi Macrae was most assuredly

a thieving, spying wench after all. She had been here in
this place, and had hidden these papers. And she had
much to explain.

A hundred yards past the point where the old ruin overlooked the highway, the road forked and plunged into
wildness both ways, toward boggy moorland edged with
craggy slopes. Rowan guided Valentine to the right
toward Abermuir Tower. The left fork would have taken
him back to Blackdrummond Tower.

Mhairi and Devil's Christie had been clever, he thought
as he rode, to watch from the Lincraig hill for the council's messengers. The isolated highway there was hardly
traveled except for those with business either at Blackdrummond or Abermuir—and those, he thought grimly,
who were intent on robbing and spying.

He was certain that Mhairi had hidden those letters in
the crypt. And she must have scooped up the broken wand
to prevent that incriminating evidence from being found
on the highway.

Such thoughts thoroughly soured his temper, and dissolved his earlier inclination to be lenient toward her. The
council documents had obviously been taken from royal
messengers, but the Spanish letter would not have been
carried by them. Mhairi Macrae had come by that through
some other means.

He shook his head in disparagement. A few hours earlier, he had been willing to regard her as a charming, stubborn, bonny lass who defended her brother honorably,
however unusual her methods and reasoning. He had even
been sure he had proof of her innocent motives. Then he
had unwrapped the bundle hidden in the crypt.

Now, riding away from Lincraig and its secrets, he told
himself that Mhairi must surely be an integral part of the
network of agents to which Iain, and very possibly Alec,
belonged. He wondered if the rest of the Spanish gold—
the missing salvage—might also be stashed somewhere
inside the old ruin.

Mhairi had used to advantage the legends of phantoms
at Lincraig. Few people would dare to venture near the
place. He wondered with fresh dismay if Devil's Christie
Armstrong was involved in this as well.

As he rode, the afternoon sun slipped lower over the dark hills, and autumn cold gathered in the air. The advent of winter, with its longer, darker nights, marked the season of reiving in the Borderlands. Rowan glanced around and behind him. Tonight would bring clear moonlight to these hills, and most assuredly a host of scoundrels with it.

After a while, he heard the sound of approaching hoof-beats, and looked ahead. Five men rode across the rolling moor toward Abermuir Castle. Their steel breastplates, helmets, and keen lances gleamed in the late sun.

Warden's troopers, he realized, as he slowed Valentine. One of the men riding in the lead saw him and spurred his horse forward. Rowan stopped to wait. Tall and heavily bearded, the man came at a stiff pace, and reached out a gauntleted hand to grasp the handle of the gun sheathed in his saddle.

"God give you good day, sir," Rowan called pleasantly as the trooper halted.

"Who are ye?"

"Rowan Scott, laird o' Blackdrummond. And you?"

"John Hepburn, land sergeant to Simon Kerr, warden o' the Scottish Middle March. Can ye prove yer name?"

"I can. And I'll show my proof to Simon Kerr."

"Then ready it, for the warden rides this way." Hepburn gestured behind him. The man who had ridden at the center of the group now crossed the moor. Even at this distance, Rowan recognized the wide build, swarthy coloring, and coarse features of the Cessford Kerrs. He folded his hands over his saddle and waited.

"He says he's Blackdrummond, sir," Hepburn called.

Simon Kerr halted his horse and glared at Rowan. His nose was reddened in the wind, and his close-set eyes, beneath heavy dark brows, snapped with fury. "You are more than a week late, Master Scott!"

"I am aware of that, Master Warden," Rowan replied easily. "I have a letter from the king's council, which I am instructed to give you personally. And I will require your signature on a return statement."

Kerr walked his horse closer and held out his hand expectantly. "Give it, then. I have been waiting weeks for official word from the council. How did you get past the damned riders that harry travelers along the Lincraig road?"

"I got through somehow," Rowan said with a shrug. He slid his hand into his doublet and extracted the water-stained letter that Mhairi had returned to him and handed it to Kerr. "The council is aware that its messengers have been plagued along this part of the road."

"Cursed tricksters, never out when I send patrols, yet always about when we ride elsewhere. 'Tis said that the haunts o' Lincraig ride this road. I might believe that, if I didna believe more strongly in thieves coveting the crown's gold," he mumbled as he unfolded the letter. "But just now there are better matters for my troopers than laying in wait for highway robbers. Jesu, this paper is near illegible. Did you use it for a rain bonnet, man?" He read the page, lips moving laboriously. Then he shot Rowan a rapid, acidic look. "Why in the name o' Christ does the council send me a Blackdrummond Scott for a deputy?"

"The council had its reasons for appointing me to the post," Rowan said mildly, though the warden's blunt, abrasive manner had already begun to wear his patience.

"I hope you mean to honor those reasons," Simon snapped as he crammed the page into the pouch suspended from his belt. "Naught I can do about it now. What else did the council send? Give it, fellow. I have been waiting weeks for the damned warrant." Simon held out his hand.

Rowan hesitated as Mhairi's impassioned words flashed through his mind. But he shut his heart to her remembered plea. The lass had hidden a Spanish document of some kind, and was likely as much a spy as her brother. And Rowan did not need another strike against his soul as far as the privy council was concerned.

"I assume you've been charged to deliver this warrant or suffer for it," Kerr snapped, wiggling his fingers impatiently. Rowan shot him a narrow look and fished the folded page from the secret slot in his pouch.

Simon grabbed the page and ripped the seal apart, scanning the contents. "Good. The English will take the rogue, and he'll hang by end o' next truce day." He slid the page into his pouch.

"When is that?" Rowan asked.

"I havena received word when the next meeting will be. I hope you are ready to ride tonight, Master Scott. We mean to take down a few rascals."

"Oh? The Lincraig riders?"

"I mean to catch Heckie Elliot and his gang, who have been riding out o' Liddesdale to rob and burn and squeeze criminal rent from the people o' this dale."

"I've heard of them. Have you had word where they mean to ride tonight?"

"Nay. But there are men throughout the dale who will light signal fires when they see them coming. Heckie and them will have black rent from this territory nae longer. Some o' the families they have spoiled live on Black-drummond land. You will ride along wi' us. Take a band o' troopers toward the Lincraig area, while I go another. We'll find 'em."

Rowan nodded. "I know the land well. Six men should be sufficient."

"Hmph. I ken how well you know the land, Blackdrum-mond, you and your brother and the rest o' your kin. Dinna forget my sergeants and I will be watching you," Simon said slyly. "I have a capable deputy at Abermuir, but the man is laid up wi' an ill foot. You are a Scott and a scoundrel, but you'll have to do for a deputy."

Rowan gave him a flat stare. "I'll ride out tonight, but I dinna come here to harass reivers for you. I have orders from the council to interview the spy who is in your custody. I am to send a report back by runner to the council."

"Send a footrunner to Edinburgh at your own peril, for the letter may never make it out o' these hills." Kerr squinted at Rowan. "Blackdrummond you may be, but you've much to learn about your new post here, man. The first lesson is that I am the warden, and you are the deputy. I dinna care if you are laird o' the moon. I give the orders here. For now, we'll head back to Abermuir and discuss plans for the trod tonight. We ride out after reivers most nights in the week. You'll ride wi' us, and learn to get your sleep in the day."

"I rode at night and slept in the daylight when I was a sapling lad," Rowan growled.

"Well, now you'll do it to *keep* the March laws and nae

break them," Simon snapped. He turned his black horse and rode away.

"Sending a Scott after a Scott? Does the council take me for a lackbrain?" Simon removed his helmet as he spoke and tossed it on a chair, then unlatched his belt. "Archie! Where the devil are you, man?" His large, thick voice echoed around the stone walls of the great hall at Abermuir.

"The council has directed me to investigate the rumors of spies in this area of the Middle March," Rowan said. "And they strongly suggest in their letter to you that I ride after Alec Scott myself."

"I couldna read the whole o' that letter—the words were spoiled. Ride after your own brother? Is this a Scott scheme?" Simon turned. "Archie!" he bellowed. "Send the lassie wi' ale!"

Rowan removed his helmet and laid it on the table. "I dinna care to help my brother or to hunt him," he said in a flat tone. "The council wants it done."

"He's a hard man to find. But if you can lead my troopers and I to him, I swear he'll be hanged by downing o' the sun on the day he's found. How does that sit wi' Blackdrummond?"

Rowan glanced away from the smug expression on Simon's face. "In addition, the council awaits my report on Iain Macrae."

"You'll speak to him only when I say you may."

Rowan watched him evenly. " 'Tisna wise to obstruct the council's orders. I will see Iain Macrae. Now or later, either will do. But I will see him." He looked steadily at Simon.

"I am the warden here," Simon growled. He yanked at the buckle on his shoulder. "Archie!" he yelled. "I'm thirsty, for God's pity!"

"Let me see the items that were taken from Iain Macrae the night he was taken," Rowan said.

"I sent a list o' them to the council. If you are indeed in their graces, then you have seen the inventory I sent."

"I have seen it. Fifty pieces of gold, thirty-five silver coins, several lengths of gold chains, and a few gewgaws. But I was with the officials on the beach near Berwick after a Spanish ship wrecked near there. If any of this gold matches the stuff missing from that salvage, I may recognize it."

"Hmph." Simon unlatched the other buckle, loosening the heavy steel breast and back pieces he wore. "Fair enough. There's nae harm in showing it to you. Archie, by hell! Where hae you been?"

Rowan turned to see a young blond-headed man hobble through the door on crutches made of stripped tree limbs. Tall and wide-shouldered, the man lurched toward them, his left foot wrapped in thick, dirty bandages. A girl in a head kerchief and simple brown dress followed him, carrying a jug and pewter cups.

"Lucy, pour the warden's ale, and some for his guest," the man said. He smiled briefly at Rowan, who noticed that his crooked nose still showed the faded bruises of a recent break. "Sir, I am Archibald Pringle, the warden's deputy." He held out his hand.

Rowan took it, noting the strong, dry grip. "Rowan Scott of Blackdrummond." Archie nodded as if he had expected him.

"Archie, help me wi' this damn back-and-breast," Simon said. Pringle reached out a well-muscled arm to lift the steel breastpiece to the bench. The warden laid the back piece down and waved his hand toward the girl. "Pour us some ale and dinna spill it out." Accepting the ale she handed him, Simon took several fast swallows, then dismissed the serving girl, who nodded and hastened from the room.

Simon crossed the length of the hall to unlock the door of a wall cupboard built into the far corner. He returned with a large metal box, which he hefted onto the table. Turning a small key in the silver lock, he flipped back the box lid.

Rowan saw a bright jumble of gold inside. He lifted a heavy golden chain out of a casket, weighing the solid links in his hand. "Spanish make," he said. "I've seen such chains before. Spanish sailors wear them wrapped around their bodies, under their clothing. A life's fortune worn constantly. We found a few on the beach last August."

"Only a few, for all the sailors captured?" Archie asked.

Rowan nodded. "Likely many of the sailors who wore such gold drowned from the weight of the chains before they made it to shore."

"Papist lackwits," Simon grumbled, and slurped his ale.

Rowan sifted through the contents of the box. Cool, bright bits of gold and silver slid through his fingers. He noted that many of the coins were identical in imprint to those he had seen collected on the Scottish beach.

At the bottom of the casket, he discovered a square of red cloth, and opened it to find a golden oval, engraved with a tiny image. He turned it toward the light and recognized, with a sudden sense of shock, the saint's medallion that he had found in the sand.

That piece had been stolen from him at the inn, by men whom his friend Geordie Bell had identified as Scottish spies. And now, suddenly, the medallion showed up here, in a horde of stuff that had some connection to Alec Scott and Iain Macrae. Had Mhairi, too, seen this little piece? He fingered the golden oval thoughtfully and swathed it again, replacing it in the box, perplexed.

"Well? Are you satisfied?" Simon asked.

Rowan nodded and closed the casket lid. " 'Tis indeed Spanish stuff, some of it taken from the wreck I saw," he said carefully. He was bothered about this, but would keep it to himself for now.

"And I hold one o' the spies who took it in my own prison."

"Possibly," Rowan said, frowning. "But I'll talk to the man first before I'll agree wi' that for certain."

"What is all this?" Archie asked. He had been watching the two men with a deep frown.

Simon looked at Archie. "Rowan Scott has been sent by the council to look into this matter o' spies. And to be your replacement as deputy," he added in a casual tone.

"I wasna told that I was to replace anyone," Rowan said.

"Well, you'll be the only deputy in this March if this Pringle doesna heal right quick," Simon answered. "Lately he's naught but a secretary. And a poor one, for

his handscript is as foul as mine. Eh, Archie?" Simon
lifted his cup and gulped down some of its contents.

"I will need to pen a letter to the king's council stating
that I gave you the warrant," Rowan told Simon.

"Archie will see to it," Simon answered. "We'll sign it,
and I'll have a pair o' troopers take it to Edinburgh." He
wiped his hand across the back of his mouth. "Will you
let this Scott do your duty for you tonight, Archie, or will
you mount and ride wi' us?"

Archie straightened on his crutches. "My foot isna yet
healed, sir. Cracked the anklebone in a football match last
truce day," he added to Rowan. "And broke my nose as
well."

"A good match that was, too," Simon said. "My
troopers had the Scotts and Armstrongs screaming for
mercy. Many a bone was broken that day." He grinned in
satisfaction.

"Did your side win the ball?" Rowan asked.

"Aye, we did, and paid well for it," Simon answered.
"Next night after the truce, some o' my own cattle were
snatched. The reivers left a flattened football behind so
we'd ken who took the beasts. Damned Scotts," he added
succinctly, staring at Rowan.

"My kinsmen hate to lose a football match," Rowan
said affably.

Simon growled indistinctly, and pointed toward his
steel breastplate on the bench. "Archie, make sure my
back-and-breast gets sanded down tomorrow. There's rust
on it again. And blacken it well wi' soot and sheep fat.
You polished it too high last time. I shine like a damned
faerie in the moonlight."

"Aye, sir," Archie said. Rowan thought he noticed an
amused glimmer in the other deputy's brown eyes. "A
warden shouldna be a beacon for reivers to find."

"Reivers, hey," Simon said, gesturing toward Archie
with his ale cup. "We'll ride out as soon as it's dark. Did
you post men on the roof to watch for beacons?" Archie
nodded. "And did you send word out to the rascals who
petitioned me last week?"

"I sent riders to their towers and houses wi' your
promise to find the Lincraig riders before week's end,"
Archie said.

Rowan looked at Simon. "What's this about?"

"Some Bordermen sent me a petition. They're complaining that the thieves on the Lincraig road are mere purse shifters, and are giving reiving men an unfair name around the March. Hah! Blast all the scoundrels to hell!"

"You promised to find the highway riders before week's end?"

"Aye. The reivers insist on justice. They threaten to ride down these highwaymen themselves, and hang 'em from the nearest tree, March laws be damned." He shifted his bulky shoulders. "Takes a braw man to deal wi' the reivers in this March," he muttered.

"But you have muckle matters to concern you now, sir," Archie said. "Perhaps you should send Scott after the highway riders. I'd go myself if I could."

Simon nodded and belched. "Aye. A Scott could handle this task well enough, I suppose." He looked at Rowan. "Act as my deputy in this matter, and deal out a dose o' the warden's justice to these thieves."

"Oh, I'll do that," Rowan murmured.

Chapter Twelve

~

Mhairi's fingers trembled as she poured a tiny stream of gunpowder into the pan of Christie's matchlock pistol. She closed the tiny lid, which made a solid click in the darkness, and laid the gun on the table. Then she glanced toward the hearth.

In the faint glowing light, Christie slept quietly on a low pallet in front of the fire, his customary bed since the day Iain had been arrested. His mother and Armstrong kin had insisted that Christie stay with them, since Jennet had refused to leave her house.

Mhairi shifted quietly on the bench and stared at the closed and barred outer door. The hour was near midnight, and the room was filled with soft breathing sounds, from Christie and the dog who slept near him, from Jennet inside her curtained box bed, from Robin asleep in his cradle.

But Mhairi could not rest. She had roused in the loft bed an hour ago with an anxious foreboding that something dangerous approached. Dressing in Iain's dark clothes, she had come down to sit at the table by the hearth. Now she waited.

For what? Her gut clenched at the thought. She did not know, but she felt something in the air like a heavy cloud, inexorable, dangerous, inevitable. That dark certainty had urged her to find Christie's matchlock gun and load it, though she knew little about using the weapon.

She sighed deeply and rested her head on her arms. Moments later, she heard the rustle of Christie's straw pallet and looked up to see him sitting in the darkness.

"Mhairi?" he whispered. "What is it?"

She shook her head. "I couldna sleep."

He came to sit beside her on the bench, clutching a blanket around his shoulders, his blond hair mussed. "You're dressed to ride out," he whispered. "Why? I heard naught o' messengers when I went to the inn at Kelso earlier."

"I know," she murmured. "But I wonder if we should ride out to the Lincraig road. Something is coming, Christie. I feel it. Perhaps 'tis another messenger."

"The messengers havena come deep in the night like this. But I'll ride out to watch the Lincraig road if you like."

She had considered that already, and had made her decision. "You stay here and watch. I'll go."

"Nay. Reivers may be about," he insisted softly.

"More reason for you to stay here with Jennet and the bairn. I'll just wait by the old ruin. I willna be seen, and nae harm will come to me there." She stood.

"Mhairi—" he reached for her, but she stepped back.

"I've loaded the pistol for you," she said.

Christie watched her, then nodded. "Take care. If you dinna return soon, I'll ride out to find you."

She smiled ruefully. "I'll be safe. Watch well, and keep awake. You'll get your sleep after dawn."

"Och, Armstrongs are kin to owls, ready to be up the night," he murmured, and went to the hearth to retrieve his shirt.

Mhairi slipped quietly out the door.

The wind rose through trees silvered by moonlight. Mhairi soothed her restive black mare and looked down the slope of the hill to the empty road. Her hands flexed on the reins.

She had been there an hour and more, and had seen nothing. Yet the ominous foreboding still haunted her, unrelieved by the action of her midnight watch. Something, someone surely rode through the wind, but she could not define it. She sighed, wishing once again that she had the true gift of Sight that her brother and mother possessed, rather than these strong but elusive sensations. She knew that she must stay alert, but did not know why, or from what source the danger would come.

Frowning, she scanned the miles of moorland and slopes laid out like a dark, rumpled quilt below the Lincraig hill. And suddenly started in her saddle.

Far off, a light winked, a tiny golden star in the blackness. As she watched, another star bloomed a mile or so off. She waited breathlessly, her eyes narrowed. The skin on the back of her neck prickled, and her stomach turned heavily.

Beacons, signaling the approach of a reiving party. Mhairi kneed her horse forward. Surely this was what had created her deep sense of unease. A band of rogues rode in the night. The half-moon was high and white enough for it.

She should have known. She should have listened to Christie and stayed home. But she had been so desperate to recover any message that the king's council might send to Kerr that she had reacted to that urge rather than to practical sense.

Anxious to ride back to Iain's house, she forced herself to wait a bit longer. A third golden light flared, brighter, closer this time.

Gasping with a sudden, intense need to be home, she spurred Peg forward. She rode down the hill and over the moor, then reined in the horse to watch again, frowning. That third beacon was much larger than the others, flaring wild and hot into the night sky.

She cried out. No beacon, but a fire on a thatched roof, a league or so away, surely set near Iain's house. Too near. Fear struck through her, a searing lightning bolt. She spurred the horse.

The distance seemed to pass slowly, though Mhairi urged Peg to a fast gallop, bent low over her neck, wind and black mane whipping into her face. Finally she reached the hill nearest Iain's rocky slope, and reined in, the horse sidestepping anxiously, her ribs heaving against Mhairi's legs.

The thatch roof of her brother's house flared as hot and bright as a torch. Mhairi rode closer, halting when she saw several horsemen silhouetted in the light of the fire. They circled in the yard, trying to herd together some cows and a cluster of sheep. She heard the beasts crying out, heard the barking of the dog, heard the eerie crackle of the thatch as it burned and smoked into the night sky.

And she heard her own scream of protest as she galloped forward.

By the time she reached the edge of the yard, the reivers had ridden away, herding the last of Iain's beasts before them. Mhairi leaped off of her horse's back, stumbling and running toward the house. Bluebell ran past her, legs pumping fiercely, barking wildly as she chased after the retreating reivers, who were now distant black specks skimming over the moonlit hillside.

Jennet knelt on the ground a few yards from the house. She raised her face in the red, flickering light. "Dear God, Mhairi," she said. "Dear God." She clutched the tiny bundle of her son to her breast, reaching out her hand.

"Was it Heckie and his lot?" Mhairi fell to her knees beside Jennet. "What—oh God! Christie!"

He lay on the ground, still as a statue, his pale face and blond hair reflecting the hot color of the fire. Sparks seared the ground nearby as Mhairi reached out gently to touch his shoulder. Blood darkened the front of his shirt.

"*Ach,* laddie," Mhairi murmured. She slipped her hand along his throat, and felt a faint, uneven beat beneath his youthful, wispy beard. "He's alive," she said. "Jennet, help me move him away from the fire. Lay the bairn over there for now."

Jennet moved to nestle Robin on the ground beside a rock, and returned to help Mhairi drag Christie through the yard and down the slope of the hill, away from the burning house. Then she retrieved her son and went toward a small stream at the base of the hill. She came back with a wet cloth, a torn scrap of her own shift.

Mhairi peeled away the bloody, sodden linen of Christie's shirt and gasped, biting her lip. A black, ugly hole in his shoulder oozed blood, and fear struck through her again. Jennet pressed the wet cloth against the wound, her hands shaking, her eyes huge and dark-circled.

"Heckie and his gang rode into the yard and broke the door o' the cow byre afore we even got outside. Christie already had his gun loaded. He lit the match and fired the powder, and missed. Clem Elliot shot him. Oh God, Mhairi—I thought he was dead when he fell."

Mhairi eased her hand over Christie's brow. His breathing was so uneven that she feared he might die. Tears stung her eyes as she looked down at his still, pale face, and at the blood seeping steadily over his sister's hand.

"They fired the roof and took the beasts," Jennet continued. "They took Blackdrummond's dappled hobbie. And Heckie"—she stopped and laughed, a hysterical titter—"told me he would leave me one cow and a sack o' grain for the bairn."

Mhairi bit her lip and raised her gaze to the roaring fire on the rooftop. "This beacon will bring help soon enough," she said. "Neighbors will surely see it and come. But I will ride out past Lincraig to fetch the Armstrongs that live that way. Your kinsmen will take you and Christie to your mother's home. You canna stay here." When she stood, her legs shook so much that her knees faltered for a moment.

Jennet bent over her brother, rocking her son against her breast. Mhairi ran toward her horse, who stood where she had left him, a reiver's mount, trained by Iain to wait placidly amid chaos and not flee. Passing through the yard, she saw Christie's pistol lying on the ground and picked it up. She mounted quickly and shoved the heavy gun into the holder on the saddle.

As she left the yard, Bluebell sped past her, barking furiously. Jennet called out, and the dog ran to her.

Smoke from the burning thatch sailed past on the overhead wind and stung Mhairi's eyes. Wiping the tears from her cheeks, she rode toward the Lincraig road.

Following the beacons in the night, Rowan galloped over moors and hills with Kerr and a fierce group of twenty troopers, well armed and determined. Not long ago, the fiery signals that warned of approaching reivers had been clearly visible from Abermuir's roof, where Rowan had stood watch with Archie Pringle. As soon as the first light flared, Rowan had called the warning to Kerr. The horses were already saddled in the barnekin yard, and the group rode out.

When Rowan saw the third beacon, blazing higher and hotter than the others, he knew its source. With a quick word to Kerr promising to investigate the fire, he took three troopers and separated from the warden's party.

Heavy dread spun in his gut as he rode. Grim, terrifying certainty told him that the burning house belonged to Iain Macrae. Urging Valentine to a faster gallop, he skimmed the ground, while three sets of hooves pounded behind him, wind howling and whipping around them.

Rowan had the sudden thought that it was not Jehovah's breath that powered the wind this night, but the devil's own, cold and dark and dangerous.

As he cleared the top of a hill near Iain's home, he saw the yellow flames that devoured the roof, soaring high to illuminate the night. Reaching the yard, he leaped from his horse, and ran toward a red-haired woman bent over a man who lay on the ground. She turned, her face pale, as he came near.

"Jennet?" he asked, dropping to one knee. "I'm Blackdrummond."

"I know," she said softly. "Heckie and his comrades were here. They took our beasts. Took your hobbie. And Clem Elliot did this to my brother."

Rowan laid a hand on her shoulder and looked at Christie, noticing the amount of blood and the lad's shallow, ragged breathing. Then he glanced up in alarm. "Where is Mhairi?"

"She rode toward Lincraig—"

"Jesu!" Rowan stood. "I'll ride after her. But you and Christie must be taken to safety. The lad needs attention."

"My mother's house is a few miles from here."

He nodded. "Walter!" he called to one of the troopers. "Make a litter for the lad, and you and the others take them wherever Mistress Macrae wishes." Bluebell circled Rowan anxiously, and he rubbed her head. "Take the dog, too," he added. "God keep you, Jennet." He turned to grab hold of his horse's bridle.

* * *

Riding furiously, Mhairi turned to look over her shoulder again, but saw only black hills beneath the floating white half-moon. Yet she felt the encroaching danger keenly, sharply, as if a hot knife had plunged through her soul. Leaning low, gripping the reins tightly, she forced herself to ride on.

The reivers had ridden this way, but Mhairi hoped they would be far ahead of her by now. Ambushes often occurred after a raid, and that knowledge made her more wary. But she was one rider, not a party of armed and fierce pursuers on a legal hot trod, carrying burning peats on lances. Surely they would not bother one rider.

She wanted only to reach the house that belonged to Jennet and Christie's Armstrong kin, who would send help. Legally or not, the Armstrongs would ride out after the Elliots and their English comrades, and a feud might well begin.

She covered another mile or so, passing the dark silhouette of the old castle on the hill. Glancing sideways, she saw the black shadows of a group of riders who cut across the moor behind her in the opposite direction, toward Abermuir and Blackdrummond. She ducked low and rode on, wondering if Heckie Elliot and his comrades were not yet done for the night. Perhaps they intended to take cattle and sheep from the warden or from the Scotts. She did not care, so long as she was not seen, so long as she was able to fetch help for Christie.

She remembered his pale face and his bloody chest, and caught back a desperate sob. Leaning lightly over her horse, she urged it to greater speed. The wind keened through the treetops and pushed against her, whipping her braid across her throat.

In the sudden noise of the wind, she had not heard the horseman who approached her from the left. When his horse pulled alongside hers, she glanced wildly at the rider and veered her mount away. Recognizing Clem Elliot by his large build and heavy beard, she knew she had to get away.

Clem grimaced at her in the moonlight and reached out to grab her. With her left hand, Mhairi grabbed the stock of the pistol, sheathed in its holder. She had no time, and little skill, to fire the powder, but she knew how to wield the ball end.

With a wild swing, she aimed toward Clem and caught him on the jaw, but lost her grip on the pistol. Stunned, Clem lurched forward, then lashed out at her with vicious strength.

Grabbing Mhairi's left arm above the elbow, Clem yanked hard, dragging her toward the chasm between their horses. She clung to the saddle, but his greater strength pulled her closer with every wild hoofbeat. Crying out with pain and fear, she kicked frantically, catching his horse in the head.

The horse whinnied and careened sideways. Thrown off balance, Clem slid from his saddle, pulling on Mhairi's arm as he went down. Hitting the ground, he yelled out and let go of her.

Mhairi yanked herself upright in the saddle, though agony slammed through her shoulder. The pain was so intense that she thought she might vomit or black out. Each movement of her left arm brought searing agony. Twisting the reins around her right hand, she held on, dazed, leaning crazily over the saddle as her horse sped onward along the road.

She did not see the other rider until too late, until he drew up alongside her. When he reached out and grabbed her around the waist, she had no strength to fight him.

Rowan pulled Mhairi across his saddle like a sack of barley grain, unresisting and awkward. He righted her quickly and smartly, seating her in front of him and strapping his arm across her chest before taking hold of the reins again.

She uttered a deep, hoarse cry and twisted a little, then stilled against him. Glancing curiously at her, expecting far more argument than she gave, he circled his horse around and caught the dangling reins of her horse to lead the animal back with them.

As he headed toward Blackdrummond Tower, he glanced at Mhairi again. She sat oddly subdued and silent in his arms. When she glanced up at him, he was struck by how pale she was, even in moonlight.

"I need to go to the Armstrongs—the other way," she

said. Her voice was so strained and low that he leaned his head down to hear her over the wind. "Take me there."

"We go to Blackdrummond," he said firmly.

"But I must help Christie—" she struggled in his arms, catching the last word on a ragged sob.

"Christie and Jennet are already on their way to their mother's home," Rowan answered. "I came to Iain's house with troopers, and we saw what had happened. The warden's men will see to their safety. Dinna fret for them. Fret for yourself instead," he added grimly. "I came over the hill, and saw that you had assaulted a traveler on the road, and were riding away. Another king's messenger?" he snapped.

"Clem Elliot," she said between clenched teeth. "He attacked me."

"Did he?" he asked in a skeptical tone. "I passed a man on the road who was trying to catch his horse, and was loudly cursing the day you were born, Mhairi Macrae."

She began to reply, but Valentine leaped to clear a narrow burn, landing on the other side. Mhairi cried out, grabbing at her arm, turning her head against Rowan's chest.

He frowned down at her. "What is it?"

"I twisted my arm," she said.

"Better that than a cracked pate," he replied sharply. She scowled at him and looked away. "You might have had much worse. Some of the Border reivers have petitioned the warden to take down the Lincraig riders, or else they would do it themselves."

"So 'tis done, then."

"I told you that I would take you down," he said softly.

She turned away. They rode the last miles to Blackdrummond in silence, beneath the white moon and the whining wind.

Chapter Thirteen

He turned her ower, and ower again,
And oh but she lookt white!

— "Edom o' Gordon"

Sharp agony swamped Mhairi when Rowan lifted her down from his horse, once inside the barnekin walls of Blackdrummond Tower. As her feet touched the ground, she stumbled, and Rowan caught her around the ribs, jolting her shoulder. She cried out and raised her hand protectively to her arm.

"Your arm hurts that much?" Rowan asked.

" 'Tis only twisted," she said hoarsely.

"Are you certain?"

Nodding quickly, she stepped away, although she wanted to tell him that the injury was far worse than she had admitted; she feared the shoulder was out of place. Yet she felt angry with him and uncertain of her safety, and could not reveal her vulnerability to him.

Rowan believed that she had attacked another rider on the Lincraig road. Acting on that assumption, he had pursued her and dragged her off of her horse just as savagely as Clem Elliot had tried to do. Rowan Scott had taken her down, just as he had promised. Now he meant to arrest and imprison her.

But she had little strength to explain this night's ride to him. The vicious pain in her shoulder dominated her thoughts. She wanted to lie down and be still, wanted to sleep until the pain subsided, until she could think again. Perhaps she was wrong about the displaced shoulder— rest might be enough to relieve the pain. Later she would tell Rowan Scott the truth.

"This way," Rowan said, taking her right arm and turning her toward the stone tower.

She stumbled along beside him. "Am I under arrest?"

"I caught you in the red hand. I told you that I would take you down—ho, can you walk? What is it?" His arm came around her waist to support her.

"I'm . . . tired," she finished huskily.

"Well, you can rest in here," he said, and banged on the heavy door in the base of the tower.

Rowan knocked loudly twice, and shouted once, and finally the latch rattled and the door opened. Sandie peered out at them, his eyes pinched from sleep, a gleaming pistol in his hand.

"Och, Rowan," he grumbled, lowering the weapon and stepping aside. "I thought 'twas reivers, bold enough to knock." He looked at Mhairi, who kept her head down as he spoke. "What—"

"We left our horses in the yard," Rowan said, guiding Mhairi past him into a dark, short corridor.

"But who's that lad?"

"The horses, Sandie," Rowan said, as he opened a second door and led Mhairi through in front of him. Sandie, grumbling loudly, went out into the barnekin.

"What will you do with me?" Mhairi asked.

"I'll confine you here until I decide what to do."

She nodded wearily. Another pain jabbed through her shoulder, and she swayed toward Rowan.

"Mhairi?" His voice, so close to her ear, seemed velvety and safe. She leaned against him for a blessed instant. Breathing in the warm scent of leather and smoke, sensing the solid comfort he could offer, she closed her eyes. "Mhairi, lass," he murmured.

Then she pulled away with a soft cry of protest and pain. Rowan Scott was the Black Laird, a notorious reiver, a deputy—and he had proven himself dangerous to her. She could not allow herself to forget that now.

"I'm fine," she said, turning away. "My arm just aches."

He hesitated. "Aye, well. Come with me." He touched her back, and she stepped ahead into a small foyer.

Torchlight crackled overhead, revealing two sets of turning steps. One stair, she knew, would lead upward to

the living quarters, where there would be light and
warmth, and hopefully some balm for her pain. If Lady
Anna were awake at this late hour, Mhairi could ask her
to tend her arm.

But Rowan guided her down the other staircase into
shadow. She missed her footing, and he put his arm
around her waist, leading her downward. At the base of
the steps, he reached past her and shoved open a creaking door.

Overwhelmed by pain, Mhairi shuffled mutely into a
small, black hole of a room that smelled dank and old.
Rowan stood behind her.

"I'll leave you here, then," he said. His voice sounded
oddly reluctant. " 'Tis where we keep our prisoners."

She started to answer, but dropped to her knees. A
frightening, powerful blackness threatened to sweep her
away in its current. She inhaled, resisting the horrid sensation that she was about to slip from this dark cell into
that void.

Rowan knelt beside her on the floor. "Jesu," he
breathed. "I canna leave you here like this. What is it you
need, lass?"

"I need a bed," she muttered hoarsely. "And a dram."
That might help the pain, she thought vaguely. She
reached out a hand, groping toward him. He caught her
fingers in his warm and solid grip.

"And I need—" she said, as darkness smothered her.

Rowan caught her deftly as she fell forward, and turned
her in his lap. He touched her cool cheek and murmured
her name, while his heart pounded heavily and his hands
shook. Cupping his hand over her left shoulder, he felt the
odd angle of her arm, even through the thickness of her
quilted doublet.

He opened the garment and slipped his hand inside,
shoving his fingers beneath her linen shirt and over the
warm, soft curve of her upper breast. As he rounded his
hand over her small, crooked shoulder, he realized that
her arm hung loose from its inner socket.

Suddenly angry at himself for bringing her here to
make his vengeful point, rather than seeing to her injury

first, he withdrew his hand and closed her doublet gently. Then he shifted her in his arms and stood.

She moaned as she woke, and lifted her head. "Rowan?" Her voice was confused and blurred. "Rowan?"

"I'm here, lass," he said. "Easy, now. Come with me." He carried her effortlessly up the steps. His boots scuffled loudly as he turned at the landing and climbed upward, past the great hall toward the upper sleeping level, his strides long and fast.

Candlelight brightened the top of the stairs. He glanced up. Jock and Anna stood on the top step, watching him. Anna, wearing only a shift and a woolen shawl, held a fat candle. Her mouth hung partly open. Jock, in a shirt and breeches, merely frowned as Rowan looked up.

" 'Tis Mhairi Macrae," Anna said in surprise, and looked at Jock. Footsteps sounded behind Rowan, and he turned.

"What the de'il is going on here?" Sandie asked, stomping up the steps. "Rowan! You left Valentine and a lathered black mare roaming free in the yard. 'Tisna like you to do that—by hell, that's Mhairi Macrae!"

"Someone open the door of my bedchamber," Rowan said as he reached the top step. "And bring me some wine. I mean to get her swine drunk."

"Rowan!" his grandmother exclaimed.

"The lass is hurt, Anna, or ill, by the look o' her." Jock moved quickly to open a nearby door.

Rowan went into his bedchamber, followed by his relatives, who jostled through the narrow door as he laid Mhairi gently on his bed. "Her shoulder is out of place. I'll have to set it right."

"Och, she'll need that wine," Sandie said, and turned to leave the room.

"Draw a flask of the Danish aqua vitae," Anna called after him. "And knock on Grace's door. Loudly." Anna turned back to the bed. "Is she awake?" she asked Rowan.

"Barely," Rowan answered, watching Mhairi's restless eyelids. He swept off his helmet and unhooked his jack, tossing them onto the chair near the hearth. Yanking off his doublet, he shoved up his shirtsleeves and sat on the edge of the bed.

Anna set her candle on the chest by the bed and bent

over Mhairi. "We'll take her doublet off, then. Why is she wearing men's gear? And how did she get hurt?" She began to undo buttons while Mhairi watched her through half-lidded eyes.

"The lad can explain later, Anna," Jock said. He handed Rowan a dirk. "Use this."

Nodding in agreement, Rowan reached past Anna's hands to slide the blade under the shoulder seam of Mhairi's doublet, slitting the cloth neatly along her left arm. Anna helped him draw the ruined garment off of her, leaving Mhairi clad in a loose linen shirt with a torn sleeve, breeches, and long boots.

Mhairi cupped her hand gingerly around her shoulder and watched Rowan. Her eyes looked haunted, dark-circled in the low candlelight, her cheeks deathly pale.

"That shoulder needs to be set straight, indeed," Anna told Rowan. "I have an ointment that will help the soreness. I'll fetch it and make sure Grace is awake. We'll prepare a room for the lass." She turned and hurried out the door.

"I was watching on the roof a while ago," Jock said. "I saw the beacons, and the fire. Iain Macrae's house, was it?"

Rowan nodded, not surprised that his grandfather already knew something about the evening's activities. Jock Scott's reiving years had given him the habit of waking often at night. "Heckie Elliot and his lot came through the dale to fetch their black rent," he answered. "The warden is trodding after them. Devil's Christie Armstrong was wounded in the raid."

"And this lass? Was she hurt by the reivers as well?"

Rowan hesitated, looking at Mhairi. She watched him with wide, uncertain eyes. In that moment, Sandie came into the room, a leather flask in his hand. Rowan turned, grateful for the interruption. He was unsure how best to answer his grandfather.

"This Danish hot water will take the sting out o' any hurt," Sandie said, handing Rowan the flask.

Freeing the wax plug, Rowan held the mouth of the flask to Mhairi's lips. She grimaced as she swallowed, and shook her head.

"You need this for the pain," Rowan insisted, and held the flask ready until she took another sip.

"Hey, good lass," Sandie said with approval. "Enough o' that fine stuff, and she'll swarf out like a candle flame, as she should. Best thing for her."

"She's already swooned, and I wouldna like to see it again." Rowan turned to his cousin. "Perhaps you should watch from the roof," he said, raising his eyebrows meaningfully. He was not eager to hear more of Sandie's suggestions just then, and knew that Mhairi did not need to hear them.

"I want to see if more beacons have been lit," Jock said. "Come ahead, Sandie. This is nae place for us. Anna will tend to the lass when she returns." He gestured briskly to Sandie.

As the door clicked shut behind them, Rowan offered Mhairi the mouth of the flask again. She sent him a wary glance before sipping.

"Well, I'm giving you what you wanted," he said. "A bed and a dram, as you said. Here, have a bit more."

She sipped, and glanced at him. "What will you do?" Her voice was soft and husky with drink.

"I'll put the arm in its proper place. I've seen it done. I had a comrade whose arm sometimes went out like that."

"I mean, what will you do with me. I am your prisoner."

He shrugged. "First we'll deal with the hurt." He put the flask to her lips again, and she drank. A clear drop of liquor slipped over her lower lip, and Rowan wiped it away, easing his finger along the sweet curve of her mouth.

She closed her eyes and turned her face, resting on the pillow. Rowan's long, slow breaths measured out time while he watched the warm candlelight flow softly over her face and studied the black, lacy crescents of her eyelashes above the gathering blush on her cheeks.

"Do you feel the spirits yet?" he asked softly.

"Mmm," she whispered, nodding. She lifted her head to take another drink while he held the flask. "Muckle strong," she said, lifting her delicate, dark eyebrows.

"You're among the privileged," Rowan said. "My

grandmother is covetous of her cask of Danish aqua vitae." He smiled.

Mhairi smiled too, a winsome lift of her mouth that, with the high pink flush in her cheeks, added a dazzling sparkle to her eyes. "Aqua vitae—that means water of life. This tastes a wee bit like our Highland *uisge beatha,* which also means water of life."

"I havena tasted the Highland stuff, though I've heard of it. How is the pain?" In answer, Mhairi grimaced, shaking her head. He gave her another sip.

She shifted her hips to slide lower on the bed, exhaling a long sigh. "*Ach,* 'tis warm in here."

" 'Tis why we call such spirits hot water," he said.

"Or is it because it burns as it goes down?" she asked, accepting another sip. He noticed the high, heated stains of color in her cheeks.

"I'll take off your boots," he said. " 'Twill cool you some."

She nodded and Rowan drew off one long boot and then the other, dropping them on the floor. When he turned back, Mhairi raised her ankle to rest it on her upraised knee. Her stockinged foot hovered in his face.

"Help me take these off as well," she said.

He drew the knitted wool down her slender leg and pulled it loose. She raised her other leg as if in silent command, and he took that stocking off too. His glance skimmed the graceful curves of her calves and ankles and the fine bones of her feet.

She sighed, shifted on the bed, and uttered a breathy little groan. The soft sound struck Rowan, unexpectedly and deeply, in his groin.

He cleared his throat. "How is your shoulder now?"

She tested it gingerly. "It hurts less. You're a fine physician, Blackdrummond." She smiled, and a drift of glossy hair fell over one eye. Rowan brushed the silky lock back with a finger and lifted the flask to her mouth.

"Just a bit more," he said. "*Slàinte.*"

She smiled. "You know some Gaelic."

"Only that much. Health, is it?"

"It is. *Slàinte,*" she murmured, and rounded her lips over the leather mouth to swallow. Drawing back, she touched her tongue to her lower lip, an unconscious, languid gesture that made Rowan suck in his breath.

She tilted her head to watch him. Her eyes, shadowed under half-raised lids, were smoky gray beneath thick lashes. The luscious curves of her breasts heaved softly beneath the linen shirt as she drew in a deep breath and sighed it out. Rowan could not seem to stop his gaze from roaming over her.

She took his wrist and lifted his hand with the flask. "When my brothers drink *uisge beatha,* they say *suas e, sios e.*" She placed her hand over his and guided the flask to her mouth, then sipped. "That means up with it, down it. Now you." She pushed the flask toward his lips. "Drink. *Suas e, sios e.*"

He repeated the phrase as closely as he could remember it. Mhairi laughed, a sound like small silver bells. Her fingers over his, on the neck of the flask, were light and soft, sending a deep swirl of need through his body. He sipped, feeling the hot comfort of the liquor, and lowered the flask.

Mhairi smiled at him, her eyes heavy-lidded, and he frowned. She had no head for spirits, he realized. She showed the effects of the aqua vitae far sooner than he would have thought, and was more than half the way to drunk.

"Perhaps 'tis enough," he said, replacing the wax stopper.

"A fine physician," she repeated. "But a foul deputy. Why did you take me down on the highway?" The glistening thrust of her lower lip sent another lightning streak through his groin.

Rowan sighed and rested his hands on either side of her hips. The feather bed sank slightly beneath them. "I did only what I promised to do if you rode out again," he murmured.

Her eyes narrowed. "Blackdrummond always keeps his word." Her breath drifted hot and sweet over his face as he leaned above her. His heart thumped heavily. He was fascinated by her soft lips and luminous eyes, by the warm scent of her in his bed.

"Aye," he whispered.

"What will you do with me now?" Her gaze wandered

over his face, returned to his mouth, flickered up to pierce his eyes.

"What should I do with you?" He watched her mouth.

She closed her eyes slowly and lifted her face.

Rowan bent down, a breath away from her lips. For the space of a heartbeat he hovered there, wanting her so much that his body throbbed with the need. But he held still, his heart thudding deep in his chest.

Mhairi looked up at him, her eyes wide and translucent in the candlelight. Rowan had the sudden wild thought that her silver-gray eyes looked like deep water, and that her fragile, beautiful soul shone through those depths.

She placed her right hand on his bare forearm. The penetrating warmth of her skin melted the last wall of his reserve, drawing him toward her like the force of a river current.

"Mhairi," he whispered, on a breath. He lowered his head and touched his lips to hers. The pillow of her mouth was soft and warm beneath his. He tasted a faint sweetness mingled with the subtle sting of the aqua vitae.

She sighed into his mouth and gripped his shirt, pulling him closer. His heart thundered heavily, urgently, as he kissed her again, slanting his mouth over hers, sliding his hand beneath her head to thread his fingers through the glossy silk of her hair. She circled her right arm around his neck, opening her lips under his, sighing again, softly, as if from joy.

Rowan shifted his hand to cup the delicate shape of her jaw in his palm, feeling the exquisite heat and velvet of her skin. His fingers traced the line of her throat as she tilted her head back. Her mouth shifted beneath his, fervently renewing the kiss. The trace of liquor on her lips heated his own breath.

As the open neck of her shirt slipped lower, Rowan grazed his fingers along her collarbone and over her upper chest, feeling warm, creamy skin, sensing the small bones beneath. The steady beat of her heart stirred under his fingertips. The delicate softness of her skin assailed him, lured him. Her body and her mouth were enticing, warm, wondrous.

Too wondrous, too enticing. Inhaling sharply, he sat up. He could not—would not—take what she offered, not in this way, no matter how much he wanted her. What she did now came from a haze of drink induced by his own hand.

Mhairi blinked up at him silently. Rowan rubbed a hand over his eyes and pushed his fingers slowly through his hair, taking a moment to steady his breath and calm his body.

"Rowan?" she murmured. "I—"

"Hush." He touched a finger to her lips. "I think I should tend to your shoulder," he said quietly, "before I forget why you are in my bed."

She hesitated, then nodded, and reached up to draw the neck of her shirt wide, exposing her left shoulder. Rowan drew in a deep breath and slid his fingers inside to round his hand over it, forcing himself to concentrate on what he must do.

Frowning, he eased his thumb carefully along the curves of her shoulder to judge the angle. Mhairi pulled in a sharp breath and bit her lower lip as he touched the side of her upper arm.

He removed his hand quickly. "I didna mean to hurt you."

She shook her head. "You were gentle. But I canna move my arm. I think 'tis out of place."

"Aye. But I can remedy that if you'll let me." He felt suddenly formal with her, his reserve back. But something profound had changed between them, as if the kiss that had flamed so suddenly had brought him to a new, strange place where he needed to reacquaint himself with her.

She nodded hesitantly, watching him with wide eyes, as if she too felt shy. Then she turned her head and her shirt slid a little over her shoulder, so that the upper slope of her left breast, pale as down, was visible. Rowan glanced away, tightening his jaw muscle against the vivid image of his hands touching her breasts, touching her hips, bringing her solace as well as pleasure. He tried to focus his thoughts on her shoulder and its awkward tilt.

"Mhairi, how did this happen?" he asked, as he looked at her shoulder. "Was it when I pulled you from your horse?"

She shook her head. "You didna do it. Clem Elliot rode

up behind me and tried to pull me off my horse. He grabbed my arm."

He narrowed his eyes. "When I saw him, he was screaming that you had attacked him."

"Well, I did hit him with the pistol," she said in a small voice.

He tried not to smile. "Ah. Your preferred weapon."

She looked at him indignantly. "I didna attack him. He chased me as I rode to fetch the Armstrongs, and I struck him."

He watched her silently, frowning, then nodded. He saw no guile in her, only sincerity. He was sure that she spoke the truth in this, at least. He would do well, he thought, to remember that she did not speak true in all matters, as that hidden Spanish letter attested.

"You took me down when I hadna done a crime," she reprimanded softly.

He sighed. "I would have taken you down, soon or late," he said. "I told you that. Better me than Clem Elliot."

"He meant to ransom me, not arrest me."

"Ransom, or something else," he answered. The thought of what Clem might have intended for her caused Rowan to tighten his lips in anger. He was tempted to offer her his own reprimand for going out on the road tonight, but he heard the click of the bedchamber door and turned his head.

His grandmother entered the room with Grace behind her. The little serving maid set a bucket of water and some cloths on the wooden chest, nodded her kerchiefed head toward Rowan and Mhairi, and left after Anna motioned her out.

Anna placed a clay pot on the chest, and pushed up the sleeves of her shift. "What can I do to help?"

"Sit behind her," Rowan said. Anna slid in beside Mhairi and urged her to lean back against her. "Hold her tight, and keep a hand behind her shoulder," Rowan said, placing one knee on the bed.

Anna wrapped an arm around Mhairi's chest and braced the other against her back. "Lean this way a bit, dearling. There. Oops, lift your head. There you are."

Anna raised a brow at Rowan. "She's had enough Danish hot water, I think," she said meaningfully.

Rowan pressed his lips together wryly and raised Mhairi's left arm as if it were made of glass. She winced, but the relaxed muscles told him that the aqua vitae had taken effect. He studied the odd angle of her arm, judging which way to best position himself, and which direction to pull and rotate. After a moment he nodded.

Kneeling on the bed, Rowan rounded one hand over Mhairi's shoulder girdle and braced his other hand against her upper chest. Beneath his fingers, he could feel fragile bones and lean muscles, and the steady thud of her heart.

"Relax, sweetling," Anna said to Mhairi. "Our Rowan is a gentle lad."

Mhairi laughed delicately and looked away.

Rowan took a deep breath. Then he nodded to Anna. "Hold firm, now."

With a sudden tug, he pulled the arm down and rotated it slightly upward to guide the arm back into its natural position.

As soon as he lifted the arm, Mhairi sucked in her breath on a high cry. Rowan heard a distinct, meaty pop as the bone found its niche. He released her arm, and Mhairi uttered a deep, throaty groan, her face drained of all color. She shuddered, her eyes rolled upward, and she fell back against Anna.

"Mhairi?" Rowan leaned over her, tracing shaking fingertips over her damp brow, alarmed by her pallor.

"She's swooned again, poor dove," Anna said. She shifted out from under her and laid her back on the feather-stuffed pillows. "She'll be bruised and sore tomorrow, and for days after that. Here, lad, help me pull the coverlet over her."

Rowan did, and sat again on the edge of the bed while Anna picked up the clay pot she had brought with her. Scooping out a fingerful of slimy brownish stuff, she smeared it over Mhairi's shoulder and upper arm, and covered it with a soft bandage.

Breathing out a heavy sigh, Rowan wiped his arm slowly over his brow, wincing as his hand bumped against the old bruise on his head, faded but still tender. He lowered his arm to see his grandmother watching him.

"You look tired," she said.

He nodded. "I'll make a pallet in the hall."

"No need. Grace and I readied the bedchamber next to this one for Mhairi."

"I'll take that, then. We willna move her this night. Let her sleep."

"Aye. I've sent Grace out to find a cold stone from the stream to apply to her shoulder for now. Tomorrow hot cloths will help the pain and stiffness." Anna brushed a damp lock of hair from Mhairi's brow and glanced at Rowan. "In the morning, you'll tell me how she came by such an injury in the middle of the night. But for now, I'm tired, too, and I'll go to my bed." She stood.

"Thank you, Granna," he murmured.

"Rowan." She touched his shoulder. "Whatever else went on between you and Mhairi Macrae this night, you did well by her just now." He nodded wearily as she left.

Reaching out, he gathered Mhairi's hand in his own, and raised her fingers to his lips.

Then he stood and went in search of his bed for the night.

Chapter Fourteen

When cockle shells turn siller bells
And fishes flee frae tree to tree
When frost and snaw turn fire-beams
I'll come down and drink wine wi thee.

—*"Jamie Douglas"*

The high winds of the previous night brought rain in their wake. Rowan went down the stairs the next morning, having slept later than he expected, and found the great hall quiet but for the patter of rain. Two narrow windows and the dim glow of the hearth provided meager light, as if the night had never lifted.

Mhairi sat alone in the room, enthroned in Jock Scott's elbow chair, a cushion under her left arm and a thick blanket over her legs. Eyes closed, head leaned back and her arm wrapped in a cloth sling, she looked pale and still. Rowan noticed that she wore a fur-lined robe of green damask that belonged to his grandfather, and beneath that, a linen shift, probably his grandmother's. Her feet, peeking out from under the robe's hem, wore a pair of his own nether stockings, a fine set made of brown silk and wool, which he had not even seen himself for three years.

Turning, he noticed a flagon on the table that undoubtedly contained Anna's cream and herb posset. He sighed and pushed his fingers through his hair. His prisoner was being coddled beneath his very roof by his own grandmother.

Last night he had been just as guilty of that coddling, and far more. But this morning he had thought about the things he had found hidden in the crypt. He had put them in a locked chest, except for the Spanish letter, which he had tucked away in the secret slot inside his pouch. He wondered now if he had nursed a spy in his bed last night.

Remaining silent, thinking Mhairi asleep, Rowan poured himself a cup of ale from the cooled jug set on the table. Resting a hip on the table edge, he watched the pure line of her profile as he sipped. Rain pounded against the windows, and the fire snapped.

After a moment Mhairi drew a sharp breath and opened her eyes, turning her head to see him. Lavender shadows beneath her eyes, and the tousled dark braid hanging over her shoulder, gave her a bewildered, innocent appearance. His feelings softened toward her slightly. She must be in a good deal of pain still.

"Give you good day," he murmured, lifting his cup. "Can I get you some morning ale?"

She groaned and shook her head, raising a hand to her face.

"How does your shoulder feel?" he asked.

"Better than my head," she muttered.

"Ah." He could not stop the faint smile that curved his lips. He smothered it with a sip. "Danish aqua vitae does have a hearty kick."

She slipped him a dark scowl and covered her eyes again. "Did you have to give me so much?"

"You took it like a bairn takes milk, my lass," he drawled.

Another scowl, blacker than the first, came his way, accompanied by a hot blush that was not due to the hearth's heat.

Rowan smiled again into his ale. No matter his suspicions of her, her current dark mood had an irresistible charm. Misery had diluted her usual boldness. He glimpsed the same tender, unguarded lass who had nursed his wound in Lincraig's dungeon, and who had held a new bairn as sweetly as a Madonna.

Her tenor this morning matched the sullen storm outside, although last night she had been as fierce and proud, and as exciting, as the high winds on the moor. He found that changeable nature not fickle, but wholly intriguing.

And, like Jock with Anna, he found that he could not

keep from teasing her somewhat. He enjoyed raising that
bonny pink blush, but he would not have her suffer for it.

"Truly, Mhairi, you didna have that much," he said
gently. "You dinna have a head for the stuff, is all."

"I know," she moaned. "I willna drink it again."

"Your shoulder is improved?" he asked.

She nodded. "But for the stiffness, aye. Rowan—I
thank you for tending my injury. And for helping
Christie."

He caught her gaze and held it. "Devil's Christie is the
son of a good comrade. I will always help Davy's kin.
And I owed you some nursing. For this." He touched the
pale yellow bruise on his forehead and cocked an eyebrow at her. "I might have died of this, if you hadna
stayed with me." He said it lightly, but meant it in part.
She had dealt the blow, but she had watched over him
with concern afterward. He had not forgotten that, or any
of it.

Mhairi frowned into the fire. "Dinna tease me. I know
you owe me naught but vengeance, and that was paid last
night, when you took me down on the highway." She
looked over at him. "Now what do you plan to do? Will
you chain me in your dungeon?"

He set down the cup. "I thought to put you there last
night to teach you the ABC's of the Border alphabet. But
I didna see that you were hurt." He sighed, and continued.
"I caught you in the red hand and I am obligated to provide imprisonment for you."

"Then you do mean to lock me in that dark cell."

"When I was imprisoned in England, I was held for
much of the time in a fine room in the warden's own
manor house, because I am a laird. 'Tis often the way wi'
prisoners of merit. So I will grant you merit, and confine
you in my bedchamber." At her soft gasp, he raised his
palm reassuringly. "I willna be there myself. But you
willna leave Blackdrummond until I say."

She watched him, her eyes silvery flashes in the firelight. "And you willna let me pledge for Iain."

"I willna."

"Will you tell Simon Kerr that you have caught me?"

He thought of the papers that he had found, which

could incriminate Mhairi along with her brother. "Perhaps later. I need to gather some answers first."

"Did you go to Abermuir?" she asked. He nodded. "So you have seen Iain."

"Simon wouldna allow it," he answered, and paused. What he had to tell her next would sit hard with her, he knew, but must be said. "Mhairi—you should know that your brother will be given over to the English at the next truce day meeting."

She stared at him, gripping the arm of the chair until her knuckles turned white. "You brought Simon that word?"

"I did," he said quietly. He stepped toward her. "With the council's signed warrant."

Mhairi looked up at him, all the lustrous color gone from her cheeks. "You had the writ," she whispered. "You had it, and didna tell me."

"There was naught you could have done about it."

"I would have taken it from you." She lowered her head. A tear slipped onto her hand. "I would have burned it."

He dropped to his haunches to peer into her face, but she tucked her chin down, refusing to look at him. Another tear dropped onto the green damask robe.

"I have tried so hard to stop this," she said in a small, breathy voice. "And now you have condemned Iain." She smothered a little sob with her trembling hand. Seeing her quick tears, Rowan realized that fatigue and pain had drained her will of its customary fire. And he realized, too, that her desire to help and protect her brother was quite genuine, whatever else was at play here.

"The council would have sent another messenger, Mhairi, and another warrant, and another after that," he said gently. Her tears disturbed him more than he wanted to admit. He wanted to touch her, wanted to soothe the wetness from her cheeks, but he remained still. "Simon would have gotten the word," he continued. "You couldna stop it. Simon himself, or the reivers who have been angered by your night rides, would have taken you down. There had to be an end to it somewhere."

"But my brother will die if the English take him."

"If he has earned it. They will give him a trial."

She laughed, a bitter huff that told him what she thought of English trials. "Would you be so harsh if 'twere your own brother?"

He set his jaw, a small muscle thumping there. "I would."

She scowled, but her moist eyes were luminous. "I dinna care how dark your dungeon is, Blackdrummond, or how strong your chains. I willna stay here with you." She stood, wavering slightly. The blanket slid unheeded to the floor.

He straightened and stood. "You will stay where I set you."

"I willna." She pushed his outstretched hand and spun away. Lifting her head with a stubborn tilt, she walked toward the door, the green damask hem sliding like a queen's train.

Rowan muttered a curse and strode after her.

Catching her at the door, he grabbed her free arm and pulled her back. The look of pain that crossed her face made him instantly regret that impulse. He let go, but towered over her, glaring, leaning his shoulder against the door so that she could not tug it open. She tried valiantly, using her right hand, her left arm snug in its cloth.

"You will stay here," he said. "If I have to chain you in that room up the stairs, you will stay here."

She pushed against his chest, ineffectively, for he would not budge. "I dinna care if you are King Jamie Stewart himself! You canna hold me here!" She returned her efforts to the door, yanking on the iron ring.

He blew out an exasperated breath. "Where would you go? To raise a host of your Kerr cousins to ride their lances against me?"

"Nay, though you are a rogue and a sneakbait," she snapped, smacking the door. "I will go to Simon and tell him that I have been riding the Lincraig road. I'll beg him to let me serve as a pledge, no matter what will come of it. 'Tis the only way, now."

"You are the most daffin lassie I have ever met," Rowan muttered, rubbing a hand over his face. "Now listen well. You are in as much trouble as your brother. I canna allow you to leave here, or you will do something daft. Your brother's fate is set, and you canna change it now. If you go to Simon and confess that you are the Lincraig rider, you will risk a charge of treason."

She stopped tugging on the door ring and looked up at him. "What do you mean? What treason have I done?"

"Attacking king's messengers is treason, lass. And holding Spanish documents can get you hanged alongside your brother."

She stared at him. "Spanish documents?"

"Aye, as well you know. I found pages written in Spanish hidden at Lincraig, along with a broken messenger's wand and some council writs. No one else but you would have put those things where I found them. Where did you get them?"

She looked down. "I—I took them from a king's messenger."

He did not miss her hesitation. "I doubt a messenger at arms would carry such foreign correspondence." He came away from the door and took her firmly above the elbow of her sound arm. "Come with me, where I can keep you safe until I have the truth from you." He pulled open the door.

"Let me go," she said between her teeth. He ignored her.

As they stepped into the corridor, Anna came up the steps from the kitchen. "Rowan! You see how well our Mhairi is this morn." She smiled and came forward to envelop her in a soft hug. "Did your rest by the fire help you?"

Mhairi shot Rowan a glance. "Nae so much."

"Well, you'll be better soon. You need more hot cloths on that shoulder." Anna looked at Rowan. "She was up before dawn, poor bird, with deep bruises, and so sore. And a headache as well—is that better now? Aye? Grace and I put hot, wet cloths on the shoulder, and I gave her an infusion of willow for the pain. She will need a few days of rest. Can you stay here with us, Mhairi? 'Twould be best."

"She can stay." Rowan moved Mhairi toward the stairs.

"Good! We'll give her your room," Anna said, climbing after them.

"Aye," Rowan drawled. "We'll do that." Mhairi cast him a dark look and went up the steps ahead of him.

Shoving open the door of his bedchamber, Rowan gave Mhairi a little push toward the bed. She glared at him and went over to the elbow chair, sitting in it with a stubborn flourish. Anna came forward to tuck a pillow under Mhairi's arm and lift her feet to a stool.

Thanking her, Mhairi lanced Rowan with another dark look, this one as ominous as the rain clouds outside the narrow window. He breathed out an exasperated sigh.

Anna leaned over the bucket of water that sat on the hearthstones and tested it with a finger. "Still warm enough to soak a cloth in for that shoulder. I'll heat a flat stone for you to wrap up and hold to your arm, but wet heat is best for now." She straightened and looked from Rowan to Mhairi. "You both look tired. Shall I have Grace bring the midday meal up here for you to share?"

Mhairi looked horrified. Rowan made an awkward grimace.

"I willna be here then," he said. "I have a meeting to attend at Abermuir. Keep Mhairi in this room, Granna. She isna to leave here."

"What?" Anna looked puzzled.

"He means to keep me prisoner," Mhairi said. Rowan sighed in dismay. He had intended to explain this to his grandmother, but not at this particular moment.

Anna blinked in astonishment. "Prisoner? Rowan, what does she mean?"

"I took her down last night—" he began.

Anna smiled. "I knew there was some secret between the two of you! You've abducted Mhairi for your bride!"

"Bride!" Mhairi burst out.

"Aye, as Jock did with me fifty years ago. Such marriages are often full of fire at first, but so much warmth later—"

"She isna my bride," Rowan ground out. "She is under March arrest."

Anna looked stunned. "Godamercy! What do you mean?"

Mhairi sighed and leaned forward. "Lady Anna," she said gently, "you've been kind to me. But you must know that I have gone against March law. I have been riding the Lincraig highway at night." She flashed a glance at Rowan. He watched her steadily, with a sudden sense of marvel at her ability to be so gentle with others, and honest about herself.

When it suited her, he reminded himself sourly.

"The Lincraig rider—you?" Anna stared at her. Mhairi nodded. "And Rowan took you down for that?"

"I thought it best to keep her from harrying the neighbors further," he said dryly.

"Then you caused her injury," Anna said, frowning.

He shook his head. "That was an accident. But I caught her in the red hand—"

" 'Twasna in the red hand last night," Mhairi interrupted. "I wasna snatching anything."

"Well, I've witnessed her at it before."

"Aye, when I took you down myself!" Mhairi snapped.

Anna blinked at Rowan in sudden understanding. "The first day you came here, you said that you had met the Lincraig rider. Did your cracked pate come from her hand?"

"It did," Mhairi said with a note of satisfaction.

He felt his cheeks grow warm, but he looked sternly at both of them. "My responsibility as the March deputy is to keep her confined until this matter is settled," he said coldly.

"What the devil is this? Mhairi arrested as the Lincraig rider?" The open door swung wider, and Jock came into the room with Sandie behind him. "Mhairi Macrae, what is this folly?" Jock asked.

She shifted in her chair to face Jock, her posture straight and proud. " 'Tis true, sir," she said steadily. "I am the Lincraig rider. No one else."

Rowan felt genuine admiration to see Mhairi face his formidable grandfather with grace and sincerity, and staunchly protect Devil's Christie by taking the whole blame onto herself. He narrowed his eyes, perplexed at the depths he continually discovered in her. She was as much an innocent as a virago.

"Why did you ride that road, Mhairi?" Jock demanded.

"I meant to help my brother," she said simply.

"Iain is held fast in Simon's prison. Raising a host o' reivers to break him out would have been better. What did you think to accomplish?"

Mhairi hesitated, looking flustered. Rowan cleared his

throat. "She meant to stop the council from sending orders to Simon Kerr," he said.

"Ah," Jock said, nodding.

"Och! A fine idea!" Sandie said. "I might have done the same, had it been Alec Scott was arrested. You did a brave thing, lassie. I like it, I do."

"Will you charge her and take her to trial?" Jock asked Rowan.

"I dinna know what I will decide," Rowan said. "But for now she is a prisoner under the Leges Marchiarum."

"March laws or none, you will not imprison this lass in a household that I live in." Anna folded her arms decisively.

He sighed. "Granna—"

"She is injured," Anna said. "How can you treat her like this? Last night you showed her kindness, Rowan. Last night you—"

"Last night she needed help," he growled. His glance flickered toward Mhairi. She watched him evenly, cheeks pink.

"You canna lock up a wee hurt lassie wi' naught but a flask o' water and a stale bowl o' porridge," Sandie said.

"I didna have that in mind, exactly," Rowan said.

"Every prisoner ever held here has been treated wi' respect," Jock said. " 'Tis the way o' the Blackdrummond Scotts."

"She isna being held for ransom. She chose to act the criminal. No one forced her to it."

"She had a good reason for it," Anna commented.

"Aye, she did that." Sandie nodded firmly.

"Kin helps kin in the Borders, even to the death," Jock said. "She's done an honorable deed. There's nae crime in aiding a brother."

Rowan avoided his grandfather's meaningful glance. "Mhairi will face the results of the risks she took."

Jock shook his head slowly. "We canna condemn her for what she's done. Blackdrummond Scotts have broken every March law there is. Will you forget that so easily?"

"How could I?" Rowan drew a quick, tense breath. "But I must follow this strictly by the law." He had reason enough for that, he thought grimly. If he did not discover the secret spy channel to Spain, his own head might be forfeit to the English. His grandparents did not know that. Nor were they aware that Mhairi Macrae was somehow an essential link in the chain.

"Pish, " Sandie said. "March law."

Rowan set his jaw, bouncing an impatient muscle. "She will stay here, and willna be allowed to leave. That, or I will imprison her somewhere else."

Jock scowled. "Verra well. An honorable confinement. Will you agree to that, Mhairi?"

"Oh, I know all about honorable confinements," Mhairi said, looking sourly at Rowan. He returned the gaze full force, but she did not look away.

"I see she's had her trial by jury in my own household," he said. "And been declared clean of all charges. You'll be held in Blackdrummond Tower, Mhairi Macrae, but without chains, it seems."

"Rowan!" Anna gasped.

"Och, woman, he wouldna have done that," Jock said.

Riding through cold, misted rain on the way to Abermuir, Rowan was grateful to escape the frustrations of watching Mhairi surrounded by her new, and very staunch, allies. As he was preparing to leave Blackdrummond Tower, Anna had been applying hot cloths to Mhairi's shoulder, while Sandie fetched more firewood. Grace had come up to the room with a trencher of hot food, and was sent out again after fresh water and a flask of good wine. Throughout, Jock looked on approvingly.

Rowan had walked away in disgust. No captive queen could have had better care, or greater admiration. Still, he had won his argument. His family had agreed reluctantly that Mhairi would stay confined. But they were determined that she would not suffer a moment's misery for her crimes. She had won the hearts of the Blackdrummond Scotts.

All but one, Rowan told himself firmly. He tightened his jaw as he rode steadily through the drizzle. Last night Mhairi had worked some kind of magic on his own heart, some charm over his body. But the cold light of a rainy day had returned him to his senses. Remembering the papers that he had found at Lincraig had been like a cold splash of reality, diluting what he was beginning to feel toward Mhairi.

But his body throbbed now at the memory of her curled warm in his bed, a sultry smile on her lips; her eyes, smoke-colored in candlelight; the feel of her soft, pliant lips beneath his.

He muttered a curse and yanked his helmet lower over his brow. Though the rain spit noisily against the steel, he vowed that he would never take the thing off in rain again, not after having met Mhairi Macrae in the midst of a storm. He was forced, more and more, to master the urges of his body each time he thought of her or was near her. That only interfered with his ability to objectively discern the truth in this matter of spies and brothers.

Ahead, Abermuir loomed above a fringe of oak trees, their autumn-gold leaves soggy and sparse. The pele tower was a massive L-shaped building of local dark red sandstone, four stories high. The silhouette against the sky was sparse and powerful, but for the odd conglomeration of conical turrets and pitched roofs added at the top, where later expansions had been made. From those watchtowers, visitors and enemies alike could be seen for miles.

Certain that he had already been sighted, Rowan drew a deep breath and rode forward. He was curious to learn if the March warden had captured Heckie Elliot and his comrades. And he meant to ask—not politely this time— to see Iain Macrae. That interview was imperative if he were to accomplish what the council had sent him here to do.

If he rode out with Kerr and his troopers on another patrol, he would not return to Blackdrummond until early the next morning. And then, Rowan thought moodily, he would do his best to avoid his own bedchamber.

That place was too crowded with Scotts courting a bonny lass who was more of a sneakbait thief than any Blackdrummond Scott had ever been.

Chapter Fifteen

~

"Now haud thy tongue, thou rank reiver!
There's never a Scot shall set ye free;
Before ye cross my castle yett,
I trow ye shall take farewell o' me."

—*"Kinmont Willie"*

"Heckie Elliot and his lot got away," Archie Pringle told Rowan, handing him a cup of ale across the table in the great hall at Abermuir. They sat with Simon Kerr and John Hepburn, the land sergeant, for the meeting. "They took a hidden path south to Liddesdale. The warden's men lost them."

"The Keeper o' Liddesdale should trod after 'em," Simon said, scowling. "But Walter Scott o' Buccleuch has been appointed to that post, and he's a worse rogue than Heckie."

"Buccleuch, Blackdrummond, or Lincraig—Scotts canna be trusted, to a man." Hepburn looked pointedly at Rowan.

"Can they nae?" Rowan narrowed his eyes. "Have you some quarrel wi' me, Sergeant?" He allowed the menace to ring clear.

"Aye, he does, as I do," Simon barked, glaring hard at Rowan, his stubble-dark face suffused with an angry flush. "We were told that Mhairi Macrae rode out last night—that she is the Lincraig thief! 'Twas you took her down and brought her back to Blackdrummond Tower."

"Where did you hear that?" Rowan asked.

"She attacked a man on that road last night and was seen. Caught in the red hand. I wouldna have believed it, but I had the report from one o' my men. He was certain what she was doing, and he saw you out there wi' her, taking her down."

"I caught her," Rowan said. "No one else. And I will say if 'twas in the red hand or nae."

"You were seen taking her down. My man said she's the Lincraig rider we've been after all along." Simon slammed the table with his fist. "By hell! The wench has lied to me for weeks. She couldna do this alone. Who's been riding wi' her? Davy Armstrong's kin? Those damned Ferniehurst Kerrs she and her brother fostered wi', my own blasted cousins?"

"She was alone," Rowan said flatly.

"Aye? And what gives you the authority to imprison her in your tower?" Simon barked.

"She rode over Jock Scott's land, and so comes under the jurisdiction of the laird o' Lincraig. She'll be held at Blackdrummond Tower, where he resides."

"By hell she will!" Simon shouted. "You and Auld Jock willna take this matter from my authority wi' such cleverness! Bring her here to sit in Abermuir's dungeon beside her brother!"

"She is injured and canna be moved."

"I'll judge that for myself." Simon swore loudly and smacked the table again. "I knew the lass had a wildcat in her. Knew it long ago, when she was betrothed to my nephew."

"Betrothed?" Rowan asked, startled.

"To Johnny Kerr o' Cessford," Archie replied. "Sweetmilk Johnny, they called him. Two years ago, he was killed by a Scott o' Branxholm."

Rowan stared at Archie, stunned. One of his own Scott cousins had killed a man who had been betrothed to Mhairi. He began to understand the animosity she had shown him at first, and her comments about untrustworthy Scotts. But she had never mentioned Sweetmilk directly. Rowan knew the name, and remembered a blond young man with a fine, notorious reputation for reiving. The Blackdrummond Scotts had regarded him with a grudging admiration. Rowan had not heard until now that Johnny Kerr was dead. Learning of it, though, roused a bitter swirl deep in his gut. After a moment, he realized he felt jealousy.

"She was spiteful and angry as a starving wildcat that night, as I remember, toward any Scott," Simon said. "Still, I've always been fond o' the lass, and this news o' her on the highway sore disappoints me. I like fire in a woman, but this . . ." he shrugged heavily.

"Females should be meek and soft as the Lord made 'em," Hepburn said. "So we can be hard, hey?" He laughed coarsely. "Bring her here, Scott, and let us interrogate her properly." He grinned, and raised his ale cup to his mouth.

"She willna leave my custody," Rowan said firmly.

"I'll look the fool if this word gets out," Simon snapped. "Bring her, or I'll ride to Blackdrummond and take her."

"Summon her to the next truce meeting." Rowan stared evenly at Simon, feeling tension swirl between them like thick smoke.

"A truce day summons would be the proper legal action, sir," Archie told Simon.

"That meeting hasna been set," Simon snapped. "This should be dealt wi' now."

"If *we'd* caught her riding last night, there would hae been Jeddart justice on the Lincraig hill," Hepburn said.

"Hang first and declare guilt afterward?" Rowan looked at him with disgust. "You canna work Jeddart justice on a woman."

"Much less on the daughter o' the king's lawyer," Archie said. "Simon, let Blackdrummond keep her safe for now. What's the harm? We risk enough trouble just holding her brother here."

Rowan glanced at him sharply. "What do you mean?"

"Mhairi and Iain's father is Duncan Macrae o' Dulsie, a king's lawyer and a Highland laird," Archie answered. "The son of such a laird canna be hanged in Scotland unless the king himself declares him guilty."

Rowan only deepened his frown, remembering what Mhairi had said of her father. "A king's lawyer could arrange a pardon for his son quick enough," he said.

"Duncan Macrae is in Denmark, and I havena notified him myself. I dinna know what the council has done," Simon said. "But the heavy storms that the Lord continues to send us make it near impossible for ships to cross to

Denmark. There's meaning in such cursed storms and freakish weather, month after month." He stared, blank and dark, into his ale cup. "Some say it signals the end o' the blasted world come upon us."

Listening, Rowan suddenly realized that he felt as tense as a drawn latchbow. He wanted no more of this conversation, or this company. "Well then, I had better speak with Iain Macrae now, before we all face our day o' judgment," he said with undisguised sarcasm. He stood and picked up his helmet. "Dinna bother to show me the way. I'll find it myself."

He turned and stalked across the room, his boots ringing loudly on the wooden floor, with its thin covering of dry, dirty rushes. Behind him, he heard Simon growl out his name.

Moments later, he heard a rhythmic thumping noise, and turned to see Archie Pringle swinging after him on his crutches.

"I'll show you to the dungeon," Archie said.

Rowan lifted a brow in surprise and glanced back at Simon, who stood, glowering after them. "Kerr will allow that?"

Archie shrugged. "I'm the senior deputy. I oversee the prisoners here. And I have a set o' keys. Simon will join us. He willna let you speak wi' Macrae alone." He waited while Rowan opened the door, then swung through.

Progressing slowly, Archie led Rowan down a turnpike stair to the lowest level of the tower, where a smoking torch gave out a rancid yellow light. Two troopers, wearing steel breastplates and helmets, moved toward them. Behind the guards, Rowan saw a wooden door trimmed in stout iron. Archie turned a key in the door, swung it open, and stepped aside.

Rowan entered the tiny room. He was immediately aware of the faint, unpleasant, familiar odors of moldy straw, sweat, and urine. Too familiar. He flared his nostrils against an onslaught of memories.

He knew what it was to spend day after day, hour after dark, crawling hour, in just such a hole. He had spent months in a place worse than this before the English had moved him to the warden's house. In that black, stinking cell, he had unfolded a pristine page with shaking fingers to learn that Maggie had married his own brother. He had felt the devastation of true betrayal in that place. Standing here now, he fisted his hand against the rising bitterness.

Then he looked toward the small window, a mere chink in the wall, where gray light revealed the huddled form of a man on the floor. The man stood, swaying, to face Rowan.

"Iain Macrae?" Rowan asked.

Iain nodded and leaned against the wall. Tall and wide-shouldered, he was too thin for his height, with straggling, dull blond hair and dark whiskers. Scant light fell over his features as he turned his head. Rowan saw that one cheek and eye were bruised and swollen, and his lip was cut and bloodied.

But the eyes that looked at him with a gaze of pure hatred were a distinct silvery gray. He had seen a match to those eyes elsewhere. Mhairi had told him that Iain was her twin. Rowan saw the proof of that in their identical, striking eyes.

"I am Rowan Scott o' Blackdrummond," he said, stepping closer. "I have some questions to ask you."

Iain narrowed his eyes, his glance alive with a cold spark of disdain. "You are Alec's brother," he stated flatly.

"I am. You rode out together one night, a few weeks past."

"We did." Iain lifted his chin, obviously meaning to say no more on that subject. Rowan saw the same stony stubbornness that he had encountered in the man's sister.

"How did you come by the Spanish gold?"

"Ask your brother," Iain said. "You'll learn more."

"Someone else must have been involved in the handling of the stuff," Rowan said. "Was it given to you by arrangement? Or did you reive it by chance?" He saw a flicker of surprise and quick thought in Macrae's eyes. Then the opening shuttered.

"Why would you think I would speak to you, Blackdrummond?" Iain sounded bitter, and thoroughly weary.

Rowan heard the rapid, heavy scraping of boots out in the corridor just before Simon Kerr entered the tiny cell. "We'll learn all we need to, do you speak or nae, Macrae," the warden said. "Rowan Scott has been sent by the king's own council to find Alec and hang you both. And who better for the task, hey? Many in this March know there's trouble atween Blackdrummond and his brother." Simon smile slyly. "Rowan Scott has brought a warrant from the council that will give you into English hands on the next truce day."

The look that Iain gave Rowan was sharp, intelligent, and condemning. "You spent time in the English warden's house, Alec told me. Did he win you to his side?"

Rowan felt a muscle pulse in his cheek. "Hardly that," he said through his teeth.

"Rowan has met your bonny sister," Simon said in an unctuous tone. "Last night he took her down on the road for her crimes. And he watched your home burn to the ground, did Blackdrummond."

Iain took a step toward Rowan. "You damned scoundrel. My sister isna a criminal. And what—"

"She's a damned thief," Simon interjected. "And I think she kens well this matter o' spies."

Iain looked angrily at Rowan. "What is this about? And what has happened to my wife?"

"Jennet is fine, and at her mother's house wi' Devil's Christie," Rowan said. "Reivers burned the house. Mhairi is at my own tower. She's been hurt, but she'll recover."

Simon leaned forward. "Bonny Mhairi was caught in the red hand, riding after travelers on the Lincraig road." He grinned, broad and dark. "And we all can guess what manner o' safety she'll receive at the hands o' the Blackdrummond Scotts."

Iain fisted his hands. "If she's harmed, Blackdrummond, you'll pay the price in your own blood to Macraes and Frasers."

"You willna live to see that," Simon said. Iain took a step toward the warden, but stopped. Rowan saw the anger that tensed Iain's body and noted, too, the self-control that stopped him.

The warden laughed harshly and turned away. "This pup is nearly tamed," he murmured to Rowan as he strolled past. "Just a matter o' days afore I get the whole truth from him. Another solid flaying, and a dry, empty belly—we'll have him." He stepped through the doorway.

"I'll see you in the great hall now, Blackdrummond. And you too, Pringle!" His voice cut like thunder through the small outer passageway.

Rowan looked at Iain. "I dinna condone the warden's manner o' dealing wi' prisoners. I want you to know that." He turned to go.

"Wait—you were at my home? You saw my wife?"

"Aye. Jennet is fine. And your house can be rebuilt."

Iain hesitated. "And—the bairn?"

A thought occurred to him, and Rowan frowned. "How long have you been here, man?"

"Seven, eight weeks. I've lost count. Jennet would have delivered her child by now, but no one here will say—"

"You have a son," Rowan said quietly.

Nodding, Iain put a trembling hand over his eyes.

"I've seen him myself. He's called Robin," Rowan said. "He's a bonny lad," he added softly.

"My thanks," Iain said, his voice hoarse. He turned away.

The guard motioned, and Rowan left the cell.

"One plow beam cost five shillings last March," Anna said, running her finger along a column of figures. "And six pounds Scots went to iron for a new plow. Some of that iron was used to make a hundred nails to strengthen the yett—Rowan, are you listening?"

Standing by the window, Rowan glanced around and nodded, then returned his gaze to the dismal view of the gray clouds and autumn-brown fields. "Go on," he said. "Iron for the plows."

"Anna, dinna read the whole blasted debit and credit list for the past three years," Jock said from his seat on the bench beside his wife. "We ken well how hard you work to keep the accounts. Just tell him the greater expenses and income we've had, so he has a sense o' the matter."

Anna pinched her lips and frowned as she picked up a paper among the several spread on the table. "We had to purchase four young plow oxen at last year's fair. Over thirty pounds Scots, that cost. I took some o' the money from Lincraig rental accounts, since the plows are shared among many."

"The price for oxen has gone up in three years," Rowan said. "What's the income in rents from our tenants?"

Anna ran her finger across one of the pages. "This year is but half collected. Eighty pounds came in last year. A good amount, but your tenants cannot always pay in coin," she said. "Some shillings from each at Whitsuntide, and again at Martinmas, and the better part in kind, from grain rent, beasts, cheeses, and such. Last June, the reckoning of the animals kept by tenants was low—the reivers have done much damage to the numbers in the herds. Many of the tenants will not be able to pay the half rent due at Martinmas, which is but two weeks away."

"Lady Anna," Mhairi said from her chair by the hearth, "I am sorry, but I must ask for an extension for Jennet on Iain's rent due you. The herd is gone—the house—" She bit her lip and looked away.

"I would extend any courtesy to you, sweetling, were it still my matter," Anna said gently. "But you must ask Rowan about your brother's rent. 'Tis his land."

"Iain's house came to him through his wife," Jock told Rowan. "He rents the holding through the custom o' kindness, for the deed is in Jennet's mother's name as main occupant, though she doesna live there. Iain has always paid his rent promptly."

Rowan nodded, and saw, in the corner of his vision, that Mhairi watched him. He did not look at her, although he had been keenly aware of her quiet presence by the hearth the entire time he had listened to Anna go through the accounts. "The custom o' kindness shallna be changed," he said. "The rent Mhairi's brother paid last Whitsuntide will be sufficient for this year."

"Thank you," Mhairi murmured. Rowan glanced at her then, while his grandmother resumed reading aloud from the accounts. He had been reluctant to let himself gaze at Mhairi; once he did, he was scarcely able to look away.

She sat as graceful and beautiful as a tinted sculpture, her elbow resting on the arm of Jock's carved chair, her chin leaned into her slender hand. She wore an old blue gown of Anna's, with a gray woolen shawl wrapped over her shoulders. Her injured arm was still suspended in a cloth sling. In the week that had passed since Rowan had brought her here, she had regained strength in the arm, for she reached up now with that hand to brush away an errant lock of hair.

A week, and hardly a word exchanged between them.
Rowan had felt the taut awareness in the air each time they
had seen each other. Though some of that tension seemed to
have relaxed on this dreary, quiet day, the air still seemed
altered somehow, as if it had a clarity that enhanced sight
and sound, and deepened his thoughtfulness.

Rowan continued to watch her while Anna murmured
on about debits and charges, about the cost of ginger and
raisins and good linen cloth, about the number of cows
that had calved last spring, and the number of milk ewes
and rams counted on his land.

He hardly heard. The amber firelight warmed Mhairi's
cheeks until they glowed like a sunset, and sparkled in her
eyes. Her dark hair, loose and glossy with recent brushing, swirled with rich red lights whenever she turned her
head. She shifted her arms and the thin shawl draped
gracefully over the round, firm contours of her breasts.

If he were to touch her now, he thought, her warm
cheeks would feel like down. Her hair would stream like
silken fibers through his hands. Her lips would taste not
of aqua vitae this time, but of the sugared ginger he had
seen her eat with breakfast. His fingers would measure
the softness of her breasts, reverently, gently, until they
budded beneath his palms and her body flourished with
passion . . .

He sighed and glanced away, annoyed at himself for
such useless, even adolescent, thoughts. A cold draft of
air sliced through the window, and he turned toward it. He
needed that blast of cold, needed whatever would dimin-
ish the heated, intense, insistent sensations that surged
through him whenever he looked at Mhairi.

She was a lyrical image of innocence and beauty who
turned his body to hard fire. He was fascinated, caught in
some spell, unable to look at her, unable to look away.

He had not forgotten those few luscious kisses the other
night. Neither could he erase from his mind the suspicion—and the fear—that she was a traitor, a liar, a spy.

At times he wanted her to be guilty. He would find that
far simpler to face than this rather alarming turn of mind
and heart. Months ago, even weeks ago, he had been certain that no woman would ever have a firm hold in his life

again. He had let Maggie do that, and only hurt and sadness had come of it.

But he knew now that his resolve had begun to crumble the day that Mhairi Macrae had struck him over the head. He had looked into her luminous, caring eyes, and was lost, and only now began to realize it.

Thrill and dread mingled in his gut, in his heart. He wanted to run from those feelings like a scared lad. He could not puzzle out this bonny, exasperating, intriguing girl with her silvery eyes and gentle Madonna's face, her intense loyalty to a brother accused of spying, and her flair for highway crime and assault.

His heart had told him all along, almost from the first, to believe her, to see the innocence and not the crime. But his head told him that she knew more than she admitted, and his instinct for survival—his desire to save his own neck from an English heading ax—told him to suspect her, and be cautious.

He sighed in dismay and gazed out the window at the overcast afternoon sky. After a while, cold drops of rain spattered on the stone sill. He closed the shutters and latched the leather loop that secured them, and turned back toward Anna, who was still talking and turning account pages.

". . . We sold a hundred sheepskins at the last market day for over fifty pounds," Anna said, as she shuffled papers into a neat pile. "Next summer we will have near that amount again, if the lambings go well and the reivers show our tenants some mercy."

Rowan nodded. "You're an able accountant and overseer, Granna. I appreciate all that you've done in my absence. Blackdrummond's ledgers are healthy. I only wish I could return to you the favors that you have done for me."

"You can," Anna said simply.

"Aye, you can," Jock said. " 'Tis well past time to fetch Jamie. Weeks have passed since we had Alec's message."

"You have not forgotten that Alec wants wee Jamie brought to safety, I hope," his grandmother said.

Rowan sighed and looked at Mhairi, a quick, involuntary glance. She watched all of them with keen, silent interest, frowning and curious. "I havena forgotten

Jamie," he said. "But there's been nae chance to ride into the Debatable Land. Sandie and I might be able to ride out tomorrow."

"Sandie must bide here," Jock said. "Wi' so many reivers about, he's too necessary. He keeps a ready watch on our flocks, and has a steady hand at the pistol and latchbow. And enough temper to match. I trow reivers willna come here willingly."

"Tales o' your temper, too, scare them away," Rowan remarked. "But I dinna care to go alone to fetch a wee bairn. Grandsire, perhaps you will ride out wi' me."

Anna leaned forward. "His joints would pain him too much on such a long ride," she said. Jock grumbled a low word to Anna, but he shook his head at Rowan to refuse the invitation.

"Then I'll ride around to the Blackdrummond tenants and find a comrade," Rowan said, frowning. "Nebless Will Scott will go wi' me, or his sons Richie and Andrew."

"Will's Richie and Black Andrew are fine men," Jock said, nodding. "They once snatched cattle from under Simon Kerr's own nose, I hear, and left a football as a trade." He grinned. "If haystacks had legs, they'd follow Will Scott's lads anywhere on a moonlit night. They can surely snatch a bairnie from the 'Batable Land. Aye, ask them."

"Will Scott's lads are too well known in the 'Batable Land," Anna said. "You would soon have every thief south of the Tarras Water riding with you, hoping to scour beasts from the hillsides. You must go quiet like to fetch Jamie, and bring him back quick." She smiled suddenly. "Take Mhairi!"

Mhairi straightened in surprise and squeaked a wordless protest.

Rowan lifted a brow. "Mhairi? She's hurt."

"Not so badly—her arm is much stronger. And I'm sure she has a fair hand with bairns." Anna beamed, as if delighted at the prospect of sending Mhairi out with Rowan. She leaned forward and began to explain the situation to Mhairi in soft, urgent tones. As she listened, Mhairi flickered a frowning glance toward Rowan.

Jock sighed and scratched his whiskered chin. "Anna has decided for you, I think."

"I see that," Rowan said dryly.

"She'll be pleased to go with you, Rowan," Anna announced, turning back. Mhairi scowled into the fire, her cheeks pink. She did not look pleased, Rowan thought; she looked as if she wanted to see the laird of Blackdrummond frying over those flames.

"Anna's decided for Mhairi as well," Jock observed. "Och, perhaps 'tis good for the lassie to gae wi' you into the 'Batable Land. Simon Kerr might ride here to get her once he learns you're gone. Still, I suppose Sandie and I could explain to him that Mhairi is your prisoner and nae his. I think we've enough powder and shot to prove the point."

Rowan sighed. "Will's Richie and Black Andrew would be the better comrades for this ride."

"Jamie will be happier with Mhairi than Will's Richie," Anna said. "They say his ugly face scares the cattle into following him. He'd give Jamie lifelong nightmares. Though he's a muckle pleasant man," she added. "Take Mhairi. She'll go."

His heart beat with heavy excitement at the thought of Mhairi riding alongside of him, but Rowan shook his head. "A woman in the Debatable Land would only attract rascals and trouble. And hold me back from fetching the bairn cleanly and getting out fast."

"I wouldna hold you back, Blackdrummond," Mhairi said stiffly. She had said so little until this point that he looked at her in surprise. "I can ride as fast and far as you can."

"With a hurt shoulder?" Rowan asked doubtfully.

She nodded. "If Anna and Jock want me to go, I will," she replied in a low voice, not meeting his eyes. "I owe them a kindness."

"Then 'tis agreed," Anna said.

"I think it a poor scheme." Rowan sighed and shoved back his hair impatiently. "She would have to wear men's gear. Two reivers riding through would be less interesting to outlaws than a man and a woman alone."

"Her doublet was ruined the other night, but we can find her some gear," Anna said, too eagerly for Rowan's

taste. "There's an old leather jack that was yours when
you were a youth. 'Twill fit her. And I'll give you some
warm clothes for Jamie. He'll need a plaything or two, as
well, to keep him happy on the journey back here."

Rowan sighed again, heavily, as if he could not expel
enough air to express his annoyance. His grandmother
had twisted matters, as she sometimes did, to suit whatever whim she had in mind. He knew that she thought of
the bairn's well-being, and he could hardly argue that.
Mhairi would be a far better nursemaid than Sandie or
Will's Richie. Or himself.

He had promised to fetch the lad, and he would,
knowing how important this was to his grandparents. But
Anna's plan was far riskier than she or Jock realized,
more terrifying to Rowan than the threat of a gun or a
blade in an outlaw's hand.

Most frightening of all was that he sensed the protective wall of reserve around his heart and feelings tumbling
down around him—and he had no idea how to shore it up
again.

He set his teeth so hard that his jaw ached. He wanted
to adamantly refuse his grandmother's suggestion. But he
knew, with a sinking sense of resignation, that he had no
choice.

Leaving Mhairi at Blackdrummond Tower would serve
as an invitation to Simon Kerr, who would attempt to take
Mhairi into his custody. And Jock and Sandie would be
more than eager to defend her. Clearly, the safest course
was to take her with him.

He sighed and rubbed his thumb and finger over his
eyes, aware that everyone watched him and waited for his
final word.

He knew Mhairi's gentle way with bairns. She would
be useful. But Rowan did not want to watch her laugh and
coo with Alec and Maggie's son the way she had played
with Jennet's child. Even the thought of such a simple joy
stirred bitter thoughts and dreams in him that he preferred
to leave undisturbed.

More than that, what hit him like a solid punch to the
gut was the realization that he would be alone with Mhairi
Macrae for the next few days.

At the same time, a rapid current of anticipation swept

through him like a heavy tide. He firmed his jaw, wanting to resist—and also wanting that current to wash through his life.

He nodded abruptly. "Aye, I'll bring her," he said. He did not look at Mhairi. "But she must remember that she is still a prisoner. She must behave herself."

"Oh, she will," Anna said, grinning.

Rowan saw Mhairi look toward the fire, her cheeks rosy, her eyes bright.

Chapter Sixteen

~

"*Tho dark the night as pick and tar,*
I'll guide ye o'er yon hills fu' hie
And bring ye a' in safety back,
If ye'll be true and follow me."

—"*Hobie Noble*"

Silence seemed to roll off Rowan like fog. Mhairi glanced at him as they rode their horses through a mist that blurred the hills and sky. Rowan's steel helmet was pulled low over his eyes, his clean profile stony, his mouth set firm. He did not seem to notice that she rode beside him, as if he were lost in his own inner landscape of intense thought.

She tilted her chin to peer out from under the brim of the helmet that he had insisted she wear. The steel bonnet, as Rowan and Jock had called it, was heavy and uncomfortable, in spite of the thick padded lining that cushioned her head. Her slender neck ached from the weight of it, and the noise of pattering rain on steel, earlier this morning, had nearly driven her mad.

Rowan's outgrown leather jack was burdensome, too, but the dark green doublet of quilted wool that she wore beneath it, which also belonged to him, was warm, if overlarge. She moved her stiff shoulder tentatively and flexed her fingers, tucked under the long sleeves of the doublet, on her horse's reins. Although she had better use of her left arm, she still wore the cloth sling to allow the healing muscles a chance to rest.

As she tilted her head to glance at Rowan again, the helmet slid down over her eyes. She shoved it back in irritation. She was tired of silences, and tension. She was tired of fog and mist, and this cursed steel helmet. She wanted to be somewhere warm and dry, concerned only with a trencher of hot food.

She knew that they rode into the Debatable Land, but no one had explained to her why Rowan had promised to fetch Alec's son Jamie. She knew that they would stop at a certain inn, where Rowan would send word to a man who would bring the child to them. And she knew, finally, that Rowan brought her along with great reluctance.

"Are we near this inn yet?" she asked.

He did not look at her. "Another two leagues or so."

"And this man, Lang Will—he lives near there?" The helmet glided over her eyes again as she spoke. She pushed the brim up.

"Aye." He glanced at her. "That bonnet is overlarge for you."

The helmet slid down again. " 'Tis fine," she said stubbornly.

" 'Tis your hair," he said, reaching out a hand to straighten her helmet. "So silky. The leather padding slides down over it too easily."

His attentions to her helmet, though he did not touch her, sent a curious whirlpool of feeling through her. She could feel her cheeks flush with warmth, sensed her quickening heartbeat.

Tipping her head, she managed to keep the helmet in place, but the back rim cut into her neck. Sighing in exasperation, she swept it off with a flourish. Her braid slipped down between her shoulder blades. "Why should I wear it?" she asked.

"Because you're supposed to look like a lad." He reached out to take it from her, placing it back on her head. When he tucked her braid under the base of the helmet, she felt a shiver go through her. "And you will dress in the gear of a Border rider, with an armored jack and a steel helmet."

"I wore but a doublet, breeks, and cloak to ride the highway. I dinna need to dress like one of the king's jackmen."

" 'Tis protection for you out here."

" 'Tis uncomfortable."

"I willna openly ride with a lass through the Debatable Land. We'd soon have an escort you wouldna care for."

She grasped the brim and lifted. "I dinna care to wear it."

He shoved the helmet down. "Wear it," he growled, "or cut your hair like a lad's."

Mhairi glanced at him sourly and lowered her hand. Rowan continued to ride silently, and she watched him from the corner of her eye.

After their argument the day after her injury, she had thought about him a great deal. At first she had been angry over being captured and confined, but his tenderness that first night had confused her and thrown her into a swirl of thought and emotion. His cool silence toward her since had hurt more than she would have expected.

She even wondered if his fleeting kindness had been a dream, conjured from aqua vitae and yearning. Had she conjured those soft, exquisite kisses as well? No. She knew that when his lips had touched her, the distinct, exciting glow that had blossomed inside of her had been utterly real.

She glanced away, keenly aware that she had indeed yearned for him that night, swept away by the burn and spin of a drink, and by Rowan's gentleness and concern for her. She had soaked in his kindness and his kisses like a dry flower stalk taking in rain. And she had wanted more, much more from him.

Heat flamed in her cheeks, and she trained her sight on the muddy road ahead, swearing silently never to behave so foolishly again. She tried to remind herself that she mistrusted Scotts because of Johnny Kerr's death and Alec Scott's betrayal of Iain. But her jumbled, conflicted emotions would not support that resentment any longer. Rowan Scott was not like his brother, or like the men who had taken down Johnny Kerr.

Having glimpsed something deep and good inside of Rowan, she could not hate him. The anger that had once glazed the surface of her feelings, like ice layered over water, had begun to melt. Beneath it she felt a warming desire. Below that, where her deepest emotions flowed, she felt a need so strong that tears started in her eyes.

Rowan had sparked a hot flare of joy in her with kisses

and with comfort, and she had thought he felt it too. But his grim silences gave little hint of that now. She must have been wrong.

She glanced at him again from beneath the heavy brim of her helmet. He stared straight ahead. Sighing, she watched the rough earthen road again. She knew that he suspected her of complicity with spies, but she could not tell him the truth—that she had found the Spanish document hidden in Iain's loft.

Her belief in her brother's innocence had faltered when she had found the papers there, but she had told herself that Alec Scott must have given him the letter to keep there. She could imagine no other explanation. She wanted no other. And so she had hidden the letter in the Lincraig crypt with the council documents she had taken, thinking no one would ever go down there, and her secrets would be safe.

She should have burned them. Rowan Scott had found them and now believed her as guilty as he believed Iain to be, and she could not defend herself. The truth might vindicate her in Rowan's opinion; she wanted that, even needed it somehow. But the truth could also condemn Iain, and so she must keep silent.

She shifted her shoulders as if she could dismiss her thoughts. When the helmet fell over her eyes, she shoved it up and muttered a Gaelic curse.

"The inn lies south, just beyond those hills," Rowan said after a while, startling her. He pointed toward the shawl of mist that covered some low hills.

Mhairi nodded and glanced around, relieved to be distracted from her glum thoughts. "Why is this called the Debatable Land?" she asked. "I thought Scotland and England agreed on their borders."

"They did. But this area—about twelve miles, it runs, tip to tip, and about two leagues wide—was disputed for so long that the actual lay of the border here, though 'twas agreed upon fifty years ago, still isna accepted by all."

"Do Scots and English still fight over the border lines, then?"

He shook his head. "But they snatch cattle back and forth and burn byres and homes nearly every night. Both

English and Scots live here, thieves and reivers who have
taken refuge in the hills and forests. 'Tis a nest of outlaws
and broken men now, though some brave souls make their
homes here as well."

"Truly a dangerous place," she said, glancing around
nervously. She had feared the reivers of the Scottish
Middle March when she had ridden the Lincraig road, but
she and Christie had fortunately encountered few such
dangers when they had taken down the king's messengers.

"Aye," he said. "Broken men ride the moors and roads
with little fear that a warden will trod after them. Vaga-
bonds are in good number as well. Neither the Middle
March nor the West March, English or Scots sides both,
want to accept jurisdiction for this place. Even the law
avoids the Debatable Land. So you, my lass"—he leaned
forward and gave her a stern look—"will wear a man's
gear and carry weapons, and use them if you must."

She looked with dismay at the gun shoved into the
holder at the front of her saddle, and glanced at the long
shaft of the Jedburgh ax, with its curved blade and sharp
hook, which thrust upward from a saddle loop. "I carried
a dagger and a pistol when I rode the Lincraig highway,"
she said. "But I dinna know how to use a lance. And I've
loaded a pistol, but never shot one."

"You dinna need to. Your aim is good enough with the
butt," he said wryly. She scowled at him, and the helmet
slipped down to cut her gaze off. Rowan gave a snort that
sounded like amusement. "I'll show you how to fire the
gun."

"What, here?" She pushed back the helmet and glanced
around the bleak, foggy moor.

"Nay," he said. "I dinna want to stop here, for 'twill be
dark soon and we need to reach the inn. But I need to
show you if you dinna know how. The gun I put in your
saddle loop there is a wheel-lock, different than the old
matchlock that you use to dent brains."

She slid him a scowl. " 'Twould crack pates as well as
any, I think," she said, looking at the heavy ball end that
thrust up out of the saddle holder. "I didna care to fire the
matchlock, and I dinna care to shoot this wheel-lock
either. I'll just use the ball end again if I must. Thank
you." She lifted the reins and rode ahead.

Rowan easily caught up with her. "If something should happen to me before we get back to Blackdrummond, you must be able to defend yourself. And I dinna want you so close to some scoundrel that you can reach over to crack his pate. Though you're admirable at that," he added in a lighter tone.

She gave him a surly look, and he grinned suddenly, as if he could not hold it back. That tilted smile rushed through her heart like sunlight through a window. But she scowled deeper. "Iain would like one of these," she said, touching the handle of the pistol. "He likes weapons, and new improvements."

"That one is fairly new, and German made. I bought it as a pair with the one I carry in my saddle, when I was a deputy in the East March."

"You were a Border officer there?" she asked in surprise.

"For almost a year, before I came back here," he said.

"And before that time, you were in an English prison."

"Aye," he said curtly, and turned his profile to her.

"You've been gone from Blackdrummond and the Middle March a long time," she said, riding close beside him.

He adjusted his reins and looked at a far hillside, where a flock of pale brown sheep grazed. "Nearly three years," he said. "Two of those spent imprisoned."

"How is it you were appointed a Border deputy in the East March, then, if you had been named a criminal?"

"The English imprisoned me, not the Scots. The privy council gave me the post after my release."

"Did they think you clean of the English charges?"

He shrugged. "There are too few Bordermen willing to take the March posts. Even notorious men are offered positions."

"What were the charges against you?" she asked.

He did not answer, though a muscle pumped rapidly in his cheek. Answer enough in itself, for Mhairi suddenly felt his unease, and his inner feeling of mistrust, as clearly as if the sensations crept through her own body. She watched him, her hands tensing. And then she remembered that Jennet had told her that some betrayal had been handed to Rowan three years ago.

"I was taken in England and declared foul of crimes I hadna done," he said after a moment.

Suddenly she understood. "What happened to Iain happened to you," she said softly.

The thin, misty light gave his green eyes a soft clarity as he looked over at her. "Perhaps," he said evasively.

"Did it have to do with Alec?" she asked quietly.

He looked away. "It doesna matter."

"It does matter," she said. "Tell me."

"I traded more than I expected to lose in order to keep my brother out of trouble. I wasna well rewarded for my kindness."

"So you were taken for what Alec had done," she said.

He shrugged. "Many know the tale. But few know the truth."

"And what is that?"

He opened his mouth slightly, then shut it firmly and shook his head.

Mhairi's breath quickened at her next thought. "When I swore to you that Iain didna do this crime, and asked for your help, you refused me. Now you tell me that a similar trick was done to you. You know just what I feel, and what Iain feels!"

He looked at her, a long, deep gaze, and glanced away.

"Why did you refuse to help me?" she asked.

"I canna take your word on Iain's innocence."

"My word is as good as your own!"

"You forget I have proof otherwise," he said. "A few Spanish papers tell me you know more than you admit."

"What does the letter matter, if you feel in your heart and your gut that I tell you the truth, that I am innocent of all but wanting my brother free?" She reached out and laid her hand on his arm. "You do feel my innocence. And perhaps my brother's as well," she added quickly, sensing there was truth there.

After a moment he shrugged, a casual gesture. But she felt the heavy tension that coursed through him. "It doesna matter what I feel, or what I want to feel," he said, his voice hard and cold. "There are other matters at risk here. I canna take your word and naught else."

She took her hand away. "And what is at risk beyond my brother's life?"

His silence was as impenetrable as steel. She thought that he would not answer her at all. Then a muscle quirked in his jaw, and he slid her a glance. Cool, green, and intense, his gaze held hers.

"My own life," he said.

If lightning existed within the soul, she saw if flash in his eyes as he looked at her. She felt frightened, as if the doom that cast its pall over his life now threatened her.

"What do you mean?" she asked, almost meekly.

"Elizabeth of England wants my head for a pikestaff decoration. Her advisers suspect that I took some Spanish booty that came off of a ship that wrecked on the Scottish coast a few months ago."

She frowned. "Did you take it?"

He huffed impatiently. "I didna. But I'll find the missing gold myself, and the spies who took it, or forfeit my life. The English will soon come hunting me unless the spies are found."

"Why would the English suspect you were linked to spies and missing gold?"

"Because they think me a rogue and a thief. And my brother is linked to these spies. Have you forgotten that? Yours is too, after all."

She stared at him, the impact of his words striking into her heart and her gut. The trouble he faced was as deep as Iain's, but he had not mentioned it until now. "I didna know, Rowan. I never thought that you might suffer trouble in this matter."

"Listen, lass," he said, his voice suddenly gentle. "This matter is my own, and none o' yours."

" 'Tis mine," she said. "You know 'tis."

He sighed almost sadly and looked around. "We should hurry. There will be heavy rain soon enough, by the look of the clouds over those hills."

"What will you do?" she asked.

"Now? Ride faster."

She huffed. "I mean what will you do about this threat that hangs over your head?"

"I will find the spies, Mhairi lass," he said softly.

She watched him, frowning, afraid to think what might happen if he learned that the Spanish document had been found in Iain's own house. "Will you find Alec, then, tomorrow, before we leave the Debatable Land? Anna and Jock said he is here somewhere."

"I dinna know." His mouth was tight with anger.

"Alec's son," she said suddenly, thinking about what they meant to do at the inn. "Why do we fetch him? You havena said."

"The child is in danger. Alec sent word to Jock that the English are searching for Jamie as well as Alec, although Alec has hidden him well away in the hills here."

"They mean to take the child as a hostage?"

"Aye. But if the English find the lad, they canna be trusted to give Jamie back to his kin, even if Alec surrenders himself."

"So Alec sent word to Jock, and you promised to fetch Jamie," she said. Rowan nodded. "But you're a deputy of the Middle March—will you try to capture your brother?"

"The council wants me to bring him to justice."

She wanted to reach over and touch him again, but the tension in his posture and his cool manner kept her away. Still, she realized that he was not angry with her, but with something inside of himself. She wondered what had happened between Rowan and his brother to create such bitterness.

After a while she sat straighter and looked around. The gray daylight had receded quickly over the hills, and heavy, cold mist still clung in the air. "Rowan," she said. "Look over there. Are those warning beacons? Do reivers ride out even before 'tis dark here?"

Scattered across the hills, lights flared in the mist, flickering and quivering like haloed stars. As Mhairi watched, three more flashed brightly on the crest of a hill. Then another pair flared away from the rest.

He watched, then shook his head. "I had forgotten the day. 'Tis All Hallows' Eve. Those are torches, lit in every yard and around every house and byre, to give thanks to the good spirits for the harvest and the beasts, and to keep the demons away."

She nodded. "In the Highlands, bonfires are lit at every castle and in every kaleyard. The fire may keep evil spirits away, but what protects the beasts from reivers in the Borderlands?"

"Some say that branches of a certain tree, woven over

the door or around the animals' necks, has power stronger than any demon, and will keep the beasts safe."

"And what tree is that?" she asked.

He smiled. "The rowan tree."

She tilted her head, amused. "And how does rowan protect beasts?"

"Ah, well," he drawled, "several years ago, Blackdrummond tenants used to say the rowan wouldna protect the beasts unless the beasts were Rowan's."

Mhairi laughed with delight. Rowan's smile widened, and his sudden laugh thrilled through her heart.

"And what else does the rowan protect, beside beasts?" she asked, teasing him then, as he had sometimes teased her. She wanted to hear the sound of his joy again, wanted it to wipe away the earlier tension between them.

His laughter stilled. "Rowan protects what is his," he said soberly. "Depend on it."

She looked at him, and a strong current of joy and yearning flooded through the gates of her heart, so quickly and completely that she knew he must have seen its effect in her eyes. Lowering her gaze, she said nothing.

As she tilted her head forward, the helmet slumped its brim over her eyes once again. This time she shoved it back without comment. Rowan did not speak.

They rode ahead in somber silence, moving closer to the flaring, haloed lights that sparkled over the hillsides like a hundred welcoming candles.

Chapter Seventeen

The morn is Hallowe'en night
The elfin court will ride,
Thro England and thro a' Scotland,
And thro the world wide.

— "Tam Lin"

Mhairi slumped her elbow on the table, leaned her cheek wearily on the heel of her hand, and stared toward the fire that blazed in the inn's wide hearth. She felt so tired she could barely lift her head, even without the cumbersome weight of the steel bonnet, which lay on the bench beside her.

The heat and light of the log fire was comforting after long hours spent riding through cold mist, but she could hardly see the bright flames. Several people were seated on benches at tables close to the hearth, and others moved past the fire, laughing and gesturing, their voices echoing inside the smoky, dim, low-ceilinged room.

Mhairi inhaled the pungent, invigorating scent of burning pine, mingled with the odors of tallow candles, ale, and roasting beef. She glanced at Rowan, who sat beside her, and sipped at the ale he had brought her. He said something to her, but she could not hear him clearly above the din. "Pardon?" she asked.

He leaned closer. "I said that I had the innkeeper send out a runner to Lang Will Croser to tell him that we have arrived. The lad will bring Lang Will and the child back with him." He frowned at her. "You look tired, lass."

She nodded, and sipped again. The threepenny ale was warm and watery, and did not sit well on her stomach after a heavy supper of beef and barley. She pushed the cup away.

"I paid the innkeeper for two beds for the night," Rowan said. "You should rest. I'll wait for Lang Will and Jamie."

"I'll stay. You brought me here to help with Jamie. And for no other reason," she added.

He watched her evenly for a moment. "Go up the stairs."

"I'm nae tired," she said. Rowan sighed, short and exasperated, and did not reply.

Beneath her elbow, the table rocked slightly, and she glanced up. At the other end of the bare trestle, four men played a game of tossing dice, cheering and swearing raucously with each throw of the bone pieces. One of the men tipped over a flagon of ale, and spilled liquid ran along the board toward Mhairi. Lifting her arm, she inadvertently leaned into Rowan.

"Spilled ale is good luck," he murmured, placing a steadying hand on her shoulder. He let his hand rest there, his thumb lightly rubbing her aching shoulder. A warm, delicious shiver ran through her. She closed her eyes, smiling softly, and felt a blush rise in her cheeks.

"Hey hey," a gruff voice said. "Nane o' that here, now."

Startled, Mhairi peered at the man who sat across the table. She saw a slightly built fellow in a dirty doublet. He had a grizzled face framed by long silver hair that barely covered his scalp, and a grin that, though partly toothless, looked elfish and charming.

"Nane o' that," he repeated. "Save it for later, I say." He winked at Mhairi, and she realized that her disguise as a lad had not gone very far. The man looked at Rowan. "Can ye nae keep yer hands off the lass—though she's bonny, hey?" His dark eyes twinkled.

Rowan chuckled. "Aye, she's bonny." At his casual remark, Mhairi felt her cheeks grow even hotter. When he moved his hand from her shoulder, she missed its solid comfort.

"Ye two lovers can behave till the morrow," the man said in a teasing tone. Mhairi noticed that his speech was slurred. He gave Rowan a mischievous smile. "Bonny lass, though she's in a laddie's gear. A long trip across the

'Batable Land, hey?" He wiggled his thick brows in a conspiratory way.

Rowan chuckled. "Long enough."

Mhairi felt as if her entire face was reddened from blushing. But the stranger smiled at her in a sweet, thoroughly charming way, and she found herself smiling in return.

"Well, if ye thought to avoid reivers, ye've found a gang o' them here." The man sat forward. "And is she yer handfasted lassie, then?"

"Ah, well—" Rowan began.

"Och, aye," the man said, nodding. "Look there. They're all here this night, like ye, reivers and their handfasted lassies, come here for All Hallows' E'en." He gestured around the crowded room at the men and women there. "This night, games and tipping o' the ale cups, and the lassies reading omens in them eggs dropped into boiled water, over there." He nodded toward a few girls gathered around a bowl on a far table. "And on the morrow—" He grinned.

"Aye, 'tis All Saints' Day," Rowan said. "What else?"

"The wedding, ye loon, d'ye forget that? 'Tis why we're all here. 'Twill be the the grandest marrying ye'll e'er see. All the lassies are here for the wedding, and brought their laddies, reivers though they be." He lifted his cup in a salute. "Here's tae us. Wha's like us?" He waited expectantly for the usual response, holding the pewter flagon.

"Damned few, and they're a' dead." Rowan held up his own flagon. "*Slàinte.*"

"Aye," the man said, and drank. Foaming ale ran down over his chin, and he wiped at it. "Och, this threepenny stuff is as thin as crone's milk. Canna get proper drunk on it. I had some fine October ale after my supper, but the tun ran dry." He belched loudly and held out his hand. "I'm Tammie the Priest. Tammie Armstrong."

Mhairi thought Priest an odd nickname for a reiver, but she had heard riding names far stranger. She nodded politely.

Rowan took the proffered hand. "Rowan. And Mhairi."

"Rowan who?" Tammie snarled.

"The Black Laird."

"Go to! I've heard that name." He frowned in earnest concentration. "Be ye notorious?"

"He's very notorious," Mhairi said. She glanced around the room at the young couples there, most of them laughing, teasing, or holding hands. "Which one's the bride?" she asked curiously.

Tammie belched again. "Och, ye'd be a fine bride. Fine, bonny bride, and this Black Laird a braw groom for ye." He grinned again, leaned his arm on the table, and then nodded his head forward, eyes half closed.

"Tammie, sir? Who's the bride?" Mhairi repeated.

"This bonny lassie'd make a bonny bride, hey, Black Laird?" Tammie winked at her again, raised his chin, and suddenly began to sing in a rich, deep voice. Mhairi blinked in astonishment. She looked at Rowan, who shrugged, suppressing a grin.

Tammie the Priest was well into a song about a lassie being wrapped in someone's plaidie and taken away to be wed, when one of the dice players at the other end of the table leaned over.

"Hey! Tammie!" he yelled, and pushed at the old man's arm. "Find yer bed, y'auld fool." He turned to his companions. "He'll be in nae shape on the morrow, hey." They laughed.

Tammie grinned and kept on singing, never losing the rhythm of his song. The men beside him chortled and went back to their gambling.

"*Ach*," Mhairi said softly. She reached over and touched Tammie's arm. "Tammie? Are you well? Can I help you?"

Tammie smiled, cheek on his hand. "By sea and sky, she shall be mine," he sang, "the bonny lass amang the heather . . ."

Rowan stood abruptly and walked around the table. "Come on, man. I'll help you find your bed. There you go, step this way."

"Och, Rowan the Black Laird. I've seen ye afore, laddie. What's yer riding family?"

"Scott."

"Go to! Anither Scott." He narrowed his eyes to peer at Rowan. "Ah! The Black Laird—I nearly forgot! Ye're like him, that wild Alec. Ye're his brother!" He looked delighted.

"Aye," Rowan said flatly, as he lifted Tammie's arm around his own shoulder.

"Och, fine lad, that wild Alec. Havena seen him for a long while—hear he's a broken man, hey?"

"So they say." Rowan stepped forward with Tammie.

"Och aye," Tammie said. "I'm a broken man too. The English warden's been on my tail for a' this year. Bed's up the stairs, God thank ye." He whipped his head around. "Where's Rowan Scott's lassie?"

"She's here," Rowan said, gesturing for Mhairi. She came around to help guide Tammie across the crowded room.

"Bonny Mhairi," Tammie crooned, grinning at her like a wizened elf. She smiled and helped him move forward. The innkeeper's wife, a wide, hefty woman, walked past them carrying a large jug full of foaming ale. Mhairi heard Rowan ask her about Tammie's bed. The woman pointed up the stairs, said something and smiled, then turned away to pour ale into a cup thrust into her path by one of the gamblers.

Rowan scowled as he turned back to Mhairi, and she wondered what the innkeeper's wife had said to displease him. With Tammie between them, they climbed several steep, loose-jointed wooden stairs to a narrow corridor with four doors. Rowan led them down the dark passage and shoved open the last door.

Tammie leaned between them as they entered a small, dim chamber. A candle burned on a shelf, revealing two beds in the crowded space. One bed was empty, and a huge, bulky shadow shifted in the other. Resounding snores floated in the air.

"The innkeeper's wife told me to put Tammie in one of these beds, and use the other for ourselves," Rowan said.

Mhairi blinked at him. "What?"

"Both the sleeping places I paid for seem to be in this room. And that bed's full already."

"Aye," Tammie said brightly. "That's my brother, Dickie the Mountain."

Mhairi looked at the bed, and did not doubt the riding name at all, judging by the shape under the bedcovers. She heard Rowan sigh heavily. "Where will you sleep lass? With Tammie Armstrong—or wi' me?" he asked in a low voice.

Mhairi stared at him, speechless for an instant.

"Och, dinna fret y'selves," Tammie said. "I may be a broken man, but I'm a priest. And Dickie's a minister. Yer lassie's as safe in here as in heaven."

"She's safe wi' me," Rowan muttered.

"Is there nowhere else for the two of you to sleep?" Mhairi asked Tammie. He shook his head.

"Our bairn will be sleeping wi' us," Rowan said, glancing at her. "Might be best if the lass slept here alone wi' the lad."

"Eh?" Tammie said. "Yer bairnie?"

"Aye," Mhairi said quickly. "He's a small lad. But loud."

"Och, ye need a wedding, ye do," Tammie muttered. "Dickie, they need a wedding, man. Shove over, now." He stumbled forward and fell to the bed, beside his snoring brother.

Rowan tilted a brow and looked at her. "You'd best come down the stairs with me, I think."

"That bed will be taken if ye leave it," Tammie muttered.

Mhairi sighed. "I'd best wait here. Tammie willna bother me. Come tell me when Lang Will arrives." But she did not want him to leave, suddenly. A wild, wonderful hope spun through her, and she wondered if Rowan would stay here with her. Her heart thudded heavily in anticipation as she looked up at him.

Rowan sighed in the dark and began to unhook his jack. Mhairi widened her eyes, thinking he shared her thoughts. "I'll leave this with you," he said, taking off the heavy garment and dropping it on the bed. "I'll come up when Lang Will brings the child," he said.

She nodded, embarrassed at her foolish thought that he would stay here. Of course he needed to wait for Lang Will.

He untied his pouch and handed it to her. "Keep this for me, if you will. My coin will be safe with you, will it nae?" He smiled, a little wry lift of his lip.

She took the pouch and grimaced at him in the dark, then sat on the bed. Covered with a thick woolen blanket, the thin straw mattress barely gave beneath her. She slipped the pouch under the linen-covered pillow.

"Keep this as well." He drew his dirk from its sheath on his belt and handed it to her, ivory hilt first.

"But I wouldna want to use a blade—" she began.

"Then hit someone with it if you must," he said. "I'll be back soon." He paused, but only looked at her through the darkness before he left the room.

Mhairi removed her heavy jack and quilted doublet, lay down on the flat, unforgiving bed, and settled her head on the pillow.

Rising winds howled outside, and rain pattered against the walls. Nearby, Dickie snored earnestly, and Tammie joined him in a rough, whining harmony that threatened to drive Mhairi mad.

After a while she sat up and punched the pillow, a lumpy sack of feathers. When Tammie snorted loudly in his sleep, she threw the pillow at him. Miraculously, both men quieted.

She snatched the pillow from the floor, pummeled it into shape again, and shifted in the flat, creaking bed, pulling up the blanket and trying to get comfortable. Finally she sighed in frustration and leaned against the wall.

Rowan's pouch lay beside her on the bed. The flap had unlatched, and a bundle of white cloth had slipped out on the bed. As she picked it up to tuck it back inside, the cloth slid open, revealing a gilt frame.

Intrigued, she unfolded the rest of the wrapping and found a dark stone with a mirrorlike polish, framed in cracked gilded wood. Frowning, she recalled seeing it once before, when she had searched through his pouch for the council's warrant. She wondered why he still carried such an odd thing with him.

As she tilted it, the black, slick surface twinkled, and she glimpsed the reflection of her face. Wide, silvery eyes stared back at her, surrounded by bedraggled hair.

Then, as she watched, the dark surface clouded over, and another face appeared, a face so familiar that Mhairi gasped.

Iain appeared in the stone. He looked haggard, one eye bruised and swollen, his lip cut. He lifted his face and looked out a small window, and gray light swamped him like a fog. His face vanished almost as quickly as it had come.

Tears welled in her eyes and spilled over, and she caught back a sob. She touched the cool black stone, but now saw only her own face, and the yellow candle flame behind her head.

Mhairi stared at her reflection. She had seen a vision of Iain in the stone—the first she had ever seen. But why? The polished black stone must have served as a natural divining surface, like a bowl of water or a blazing hearth. Visions occurred in such ways for those with the Sight, she knew. But she had gazed many times into water and flames, and had never yet seen a vision. Why now?

Then she remembered that tonight was All Hallows' Eve. At such a time, when the beings of the otherworld were said to ride through this world, visions might happen more easily.

She gently bit her trembling lip, squeezed her eyes shut, and prayed that the Sight would come again. But when she looked, she saw only her face again, her tear-filled eyes shining like crystals.

Then her image faded. A mist formed in its place, swirling through the depths of the stone until it became the black-and-silver pattern of rain falling at night. A vein of lightning, tiny and white, licked across the stone.

A man appeared, dark-haired, etched in miniature. He rode a dark horse along the crest of a hill. When he turned, a new burst of lightning gave his features brilliant clarity, and Mhairi saw his face.

Rowan. She gasped. And then he was gone, as if washed away by the rain. Mhairi cried out, gripping the cracked frame with both hands, and saw only her own face again, frightened and pale. With trembling fingers, she rewrapped the mirror, thrust it inside the pouch, and crammed it under the pillow.

She covered her face in her hands and drew her knees up, seeing again in her mind that vivid image of Rowan in the storm. In the past weeks, she had somehow forgotten Iain's vision, though it had once troubled both of them. Now she remembered her brother's description of the strange premonition he had seen months ago: a man riding through a heavy storm, a Borderman, desperate to find someone—Mhairi, Iain had said. The man loved her profoundly, and searched for her, but brought danger.

She was certain that she had just seen the same vision. And now she knew that Rowan Scott was the man Iain had seen.

Tears ran freely down her cheeks. She wrapped her arms around her knees as a sob burst free. Iain had said this man would search for her in a dangerous storm—just before Iain's death.

Rain and wind battered the sides of the inn, and with that pummeling, the truth, or her fear of the truth, hit her like a hammer. She tightened into herself, sobbing, afraid that Iain would not survive. Rowan Scott had already delivered the warrant that would seal his death. He had indeed brought danger.

She cried until her body hurt with it, until she had no breath left, until her head ached as desperately as her inner heart. The pain felt like mourning, as if she had already lost Iain—and as if she would lose Rowan too.

Then she felt a gentle hand on her shoulder.

"Mhairi," Rowan said softly. "What is it?" He was there, though she had not heard him come into the room. He sat beside her, the wooden platform of the bed creaking. "Mhairi—did Tammie—"

"Nay," she said quickly, wiping her hand over her eyes. "I'm fine."

His palm traced a warm circle on her back. "Tell me what 'tis."

She shook her head and tucked down into her folded arms.

"Och, lass," he murmured. His arms came around her, warm and strong, turning her, curling her into his embrace. Weakened by crying, she leaned her head against his chest, where his doublet lay open over the soft folds of his shirt. She inhaled a blend of pine smoke, ale, and the warm scent of Rowan's skin. Tears shook through her, but she bit her lip to stifle the ache.

"Hey, lass," he whispered. "What is it? Let me help."

His words—those particular words—broke through some trapped reserve of unhappiness. *Let me help.* She had wanted to hear those words from him, offering help for Iain, and now it was too late. Fresh, painful sobs spilled out of her.

Rowan streamed his fingers through her disheveled hair, each stroke a caress, coaxing the sadness and the tears from her. After a while she felt an emptiness, almost a peacefulness, move through her. He murmured something indistinct, something patient, his voice deep and soft as velvet in the dark, his comforting touch offering succor for her misery.

"Tell me," he said then. "Let me help you."

"I asked f-for y-your help before," she said, her breath heaving. "B-but you wouldna give it me."

"Mhairi," he sighed. "Nae that."

"Ay-aye, that," she answered. "I sh-shouldna have spoken to you again. Ever. I should have run from you."

"Why?" he asked, the word a mere breath.

"Be-because now—" she stopped and shook her head. *Because now I love you,* she thought. Her own inner words hit her with strong force. She nearly lost her breath with the realization. *Because now I love you, but you will destroy my brother.*

But she could say none of that aloud. A thrust of anguish tore through her and she sobbed again.

Rowan whispered something against her temple, his beard prickly against her skin. He smoothed his hands over her back, through her hair, and shivers cascaded through her as the warmth of his body penetrated hers. She looped her arms around his neck and held onto him.

"Tell me what you need, lass," he murmured.

She made a little sound and shook her head, though she knew that this was all that she needed—Rowan's arms around her, Rowan's heart beating beside hers. Nothing more, in a perfect world, for there was a rightness to this that glowed like a light deep within her. She felt the hunger and power of the need that fueled the flame.

But this was no idyllic world, and what could bring her joy also brought her deep distress. The mirror had given her some kind of warning, which she had to heed. She had reason to fear Rowan. Instead, she let the curves of her body meld to his, allowed the slow rhythm of his breath to set the rhythm of hers. She knew she should not, and yet did.

After a moment, she tried to break out of the circle of his arms, but he pulled her back easily and settled her against his heart. She felt the steady, warm thud of it beneath her cheek. Exhausted, she slumped against him, her heavy sniffling breaths gradually quieting beneath his calming touch.

"Mhairi, lass," Rowan said. "If all this is because I refused to help you with Iain—"

"And you took me down," she whispered stubbornly. "Like a criminal."

"Mhairi—"

"And you brought Simon the warrant. Iain will die—" She swallowed back a fearful sob.

"I didna mean to hurt you." He lowered his mouth to her ear. "Truly, I wouldna do that." His whisper thrummed through her body like a harp string plucked and released.

Her breath quickened. She craved more of his safe, soothing touch, and wished she could let the rest go. She did not want to feel sadness or fear, or think about visions and danger. She wanted only comfort. "Rowan," she whispered. "Hold me."

"Oh, God, Mhairi," he breathed out. As she tilted her face to look at him, he found her mouth with his own.

His lips touched hers, and she felt as if she plummeted from a great height, as if he caught her and held her safe. He kissed her again, a soothing touch, quite gentle, but her knees and her abdomen quivered. She rounded her trembling hands around his back.

Rowan enclosed her face in his warm, strong hands and kissed her into breathlessness, tilting her head to fit his lips to hers again and again. A burst of sheer, delicious joy flamed inside her like a new candle. She arched her head back as his thumbs traced the line of her throat, creating a thrill of pleasure that sank into her deepest center.

Her heart pounded heavily, her blood pulsed. She skimmed her fingers over his face, feeling the texture of his beard against her fingertips, touching the strong frame of his jaw and the warm carving of his ear. She slid her fingers over the stiff buckram neck of his doublet and splayed her fingers against his chest. Beneath his open doublet, the folds of his shirt parted, and her fingers touched warm, bare skin.

Rowan exhaled a muted groan and lifted his mouth from hers. He traced his lips over her cheeks and over her closed eyelids, small, exquisite kisses, soft as a butterfly alighting on a flower. Mhairi moaned and found his lips again.

Now she opened her mouth beneath his, and felt the warmth and wetness of his tongue as it gentled over hers. A plunging heat spun deep inside of her. She pressed closer against him, one hand on his chest, sensing the deep beat of his heart, the other hand lifting, her fingers sinking through his hair. The black locks slipped sensuously over her hands like heavy silk, cool and thick.

Spreading his hands over her back, he leaned her down onto the bed, then lay down beside her. Drawn to his solid strength, she shifted toward him, fitting her body against his. The low groan that he emitted drifted soft into her mouth.

He touched his lips to her chin, then skimmed along her arched throat, his breath warm, his beard rasping over the sensitive skin below her collarbone. Mhairi sighed, streaming her fingers through his cool, soft hair. Then she slid her hands over the width of his shoulders, pulling him closer, needing more from him, wanting more.

He groaned and slanted his lips over hers with a fierceness that snatched her breath away. As the palm of his hand rested on one of her breasts, she inhaled sharply. His touch floated past, stirring the cloth of her shirt, tracing down over her abdomen, creating a peculiar flutter, almost an ache, deep within her.

She sighed and shifted in his arms, breathing out softly against his lips, so warm and pliant and insistent over hers. His hand circled her ribs just under her breast and slid up slowly, until his long fingers kneaded and stroked first one breast, then the other, with exquisite care. When Mhairi pushed her hips instinctively against him, he slid his other hand behind her, holding her against him. She felt the heated, pulsing hardness of him press against her, and her knees trembled like flowing water.

Wrapping her arms around him, she kissed him again, sensing her sadness and fear abate, replaced by the luxury of touch and blissful comfort that he offered. She did not want to think; she only wanted to feel the texture and warmth of his hands on her skin, wanted to taste the moist, hot sweetness of his mouth on hers, wanted to cleave her body to his. She felt herself sink into the heated pool of sensation that swirled inside of her.

But when she heard a soft mumble from the other bed, followed by a sharp snort, she started, as if a cold blast of air had chilled her. She inhaled and lay still, her hands on Rowan's chest. His heartbeat thundered beneath her fingers, echoing her own. She let out a shaky breath and listened.

In the other bed, a few feet away, Dickie snored steadily on, but Tammie muttered a few indistinct words and shifted restlessly.

Rowan skimmed his fingers up to touch her shoulder. He raised his head, his hair brushing against her brow. She heard him sigh, long and low, then felt him place a light kiss on the corner of her mouth. She turned toward him, but he shook his head and sat up.

She watched as he slid his legs over the side of the bed. Breathing out deeply, he rubbed his fingers wearily over his eyes. That ordinary gesture, which she had seen him do often, now tapped a welling ache of sympathy and yearning in her. She reached out to touch his arm.

He took her hand in his, palm to palm. "Mhairi—my pardon," he murmured softly. "You didna want that from me. 'Twas thoughtless."

"Hush," she said. "Hush. I wanted it."

He paused. "Did you, lass?" His voice, low and sensual, held a warmth in it, a fondness, or more. Her heart pounded.

"I did," she whispered. "I do, Rowan."

He bent and touched her lips with his, a soft, warm press. "You were muckle upset wi' me when I first came in here," he whispered, his voice gently amused, his breath flowing softly over her cheek.

"I was." She frowned. "And I may still be, when I gain my reason back." He chuckled and sat up again. As the bed creaked beneath him, Mhairi heard a light tap at the door.

"Aye, what?" Rowan called softly.

"Sir, I'm the runner," a light voice said.

"Dear God," Rowan muttered. "I swear I forgot." He

went to the door and opened it. Mhairi rose from the bed, her knees trembling for a moment, and followed him to the door.

A lad stood in the dark corridor. "Lang Will says he willna come," he said. He was no more than twelve or so, Mhairi thought, but he held a cup of threepenny in his hand, and she watched him down it as fast as any reiver, swallowing heavily and wiping his mouth on his sleeve. "He says where were you a week past. And his mither willna let him bring the wee laddie out in the murk and the mist."

Rowan, leaning in the doorway, uttered a soft curse. "You'll earn another coin to make certain he's here in the morn, with the laddie."

"Och, well, he'll be here for the wedding. His mither and his lassie will see to that."

"Well, you see to it, too. Early," Rowan said. The boy grinned and thanked him, then walked away.

Rowan shut the door and turned to Mhairi. "We'll leave at first light if we can."

"Or whenever Lang Will arrives," she said.

"Aye," he agreed. He leaned his back against the door and looked down at her. Deep shadows shaped a dark, beautiful sculpture of his face, his eyelids heavy, his jaw strong, his lips sensuous. Her heart thudded like a storm, but she felt suddenly shy and uncertain under his intense gaze. The spell that had wrapped around them only moments ago had broken with the intrusion. She glanced away, wanting that heated magic back again, but unsure how to regain it.

He tipped up her chin with his finger and thumb. "Hey hey, lass," he murmured, a soft, teasing tone. "Remember. You're as safe here as in heaven."

She looked up at him. "I know," she breathed out.

He stroked his thumb over her chin, watching her, then leaned forward to touch his hips to hers. The kiss was light and dry, but she sensed passion in the heat of his hand on her face, in the swirling current that seemed to pull between their bodies. She fell back into that warm, luxurious pool of comfort and desire at the simple touch of his lips.

" 'Tis just as well the lad came," he whispered, drawing

back slightly. He put his arms around her and rested his chin on her head. She heard his heart pound beneath her ear.

"Is it?" She felt a quick dread as she waited for his answer. He might say that he could not trust her.

"Aye. Tammie might have my head otherwise," he murmured.

She breathed out in relief. "Och, but he's a priest."

Rowan chuckled softly against her hair, and she rested her cheek on his chest, wrapping her arms around his waist, smiling.

"Hey?" Tammie mumbled, half sitting up. "Did ye call for me? Is it a raid?"

"A priest with a reiver's ears," Rowan whispered. "Nay, man," he called out. "Go back to sleep."

"Ah, the Black Laird," Tammie said, lying down again. "The Scott. Wait till the morrow, lad, hey."

"What's that?" Rowan looked up, but the only answer that came was a loud, sloppy snore.

Rowan took her hand and led her back to the bed. She lay down, and felt him sink down and stretch out. When she turned on her side to face him, he wrapped his arms around her in silence.

Nestled in the circle of his warmth, with his breath caressing her brow and his body strong and solid against hers, Mhairi closed her eyes, and slept.

Chapter Eighteen

~

There's ancient men at weddings been
For sixty years or more
But sich a curious wedding day
They ne'er saw before.

— "The Earl of Mar's Daughter"

Rowan leaned his shoulder against the wall near the blazing hearth, and watched Mhairi cross the room. The mulberry-colored dress she wore—he had no idea where she had gotten it—swayed slow and bell-like on her hips, and the stiffened bodice made her appear even slimmer than she was, though it swelled gently over her breasts. He tilted his head and was content for that moment, as he had been another time, just to watch her move.

She walked through the crowded main room of the inn as gracefully as if she walked through a field of flowers. Rowan did not miss the glances that several men gave her as she passed. Her hair, newly braided, peeked demurely from under a white head kerchief, which framed the sweet oval of her face and heightened the dewy pink in her cheeks.

"You look bonny this morn," Rowan said, raising a brow to mark his appreciation. She smiled, and all of heaven seemed to look at him through those soft gray eyes.

"As do you," she said. "You've shaved."

"Aye." He rubbed his clean jaw self-consciously. "Tammie made sure I shaved and bathed for the wedding. He even brushed my doublet." He glanced down at her. "I didna know you'd brought a gown with you."

"I didna," she said, passing her hand over the skirt.

"Tammie borrowed it from the innkeeper's daughter, for me to wear for the wedding. And had the serving girl show me to a bath as well. Very insistent, he was."

He chuckled, and she did, too, her cheeks glowing above the rich color of the gown, its high neck accented by a narrow, cream-colored starched ruff. She turned and lifted up on her toes to see through the throng that filled the room.

The low-ceilinged room seemed even more crowded than the night before, Rowan thought, as he looked over Mhairi's head. The trestles had been pushed against the walls, and loaded with roasted meats and platters of food for the wedding feast. The men were dressed in clean doublets and breeches, without a jack or steel bonnet in sight. The women wore gowns similar to Mhairi's, simple, pretty dresses of wool or linen with narrow ruffs or touches of lace, and neatly arranged head kerchiefs. A few small children ran underfoot, while several bairns were held in their young mothers' arms, wrapped in bright blankets.

The adults wandered about, talking and laughing, apparently among friends and kin. Nearly every face he saw seemed to have a smile, or even a glow of excitement or anticipation, although he saw a few serious faces among the men. He had not, as yet, determined which one of the couples was the bride and groom.

Rowan smiled slightly as he watched, and realized that the lighthearted atmosphere among the wedding guests had affected him. He, too, felt a lightness inside, a lifting of the heavy, dark mood that he had brought with him yesterday. Or perhaps his mood had changed last night, when he had held Mhairi and kissed her, and had let himself begin to love her.

That startling, sobering thought felt less like a glow of excitement than a distinct punch to his middle. His heart hammered in his chest, and he felt sweat break out on his brow.

But he could not deny the truth of it. Last night, with Mhairi in his arms, he had wanted her so much that his body had burned and ached with it, hard as new iron. But he had realized, somewhere among the heated kisses, that he cherished her as much as he desired her. He would not allow himself to take her like that, rapid as a drunken thought.

He glanced at her. She stood by his side and looked around, oblivious to her charm and sensuality, to the gentle beauty and distinct self-will that blended together and made her fascinating to him.

He watched her, and knew that when he took her, finally, there would be a slow, aching, beautiful passion between them. He would wait until she desired it as much, even more, than he did. Fisting his hand behind him, he drew in a heavy, long breath.

She turned to him and smiled. "Has Lang Will come yet?"

He shook his head. "I dinna know. He could be outside, where there's a host o' people who canna fit in this room."

She looked surprised. "Are there so many here?"

He nodded. "Tammie said that many handfasted couples had come here for All Hallows' Eve, and to attend the wedding today."

"Handfasted?" she asked, looking around. "So many of them seem to have bairns of their own."

"Aye, handfasting custom allows couples to live as man and wife for a year and a day. Some do for even longer. If they agree wi' one another, they eventually decide to wed."

"So one couple here has made the decision," she said. "I wonder who 'tis. Could it be Lang Will? The runner said his lass and his mother would make certain he was here." She smiled as she glanced around.

Rowan began to answer, but saw the young runner in that moment. The lad stood near the open door of the inn, looking around the noisy crowd. Rowan raised his hand and called out. The runner saw him, called back, and turned toward the door.

A tall man stepped into the inn, ducking his head down as he came through the door. In his arms he held a small, dark-haired child. The runner directed him toward Rowan, and the man made his way through the crowd.

Rowan touched Mhairi's shoulder, and she turned. Stepping forward, Rowan held out his hand. "Will Croser?" he asked.

"Aye." The man, his features craggy, his dark eyes kind, looked gravely at him. The child he held clung to him, his face buried in his shoulder. "I would've known that braw face where'er I saw it," Lang Will said, grasping Rowan's hand in his. "You're nearly a mirror to your brother Alec. And this is his son. Jamie, here's your uncle Rowan. Your da wants you to go home wi' your uncle to see Jock."

Rowan's heart thudded heavily, suddenly, as the boy looked around. His small face was pale and clean, his features sweetly shaped, his pink mouth wrapped around one finger. Even more striking than his abundance of glossy black curls were his eyes, which were round, black-lashed, and startlingly blue.

Maggie's eyes, Rowan thought, and drew in his breath. "Jamie," he said, softening his voice. "I'm Rowan Scott, your uncle. I've come to take you to see Jock and Anna."

Jamie nodded, sucking his finger, eyes wide. He removed the finger with a wet popping sound. "Jock," he said clearly. "Jock." Rowan saw that the child had white, well-shaped teeth.

"Aye, Jock wants to see you," Rowan said. Jamie nodded, then laid his head on Will's shoulder and stared at Rowan.

"*Ach,* a bonny lad," Mhairi said softly, and smiled at Jamie. "I'm Mhairi. I'll help bring you home to Jock."

Jamie nodded earnestly, and looked around the room, turning in Lang Will's arms. Rowan felt a sense of relief. At least the child appeared to understand what was said to him.

"Can he walk? Or talk much?" he asked Lang Will.

Will laughed. "Och aye, this one talks all day if you let him. And walks faster than I do. He's shy now because o' the people here, I think."

"Well," Rowan said, feeling awkward somehow. "Well." *What now,* he thought. He looked helplessly at Mhairi, who smiled at Jamie. He looked again at the boy. "Well, then, lad"—he cleared his throat—"I'm your uncle, your da's brother," he repeated.

"Da," Jamie said, and reached out to Rowan so quickly that Will nearly dropped him. Rowan caught him around the middle, surprised at the solid weight and strength in the little body.

Jamie looked at Rowan. "Da na here. Na here." His face crumpled. "Da. My Da." He repeated the phrase fretfully, whipping his head around as if he looked for Alec. Rowan looked questioningly at Will.

"Da said to go wi' Rowan," Lang Will told Jamie, touching him gently. "Go wi' Rowan, and see Jock."

"My Da, mine," Jamie whined. Rowan jiggled him awkwardly and looked at Mhairi, hoping for some help. She watched Jamie, her lip protruding in sympathy, a glaze of tears in her eyes.

God's good night, Rowan thought in irritation as he wobbled the fretful child in his arms. The lass was supposed to help him out with this. "My Da, my Da," Jamie wailed.

"He's muckle attached to his father," Lang Will explained over Jamie's repeated litany. "We just left him, y'see."

"Alec is here?" Rowan asked sharply.

Lang Will shook his head. "He rode wi' us, and left us near here. He didna want to see you."

"I canna blame him for that. Is he well? My grandmother will want to know."

"Aye, but fretting over his laddie some. Wants him safe, y'see. When the runner told us that 'twas you come to fetch Jamie, Alec was muckle glad o' that."

"Was he?" Rowan frowned, surprised. "What are his plans?"

"Jock," Jamie said suddenly, changing his song. "Jock." He wrapped his little arms around Rowan's neck and peered into his face, nearly touching noses. "Jock here?"

"Nay, Jock is at home," Rowan answered, looking over the glossy little head toward Lang Will. "And what of Alec?"

"Na here," Jamie said knowingly, shaking his head. "Da na here." Rowan nodded, distracted, trying to listen to Lang Will.

Lang Will shrugged. "The Debatable Land has hills and valleys enough for a man to hide a lifetime," he said. "Alec doesna know where he'll be from one day to the next. But troopers have come through here looking for him, and some have asked around after his son, claiming to be sent by the lad's great-grandsire to bring him to safety. Alec wants Jamie gone from here as fast as can be managed."

Rowan nodded. "Tell him 'tis done."

"I will. And he wanted me to ask you about Iain Macrae."

Beside him, Rowan felt Mhairi stiffen. He glanced down at her, and saw a cold, silver snap in her eyes. "Iain is in Simon Kerr's dungeon," Rowan said, "awaiting the next truce day between the Scottish and the English Middle Marches."

"Where he will be condemned to die for Alec Scott's crimes," Mhairi added in a bitter tone. "Tell Alec that Mhairi Macrae sends that message to him."

"I will," Lang Will said mildly, raising his eyebrows and looking at Rowan. "I must find my lass and my mither. Will you be staying for the wedding? There's Tammie the Priest and Dickie the Mountain coming in the door, see, so they mean to start." He smiled and laid a hand on the child's head. "I'll see you again, wee Jamie," he said fondly. He glanced at Rowan. "There's a sack o' his gear by the door, clothes and suchlike. You watch him well, Rowan Scott."

"I will," Rowan said. Jamie raised his hand and waggled it as Lang Will turned away and pushed through the crowd.

Rowan sighed and looked down at Mhairi. She smiled and brushed at Jamie's curls. "He's a fine laddie," she said.

"Hey hey, the bonny lassie and her braw Black Laird!" Tammie shoved toward them, waving vigorously, his thin, weathered face beaming. "Here ye are. Och, and yer bairnie, this is! He do look like his da, hey! A wee Black Laird! Greetings, laddie!" He grinned close at Jamie, who pulled back in Rowan's arms, frowning cautiously.

"We'll be starting the wedding now," Tammie told them. "Och, here's Dickie." Tammie waved and shouted to his brother.

The crowd seemed to part in a wave a moment later, as a huge man walked toward them. Rowan had not seen Dickie the Mountain outside the bedcovers, for the man had slept later than the others, but he recognized him by his fitting name, and by the elfish grin that was identical to his smaller brother's.

"Ho, Tammie," Dickie said. "We're ready. I've spread the word, see, and they're coming inside now."

"Good, good," Tammie said. He took Rowan's arm and moved him to the side. "Here, stand over here, and yer lassie and yer bairn wi' ye."

"We'd best stand out of the way of the bride and the groom," Mhairi said, nodding at Rowan. He could see her cheeks pinkening again, as if the excitement of this event appealed greatly to her. He had little interest in it himself, since he had earlier decided that they would leave here as soon as they had Jamie. But since the wedding was about to start, they could hardly depart just yet.

He stood beside the hearth, with Mhairi's shoulder pressing against his chest, and the child's warm weight in his arms. He felt good, strong, warmed somehow by their presence, and was content to wait.

Dickie the Mountain and Tammie the Priest stood side by side in front of the hearth, an odd pair with twin smiles. The crowd that had packed into the inn's single room hushed expectantly.

"Greetings all, and God bless yer heads," Dickie said in his large, thick voice. "We're gathered here this day for a solemn, sanctified reason, to perform a wedding."

Rowan glanced around curiously, wondering when the elusive, obviously modest couple would appear. He had half suspected Lang Will to be the groom, especially when he saw the man's craggy face above the crowd at the back of the room, and saw a tall, pretty blond girl beside him.

"And because some o' ye dinna care for the teachings o' the new kirk, my brother Tammie the Priest is here to say papist blessings for those who want 'em," Dickie said magnanimously.

Tammie nodded, grinning. Then he stepped forward and pulled on Mhairi's arm, drawing her toward Dickie. She glanced over her shoulder at Rowan. Tammie beckoned to him next, and he took a long step forward, wondering if perhaps Tammie wanted the child to spread flower petals or some such wedding nonsense.

Tammie turned to the crowd. "And who's to be married this day?" he asked in his booming, mellow voice.

"We are!" came shouts from the crowd. Rowan looked around, startled. Throughout the room, all the couples who had gathered there had raised their hands. "We are!" they cried, a sea of smiling faces. Lang Will's hand was raised with the others.

Rowan whipped his head around to look at Mhairi. She stared up at him, her eyes huge and silvery, surprise and confusion in them. He must look the same to her, he thought wildly.

"And these two lovers," Tammie said, pulling them both forward by the arms, "Rowan Scott the Black Laird, and his lassie bonny Mhairi, hae been handfasted so long that they hae birthed a fine bairnie atween 'em." He grinned. "And this bonny pair will stand up and take the vows for all o' ye in this room who've been handfasted a year and more, and have come here on All Saints' Day to be wed, as is the custom o' this glen."

"What?" Rowan said, staring at Tammie. But the priest did not hear him above the outbursts of cheers and laughter.

"What?" Mhairi said beside him.

"What?" Jamie repeated precisely, content in Rowan's arms.

Tammie grinned up at them. "Be ye papists or protestants?" Rowan gaped at him an instant too long. "Protestants," Tammie said knowingly to Dickie, who stepped forward and began to recite the marriage rites in his deep voice.

The crowd of couples stilled in reverence, bowing their heads and joining hands. As Rowan opened his mouth to stop the proceedings, he looked out over the hushed crowd.

He saw tears in the eyes of some of the girls, saw pleased flushes on the cheeks of the men. He saw young mothers who held their bairns and stood proudly to be wed to the fathers of those children. He saw Lang Will holding the hand of the tall girl. Will nodded to Rowan, his leathery face as handsome, as glowing, as any other in the room.

Rowan gazed at all of them, while Dickie spoke the

wedding rite, and wondered how to disclaim his own part in this. But these people were being married in this moment. If there ever was a time for silence, it was now.

He glanced at Mhairi. She, too, looked out at the crowd, her cheeks a high pink, her eyes sparkling like dewdrops. She glanced at him then, and Rowan could not speak.

He could not protest. He did not want to. Suddenly he wanted this woman with a fervency he had never felt before in his life. He wanted all of her, body and heart and soul, wanted her past and future, regardless of who or what she might be. Whatever came of this moment, whatever he might discover about her that he did not know now, he was certain that the kind of betrayal he had suffered before, through another woman, would never be repeated with Mhairi.

Truth and rightness somehow blended with a new, stunning sense of peace. He drew a long, long breath, knowing that his silence required greater courage than speaking out.

He took Mhairi's hand in his, and balanced Jamie in one arm. The child looked around curiously, silently.

Mhairi watched Rowan, her eyes full of apprehension. He lifted a brow to form the question that was in his mind.

Mhairi swallowed once, touched her teeth gently to her lip, and squeezed his hand.

And stood beside him, as silent as he.

God have mercy, he needed some fresh air. Rowan sucked in a breath, but the room smelled stale and sour with the mixed odors of smoke, ale, roasted meats, and sweat. He rubbed at his aching brow. The chattering and laughter had risen to a near deafening level, and now Tammie added his powerful singing voice to the blend. He was joined by many in the crowd, including someone who had an enthusiastic hold on a hand drum.

Rowan looked for Mhairi, and saw her standing beside one of the trestle tables, her back to him. She held Jamie in her arms, choosing food for him while she laughed with Lang Will's new wife.

God, he thought, she was beautiful. She was a haven of serenity and smiles, and he could hardly think. In the hour

or so since the wedding, he had been struck by the depth
and breadth of the risk he had taken. Somehow, underneath his fear and astonishment, he did not regret it, and
that alarmed him most of all. He could hardly compre-
hend how, or why, he had made the impulsive choice that
led him to this moment, where he watched his wife—his
wife!—across a roomful of revelers.

Dread, confusion, anticipation, and a fledgling sense of
happiness spun recklessly in his gut. He had never before
acted so spontaneously, without careful thought or reserve. He was not the sort to snatch at something that
promised happiness and love. He had always approached
such things with greater caution than he did matters that
involved physical danger and risk.

Sucking in another breath, he wondered if he had lost
some essential faculty of reason an hour past. He had
somehow overlooked that he suspected Mhairi of spying,
forgotten that he knew little about her and needed to sort
out much. Aware only that she was delectable, gentle, and
appealing in that moment, aware that he wanted her with
his body as well as his heart, he had taken the chance
before he truly knew what he had done.

He shoved his hair back roughly and spun for the door.

Outside, he inhaled the cold, damp air gratefully and
moved across the yard to lean against an oak tree. The
singing was almost as loud out here, and the yard was
nearly as full of people as the inn. He pressed a shoulder
into the tree and watched the crowd in the yard, glad to let
go of the turmoil of his own thoughts, relieved to just
observe.

These people were of a different sort than those inside
the inn, mostly men, many of them rough-edged in
appearance, wearing jacks and helmets, with weapons
thrust through their belts. Reivers, he thought—or possibly warden's troopers. Some of them tipped full flagons
to their mouths and watched each other suspiciously.

As Rowan stood there, narrowing his eyes and studying the crowd, Dickie the Mountain emerged from the
door of the inn. He saw Rowan and came toward him.

"Och, look there," Dickie said quietly, gesturing
toward those in the yard. "Rogues and troopers, come to
the inn for a midday threepenny and bowl o' meat and

broth, and finding instead a wedding feast and nae benches left to sit on." He grinned.

Rowan nodded. "Do you know many of them?"

Dickie scowled. "Och aye, me and Tammie ride wi' some o' these men ourselves. But we willna ride wi' that naughty lot over there." He tipped his head to the left. "Heckie Elliot and his brothers. His Bairns, he calls 'em. Though they dinna usually ride into the 'Batable Land from their nest in Liddesdale. I wonder what they want here in this glen."

As he listened, Rowan watched the three men standing together at the opposite end of the yard, holding flagons of ale and eating hunks of roasted meat with bare hands.

The tallest of the group, a wide, burly man, muttered something to his equally burly brothers and loped away, running to catch up with a girl who carried a brimming jug and a handful of cups. The man's shoulders and long arms dipped in a clumsy rhythm as he walked, reminding Rowan of a mummer's trained bear.

He frowned at his sudden thought. "Which one is that?" He nodded toward the man, who now flirted with the girl.

"Him? 'Tis Heckie, that one. Fancies himself a braw man for the lassies, and him wed, too. But most canna abide him. The other two are Clem and Martin, his brothers."

"We've had some trouble with Heckie and his brothers in the Middle March. And I've met him myself, elsewhere," Rowan added in a low mutter. "Outside an inn."

"Eh? Inn? Hey, I hear you are a deputy in the Middle March. And brother to Alec Scott, hey." Dickie grinned.

"Aye," Rowan answered. "Tammie told you?"

"Och, I knew that when I saw you. Many know you, man, the Black Laird o' Blackdrummond," Dickie answered. "Hey, now you've a bonny new wife, man. My blessings on you both. You'll be muckle happy wi' her, I can see. And that bairn needs a father and a name." He wiggled his brow.

"He has both," Rowan said. He felt that he could trust Dickie, and he wanted to learn what the minister knew about Alec. He had not yet had a chance to question Lang Will about his brother. "The lad is my nephew," he said. "Alec's son."

Dickie's mouth dropped open, his chins wobbling. "Tammie told me that you and the lass were handfasted, and parents to the bairn. He said you'd come here to fix your handfasted marriage legally, wi' the other couples."

"Your brother is a fine man, but he has a way o' half listening, and then deciding matters to his own liking," Rowan said affably. Dickie nodded, looking stunned. "What do you know of my brother, then?" Rowan asked, keeping the Elliots in sight.

Dickie shrugged. "I met him a few years past, riding forays wi' Lang Will Croser and some o' the Armstrongs and Scotts." He glanced at Rowan. "Tammie and I rode wi' you, too, four years ago, but you willna recall us. That raid ran to near a hundred men, Scotts and Armstrongs after the Kerrs. But I recall you, the Black Laird, riding at the head o' the pack wi' your grandfather and your brother. My own cousin, Devil Davy Armstrong—bless that rogue's soul—was wi' you too," he added. "We heard you were taken down later by the English. Welcome back. Will you ride reiving again? I'll ride wi' you if you like, and proud to do it. Tammie as well, I trow."

Rowan smiled a little. "My thanks. Tell me what you know of Alec lately."

"Och, that lad's had trouble, hey? Three years past, I think, I said the marriage vows for him and a lass—'twas just after you were taken down. I heard she died, but I didna ken she'd left him a son."

"Aye." Rowan set his jaw so hard that it hurt.

"And now this for him. He's been here in this glen the past several weeks," Dickie continued. " 'Tis known he's hiding in these hills, a broken man. He's well liked here, is Alec Scott—as are you, Rowan. We dinna care what Alec's crimes might be. None here will give him away to the warden's troopers that come through looking for him. So that's his wee bairn, hey?"

"Aye. I've come to take him safe to his kin."

"Och, Alec canna ask for a better brother than that, hey." Dickie grinned. "I'll go in now, afore that feast is picked clean. Will you come in and eat?" Rowan shook his head, and Dickie went back inside.

Canna ask for a better brother. The words rang in his head. He sighed heavily. The burden that he had carried in his heart and mind, from which he had had some relief, was back again.

He eyed Heckie Elliot, who was laughing with his brothers and quaffing ale. When Heckie turned and caught Rowan's eye, he paused momentarily, his grin fading. Then he spoke to his brothers in a low voice, and they sauntered toward the inn door.

Unsure if Heckie remembered Rowan from the inn as clearly as Rowan remembered him, he decided he should make certain that Valentine and Peg were both saddled and the gear pulled together, with the weapons readied and loaded onto the saddles. He strode quickly toward the barn.

He did not yet know what action he would take now that he had found the man who had attacked him. Heckie Elliot and at least one of his brothers were somehow linked to the spy chain Rowan sought. They had also harrassed Iain Macrae, who had ridden with Alec—and Iain had been caught with Spanish gold, including the medallion that Heckie had taken from Rowan not so long ago.

He frowned, unable yet to sort out the various scattered threads of intrigue and theft in this bit of weaving. Some element was not right in the pattern. As he walked on, the sounds of the celebration faded behind him, replaced by the quiet crunch of his boot soles over stones and frosted blades of grass. Sunlight sliced through the overhead clouds, giving a crisp clarity to the round blue hills that surrounded the glen.

He looked up. On the crest of a hill, a solitary horseman sat unmoving, as if he watched the inn. He wore a dark leather jack and a helmet. The peaked tip of the steel bonnet caught a quick gleam from the sun as the man turned his head.

Rowan stopped, staring. Something looked familiar about the man, perhaps the distinct shape of his morion helmet, or the wide set of his shoulders, brushed by black hair that whipped out below the steel brim.

Then Rowan felt an icy shock of recognition pour through him. Alec Scott sat that hill, watching the inn.

Watching Rowan, now. Rowan knew the instant that their eyes met and held, even from such a distance. He did not move, nor did Alec. Rowan felt frozen where he stood, stilled by shock, by anger—he knew not what held him there. Nor did he know why, in that moment, he did not seize the chance and fetch his horse to ride after his brother. That, after all, had been one of the assignments the council had given him.

Hearing his name through the fog of his thoughts, he turned stiffly. Mhairi ran toward him, carrying Jamie and a cloth sack. She reached his side and thrust the sack at him.

"We must go! Rowan—we must leave! Now!"

He stared down at her, confused, vaguely wondering if she, too, had seen Alec. Was she set on pursuing the man, even with a bairn in her arms? "What is it?" he asked.

"Those men over there—look! 'Tis Heckie Elliot and his brothers. Rowan, we must leave. They havena seen me—and they dinna know you, I think—but please, for Jamie's safety, we must be gone from here." She pulled on his arm.

"Wait." Rowan looked again toward the hill where Alec sat his horse, as unmoving as a statue, silhouetted on the hilltop. Mhairi stopped beside Rowan and looked around with him, holding Jamie tightly.

As Rowan watched, Alec touched a hand to his helmet brim and then held his hand high and steady, palm up.

Rowan's heart pounded heavily. He knew, suddenly, why Alec was there. His watchful presence on that hill had nothing to do with spies, or Heckie Elliot, or an old feud of the heart between brothers. Those were matters for another day.

Lifting his own palm up, Rowan reached out with his other hand and touched Jamie's head lightly.

Alec nodded, gathered the reins, and rode away, disappearing behind the hill.

Chapter Nineteen

Then out it spake his brother,
"O were I in your place,
I'd take that lady home again,
For a' her bonny face."

— *"Bonny Baby Livingston"*

"R ow-an," Mhairi enunciated carefully. "That's Rowan."

Jamie looked at Rowan and pointed. "Roon."

She laughed in delight. "Aye, he's Roon. And who am I?"

"Marr," Jamie said in his light voice. Mhairi chuckled and shifted him in her lap, where he sat as they rode. She smiled over at Rowan, but he proceeded in silence, glancing quickly at her before guiding his horse ahead of hers down a rocky slope. She descended after him, walking her mount through a shallow, rushing burn and up another hill to ride abreast with him again.

She sighed, unsure of what he was thinking. They had left the inn quickly, grabbing their gear and riding out, and had spoken little to each other since they had said their wedding vows. She wondered if his grim manner now came from concern over Heckie or Alec—or if he regretted his spontaneous decision to marry her. She did not think that Rowan was accustomed to impetuous, emotional action, unlike her.

Riding beside him now, she cherished one memory. After Dickie had said the final blessing, Rowan had leaned down to give her a quick kiss. "God have mercy, Mhairi, I'm glad for what we've done," he had whispered.

She had nearly melted from the heated yearning that

had poured through her. But since then, he had said almost nothing to her that did not concern horses, or gear, or the bairn.

He was her husband now. A tumultuous feeling spun inside of her. She wondered what had led her, and Rowan as well, to agree to the marriage so quickly. But she thought she knew.

Caught up in that beautiful, reverent moment, they had both reached out impulsively to embrace it for themselves. Mhairi had never witnessed anything as touching, or felt so much love in one place, as existed in that roomful of young couples. Eager to forget the fears and dilemmas in her own life, she had wanted desperately to share in such happiness.

Still spinning from the heady passion of the night before, she had taken Rowan's hand as they stood before the minister with a sudden, intense feeling of hope, and even peace, in the center of her soul. She had felt the rightness of the deed then.

Now, looking at his dark, private scowl, she wondered if she had been foolish. She had looked only at the dream, and not at the reality. She wondered if Rowan regretted their hasty marriage, or if he was angry with himself for his impulsiveness.

But an inner sense told her that he would never have taken her hand and said those vows if he had felt doubt. He was not a man to follow the lure of a dream without the structure of sense and knowledge to support what he did. She felt certain of that.

And she felt sure that, for those moments in the inn, they had tapped some deep well of hope and of needs fulfilled. She wondered if she would ever again know a moment as pure, as simple and as beautiful as that.

But the conflicts between them would not dissolve with vows, however quick, heartfelt, or hopeful. How could she have forgotten who he was, what he wanted? She had risked her life to prevent Simon from getting the council's warrant. And Rowan had brought it to him, knowing it would guarantee her brother's death, knowing she had begged him to help her. He relentlessly suspected Iain of spying, and yet had not pursued his own brother this afternoon when he might have.

She sucked in her breath as a confusing onslaught of remorse and doubt, and of hope and wanting, surged through her. She looked away from him, dismayed that she had let a fancy of safety and happiness sweep her rational thoughts and her fears clean.

And yet, in spite of all, some deep, pure part of her wanted him, wanted this bond to exist, to grow, to flourish.

"Jorn," Jamie said. "Jorn."

She startled out of her thoughts, realizing that the child had been chattering on to her and she had hardly listened. "What, lad?" she asked.

Rowan looked over at them. "What's he saying? He hasna been quiet since we left the glen."

"Maybe he's hungry. Do you want some cheese?" she asked Jamie. But he shook his head vehemently.

"Jorn," he insisted. "Jor-nan."

"Ah," Mhairi said, suddenly understanding. "I think he wants a jordan pot. We need to stop."

"What, again?" Rowan pulled on Valentine's reins. "We stopped once for a meal and a drink of water from a burn, and then again because he insisted on chasing ravens out of a tree. And that time you took him somewhere to empty himself."

"He isna a horse," she snapped, letting her uncertain mood make her irritable. "At least he can use a pot. You might be out here alone, changing a bairnie's cloth. 'Twould have done you good to do that," she muttered, halting her own horse. "I should be sorry I came with you."

"And are you?" His voice was cold and curt.

She drew a breath to reply, then looked away silently. There was too much to say, and no opportunity to say any of it.

"Pot," Jamie said, squirming fretfully. "Jornan."

"Aye, laddie, hold on," she said, trying to balance Jamie in the saddle while she climbed down.

Rowan dismounted, then came over to lift the child away until Mhairi got down. "Well, go on," he said, handing Jamie to her. "And remember we dinna have the leisure to chase birdies and go splashing in a burn. Heckie may be riding after us, or have you forgotten?"

Casting a sharp look over her shoulder, Mhairi walked
with Jamie into a stand of alder trees. Lifting the tail of
his thick, square little coat, and the hems of his long
woolen tunic and two linen shifts, she waited. He relieved
himself, smiling blithely up at her. Then she readjusted
his layers of clothing, speaking softly to him about some
nearby swallows—she had noticed that he was fascinated
by birds—and about what a fine lad he was, and how
brave and strong.

She was keenly aware that Jamie had no mother at all,
that he was with strangers now, and that he adored Alec
Scott. His plaintive, repeated calls for his father pulled on
the string of her heart each time she heard them. She
would do whatever she could to help him feel comfortable
until they reached Blackdrummond, where the faces
would be familiar to him again.

"Come, Jamie," she said, taking his tiny hand and
patiently strolling back to the horses with him. "We'll
leave with Rowan."

"Roon!" Jamie said, holding up his arms. Rowan
picked him up wordlessly, holding him while Mhairi
mounted her horse. Before they had left the inn, she had
changed out of her borrowed gown, and now wore the
same breeches, boots, shirt, and green doublet that she
had worn on the journey into the Debatable Land. Rowan
had insisted that she wear the heavy jack again, but
she had refused to put on the helmet, which hung suspended from her saddle. Over the jack she had added her
own hooded black cloak, which she now pulled closed in
the chilly air.

"Roon!" Jamie grabbed Rowan's face between his
hands. "Go see Jock," he said earnestly. "Go see Jock.
Roon go see Jock."

A reluctant chuckle burst from Rowan as he looked,
nose to nose, at his nephew. "Aye, I'll see Jock too," he
said. "And so will Mhairi." Jamie nodded at this, obviously satisfied.

Mhairi held out her arms while Rowan lifted Jamie into
her lap. As he wrapped the blanket around the child, his
hand grazed hers, a startling warmth and pressure. She
glanced at him.

Rowan's green eyes were keen as he looked at her. His

expression faded into soberness as he turned away to remount.

They rode on in silence. After a while, Jamie leaned against her, slumping gradually until she knew he had fallen asleep. She pulled the blanket higher to cover his head, and glanced up at the gray veil of clouds that covered the sky.

" 'Tis growing muckle cold," she said.

"Aye," Rowan agreed. "Those clouds could bring rain later." He looked over his shoulder again. She had noticed how often he had done that as they had ridden over the moorland.

"Do you think they are following us?" she asked.

"Most likely." His quiet words sent a chill up her spine.

"But Heckie doesna have a reason to follow me," she protested. "And he doesna know you."

"He knows me," Rowan said grimly.

"Did you ride out after him with the warden's men?"

Rowan slid her a glance, then gazed ahead. "Do you remember that I told you about a Spanish galleon that wrecked not long ago? I was there, on that beach, as a Border official."

She nodded. "And the English blame you for some of what's missing from the salvage. But what has that to do with Heckie?"

"Shortly after that, two men attacked me and stole some Spanish gold that I had in my possession. Those men were there today at the inn. 'Twas Heckie and one of his brothers." He looked at her directly, almost accusingly.

But she could only frown, thoroughly puzzled. "I dinna understand. Why would Heckie and his kin attack you? Why would they follow you now? Did you take something from them that day, that they want retribution? Though if you insulted Heckie, or pummeled him, he would come after you," she added sensibly.

"You dinna know," he said simply, sounding surprised.

She tilted her head. "What should I know? I know Heckie is a sneakbait thief."

He gave a perplexed huff, and shoved his helmet back on his head. "You dinna know that Heckie is part of this spy ring."

She looked at him in disbelief. "Go to," she said,

almost laughing. "He hardly has wit for reiving and black rent."

"A gold medallion, a Spanish piece, was stolen from me. Heckie took it. I saw it again recently, when Simon showed me the Spanish booty taken from Iain the night he was caught."

She stared at him. "Nay," she said hoarsely. "Nay."

"Somehow Iain and Heckie are connected to this Spanish gold."

"Iain isna one of your spies," she said vehemently, through set teeth. "And neither am I. You think that I should know about Heckie and these spies because you think I am one of them!"

He looked ahead again. "I dinna know who is innocent and who isna in this. 'Tis a puzzle," he murmured. "But I will sort it out, be sure of that."

Jamie shifted in his sleep and nestled against her. Mhairi hugged him close, shielding him from the cold. "Perhaps you should listen to your heart, Rowan Scott," she said, watching him over the child's blanketed head. "Then you will know who is clean and who is guilty in this matter."

He looked at her intently, his silence deep and long. In the cool green depths of his eyes, Mhairi sensed a craving, a need of some kind. But he smothered it quickly and turned away.

"The times I have listened to my heart have only brought me trouble," he said in a flat voice.

"Then you should have spoken up at the wedding," she said primly, defensively, though inside she felt a hurtful twinge.

"Och, I didna mean the wedding," he muttered. "I meant other times."

She saw a hint of something deep hidden in those quick glances, and wanted to know what he held back from her. "When have you followed your heart and found only trouble?"

"Three years ago when I helped my brother," he said.

"You were imprisoned because of him. What happened?"

He shook his head. " 'Tis over and done."

"Naught is done that still hurts," she said softly, feeling

a wave of sympathy, suddenly, that overtook any resolve she might have made to hold back her feelings for him. "Tell me, Rowan."

He sighed, and sighed again, heavily. "Alec and I rode out on a foray one night," he said, "over into England, with a large group of Scotts and Armstrongs. Crossing the border at night is March treason, but we didna mind that. We rode after some English riders who had been taking beasts from Blackdrummond lands. A party of Englishmen and their warden chased us over the Scottish border. Alec shot the warden when the man fired a pistol at us. He didna know 'twas the warden until too late."

She gasped. "He killed the English March warden?"

"Aye. I had been wounded in the leg by the warden's shot. The English took me down easily. They claimed I did the killing."

"You didna deny it?"

"If the English had caught Alec instead, they could have hanged him then and there. But I was a laird, and they couldna execute me so quick. I had to be given a trial."

"So you said naught, and let them take you, to spare Alec."

He nodded. "I expected a fast trial and a fat fine on truce day, and perhaps a brief time in an English prison. But the new English warden wasna as lenient as most Border officials. I was condemned to death for the murder, and for the sum of all my previous crimes— March treason and years of reiving—and sent to the dungeon in Carlisle Castle."

She furrowed her brow in dismay. "I thought you were kept in a noble's house."

"Later. I spent the first few months in a dark, cold cell nae larger than a curtained bed. And hardly as comfortable," he added with a bitter laugh. "After a while, at the request of Scott o' Buccleuch and the privy council, the English remanded the sentence of death. I was moved to the warden's own house and kept there in a fine chamber, though I couldna leave the grounds, until two years total had passed."

"But you didna come home then," she said.

"I didna." Mhairi watched his jaw tighten, and realized

how painful this discussion was for him. "I took a post on the Scottish East March for nearly a year. Then I was sent to the Middle March as Simon Kerr's deputy."

Mhairi was silent for a while, absorbing what he had said. "Alec killed the warden, but you willingly took on the blame. He didna truly betray you."

"He did." He bit out the words violently. She glanced at him. His mouth was white-lipped and hard, and a muscle pumped in his cheek. She knew that some intense feeling coursed through him, as powerful and dangerous as a swollen, rushing stream, but she was not certain of its source.

"How did he betray you? I dinna understand." She looked down at Jamie, who slept, slumped and trusting, in her lap, then returned her gaze to Rowan. "Alec was near the inn today. He came there to watch over Jamie. You knew that, I saw it in your face. You love your brother, Rowan. I saw that too."

He lifted his chin at that, as if she had struck him. But he said nothing.

Mhairi drew a breath and went on. "He risked his life to come out in the open today. A man who loves his child like that wouldna betray his brother." She paused. "Perhaps he didna betray Iain as we think. Perhaps we've been wrong about Alec."

"Nay."

"But he—"

"Nae more!" he snapped, raising a hand to command her silence. She drew an angry breath, undaunted, ready to speak again. "Nae more," he said gently, and stepped his horse sideways, closer to hers, his lower leg pressed against hers. He took her chin in his hand and looked at her for a moment. "Those silvery eyes see too much of what is inside of me," he murmured.

"Nae enough," she whispered, leaning toward him.

"Too much." His face was a breath away from hers. "Far too much." She looked into his eyes, leaning toward him, unwilling to let go of that joined gaze.

"Tell me," she murmured. "I want to know."

He dropped his hand and pulled back. "We have enough troubles between us," he said, gathering his reins.

"You mean the wedding," she said in a tight voice.

Rowan paused, then reached out to touch her cheek gently. "I dinna regret that," he said softly. "At least nae yet."

She glanced up and thought she saw a teasing glimmer in his eyes. "Well, neither do I—yet," she said.

"Ah." His tone was sage and mysterious, and the gleam was still in his glance. Then he looped the reins over his hand and rode ahead.

Rowan looked back over his shoulder once again. Each time he scanned the countryside, he saw only the empty moor, or scattered herds of sheep and cattle, or an occasional ragged shepherd uninterested in the passing of two riders. The Debatable Land could be as peaceful in daylight as any other area of the Borderlands. And the wedding celebration in the glen behind them still occupied reivers and their kin for miles around. Wedding or none, had he and Mhairi ridden these moors in moonlight, their safety would have had no such assurance.

But he could not dispel the sense of unease that had settled on the back of his neck and between his shoulder blades. He was certain that Heckie would follow them, though he did not know when. Heckie Elliot had definitely marked Rowan's presence today, just as Rowan had recognized him as the man who had held a knife to his throat outside that other inn, while Clem Elliot had been the bearded man who had rummaged through Rowan's leather pouch.

If he had been alone today, Rowan might have considered pursuing Heckie then and there to take him down for a thief and a spy. Without an extra hand to help him, that course would have been dangerous. With Mhairi and Jamie beside him, the idea was thoroughly foolish. He could only hope that Heckie would bide his time, knowing where to find Rowan Scott.

He had no wish to meet reivers and outlaws just now. He glanced sideways at Mhairi as she rode. Jamie was awake once again, sitting up in Mhairi's lap and chattering like a jay while she listened intently. He took her face between his small hands and earnestly repeated something to her until she nodded, laughing.

"What's he saying?" Rowan asked, curious.

She looked up, smiling. "He says that Jock likes birds. He canna wait to see Jock. He adores your grandfather."

"Och aye, Jock's an adorable sort," Rowan said dryly. Mhairi chuckled and bent her head to listen to another question from Jamie.

He watched their heads touch, Jamie's curls glossy and black against the rich, deep brown of Mhairi's hair. She laughed at something Jamie said, and glanced at Rowan briefly. He only gazed at her somberly. A frown puckered her brow, and she turned her attention back to Jamie, pointing with him toward a raven that flew down to land in a bare tree.

Rowan remembered another day when Mhairi had shared a similarly proud smile with him over a child. He had stood in Iain's cottage watching her tend to Jennet's bairn, all the while feeling an ache, like a dull sadness, centered in his heart.

Now, watching Mhairi with Jamie tugged at that same store of sadness once again. But something had changed. The child was not his—but the woman was his wife. He still had not had time to absorb that. This morning he had been caught in a whirlwind of hope, mingled with simple lust and something far deeper, a complex emotion that he hesitated to name.

He wanted Mhairi, with her soft gray eyes, her sharp wit and her loyal heart, with her supple body and her gentle hand. He wanted her and he had reached out for her. And even though his cautious, reserved side was uncertain, he felt, overall, oddly content with his unaccustomed spontaneity.

When he looked at Mhairi with Jamie in her arms, the memory of a lost, early dream sparked again. That dream had been born when he had courted Maggie and had loved what he thought was her sweet, simple nature. He had wanted Maggie too, but he felt now as if he had wanted her with eyes closed, like a newborn calf, blindly going toward what comforted and pleasured him. He had been immature then, though a man. Now, seasoned by time and tragedy and experience, he knew what he wanted.

Some deep inner instinct told him that he had taken the right road this morning when he had said wedding vows with Mhairi Macrae, although he did not know what lay ahead on the path.

He watched Mhairi and the child. Jamie had Maggie's eyes, the color of bluebells in sunshine; and he saw her, too, in the dimple that deepened when Jamie smiled. He realized, suddenly, that it was Maggie's friendship that he missed most of all. She had been a part of his life since childhood.

He saw Alec in Jamie as well, in the dark hair, the straight brows, the firm jaw of the Blackdrummond Scotts. He felt a surge of loss, and knew that Mhairi was right. He had always loved his brother deeply. Jamie's small, bonny face combined elements of both of his parents, and created in Rowan a keen awareness of what was irreparably gone from his life.

Looking at Mhairi, he knew what he had gained. She was serenely beautiful to behold, and possessed such fire and pride and compassion in her soul that it nearly took his breath away to think of it. Yet he was not ready to give up his guarded heart to her. There was too much that he did not know, too much he did not understand.

He watched her laugh in harmony with Jamie as they slapped their flattened palms together in a simple rhythm. Mhairi smiled over at Rowan. "He's a joy, this lad," she said. "And witty. He's only just learned this. Watch." She held up her palm, and Jamie held up his to match. "Go on," she told him.

"Come east, come west—" Jamie said, enunciating carefully.

"And pick the one that ye love best," Mhairi finished with him. Jamie slapped her hand vigorously. They laughed together, and both looked at Rowan. He smiled, the rhyme familiar from his own childhood.

"Roon!" Jamie said, stretching out his hand. "Do it!" Rowan leaned over and held up his palm. "Come ye east and come ye west," he said in unison with the child, "and pick the one that ye love best." Jamie slapped his hand with enthusiasm, and Rowan glanced at Mhairi. Something flashed in the silver-smoke depths of her eyes, and a quick blush brightened her cheeks. He glanced away, feeling heat in his own face.

"He's a clever lad," he said.

Mhairi hugged Jamie to her, looking at Rowan over his head. Jamie sucked on two fingers and settled against her. "Clever as his da, perhaps," she said. "Or his mother. Did you know her?"

"Aye," he said in a low voice. "Her name was Maggie."

He felt Mhairi's gaze on him, but he did not turn as he guided his horse alongside hers. Jamie yawned and Mhairi spoke softly to him. Then Rowan felt her gaze return to him.

"Rowan," she asked slowly, after a moment, "did Maggie have aught to do with Alec's betrayal of you?"

He felt stunned, for an instant, by her question. Yet he was not truly surprised that she had guessed. He set his jaw, feeling a tense thumping in his cheek, and realized that his subtle action revealed more truth than he intended. "You see too much, as I said."

"What happened?" Her tender tone nudged at something within, peeling away a hard layer over his heart. He drew a breath, surprised to feel it shake inside his chest. "Did you love her?" she asked.

Those words, so gently spoken, had a hidden strength that cracked another unyielding layer. He glanced sideways. Mhairi watched him steadily. He saw Jamie lean his small head against her chest and close his eyes, those Maggie-blue eyes, trusting, unaware that he stirred a well of hurt and longing in his uncle.

"Rowan?" Mhairi asked.

He stared ahead. "When I was in the dungeon at Carlisle"—he spoke in a flat tone—"I received a letter from Anna. She said that less than a month after the trial, Alec had married."

"Ah," she said softly. "He wed Maggie."

"Maggie Maxwell," he said, slowly, fiercely, "was my betrothed. Later in the year, Anna wrote to tell me that Maggie had died in childbed."

Mhairi said nothing, though he knew she watched him. What could be said, he thought to himself, watching the road.

Then Mhairi reached out and laid her cool, slender fingers over his. After a moment, Rowan turned his palm up and entwined his fingers with hers. No one had ever comforted him over this matter. He had carried the pain alone until now.

As he cradled her small hand in his, a pure, simple, warm feeling welled in him. He felt, in that instant, cared for, cherished. Loved. And he felt humbled that she could offer this so freely and generously to him, despite their differences.

They rode side by side in silence. After a while she took her hand away and pulled on the reins. "Rowan, stop, if you please," she said, shifting the sleeping child awkwardly.

He glanced at her and halted his horse. "What is it?"

"Can you take him for a bit? He's muckle heavy against my shoulder. 'Tis beginning to ache."

Rowan nodded and reached out, gathering Jamie's limp, slumped form into his arms. Mhairi handed him the blanket and he tucked it around the child, settling the slight weight into his lap before lifting the reins and riding ahead.

Jamie was warm against him, a comforting burden. He murmured and giggled in his sleep, and Rowan glanced down to see the sweet dip of a dimple in his cheek. Rowan smiled, a sad, private lift of his lip, and hugged Maggie's child close to him.

He rode on slowly, and the warmth from the small body seeped into his bones, and somehow into his soul, and began to melt the core of pain and anger that he had stored away years ago.

Rowan felt an unfamiliar sting in his eyes. He blinked it away, and rode ahead. And he suddenly knew that the hurt that had ached within him for so long had begun to heal.

He looked at Mhairi. She watched him with a knowing depth in her gray eyes, wise and patient. And he knew that she had handed him the child not because her shoulder hurt, but because she knew that Rowan might need to hold him.

He nodded to her, and glanced away, and tightened his arm around Jamie as he rode on.

Mhairi glanced up at the sky. " 'Tis nearly dark, and the wind is stronger. We'll need to stop for the night." She shifted Jamie's boneless, sleeping weight in her arms. Rowan had handed him back to her not long ago so that he could stay watchful as they rode in the dusk, though they had left the Debatable Land.

She waited for his answer. He had ridden without comment beside her since entrusting Jamie back into her arms. But his silence this time was less tense, almost tranquil. She tilted her head and watched him. He turned and nodded wearily.

"Aye, we can stop," he said. "We're near the Tarras Water and Roan Fell."

"Jean Armstrong lives near here," she said, brightening. "Jennet and Christie are with her."

"Aye. When Devil Davy and I rode reiving together, Jean Armstrong always kept a warm fire and a full kettle to welcome visitors. We'll rest there for the night. And hope that we havena been followed." He gathered the reins and surged forward into the twilight.

In a short while, Mhairi saw two warm yellow lights glimmer in the narrow windows of Jean Armstrong's small house, tucked in the lee of a hill. Built of fieldstones with a roof of heavy thatch, the bastel house was more fortress than farmhouse. Two slit windows pierced the front, and the ground floor level, which had no front door visible, was used for storage, with an enclosed cow byre that Mhairi knew opened at the back. The entrance to the upper level, where the main room was located, was accessible only by a ladder that had already been pulled in for the night.

Weary, stiff, and hungry, with the wind beating at her hooded head, Mhairi waited while Rowan called a greeting and tossed a stone at the entrance. After a moment the door opened wide, held by Devil's Christie, who hollered in delight and ran to fetch the ladder. Silhouetted in the doorway, Bluebell barked and yelped in fervent ecstasy. Jennet waved at them, holding Robin in her arms, and her mother Jean smiled behind her.

Rowan took Jamie from Mhairi, holding the sleeping child against his shoulder while she dismounted. "They'll make us welcome," he murmured. "We'll spend our wedding night here, and be glad for the company."

She blinked up at him. *Wedding night.* Her heart hammered inside of her. "I suppose we should tell them we're wed." She had not thought about it until now.

Rowan smiled, a little quirk of his lips in the moonlight. "We may as well, lass," he drawled. "I have a feeling that Tammie the Priest and Dickie the Mountain will spread the word quick enough, from the Debatable Land to the Yarrow Water, that the Black Laird has wed a bonny lass." He tilted a brow.

She knew he teased her, but she felt a trickle of joy at his words. Then she turned and was swept into Christie's arms, and did not look at Rowan again until she was safely up the ladder and seated by the blazing hearth with a bowl of broth in her hands.

Chapter Twenty

~

Near me, near me,
Lassie lie near me,
I woo'd thee and wedded thee,
Lassie lie near me.

—*"Lassie Lie Near Me"*

Mhairi slipped gently off the feather mattress, careful not to wake Jamie. She had rested with him until he slept at last in Jean Armstrong's curtained box bed, one small fist grasping the woolen coverlet, another grasping Bluebell's coat. The dog snored quietly beside the child, tail thumping slowly.

Pushing aside the curtain, Mhairi stepped into the main room, and into the circle of light from a fat, fragrant beeswax candle on the trestle table. Christie and his mother, who sat at the table, looked up as Mhairi approached. She passed the cradle where Robin slept, and glanced toward Jennet, who sat with Rowan on a bench in the far corner, talking quietly.

"Jamie's asleep?" Jean asked. Her thin, handsome face, framed by a white kerchief, tilted up in the soft light.

"Aye," Mhairi said, sinking down beside Christie. "Thank you for lending him your bed. The hound is in there too."

"Och, Bluebell has slept at my feet each night since Jennet and Christie came here," Jean answered. "I'll gladly share the bed wi' Jamie this night, and for as long as you and the Black Laird stay wi' us. You and your husband will have Christie's bed in the loft, and he'll take that wee pallet by the hearth." Blushing at the thought of sleeping alone with Rowan, Mhairi nodded her thanks to Jean.

Christie grinned at her. "Wed to the Black Laird," he crowed in a soft voice. "I still canna believe it!"

"Hush, Christie. They're a bonny pair," his mother said.

"Mhairi, d'you think Heckie followed you from the inn?" Christie asked.

She shrugged. "I dinna know."

"Those clouds and wind may bring rain tonight," Jean said. "Most reivers willna ride out in poor weather. We'll be safe, I think, until the weather clears."

"I wonder why Heckie and them were at that inn," Christie said. "They wouldna have been in the 'Batable Land for reiving. The tenants there are tougher game than those Heckie preys upon here in the Middle March. But for us, o' course," he added. "I wonder if they were looking for Alec?"

Mhairi frowned. "They might have been," she said slowly, remembering that Rowan was certain Heckie was involved somehow in the spying ring in which Alec was also implicated. She glanced at Rowan, who still spoke quietly to Jennet. She saw Jennet lean forward and hug him, then kiss his cheek, a gleam of tears in her eyes. Mhairi wondered what they had said to each other.

Moments later, Jennet stood and murmured good night, moving toward her own bed behind a curtain at one end of the room. As she passed Mhairi, she leaned down and kissed her cheek. "He's a fine man, your Black Laird," she said. "I owe him a kindness."

Mhairi watched her wordlessly. A moment later, Jean also bid them good night, and slipped behind the curtain of her own bed, where Jamie and Bluebell snored softly together. Christie yawned and stretched, firelight sheening his blond head.

"I'll stay up and watch for reivers," he said. "You two go on to bed." Mhairi could see the grin he suppressed, and she wanted to grimace at him for all his delight in this.

Rowan walked to the door and tugged on the wooden bar, then peered through the shutters over each small window. "That outer door in the byre below us," he said, turning to Christie. "Have you secured it?"

Christie stood, his expression immediately serious. "I pulled the door bar across after I put your horses there, alongside my horse and my mother's milk cows and milk ewes," he answered. "But I didna roll the great boulder across to block the door."

"Do it," Rowan said bluntly. He crossed the room and picked up one of his wheel-lock pistols, which he had left on top of a wooden cupboard along with his other weapons.

Without comment, Christie went to a small trapdoor in the wooden floor. He raised it and climbed quickly down the ladder into the byre. Mhairi smelled the odor of animals and hay, and heard the lowing of the cows and bleating of sheep.

She stood and went to Rowan. "You think Heckie will come."

"He may," he said. She watched him load both of his guns with powder and lead shot, then take out the small metal cylinder that he wore on a string around his neck. He fitted the key to a stud in the gun casing, and wound it tightly to set the trigger mechanism. As he readied the second gun, Christie clambered back up through the trapdoor.

"The byre is safe," Christie said. "But those winds are high, and might bring a storm. We willna see reivers."

"I think we will," Rowan said quietly.

"But we willna need so many weapons against them. This house is strongly fortified," Christie said. "They might take some o' my mother's cattle and sheep, left out on the far hill, but they canna get our gear unless they break down the door and climb in. And you ken well that most reivers willna take lives unless they must. Most reivers willna start a blood feud for a bit o' gear or a few beasts."

"Most," Rowan said, checking the mechanism on his latchbow. "Christie, you'll take the first watch."

Christie nodded soberly. "They want more than gear and beasts, I think. What is it?"

"Something that I have and willna give up. Load your matchlock, and ready your latchbow. Your father had a steady hand with one, and I dinna doubt he taught the skill to you."

"He did. I'm a bonny shot wi' the latchbow, and a long bow as well. And I can fire a pistol and wield a lance and a long ax, too," Christie detailed proudly. He rubbed his upper shoulder, where a lead ball had taken him down. "And I would have shot Clem Elliot the night they burned Iain's house, if my pistol had not missed fire."

"You did your best to protect your kin that night," Rowan said. "And you'll do your best this night as well, if they come riding here." He took Mhairi's elbow as he spoke. Shivers spiraled through her at his warm touch. "Call me if you hear aught, lad. Good night to you, then." Christie nodded and went to the window, peering out through the slightly opened shutter.

Mhairi went to the loft ladder and climbed up, her heart thumping and her hands clammy. Tension sharpened all of her senses. She heard the shriek of the wind outside, heard the baby whimper in his sleep, smelled the musty smoke of the blazing peat bricks. And she knew with another, deeper, sense that before the night was through, reivers would ride into the yard to threaten them all.

Most of all, she was keenly aware, just then, that Rowan climbed the ladder steadily behind her.

In the loft, faint blue light seeped through a small shuttered window in the end wall. Rowan went to the narrow opening and looked out through a crack in the shutter. In the soft, shadowed silence, he heard Mhairi walk to the bed and sit.

The muted whine of the wind outside made the loft seem close, safe, and warm. Rowan scanned the dark landscape, but saw only the sweeping movement of trees, heard only the wind. The moon glowed white through dark, rapid clouds, and Rowan saw that the hills were deserted.

So far he had seen no indication that Heckie had followed them. But Rowan could not assume that they were free of a threat, even sealed as they were in Jean Armstrong's fortified house. He could not ignore the feeling, deep in his gut and honed to sharpness by a lifetime of reiving, that riders approached. He only hoped they were still distant.

"Do you see aught out there?" Mhairi asked softly. The tremor in her voice carried clearly.

"Nay." He continued to look out the window.

"They will come," she murmured. He looked at her. Her glossy braid shone like black fire as she turned her head. "They will come. I feel it."

He felt it too. He turned and glanced out the window again, and said nothing. A few minutes dragged past. Behind him, he heard Mhairi yawn, heard her shift quietly on the bed. He looked back at her again.

She had removed her doublet and sat there in her pale linen shirt and dark breeches, stifling another yawn with the back of her hand. She flexed her white-stockinged feet in the shadows; both she and Rowan had removed their boots almost as soon as they had arrived, and had left them lined up beside Jean's hearth.

"Tired?" he asked. She nodded, her face pale, her eyes like shadows in starlight. "You should sleep," he said, looking away. She did not lie down, and he felt her watching him.

"What did you tell Jennet?" she asked. "She seemed pleased with you for it."

He shrugged. "Jennet was glad to hear that Iain was well. When I saw him last week, he hadna heard of Robin's birth. I told him he had a bonny lad. She was pleased about that."

She gaped at him. "You saw Iain at Abermuir? You spoke with him, and didna tell me?"

He paused, inwardly cursing himself for forgetting to tell her, in the rush to fetch Jamie, that he had seen her brother. But at the time, he had suspected her of duplicity with Iain. "You didna ask, and I didna think to say it," he said in an effort to apologize. Her scowl told him that it was not well accepted. "I only saw him briefly. We said little. He wasna willing to talk about the night he was taken."

She hesitated, biting at her lower lip. "Rowan—was Iain very thin, and bruised beneath one eye? Did he have a cut lip?"

He turned from the window. "Aye. How did you know that?"

"I saw his face in that wee dark mirror in your pouch," she answered in a faint voice, looking down at her clasped hands.

"You saw Iain in the mirror?" She nodded. He stared at her, astonished, intrigued. He got up and came over to sit beside her. The bed, a feather mattress on a wooden frame, sank a little beneath his weight. Mhairi's shoulder brushed his arm. "Tell me what you saw," he said, a low, somber order.

She shrugged. "I found the black stone in your pouch. I looked at it, and saw Iain's face. He was bruised and cut."

He nodded. "He looked like that when I saw him. Did you see aught else in the mirror?"

She hesitated. "Only my own face," she said softly. "I have never had a vision of my own until now."

"Until now?" He narrowed his eyes. "What do you mean?"

"Dà-Shealladh." Her Gaelic was so soft that it sounded like an exhalation. "The Second Sight—it runs in my mother's blood. She has the Sight, as does my brother Iain. They both have true visions. But I never have—until I looked in that mirror." She looked up at him. "Rowan, could it be a charm stone? I know there are such things, though I havena seen one."

He frowned in the dim blue shadows. "I dinna know. I found it on the beach, washed up from the Spanish wreck." He looked intently at her. "I saw something in that mirror, too, once," he murmured. "I saw your face." Slipping his fingers along the side of her face, he traced the velvet angle of her jaw. "This face. 'Twas before I knew you."

She stared at him. "What is this stone, Rowan?"

He shook his head and took his hand away. "Whatever 'tis, Heckie and his lot seem to want it. When they attacked me, they demanded something they called the raven's moon. I didna know what they meant. Later I realized that I had the black mirror inside my jack. I think they sought that—although at the time I thought it an unimportant thing, broken and ugly."

"The mirror has significance to someone. But why?"

Rowan opened his leather pouch and took out the stone. Unwrapping the cloth, he cupped the mirror in his palm. "I doubt Heckie would care about a charm stone, though he's surely tied into the spy ring. Perhaps there is something else about it . . ." He touched the stone, which winked like a slice of the night sky.

"It doesna look valuable," Mhairi said. "What else could it offer but this strange power we have seen?"

He shrugged. "Heckie must have been sent by someone who knows."

"I wonder if everyone who looks in it sees visions?"

He shrugged. "I dinna have the Sight, and I saw you. There are prophets and seers who use such things for divination. The English queen has her own magus, an astrologer. I've heard he uses a similar stone, black and round, to show him visions." He stopped, chilled by what seemed too obvious. He kept silent.

"What is it?" She sounded alarmed.

He looked at her. "You said that Iain has the true Sight?"

"Aye, but—Rowan, he isna part of this!"

"Whoever sent Heckie for this stone knew 'twas on that Spanish ship. Whoever wants this stone must know something about its powers," he said, his voice grim and stern.

"Who else but a man with the Sight?" she asked bitterly. "Do you suspect me as well, since I saw something there too?" She stood and scowled down at him. "I know naught of this raven's moon, nor does my brother."

"Mhairi—"

"Iain isna the one who sent Heckie after this stone!"

"The clues are there, Mhairi," he said wearily.

"Then you are seeing them wrong!" she shouted. She turned away to pace the loft floor in a panicked manner, back and forth, her hands fisted. "He didna—he couldna—" She stopped, clapped a hand over her mouth, sobbed a little, and turned, desperately, turned again. "Nay, nay," she said.

Rowan's heart ached to watch her. He remembered the devastation he had felt when his brother had betrayed his trust. He wished he could take this from her, but could not promise her falsely that her brother was innocent. He simply did not know.

Mhairi stopped pacing and pressed her fist to her mouth. He heard a slight sob burst from her, and her pain suddenly became his. He stood and reached out to touch her shoulder. She stilled at his touch, tense as a trapped hare.

"Mhairi, if Iain did this, he must have had reasons," he said calmly. "He may have wanted coin to gain land or a title. He has a family."

She shrugged off his hand and stepped away to stand still. He saw how anger and hurt tightened her shoulders. And he saw how much of a shock this was to her. Perhaps she had truly had no involvement in any conspiracy. Whatever she had done may have been done entirely out of genuine love and concern for her brother.

"The evidence isna in his favor, Mhairi," he said gently. "But I was wrong about you, I think."

She lifted her chin in a gesture that was proud and graceful, and yet sad, vulnerable. She said nothing, and kept her back turned stiffly to him.

"Mhairi, I dinna know what is true here," he said, and sighed, aware of how tired he was, and how confused he felt over the whole matter just now. He stepped toward her again, cupping his hands over her slight shoulders, rubbing his thumbs over her taut muscles. She did not relax under his touch, as if the burden of her grief were too heavy. He knew that burden, had carried it himself for three years. He, too, had loved his brother deeply and had been shocked by the betrayal. But his feelings, after that, had hardened, comforted only by his own bitter thoughts. He would not let that happen to Mhairi.

He drew a deep breath. "We may both have wayward brothers. Or I may be wrong," he said softly.

"You may," she whispered. He heard the agony in her voice, felt it curdle in his own gut. "Iain is my *leth-aoin*, my twin. I would know if he had done wrong."

"Your loyalty to Iain is a fine thing, like a pure fire," he murmured. "Dinna let it burn you." He watched the side of her face, the simple beauty of her profile, the moonlight purity of her skin, the glint of a single sliding tear.

"I rode out each night for weeks to save his life," she whispered. "I might have killed you one night, for his sake."

"But you didna." He touched the dark sleekness of her hair.

"I canna bear it if Iain is guilty," she whispered.

"If he is, then aye, you can, and you will." He turned her in his arms and looked down at her, holding her by the shoulders. "Mhairi, you are strong. Whatever comes, you will bear it, and be stronger for it."

She kept her head tucked down, and he felt her shoulders straighten, felt her fill with a resolving breath, as if she had looked at her doubts and fears and was done with them.

"I know my brother," she said, looking up. "I swear to you that he is clean. I want you to believe that. I do."

He opened his mouth to speak, then suddenly wondered if he had somehow wanted her brother to be guilty, wanted it because his own brother might be involved in this league of Scottish spies. No matter the truth, he had been wrong to assume that Iain and Alec were guilty of spying, without knowing. In a way, he had betrayed Alec too, by accepting the worst as truth.

Mhairi gave only loyalty to her brother, consistently, without question, in spite of the evidence. She believed in him, and listened to her own heart.

The realization humbled him. Once again, she had taught him something through her behavior, through her purity of intent. He did not know the truth of this matter, and until he did, he should reserve his judgment. And he should not try to convince her to take on his beliefs.

He looked into Mhairi's tear-glazed, solemn eyes, and admired her strength in the face of this. And knew then that he had to help her. He would not feel at ease himself with this until he had eased it for her.

"Come here," he said, wrapping his arms around her, pulling her against his chest. "Mhairi, if you are right and I am wrong, if Iain isna guilty, I promise you that I will find it out."

She sobbed then, a small, muffled sound of relief. He held her close, wanting to soothe her, to make her feel safe. She had given him compassion when he had spoken of Maggie; now he wanted to return it to her.

He lifted her face with his fingers, lowered his head,

and kissed her trembling lip. He had intended it to be a gentle, light touch, reassuring, caring.

But the sensation that shot through him at that simple touch spooled like lightning, hard and fast and sure, striking from his head through his groin, even down to his feet. Her mouth moved beneath his, and he felt as if that small, moist touch ignited a flame deep inside him. He covered her lips fully with his own and his heart took up a thunderous pace.

Last night in the inn, he had been overwhelmed by a passion that had taken all of his will to subdue. Now she had become his wife through means that seemed almost miraculous, as if designed by heaven itself. Despite all that separated them, a bond had begun to form between them. He felt stunned, awed, privileged.

He sucked in a deep breath, pulling in her breath with his own, sipping a little of her spirit with that soft breath. He sensed her vulnerability, her wounded emotions. He knew he should go gently, calmly. But the power and the urge that swept through him was nearly overwhelming.

He pulled away from her lips, drawing back, but could not tolerate even the width of a breath between them. He lowered his lips to hers again. With a small moan, she tilted her head and accepted the full caress of his mouth. A few tears slipped from her eyes like an overflow of sorrow. He kissed it away from her cheeks. Holding her head in his hands, he fitted his mouth to hers, wanting to soothe the sadness from her, wanting to quicken her heartbeat to the insistent rhythm of his own.

He lifted his head. "Mhairi," he whispered, and heard the sound echo in the loft. Soft as velvet, reverent as a prayer. "Mhairi—" He covered her lips again.

She pressed closer, silent, breathing fast. She slid her hands up his back and pulled him toward her. He kissed her with even greater fierceness, his hand cradling the back of her head, his fingers threading into the woven silk of her hair. Her braid loosened under his touch, and he streamed his fingers through that soft coolness, gathering its dark weight in his hand.

He felt her hands glide along his back as she returned his kiss with a hungry, compelling shift of her lips beneath his. He parted her lips with the patient tip of his tongue, tasting her heated inner moisture, licking gently. He met her light, sweet thrust with his own and felt her breath catch, felt her small sigh slip into his mouth.

He skimmed his fingers over her jaw and throat, feathery touches that seemed to constrict his own breathing for an instant. Slipping his hands over her shoulders, down her back, he traced the firmness of her hips and pressed her close. As he fitted her body to his through their layered clothing, as his body pulsed against hers, he continued to taste her mouth, drinking in the sweetness there.

Mhairi wavered for an instant in his arms, moaning softly as if she were unsteady on her legs. He tightened his grip on her lower back, and with his other hand traced a path down her throat and over her shirt, easing his fingers over the soft fullness of one breast. The peak rose against his palm, and he felt the quick thud of her heart beneath his touch. He let his fingers graze downward until he pulled the tail of her shirt out of the waist of her breeches.

Slipping his hand under her shirt, gliding up the smooth skin of her torso, he cupped his hand over her breast and kneaded its incredible softness with his outspread fingers. Her nipple budded firmly between his fingers like a warm pearl.

Mhairi gasped and arched her hips against him. He felt the insistent tug of her fingers on the hooks that closed his doublet, felt the garment opening, and then her hand slipped inside, burrowing beneath the doublet and the cloth of his shirt to find his bare chest.

Rowan plunged his tongue into her mouth, and captured her other breast in the warm, gentle cage of his fingers. Another pearl blossomed against his hand.

Touching her was sweet agony, being touched by her was equally as sweet, filling him to such aching stiffness that he groaned softly and pressed her closer. Reaching down, he lifted her into his arms and stepped to the bed, easing her down and kneeling alongside. Mhairi circled her arms around his shoulders and pulled him toward her. He took her lips again, quick and hard, and drew back, breathing rapidly.

The cool air of the loft cleared his senses a little. He glanced at the narrow window, where the shutter moved slightly with the outside wind. Mhairi glanced there too, her eyes wide, smudged with passion, edged with apprehension.

"Rowan—"

"Hush," he murmured, kissing her, the words lost in sensuous warmth. "We have time." He hoped that was true, though he sensed danger moving toward them like the storm in the wind, filled with its own thunder.

"Oh God, Rowan." She glided her hands up his arms, slid them down again, her small hands telling him how eager she was, how frightened. "We should stop, but I dinna want to stop—"

"Hush," he said again. "We have time for this." He wanted her fiercely now, utterly, his body urging him onward despite the danger. He stroked his lips along the velvet curve of her cheek, found the shell of her ear with the tip of his tongue. They might have no time, or there might be all the time they needed. He did not know. He only knew he could not stop touching her.

"Hurry," she whispered, and turned her mouth to meet his.

He sucked in a breath as if he had been starving for air, and gathered her shirt in his hands, sweeping it over her head, flinging it aside. He yanked off his doublet and his own shirt while her warm, slender hands trailed up his chest. She grasped his arms and pulled him down to her.

He had vowed, only that morning, that he would take her only when she desired it as much as he did. That moment had come, far sooner than he expected. The deep emotional currents that bound them together seemed to sweep him along with her now, swiftly, forcefully, like the heavy winds that sailed outside.

Whatever approached out there now, storm or worse, sailed toward them like thunder riding on scudding clouds. Urgency swelled in him and pulled him along with that kind of power, so that his heart echoed what his body already felt. Impatiently he pulled his breeches loose and stood to kick them aside.

Cold air swept over him as he stood beside the bed, a cushion of chill that separated him from where he wanted to be, where he needed to be, with her, beside her. Languid and beautiful, she gazed up at him, the supple contours of her body edged in blue-gray light. He wanted to touch her, taste her, enter her fully. He could not stay apart from her, not physically in this moment, or ever, in his heart and in his soul.

He was as lost then as he had been the day she had taken him down on the road. But this time he surrendered his heart, just as swiftly as he had surrendered his consciousness to her that day. This time he was willing. This time he knew what he wanted from her, with her. He lay down beside her, and she reached up to welcome him with her arms.

He embraced her and pressed her warm, velvety soft body against him. She arched her hips against him, and he pulled at the drawstring of her breeches, sliding them off of her, all the while capturing her mouth in another kiss.

He traced his lips down her throat, lowering his head to kiss the unutterably soft skin between her breasts. Letting his tongue slip over her skin, he found the sweet, firm nipple and sucked there. She cried out and grabbed at his shoulders, then slid her hands down his chest, over his abdomen, stopping there.

He sucked in his breath as she wrapped her fingers around his turgid length, her sweet breath sighing into his mouth while her hands explored him tentatively, then boldly.

Heart pounding, heat flooding through him, he skimmed his hands up the sensuous curves of her inner thighs until he slid a hand between their bodies. He could not wait, but he would, stilling his body, stilling his breath if he must, so that he could hear her cry of pleasure mingle with his own.

His fingers glided until he found her opening, slipping inside where it was warm and honeyed, where he found the pulsing bud within. Touched there, she gasped; stroked, she moaned, and he kissed her lips, pulling gently at her tongue while he eased another moan from her. When her body found its rhythm, when she arched and soared toward him, he shifted and covered her.

She opened, undulating beneath him, and he pressed forward, gingerly, slowly, though his body thundered its own insistent rhythm. He sucked in his breath and eased into her heated moistness with exquisite care, knowing he was causing her pain. He pushed slowly, feeling her inner resistance. She gasped and tensed, and he waited until she relaxed, wrapped with her in a silent, urgent harmony of breath and pounding hearts.

"Now," she whispered. "Oh, hurry—"

But he would not hurry now. Time unfolded, spinning out into waves, into a languid existence of extraordinary sensation without measure. She eased her hips upward and he pushed through into her, plummeting, thrusting. Overwhelmed by the welcoming heat and lusciousness inside of her, he thrust again and pulled back, trembling, aching inside for freedom, forcing himself to wait until she was ready, until she ached for it as he did.

She arched and gave a small, poignant cry, wrapping her arms, herself, around him. And the gathering storm rolled and streamed and exploded through his body, as if his soul rushed into her, as if all the desire, all the need that had been trapped inside poured out of him.

She rocked with him, and quickened beneath him, and he felt the force of whatever bonded him to her. Blood and flesh and spirit whirled together, releasing him into her, where he knew, now, that he belonged.

"Soon," Mhairi said, and sat up, looking down at him. "Soon. Do you feel it?"

He did. He tipped his head to the side and listened, his hand on her hip as they waited silent, interminable moments. At first he heard only the wind buffeting the roof, and the muted thudding of his own heart.

Then another sound emerged. He reached for his clothing, and stood quickly to dress in the dark. Mhairi reached down and found her own clothes and put them on, as silent and swift as he.

The rhythm that grew through the air was regular, fast, and far more dangerous than any storm. Below, he heard Christie call his name softly. The thundering became the thick, steady beat of hooves nearing the yard.

Rowan turned toward Mhairi. "They've come."

She stepped into his arms. He enfolded her against him for a moment, their bodies familiar, fitting easily together.

The curves and hollows and planes of her body merged more fully to his now, even in a simple embrace.

He kissed her, releasing her reluctantly. Then he stepped over to the ladder.

Chapter Twenty-one

They were three brethren in a band—
Joy may they ne'er see!
Their treacherous art, and cowardly heart,
Has twin'd my love and me.

—*"Lord Maxwell's Goodnight"*

When Mhairi reached the bottom of the ladder, Rowan was strapping his belt over his leather jack and speaking in urgent tones to Christie. Outside, the first echo of Heckie Elliot's voice rose above the wind. The dog barked and burst through the bed curtain, circling anxiously near the door. Mhairi heard Jean and Jennet stir in their beds, and heard the children whimper.

Bluebell came to her side, and Mhairi brushed her hand distractedly over her rough coat, feeling the dog's quivering tension. Mhairi trembled too, but from an urge to run from the disturbing onslaught of danger and fear that she felt here. That harshness was even more disturbing because her body, her soul were still finely tuned from the deeply sensitive and sensual loving that she had found with Rowan only a little while ago.

As Rowan sheathed his broadsword in the holder looped onto his belt, Mhairi crossed the room and laid her hand on his arm. "We are safe in here. You dinna need to go out to them!"

"I'm just preparing, Mhairi," he said quietly, shoving one of his guns into his belt. He turned to load a short, steel-tipped quarrel bolt into his latchbow, and pulled back the bowstring to set the long metal trigger. "Go sit with Jennet."

"I willna," she said stubbornly. Hands shaking, she

picked up his second wheel-lock pistol. "I'll stay with you. I've fought reivers before this."

He looked at her, then sighed in acceptance. "I dinna have time to argue. That gun is loaded and spanned, and dangerous. Hold it more carefully—aye. Do you know how to fire it?"

"I'll watch you," she said.

He nodded. "Just aim it, and pull the trigger when you must. And mind the recoil—it could knock you back." He stepped to one of the windows to peer out through the parted shutters.

Mhairi heard Heckie's loud bellow as Rowan opened the shutter wider. "Rowan Scott o' Blackdrummond! If you're in there, then come out, man!"

Gripping the heavy pistol in both hands, Mhairi went to the window and peered out beside Rowan. He shoved her gently away from the exposed center, shielding her with his broad back and cutting off her view. She looked out through a gap in the hinged side of the shutter.

Weapons glinted in the moonlight as several men sat their horses in the yard. Two of the riders had sputtering resinous torches. Beside her, Rowan lifted his gun to the window and rested the barrel in the shutter opening.

"Come out, Rowan Scott!" Heckie called again. "We've borrowed some fine cows here, and some sheep as well. Now we'll have what you've been holding from us!"

"Be gone from here, Heckie Elliot!" he called out. "There are women and bairns in this house!"

"Then come out and bring us what we want!" Heckie yelled.

Christie, holding a loaded latchbow in his hand, went to the other window, opened the shutter, and aimed his weapon. He glanced at Rowan, who held up a cautioning hand.

"One chance, Heckie," Rowan called. "Be gone!"

Heckie lifted something to the level of his chest. Mhairi saw the hard glint of metal, then saw a bright spark.

The gunshot burst against the door, shaking it, but the lead ball did not penetrate the wood. Jean and Jennet, holding the children at the back of the room, gasped. Bluebell ran to the door and barked furiously at it. Mhairi heard Robin whimpering, his tiny cries muffled against his mother's shoulder. She turned to see Jamie fling his arms around Jean's neck and bury his dark head in her shoulder.

Rowan motioned to Christie, who released a crossbow quarrel. Then leadshot and splintering noises shook the oaken door.

"You ken well what 'twill take for us to be gone from here, Rowan Scott!" Heckie shouted. "Come out and give o'er the raven's moon! I'm sure you have it, man! We know you picked up something on that beach. We should have gotten it from you then!"

"What the devil is he talking about?" Christie asked.

"A long tale, lad," Rowan said. He held his gun balanced against his shoulder as he aimed it. When he pulled back the trigger, the explosion was so loud that Mhairi covered her ears instinctively. Behind her, Jamie and Robin wailed in unison. Bluebell leaped toward the door, barking and snarling, and Jennet dove forward to drag her back toward the bed.

"You caught that rogue in the shoulder, Rowan, but he still lives. D'you want to try it again?" Christie asked dryly, sliding another bolt into his latchbow.

"I didna mean to kill him, nor will you, Christie," Rowan said. "We willna start a deadly feud among Elliots and Scotts and Armstrongs."

"Hey! Blackdrummond! We willna be gone!" Heckie shouted. "We'll burn all o' you if we must, to get what we want!"

"They dinna have a principle against starting a feud," Christie commented.

"Bring the moon out, Blackdrummond!"

"Why does he keep asking for the moon? Has he gone mad?" Christie asked.

"We'll explain later," Mhairi said distractedly as she peeked through a crack in the side of the shutter. She saw the men with the torches ride across the yard.

"We'll smoke you out, Blackdrummond!" Heckie yelled.

"Jesu," Rowan muttered low. He sighed heavily and leaned his shoulder against the wall. Glancing at Mhairi, he shoved a hand through his hair. "I'll have to go out," he said. "The children—"

Susan King

"Rowan, stay!" She grabbed his arm. "You willna come back—they're waiting for you. Dinna go!"

"We can shoot all o' them from in here afore they can get to the thatch," Christie said grimly, and let loose another quarrel. A cry rose above the howling wind. "Och, just his leg. But they refuse to take our warnings, I think." Christie turned and sent Rowan a flat, humorless smile.

Another shot rang out, this one chipping loudly against the stone wall near the window. An arrow followed that, thudding into the shutter and banging it toward Mhairi. Struck by the edge of the frame, she stumbled and raised her hand to her temple. Rowan grabbed her elbow and pulled her back.

She looked at her palm, and saw that a trickle of blood darkened her skin. "I'm fine," she said. "Just a wee cut."

"Aye, but it might have been far more," he said fiercely, gripping her elbow so hard that it hurt. "I canna risk harm to you, or to them—" He gestured toward Jennet and Jean, who sat together on one of the beds, holding the crying children and trying to subdue the wolfhound.

Mhairi knew what he planned, as if he had said it aloud. She took his arm and pleaded with him through touch and gaze to stay in the house. He watched her silently, shook his head firmly, and turned back to the window.

Heckie bellowed out again, the details of his threats lost in the whining wind. Christie released a latchbow bolt that must have found a target, for Mhairi heard another scream, followed by angry shouts and a flurry of arrows that struck the shutters and the outer wall of the house.

"You winged him in the arm, Christie," Rowan said wryly.

"I told you I'm a careful shot, even in the dark o' night."

Rowan chuckled softly, then picked up his latch-bow and let loose a bolt that whistled past Clem Elliot's head. Clem bellowed and raised his pistol. The lead ball slammed through the window and hit Christie, who fell backward.

Mhairi cried out and ran across the room. By the time she reached him, Christie had risen to his feet. Blood darkened his white sleeve. "I'm fine," he muttered, shaking off her hands as he picked up his latchbow and went back to stand by the window.

Rowan swore quietly and turned away to reload and wind the wheel-lock. Then he picked up his helmet and shoved it onto his head, grabbed his lance and latchbow, and went to the trapdoor to yank it open.

Mhairi ran toward him and grabbed his arm. "Rowan, they only want that cursed black mirror. Just toss it to them!"

He took her hand from his arm, grasping her fingers tightly. "If I let them have it, what becomes of my head? The English will be after me unless I catch these spies." His gaze was dark and intense in the dimness. "This is the better chance. For all of us."

He loosened his fingers, but she kept hold of his hand. Rowan leaned down and gave her a quick, firm kiss, sending a surge of yearning, tinged with raw fear, through her. "Hey, my lass," he murmured against her lips. "I'll come back. Naught could keep me away from you. But let me go for now."

"Rowan—" She held tightly to his fingers, suddenly afraid that he would never return, and knowing that she could not convince him to stay.

"Let me go," he murmured as he stepped back. She released his hand, her breath heaving, and watched him turn and drop down onto the ladder. As he lowered into the byre, Mhairi heard the sounds of the beasts shuffling. Rowan glanced up at her.

"Stand by the window for me, and hold the gun high and ready. You'll see what I mean to do. Jean Armstrong"—he called out softly, looking toward her—"I thank you for your hospitality. Tend to my wife's cracked pate, if you will." Then he was gone, closing the small wooden door over his head.

Mhairi ran to the window and lifted the loaded gun to the gap between the shutters. Warm blood trickled down the side of her face from the stinging cut at her temple. She wiped it away impatiently with the heel of her hand. Aiming along the metal barrel, she looked past its cold glint toward the shifting, shadowed forms of the men in the yard.

She glanced over at Christie, who held his reloaded latchbow balanced on the windowsill. He met her gaze, then turned toward the window again.

They waited. An eerie silence filled the small house. Even the dog ceased to bark, and the children became oddly quiet. Mhairi looked out the window and saw Heckie mutter to his comrades. Tension seemed to constrict the surrounding air.

Moments dragged past. Muffled sounds from below told her when Rowan left through the outer door of the byre. She bit anxiously at her lip, watching Heckie and his gang, and waited for Rowan to appear.

She squeezed her eyes shut for an instant as she remembered another man who had also gone out to meet reivers in the dark of night. Chills went through her. Johnny Kerr had smiled at her and assured her he would return. But he had ridden to his death.

And Iain had gone out with Alec Scott one night, and had been arrested and imprisoned. She was terrified that she would not see Rowan again if he went out there alone, and yet she could not help him. She was not even sure how to fire the pistol, but knew she had to try.

She drew a shaking breath and looked out again. A moment later, she saw the men startle and gather their reins, heard them shout and wave to each other. At the side of the yard, she saw a dark gleaming flash as a rider galloped past.

Rowan, on Valentine, rode furiously away from the house. Heckie shouted and turned his horse, then galloped after him, waving toward his men.

"Now!" Christie yelled to her. "Fire now!" He released his latchbow bolt and reloaded, holding it ready.

Mhairi held the heavy gun to her shoulder as she had seen Rowan do. Sighting along the barrel, she pulled back the trigger, finding it far stiffer than she expected. A whirring sound, a click, and then the gun fired with a blue flash, so hard and fast that it knocked her back. She stumbled and fell, her shoulder jarred, her ears ringing.

"Recoil," she muttered, and stood. She had no idea if she had caught anyone with her shot. "Oh! The key," she called to Christie. "He didna leave me the key for the wheel-lock! I canna fire it again!"

"Nae matter," Christie said, as he stepped back and closed the shutter. "Rowan is gone. They're all gone. He lured them away from here, Mhairi." He shoved trembling fingers through his golden hair, and sat on the bench, laying his latchbow on the trestle table. "He rode off so that they would follow him, and leave us be." He shook his head. "They've snatched a good dozen o' my mother's sheep and a few cows, too, that werena in the byre below."

Mhairi sank down to sit on the bench beside Christie. Her legs trembled, and her shoulder ached sharply from her fall after the recoil of the gun. But all she could think about was Rowan. "He's left us safe here," she said. "But what about him?"

Christie looked at her, his eyes dark with concern. "I'll ride out after him. He'll need another gun and bow behind him."

"Nay, Devil," she said, touching his blood-soaked sleeve. "You're wounded."

"Och, the ball only bit at me, it didna pierce below the skin." They both glanced up as Jean Armstrong walked to the hearth and took down a bowl from a shelf, filled it with cool water from a bucket by the hearth, and took a pile of cloths from a wall cupboard. She turned toward them.

"Let me see," she said brusquely. "Both o' you need tending." Within moments, she stripped Christie of his shirt and began to swab at the gash in his upper arm with a cloth soaked in cold water. He winced and complained, and his mother hushed him sternly. Then Jean turned to Mhairi and bathed her forehead with another cool cloth.

"You'll be fine, do you press this against your head to stop the bleeding," she told Mhairi. "But Christopher will need a bandage and a few bits o' silk thread to close the wound." Christie protested, but his mother scowled at him as she vigorously tore bandage strips from the pile of linens on the table. "You willna ride out this night. Dinna forget you're still recovering from the last time the Elliots came around."

"Rowan needs my help," Christie muttered, and winced again as his mother wiped at the fresh blood streaming down his arm.

Mhairi pressed the cloth to her temple, hardly feeling the sting of it. As she thought of Rowan riding out there with a gang of reivers on his tail, her stomach constricted in fear.

She wanted to be with him. She had no desire to wait here, fretting and wondering, until the warden rode back to bring the news that he had been taken, or killed. She did not think she could survive that again. She could not lose Rowan, too.

Once Christie's arm was wrapped, Jean fetched him a clean shirt. Then she peeled away the cloth from Mhairi's brow.

"You'll do well enough," she pronounced.

"Good," Mhairi said, standing. "I'm going after Rowan."

"What?" Christie said. "You canna—"

Mhairi crossed to the hearth and hastily pulled on her long boots, then ran to the wooden chest where she had left her leather jack. Pain struck through her shoulder when she shrugged on the heavy vest, but she ignored it, latching the hooks as fast as her trembling fingers would allow.

Christie and Jean watched her. "You're daft," Christie said. " 'Tis nae ride in the moonlight, chasing a messenger. Those are hard rogues out there. I'll go, and fetch help."

"You do, and you could bleed to your death," Mhairi said. She picked up the cumbersome steel bonnet, looked at it with dismay, and set it down again. "Rowan needs someone at his back out there. If naught else, I can ride for help to the Armstrongs in the next glen. Or I can go north to Blackdrummond and fetch the Scotts." She grabbed Rowan's wheel-lock and shoved it into her belt. Though it was not loaded, the ball-butt was sound enough.

"I'll ride out wi' you," Christie said, standing.

"You willna," Jean said, reaching up to push down firmly on his shoulder. He sat, holding his arm and turning pale. "Mhairi has ridden out many a night, you said. She can do it again. Go east to Johnny Armstrong's house and fetch him and his kin," she told Mhairi. "Jennet, help her saddle her horse."

Jennet nodded and laid the baby on the bed beside Jamie, whom she had just soothed back to sleep. Mhairi grabbed her black cloak and climbed down the short ladder into the byre. Jennet followed, carrying a candle.

The smell in the byre, from the various beasts separated by low wattle walls, made Mhairi catch her breath for an instant. She found Peg in the darkness, and ran her hand soothingly over the mare's black muzzle. With Jennet's help, she saddled the horse and tightened the girth.

Jennet grabbed Mhairi in a quick hug. "God be with, Mhairi," she whispered. Then she pulled away to open the door.

Mhairi nodded her thanks and led Peg outside, mounting swiftly. As she rode out, she drew up the cloak of her hood against the wind.

Rowan cast a quick glance over his shoulder. The moon was high and full, and shone brightly over the hills. He saw several horsemen riding pursuit across the moorland.

Smiling grimly, pleased that he had lured Heckie and his comrades away from Jean Armstrong's house, he bent low over his horse's neck, riding as fast as he dared through the darkness. Icy winds buffeted him, and he ducked his head against their strength, never slowing.

If he could keep a good distance ahead of Heckie and the rest, he could make it to the Lincraig road and to Blackdrummond. Once near Lincraig, he could ask assistance from his kinsmen, Will Scott and his sons, in apprehending the lot of them. Heckie and the others, driving cattle and sheep along with them, would not be likely to catch him before he reached Will Scott's land. If they sent riders ahead, he would deal with them as they came.

For now, it was enough to know that Heckie and his gang had been led away from Jean Armstrong's house. He crossed a shallow burn that glinted in the moonlight, its banks rimed with ice, then rode swiftly over a long moor. Drops of cold rain occasionally pelted his hands and shoulders. He looked up again at the white glaze of moonlight through the drifting clouds, and rode on.

Another quick glance showed him that they rode steadily and were coming closer. He saw the dark silhouettes of the riders, and saw the cows and sheep that the men had taken from Jean Armstrong's land, and clearly heard the beasts' disgruntled noises.

He looked ahead. The Lincraig road lay a league away across the open moor. To the right was a long, rocky slope that led down to the Lincraig road. Heckie and his men would have to drive the beasts the longer way, but Rowan knew he could take the shorter route. Fording a stream in moonlight would be far more risky than crossing the open moor, but he would take the chance willingly to reach help sooner.

He turned Valentine and headed for the slope. The bay slowed, nickering softly, as Rowan guided him down the rock-studded, steep incline. Difficult in daylight, the way was treacherous in moonlight and howling wind. At the bottom of the slope lay a wide, rapid stream, rushing loudly, its white-whipped surface pale and constantly changing in the moonlight.

The wind rose high and bitter as he reached the usual fording place on the bank. About to urge Valentine forward into the stream, Rowan pulled back. The waters, swollen with recent rain and rocking with the winds, appeared too deep to ford. The bay circled restlessly, balking and whinnying, and Rowan guided him along the slippery bank to look for another place to cross.

Rushing water filled the streambed to its brim, swirling fast and deep. Realizing that fording at any point might be foolhardy, Rowan tucked his head against the cold bit of the wind and headed along the bank, which inclined and hung out over the water at one point.

Valentine sidestepped nervously, and Rowan steadied him, glancing around. The whipped surface of the water rushed past him, pale and eerie in the darkness. Glancing up the long slope, he saw the swift, dark shapes of Heckie and the others as they herded the beasts onward over the moor. But he could not tell if they had seen him down here.

Unable to ford the stream as he had planned, Rowan knew a quick, risky solution. The bank rose out over the water, and the opposite bank was nearly as high, forming a chasm of two low jutting crags above the surging water. The stream narrowed at this point, so that the banks were separated by several feet.

He and Valentine had made this jump a few times before, accompanied by Devil Davy and Alec, once with a host of English troopers on their tail. Even in the wind and the dark, he knew the bay could clear the gap easily. He cantered Valentine as far back as possible, then turned him to face the stream.

As the wind howled around them, Rowan leaned low and pressed with his knees. The horse strode rapidly ahead and then sailed over the crag's edge to land strong and sure on the other side.

About to ride toward the Lincraig road, Rowan spun around to see if he had been followed. Glowing moonlight spilled downward, and he easily saw the silhouettes of Heckie and the others as they moved past. But he was alarmed to notice a commotion at the top of the slope, and stilled his horse for a moment to watch, wondering if he had been seen.

In a bright swath of moonlight, Rowan suddenly noticed that someone else came behind Heckie and the others, riding the crest of the hill like a black phantom. The reivers had clearly seen this rider too, for Rowan heard the echo of their shouts even from where he sat. They turned in pursuit.

The isolated rider turned, his black cloak filling with wind. The dark hood slipped back, and Rowan saw a delicate oval-shaped face catch the scant light.

Mhairi. He sucked in his breath, then swore out loud, the curse lost in the combined rush of the water and the wind. He had not thought she would be reckless enough to come after him. He certainly would have thought that Christie would have come with her, but she appeared to be alone. Rowan swore again as he sat Valentine on the edge of the crag and watched Mhairi, knowing that a spating stream and a long slope lay between them.

A whirl of wind picked up her cloak and spun it around her as her horse sidestepped on the hill. Heckie approached her, bellowing—Rowan heard the echo even over the rushing water—and rode toward her.

Mhairi looked down toward Rowan, her cloak whipping high. Raising her arm, she gestured wildly for him to ride on.

He swore again, feeling a rising, frustrating blend of

fury and fear. Steadying the circling, anxious bay beneath him, he judged the leap from this side. But the first bank projected higher than this one, and the horse would not be able to make the jump back again.

Rowan cantered Valentine along the bank, looking across the swollen stream and up the long slope. He saw Heckie and the others surround Mhairi. She lifted her arm, fingers splayed and pale in the darkness, before Heckie grabbed her from her horse and she was swallowed up in darkness.

Galloping in tandem with them, Rowan scanned the treacherous water for a place to ford. His urgent need to follow Mhairi was stronger and more dangerous than any spated stream.

Gathering the reins, easing the horse forward, he plunged into the chilly, rushing water.

Chapter Twenty-two

~

"He is either himsell a devil frae hell,
Or else his mother a witch maun be;
I wad na have ridden that wan water
For all the gowd in Christentie."

—*"Kinmont Willie"*

"Jesu! Look down there!" Clem Elliot said, pointing down the slope. "He's breaching the stream!"

Heckie turned. "By hell! He is!"

Mhairi turned too, though less easily. She sat her own horse between Heckie and Clem, but her ankles were tied by a single rope slung under the mare's belly, and her hands rested on the saddle pommel, bound at the wrists. The changing clouds had blown past the moon again, and she peered through the darkness, past the riders herding Jean Armstrong's stolen beasts, down the rough, long slope to the whitened rush of the stream at its foot.

Far below, dark moving shapes cut through the pale foam: a man and a horse, partly immersed in the wild water. She gasped, fear curling inside of her as she watched Rowan and Valentine struggle forward.

"He'll drown, the fool," another man chortled.

"He'll make it," Heckie said, turning back. "Damned Black Laird. He used to ride wi' Devil Davy Armstrong and Alec Scott. A floody river wouldna hold back any o' that wild lot."

"He's got some demon in him, to attempt that water," Clem muttered.

"Demon or nae, he'll clear the stream and be on our tail soon," Heckie said. "Ride on!" He yanked on the rope clutched in his fist, with which he led Peg by the bridle.

Mhairi gripped the saddle more tightly, though her wrists ached with the effort. Her horse picked up pace beside Heckie's mount. Clem cantered briskly on her other side.

Mhairi glanced back awkwardly, unable to see the stream any longer. But she felt certain that Rowan would clear the water. She sensed his determination like a warm, solid glow that sustained them both, as if her spirit were linked to his somehow. The security of his presence behind her gave her hope and strength. "Rowan Scott will take you down before this night is through," she said confidently. "He willna stop until he finds me. You canna hide from Blackdrummond."

"I dinna mean to hide from him," Heckie said. "He has something that I want. But I have what he wants. I heard in the 'Batable Land that you're his wife now." He grinned at her. "The Lady o' Blackdrummond—a fine bartering coin, hey! You're a valuable lassie." He turned and looked behind him. "Martin, take a few men and ride ahead wi' the word that we bring something to trade. You ken where to go." His brother nodded and he and two others broke away from the group, galloping fast over the nearest hill.

"Trade?" Mhairi asked. "You mean ransom."

Heckie leaned toward her. "I dinna have time to collect a ransom. I mean to bargain you this night for what I want."

"Bargain with whom?" she asked.

He grinned at her through the darkness and did not reply.

"Rowan willna trade," she said. "He'll see you and your gang declared foul for this deed, and for all else you've done."

"I will meet your Black Laird and claim that thing we've been searching for. But just now, I'll barter you to someone else who wants you, in exchange for something dear to me."

"Someone else wants me?" She stared at him, perplexed.

"Aye. You'll bring me a good price, too."

She swallowed uncertainly, then lifted her head. "You willna get ransom coin for me. You may as well let me go."

"Let you go! Hah! Hey, a lass wi' wit!" He grinned as he looked over at his brother. Then Heckie reached out and grabbed her chin in his thick fingers. "I willna let you go until I've had something for my trouble."

Mhairi jerked her head away and stared ahead, her heart beating heavily, her back straight and stiff.

"She's quiet now," Clem sniggered. "Such a canny lass, and yet doesna ken a' the answers, hey."

Heckie glanced over his shoulder, then back again at Clem. "Damned scoundrel! He's back there. I swear I saw the flash o' a steel bonnet on that far hill."

"Aye," Clem said. "He's there. I've been feeling him on my back all along. Like leeches on my skin." He shivered. "I'll ride back and shoot him."

"You willna," Heckie snapped. "Wait until we have that blasted stone."

"Mhairi Macrae might ken where 'tis," Clem said, peering at Mhairi. "Hey, lassie? Have you seen a stone, round like, and black as a raven?"

She stared at Clem. "I havena heard of such a thing. What is it? A stone from a streambed? Or is it a jewel, like a ring, or a pendant?"

"Och, she doesna know," Clem muttered.

"You ne'er saw a fine black stone among your laddie's gear, set like a mirror?" Heckie asked. "There's a good price in it for you if you ken where 'tis."

"Och aye," Clem said, nodding. "Your life." He laughed.

Mhairi stared at him flatly and looked away.

"Bah," Heckie said, and spat. "If that blasted gewgaw had wings, it couldna be harder to catch."

"What do you want with such a black stone?" Mhairi asked. "Do you steal jewels now?"

"Nae Elliot would snatch a purse," Heckie growled. "Unlike some, hey, lass. Clem and me saw you that night, riding the Lincraig road, the night Clem tried to take you down—but Blackdrummond snatched you away. We ken well you were part o' those highway riders." He turned quickly. "By hell! Was that him, again, just there?"

Clem turned. "My neck is a' prickles," he said. "Let me go back and shoot him."

"You yammer like a bairnie," Heckie snapped. "I'll let

you fire on him when I have that raven's moon in my hand."

"Raven's moon?" Mhairi asked. "What does that mean?"

"Am I some damned poet?" Heckie asked irritably. "I didna name the thing. I'm paid to find it. A round, blasted black stone. Do you ken aught, you tell me now." He glared at her.

She sent him another purposely blank look and turned away again, clenching the hard wood of the saddle pommel. She knew too much about the raven's moon—too much and not enough. But she would not utter a word of what she knew.

Rowan searched for her. She felt his presence in those hills, more keenly than Heckie or Clem ever could. And he carried the black stone with him. If there had been any substance to the vision that she and Iain had seen, to the danger they sensed, then the black stone, with its strange power and its unknown importance, somehow was part of the force that led them all into danger.

Furrowing her brow, she hung her head down as they rode through the cold, windy darkness.

A drizzle began, thin and chilly. Mhairi hunched her shoulders against it, unable to pull up the slipped hood of her cloak. Beside her, Clem on her left and Heckie on her right rode silently. From behind, she heard the fretful bleating of the sheep, the grunts and moans of the cows, and an occasional curse from the reivers who drove them forward.

At first, she had expected Heckie to head south for Liddesdale, to take his newly snatched cattle and sheep, and his hostage, to his robber's roost. But she soon realized that they rode north into the heart of the Middle March.

Puzzled, she wondered if he intended to reive again, even in this increasingly poor weather. Looking around, she straightened her posture, her attention caught. "That's the Lincraig road ahead," she said. "Where are we going?"

Clem grunted. "Hush up," he said. He turned again, as he had so often, and looked back over his shoulder.

Heckie turned too. "I swear I saw a shadow at the top o' that hill, back there. D'you see?"

"Relentless bastard. I'll ride back and find him. If he has the black moon, we'll end it here." Clem gathered the reins.

"Halt," Heckie said. "Look ahead."

Mhairi saw a pinpoint of yellow flame ahead, bobbing in the night. As the flame grew, she saw that it was a sputtering torch held by a horseman who rode in the midst of a large group of men. Twenty or more shadowed forms advanced steadily across the moor.

"Hey," Clem said. " 'Tis the warden."

Mhairi felt a wash of relief go through her. "Simon!" she screamed out. "Simon!"

"Hush up, lassie," Heckie growled. But when she expected him to gather his reins and retreat, he held his place and waited while Simon Kerr and his troopers came toward them. A few of them carried burning chunks of peat on the ends of their lances to signal that the warden rode out in pursuit of reivers.

The warden halted his horse and steadied it, staring at them, his helmeted face shadowed and grim. "What's this?"

"Simon Kerr," Heckie said pleasantly. "Greetin's to you."

"Heckie," Simon said slowly. Then he looked startled. "Mhairi! What are you doing wi' these ruffians? Rowan Scott told me he had confined you in his tower!" He shoved back his helmet and glowered at them. "What the devil is going on here?"

"I've been taken—" Mhairi began, but her words were cut short when Clem reached out and yanked on her left arm, keeping a heavy grip on it. A sudden, vicious pain shot through her weak shoulder. She gasped.

"Och, we're out on a wee night stroll," Heckie said loudly.

Simon gave him a flat, dark glance. "I've been trying to catch you on one o' your midnight strolls for a time now," he said. "Whose cattle and sheep are those?" He gestured toward the beasts with his thumb, then turned and barked an order behind him. Several of his troopers aimed pistols and latchbows at the reivers.

"Those, well," Heckie said, looking over his shoulder, "those are mine. We were ridin' to Abermuir to present them to you. A bit o' meat and cheese, you see, toward my Martinmas rent." He smiled.

"You pay nae rent to me," Simon snapped.

"Nay?" Heckie looked stupefied. "I thought I did." Then he grinned.

"What jest is this? How many households have you ransacked this night? You've earned your arrest, by hell!"

"You willna accept my Martinmas tribute?" Heckie asked, and then laughed heartily. Simon snatched his pistol from its holder and aimed it at Heckie, who stopped chortling and pulled out his own pistol.

Mhairi drew breath to speak again, but Clem twisted her arm so hard that she cried out.

"What's amiss there?" Simon demanded, glancing at her.

Heckie pushed the barrel end of his gun against Mhairi's temple. "Hey, Simon," he said in a smooth voice. "I've brought you good meadow beasts, and this wee lassie."

"Why would I want her?" Simon said, his eyes shifting swiftly. "Let her go."

"She's a traitorous wench. You said so y'self."

Simon leveled his pistol at Heckie. "Now when did you hear me say that?"

"Och, I heard it," Heckie said easily. "And I heard that the summonses for truce day have been delivered. There's several, I hear. One was delivered to me, but your trooper gave it to my wife—she was muckle upset, too."

"I doubt that. She kens well who she married," Simon said. "I sent all the summonses out in the past two days. Truce day has been set for Friday next at Kershopefoot on the border. You will be there, Heckie Elliot."

"I hear you sent a summons for Mhairi to appear at court at the truce meeting also."

Mhairi squeaked dryly, but remained still. The cold metal of the gun hurt her temple, and Clem's grip grew more painful with each moment. She flashed her gaze back and forth between Simon and Heckie as they spoke.

"Aye, I issued a summons for Mhairi Macrae for her

highway crimes," Simon said. "A rider took it to Black-drummond Tower. How is that your concern?"

"I have her. But I'll let you take her, and this fine herd too. For a price, that is. Or I'll fire on her and be done wi' this night's work."

"What price is that?" Simon asked.

"You can have her whole and well, for whatever purpose you want her, if you cancel my summons."

"Cancel your writ? I willna!" Simon held up his pistol.

"This is a wheel-lock," Heckie said. " 'Tis spanned and loaded. I only need to pull the trigger. That one you hold is a matchlock. Have you got a light at hand?"

Simon glared at Heckie, and lowered his gun.

"This is a wheel-lock too," a voice growled through the darkness. "Spanned and loaded, and ready to fire. And aimed at your back, Hector Elliot."

Mhairi gasped at the sound of Rowan's deep voice, safe and strong and angry, somewhere behind her. She turned slightly, but the heavy threat of the gun against her temple stopped her.

"Damn," Heckie muttered, and twisted in his saddle.

"Let her go," Rowan said. She heard him ride forward, and heard the sheep bleating and shoving around him. Neither Clem nor Heckie released her, and Clem's grip tightened so much that she gasped and feared that he would pull her shoulder out of position again.

"You have twenty troopers at your back, Sir Warden," Rowan said. "Will you sit there and let these scoundrels threaten my wife?"

"Your wife!" Simon jerked as if he'd been hit. "What d'you mean, your wife?"

"Twenty troopers, sir," Rowan said. "Or I can shoot this ruffian here and now. And then arrest you, on my authority as council-appointed deputy, for neglect o' your duties."

Simon turned to Hepburn, who sat his horse beside him. "Take them, then," he grumbled.

Hepburn nodded and motioned to the troopers, who stepped their horses closer and raised their weapons, deliberate and cautious. Mhairi felt Heckie lift the gun barrel away from her head, although Clem kept his hold on her arm. Able to move, she spun in her saddle.

Rowan sat on Valentine a few feet behind her, the horse's legs surrounded by sheep. He aimed his pistol at Heckie and glanced toward her for an instant, his gun never wavering.

"Are you harmed?" he asked. She shook her head. He jerked his chin toward the open, empty moor. "Go over there."

"I'm tied," she said. "I canna guide my horse."

Rowan growled something and edged Valentine forward, cleaving a path through the sea of sheep.

"Och, cut her loose," Heckie muttered to Clem. He bent down, still holding Mhairi's arm, and sliced a knife through the ropes that bound her ankles. She shifted her stiff legs in relief, raising her knees, and suddenly felt Clem tighten his grip on her arm.

He yanked her off the horse violently, flinging her toward the clustered sheep. She fell into their midst, her landing cushioned by a pair of woolly backs. As she went down, she heard a pistol shot rip through the wind.

Rolling over, gasping for breath, she dodged frantic hooves as the sheep scattered. She heard bleating mingle with shouts, and saw, through the screen of sheep, several troopers gallop away. She realized that Heckie and Clem had used the distraction of her fall in order to escape.

Dazed and shaking, she sat up in the darkness, still hearing shouts, though they were distant now. Sheep butted into her, knocking her over again. Breathing hard, she sat up once more, awkwardly, lacking the use of her hands for balance, since they were still bound at the wrists. Her shoulder hurt so sharply when she moved that she just sank back into the sea of sheep and sat, hanging her head down to her upraised knees.

Moments later, she heard the thud of hoofbeats, and looked up. A horse cantered toward her and stopped, and booted feet stepped down into the midst of the sheep. A hand touched her shoulder.

"Mhairi—" Rowan knelt and took her into his arms, pressing her head to his shoulder, lifting her gently to her feet. She leaned against him as a feeling of safety, of relief, poured through her.

He took her hands, bundled by hemp, and turned them

in his. Then he withdrew his dagger to slice at the ropes. "Are you harmed at all?" he asked, just as softly.

"I'm fine," she said. "My shoulder aches. But I'm fine."

"I would have killed them, Mhairi," he murmured as he worked the blade. He glanced at her, and the intensity in his eyes, glinting in the darkness, caused her breath to catch. "God help me, I would have killed them if I had caught them."

She nodded, biting her lower lip. "They got away, then."

"Aye," he said curtly. "Simon and Hepburn gave up the chase. I did too—only because I wanted to make certain you were safe." Mhairi felt the rough bonds release, felt his strong fingers surround hers. He looked down at her while sheep surged and swelled around their legs like a bleating, foaming ocean of heat and wool.

When he leaned down and kissed her in the dark, the feel of his lips, soft and quick over hers, took away for a few floating moments the discomfort of pain, and cold, and fear.

Some of the troopers rode back and began to herd the sheep away. Mhairi watched them. "What happened to the men who were herding the beasts—Heckie's men?"

"I came up behind them and cracked one on the pate wi' the butt of my pistol," Rowan said. Mhairi glanced at him and laughed suddenly. He tipped an eyebrow. "I caught the others wi' my long ax. I was saving the lead ball for Heckie," he added quietly. "But I missed the rogue. Can you ride now?"

She nodded and turned toward Peg, who waited placidly in the midst of the sheep. Rowan helped her mount, then stepped away to leap up onto Valentine's back. Mhairi looked around then, and saw Simon, on horseback, wading through the teeming sheep toward them. A trooper rode beside him, holding an upright lance on which a burning chunk of peat was impaled, its scant light glowing and spitting over their heads.

"Hepburn has just ridden back," Simon said. "Heckie and Clem have escaped into the hills. They're slick rascals. Martin Elliot and two Englishmen who usually ride wi' them came across the moor and helped them fight off the troopers wi' pistol shots and arrows. Hepburn turned back."

"Your land sergeant is a fool, Kerr," Rowan said. "And you're one wi' him, I suspect."

Simon sputtered. "Anyone would have lost them. We'll find them again. I'm already in pursuit o' three English outlaws who took a dozen head o' cattle and a horse from Nebless Will this even. You go on wi' a few o' my troopers and ride patrol after Heckie."

"I willna," Rowan said. "You and Hepburn can find them. I'm taking my wife home to Blackdrummond." As he spoke, he reached out a hand to gesture Mhairi closer. She edged Peg beside him.

"How is it she's your wife now?" Simon snapped. "A week past she was your prisoner."

"We've been wed," Rowan said simply.

"Hah!" Simon stared at them. "Wed! By hell! You let your lust blind you to her guilt!"

Mhairi opened her mouth to reply, but Rowan held up the palm of his hand to her, as if he sensed her imminent outburst and warned her to silence. She subsided reluctantly.

"Actually, I see matters more clearly than ever before," Rowan said. "Good night to you, Warden." He nudged Valentine forward. Mhairi followed, sliding Simon a scowl as she passed him.

"You're deputy to me," Simon called out, moving after them. "You'll do as I say. Ride out now after Heckie. You want him as much as I do."

"More," Rowan said. "Much more. But I'll find him another day. I'm going to Blackdrummond." He gathered the reins.

"Rowan Scott!" Simon bellowed. "Mhairi is to be escorted to Abermuir."

Rowan turned, his glare hard and cold. Mhairi saw its glint in the darkness. "Abermuir?"

"She'll be confined there for her crimes until truce day," Simon said. He called over his shoulder to a couple of his troopers, who moved forward.

Mhairi drew in her breath, watching them come toward her. Bleating sheep milled stubbornly about the horses' legs, impeding their advance. Simon, riding forward, kicked at a particularly reticent ewe.

"Peace, men," Rowan called to the troopers, holding up a cautioning hand. "This lass goes wi' me, and no one else." His voice was low and dangerous.

"I've served a complaint against her," Simon said. "I sent the summons to Blackdrummond Tower by runner, who gave it to Jock Scott. You told me the lass was there. You must have known about the summons." He paused. "But you dinna seem to, either o' you, and the runner said you werena at Blackdrummond. Where have you been these past days?"

"I rode south to fetch a kinsman," Rowan said succinctly. "Mhairi went with me. When and where is the truce meeting set?"

"Friday next. Kershopefoot at sunrise."

"Consider your summons well served. She will be there." Rowan stepped the horse forward.

"Halt!" Simon roared. "D'you take me for a fool? She'll go wi' my troopers now!"

Rowan turned once again, patiently, coldly. "Scots law is based on trust. Have you forgotten that? She will be there on the day of truce. The summons requires only that of her. 'Tisna an arrest warrant. She goes with me."

"I dinna trust you, Blackdrummond," Simon growled.

"Nor I you," Rowan answered smoothly. He spurred his horse, and Mhairi followed alongside.

"Rowan Scott!" Simon bellowed across the waving sea of sheep that separated them.

"Friday," Rowan called over his shoulder. "At dawn."

"I'll serve a summons to you as well for taking a prisoner unlawfully! I want her in my custody!"

"We'll both be there," Rowan called. "And Simon—have your troopers escort the sheep and cattle back to Jean Armstrong at Roan Fell." Rowan cantered ahead, and Mhairi pressed her heels into Peg's side to catch up. She looked over her shoulder, and saw Simon staring after them. Then his troopers gathered around him, and they rode off across the moor, the burning peat brick still glowing on its lance like an amber star in the darkness.

After a while Rowan turned to glance at her. "Let's ride home to Blackdrummond," he said quietly. She smiled wearily and nodded. They set a steady pace between them and rode across the moorland and down a slope to the Lincraig road.

As they rode, her arm and shoulder ached more and more with every footfall her horse made. She held the reins in her right hand and shifted her arm, trying to ease the discomfort. The weight of the heavy jack she wore added a further burden to the sore muscles. Finally she just cradled her arm against her.

Beside her, Rowan rode through cold rain, his helmet pulled low over his eyes, one hand resting on his thigh. She glanced again at his profile beneath the dull gleam of his steel bonnet, wondering what thoughts were going through his head.

"Rowan," she said. "You didna ride after Heckie, though I know you could have caught him. Why?"

"I needed to see that you were unharmed, and to get you back to Blackdrummond Tower," he said. "And—" He paused.

"And?"

"And I'm freezing," he said bluntly. "I rode through an icy stream for you, my lass, and I'm soaked. And we're both cold." He looked sideways at her, and she saw him smile faintly in the darkness. She felt filled with a kind of warmth, in spite of the wind and the dark, and the miserably cold drizzle that soaked her head and breeches. "And I willna have to pursue Heckie Elliot," he added. "He will come looking for me soon enough. I still have the thing he wants."

"The raven's moon," Mhairi said. "He said that someone paid him to find it. I dinna think he knows of its powers, Rowan."

"Someone paid him? I thought as much."

"Aye. But it couldna have been Iain," she said. "He wouldna have hired a ruffian like Heckie to do aught for him. Heckie was after him for black rent, remember?"

Rowan did not reply as he rode beside her. He nodded once, thoughtfully.

"Rowan—Heckie told Martin Elliot to ride off and meet wi' someone. He said he wanted to barter me for something. Nae the raven's moon, I think, but something else. I dinna know who Martin went to meet. Later, when we met Simon and his patrol on the moor, Heckie tried to trade me for his freedom. He told Simon to cancel his summons, but the warden refused to have any part of it."

Rowan nodded. "I heard them talking as I rode up."

"If Simon hadna ridden through when he did, Heckie might have had you killed. Clem was ready to ride back and shoot you. Simon was angry with Heckie and ready to arrest all of them. The warden and his troopers saved both of us."

"Perhaps," Rowan said thoughtfully. "Perhaps. I've much to think about. I hope by truce day, though, I'll have this maze sorted out. This night has given me a few ideas to ponder."

"What about Heckie? He willna show up for his summons."

"If he wants the raven's moon, he'll find me."

She nodded, frowning. "I've never been to a truce day."

"Few lassies have, but for alewives and merchants' wives."

"I've heard they're wild, unruly affairs, more like a gathering for drunkards and gamblers than a judicial meeting."

He smiled. "On occasion. But most truce meetings I've been to have been fairly dull. If naught else, this next meeting will be talked about for a long time to come."

"Why is that?"

"A lass has never been summoned that I know about," Rowan said. "Many will come just to see that."

"Oh," she said, fighting a sudden onslaught of dread that seemed to go right to her stomach. She feared deeply what might happen at the truce meeting, not only to her, but to Iain, who would be handed over to the English.

But she was far too tired to think about it. She would face the fear, and the challenges, when they came. She had no choice. At least she was certain that she would see Iain that day.

Rowan spurred his horse, and she pressed Peg forward as well. After a few minutes, he turned. "Come ahead, Mhairi o' Blackdrummond," he said. "Your tower is just there!"

She looked where he pointed. The tall, square-cornered building soared upward from its rocky perch, impermeable stone blacker than the night, surrounded by the shimmering drizzle.

At the top, a beacon flared like a welcoming torch. And suddenly she longed to be inside, where it was warm and dry, where there was fire, and food, peace and safety.

She guided her horse carefully up the rocky slope, following Rowan. Then the gate opened and Jock and Sandie stepped forward to usher them inside.

Chapter Twenty-three

~

O hold your tongue of your former vows,
For they will breed sad strife
O hold your tongue of your former vows
For I am become a wife.

— *"The Demon Lover"*

"Where's Jamie?" Anna asked as she hurried forward to embrace Rowan and then Mhairi. "You did find him?"

"Aye, we did," Rowan answered, as he took off his cloak and helmet and began to unhook his jack. "The lad is fine. But we left him with Jean Armstrong for the night. I'll go back and fetch him in the morn." He glanced at Jock, who had come through the doorway of the great hall behind him. "Will you ride wi' me then, sir? Jamie has been asking for you."

"Aye," Jock said gruffly. "I'll come."

" 'Tis a muckle poor night to be about." Sandie came in after them, brushing at the rain on his doublet.

"Some would disagree wi' that," Rowan said wearily. He set his heavy jack on top of a wooden chest, and advanced toward the hearth, stretching his hands toward the intense warmth there.

"What do you mean?" Jock came forward to frown at him. "You've had trouble, then."

"Some. I'll explain later. We're cold and hungry just now." Glancing at Mhairi, Rowan pulled a carved chair closer to the fire and gestured for her to sit. She handed her jack to Grace, then sat wordlessly, her face pale and drawn. Anna came forward with a blanket, and Mhairi accepted it with a soft, weary word of thanks, spreading it over her lap. Anna handed one to Rowan as well, which he threw around his shoulders.

Rowan frowned and turned to watch the flames lick around the pine logs in the hearth. The rapid pace of the last few hours had not yet left him. He felt its uneasy, restless residue still stirring his blood, still sobering his mood. Looking around, he saw Mhairi give him a tentative flutter of a smile, yet he could not return one to her.

He splayed his palms and felt the heat penetrate his skin as he gazed into the flames. The fear of losing Mhairi had ended, but the tension still lingered, partly because he knew that she would have to face a hearing at the truce meeting in a few days. And he was vexed with her for leaving Jean Armstrong's house and putting herself in such danger. And for frightening him so deeply.

He would say nothing to her about that now. He wanted to see the bloom return to her face, needed to know she was not hurt. He sucked in a quick breath, overwhelmed by an urge to ensure her safety, her comfort, to fulfill whatever she wanted. He was astonished at the depth and variance of the feelings that she stirred in him.

He turned. "Mhairi is cold and wet," he said to Anna, more briskly than he meant.

Anna nodded. "I'll have Grace set up a hot bath for her."

"Rowan is more wet and chilled than I am," Mhairi said. "He should bathe first."

"I can wait. Mhairi will go." Rowan sat on a bench and tugged off his long boots, intending to warm his chilled feet and toes before the fire. He glanced up at Anna, who narrowed her green eyes at him speculatively. Then she turned away to pour the contents of a flask into two pewter cups, handing one to him and the other to Mhairi.

"Spanish sherry," she said. " 'Twill warm you nicely. And I'll heat up some chicken broth for you both while Grace is filling the bath. Then I'll have her put warm stones in your beds. Rowan, you will not mind if Mhairi takes your bedchamber again, will you?" She frowned. "Is she still your, ah, prisoner?" she asked hesitantly.

Rowan glanced quickly at Mhairi, but she lowered her eyes. "She can sleep in my bedchamber," he answered succinctly. Far more needed to be explained, but he would wait.

Tossing his boots aside, he peeled off his damp nether stockings and dropped them on the hearth stone. Then he dried his feet with the blanket and stretched his legs out before the blazing yellow fire, sighing at the simple, comforting warmth as he sipped the sherry.

Mhairi began to tug awkwardly at her own long boots, favoring her left arm. Rowan left his bench to kneel beside her, and reached out to pull off first one boot, then the other.

"You look pale," he said. "Does your shoulder hurt?"

"Nae so much. I'll be fine. Thank you," she added softly, reaching out to touch his arm.

He nodded, warming her bare feet between his hands for a moment. Then he stood and turned to see his grandparents and Sandie staring at them.

"Well then," Anna said, fisting her hands on her hips, "just how was that ride into the Debatable Land?"

He hesitated, glancing at Mhairi. A high blush glowed on her cheeks as she turned to Anna. "Oh," she said, " 'twas—well, 'twasna what we expected," she finished.

"Nay?" Jock asked. "What happened there?"

"Aye, lad." Sandie glowered at Rowan. "What happened?"

Rowan cleared his throat. "Well, ah, we went to a wedding."

"Whose?" Anna asked sharply.

"Lang Will Croser got married," Mhairi said.

"Oh! How lovely," Anna said.

"What else happened?" Jock asked brusquely.

"You two look as guilty as Scottish riders in the dark o' night, herding a muckle lot o' English sheep," Sandie said.

Rowan glanced again at Mhairi. She nodded her head gently. "Well," he said, rubbing his hand over his jaw, "there were other weddings that day, too."

"Several other couples were wed, all at once," Mhairi said.

"And so were we," Rowan added.

Silence fell over the room. Rowan glanced from one face to the other. Anna slowly smiled; Sandie scowled as if he were deep in thought, and then broke into a raw grin;

and Jock's expression was somber, but his blue eyes were
curiously bright.

"Wed? You're wed?" Anna asked.

"Aye," Mhairi said. " 'Twas sudden," she added un-
necessarily. Anna stepped forward to fold her arms
around Mhairi, then turned to Rowan to embrace him.
Jock stepped forward as Anna released him, and clasped
Rowan's hand without a word, though Rowan could see
that he was pleased. Then Jock turned to Mhairi, covering
her hands with his and murmuring softly to her.

Sandie went to the table and poured sherry into three
wooden cups, giving two to Jock and Anna, and cradling
one in his own hand. "A toast," he said. "To all the blessings o' life—" He raised his cup.

Rowan drank with the rest, feeling the natural heat of
the sherry warm him again. He looked at Mhairi over the
rim of his cup, and thought how bonny she was, with the
firelight shining in her eyes, and her cheeks glowing like
summer roses from the drink and the moment.

Sandie gave them a sly grin. "I guess you needna argue
about who has the first bath. You'll have it together,
hey?"

"Alexander!" Anna said, her eyes widening. Sandie
chuckled.

"You auld scoundrel," Jock said, huffing a low laugh.

Rowan suppressed a smile and glanced at Mhairi. Her
cheeks had deepened in color, and she tucked her head
down quickly, touching her cup to her lips. He sipped at
his own sherry, feeling the sweet burn as it slipped down
his throat, and briefly considered how pleasant such a
bath might be.

" 'Tis no proper wedding feast," Anna said, "but I'll
fetch that hot chicken broth now."

" 'Twould be a fine wedding feast," Mhairi said softly.

Watching her, Rowan smiled, a slight lift of his lip that
expanded, warmed by the glance she sent back to him.

"Bring enough for all o' us, Anna," Sandie said. "We'll
sup on broth and barley, and keep reiver's hours on
the morrow." He grinned again. "Meaning we'll sleep
through till gloamin' if we like, hey." He wiggled his eyebrows at Rowan.

While Anna admonished Sandie for his boldness,

Rowan smiled and turned toward the fire. Even that heat could not warm his heart as this welcome had done.

But beneath all of that, like dark clouds sailing toward the sun, he could not free himself from a taut sense of approaching danger.

Reclining in Rowan's bed against feather-stuffed pillows, Mhairi stretched her feet between soft linen sheets. Dark red damask curtains surrounded the bed, enclosing all sides but one, creating a warm nest of deeply piled feather mattresses and woolen blankets. She stretched again and yawned, sliding deeper in the bed, savoring the delicious comfort against her bare skin.

A fat candle flickered on a wooden chest beside the bed. Peat crackled and glowed in the hearth, offering low light and much heat. The wooden tub, in which she had soaked in hot water and fragrant herbs, was still full and still warm near the hearth. She sat alone in the dark, warm room, waiting for Rowan.

Yawning again, she wondered when he would come up the stairs. When she and Anna had left the great hall more than an hour ago, he had been involved in an earnest, quiet conversation with Jock and Sandie concerning truce day and her summons. She had heard Rowan explaining about the curious black stone, but she had been too tired to listen, almost too tired to care what was said.

She combed her fingers through her damp hair as she relaxed against the pillows, and gradually closed her eyes.

When she woke, startled, to the sound of splashing, she realized that she had fallen deeply asleep. Blinking, she looked toward the hearth.

Silhouetted in the scant light, Rowan stood in the tub and stepped out, the water sloshing quietly. His back was turned to her, and his hair, black as a raven's wing, swept between his wide shoulders. Candlelight flowed over the sculpted hardness of his body, over the powerful contours of his wide shoulders and muscled back, tapering to narrow buttocks and strong legs. Mhairi thought suddenly of a depiction of Adam that she had seen once in an illustrated Bible: potent strength and supple grace held in perfect balance.

Fascinated, she rested her head on the pillow and

watched the gleam and surge of his firm muscles as he
dried himself with a linen towel. She wanted to touch the
soft, sleek wave of his hair, wanted to feel that hard,
warm, solid body against hers.

A blush heated her throat and her cheeks, and her heart
beat rapidly. As Rowan turned toward the bed, the low
light revealed the tight modeling of his torso beneath the
black hair that swirled across his chest, and plunged in a
wedge over his flat abdomen, clustering at his groin.

With a quick, easy motion, he pulled the red damask
curtain closed, leaving a narrow open space. Candlelight
spilled inside, giving the quiet interior of the bed the color
of dark rubies.

He sat on the bed beside her, the mattress sinking
beneath him. Mhairi inhaled the clean, herbal scent that
drifted toward her from his skin and hair. As he shoved
his fingers through his wet tousled hair, she saw that it
curled gently, reminding her, suddenly, of Jamie's glossy
head. He sighed and turned to look at her.

"I thought you were asleep," he said softly.

"I was, for a while," she answered.

"Did I wake you? I tried to be quiet while I bathed."

She shrugged. "Nae matter."

He nodded and shifted so that he faced her, his knee
close beside her hip, his arm draped over his leg, his chest
wide and powerful. The torsion of his body concealed the
rest from her, but she felt a blush rise from her chest to
her brow.

"Since you're awake," he said, "there is something I
wanted to talk to you about."

She heard his grim tone and sat up against the pillows,
drawing the linen sheet securely over her chest. The
power and boldness of his nudity and his somber attitude
within the small, intimate space disconcerted her. Equally
nude, she shielded herself beneath the blankets.

What did he mean to ask her—dear God, she thought,
not more about spies, or about Iain's supposed role in this
conspiracy to acquire the black stone mirror. And although she was worried about what might happen on
truce day, she did not want to speak about that now. She
had hoped for another kind of encounter with him that

excluded all those concerns, that possessed all the fervent joy of the brief time spent in Jean Armstrong's loft.

Rowan looked serious, even angry, his brows lowered as he waited for her to respond. "What is it?" she asked cautiously.

"First of all," he said, reaching out to touch her shoulder, "I wondered if you were in pain."

Something wild and strong plummeted through her at the warm brush of his fingers over her shoulder. Her heart beat fast and hard. "It aches some," she said, a little breathlessly.

His fingers curled over her shoulder, rubbing gently. Shivers swirled through her. "Only some?" he murmured.

"Aye," she answered. "The hot bath helped."

Rowan stroked her aching muscles with his thumb and fingers, and looked at her. Above his shadowed jaw, his eyes reflected the candle flame with green clarity. "There's another matter I wanted to ask you about," he said carefully.

"What is that?" Her heart pounded.

"Why did you leave Jean Armstrong's house?"

"To follow you," she said simply.

"You should have stayed there." His fingers circled and pressed, creating heat, releasing some of the ache. She moved her head languidly, stretching the muscles in her neck, lured into relaxation by his touch.

"I couldna," she said quietly, shivering slightly as she felt an echo of the compelling need that had moved her to ride after him. "I had to ride after you."

"I wanted to lead Heckie away from Jean Armstrong's house. I didna mean for you to follow me." His words were curt, in contrast to his gentle, massaging touch. "Christie should have gone out in your place if you wanted to fetch help."

"He's injured. And I didna go for help. I rode out to be with you."

He sighed as if in mild exasperation, his fingers pushing deep into her muscles. Moments passed before he spoke. "When I saw you there—when I watched Heckie take you down . . ." He paused, although the firm rhythm of his fingers continued. "I dinna want to see such a thing again," he finished in a low, flat voice.

She felt a sense of dismay, for he was clearly displeased, even angry with her. That had not been her intent. "I only meant to help you," she murmured.

"You put yourself in danger. Since you had to be out there, you might have at least jumped the cliff wi' me. We could have ridden away." Now he looked at her, his frown deep and sincere, his hand on her neck. " 'Twas a lackwit thing to do."

She scowled in quick indignation and jerked her shoulder away from his hand. "And you did a muckle dangerous thing when you rode out from Jean's house," she said. "I havena reprimanded you for that, though you think it fine to reprove me."

"I rode out and left you safe, or thought I had. But you went out and risked getting killed."

"You risked your life as well," she snapped, hurt by his words. She had wanted only to be beside him. Pressing her lips tightly, she glared at the flickering shadows on the red curtain.

He watched her for a moment. "If you had a riding name, 'twould be Firebrand," he said, his voice suddenly gentle.

She slid him a petulant glance. "Nae Lackwit?"

"Firebrand." He smiled slightly. "Your hair is dark, but you have the hot temperament of a redhead."

"My mother has coppery hair," she said, still looking stubbornly away from him.

"Ah, there 'tis, then," he said. He sighed and ran his fingers slowly through his thick, damp hair as he considered his next words. "Mhairi, I know you thought to help me. But I needed you to stay at Jean's house. Seeing you in danger like that"—his voice caught—" 'twas hard."

"Harder than risking your own scoundrel's neck?" she asked.

He lifted a brow in casual response, but Mhairi saw a muscle pump in his jaw. That unknowing impulse of his told her so much. A surge of compassion flowed through her, and she reached out to touch the back of his clenched hand. Rowan feared losing her. That realization nearly took her breath.

She smoothed her fingers over his. "When you rode away from Jean's, I thought . . ." She closed her eyes as

hurt and fear welled inside of her, like a basin over-
flowing. "I was afraid that I wouldna see you again. I had
to come after you."

"That ride was nae threat to me," he said quietly. "I told
you I would be back for you."

"I know. But near two years ago"—she looked toward
the fluttering candle flame, easing through the hurt of the
words by focusing on that yellow light—"near two years
ago, on a poor, misty night, I watched my betrothed ride
out after reivers. He laughed when I asked him not to go,
and he said he would be back soon." She paused. The
flame lengthened and brightened. "He was killed that
night. Iain and Simon brought his body back."

He was silent. She watched the flame while a wave of
old grief swelled and ebbed. She expected Rowan to ask
her about the betrothal, or simply to ask if she had trusted
him so little because of that night that she had to follow
him out.

But he only turned his hand, caging hers gracefully in
his long fingers. "Sweetmilk Johnny," he murmured.

She glanced at him. "You knew about him?"

"Aye. Simon mentioned it. I knew Johnny Kerr. He was
a bonny lad. Overbold, perhaps, and too quick to act, but
a charming rascal, with cream-colored hair that reivers
used to tease him about, as I remember."

She nodded, and saw only sincerity reflected in his
eyes, only concern and no jealousy in his handsomely
shaped, caring face. She felt his warm fingers wrap protectively over hers.

"My kin killed him, I think," Rowan said softly.

She had carried this burden of resentment for a long
time, but the sadness seemed to ease out of her without
effort, as if it were a mist she breathed away. "Aye," she
said. "Scotts of Branxholm."

"I couldna blame you if you hated me for their crime.
Blood feuds run as strong in the Borders as they do in the
Highlands."

She shook her head. "I couldna hate you," she whispered. "I resented all Scotts, and you at first, but I couldna
hate you now for it. Johnny is gone. His own wild ways
brought him to that night. Iain told me that Sweetmilk
rode at the Branxholm Scotts when they pulled out their

weapons, as if he thought he couldna be killed." She looked at the candle flame, which wavered suddenly, seen through welling tears. They slipped down, but no others followed. She felt calmed by Rowan's steady presence beside her, as if she absorbed strength from this touch. " 'Twas long ago. He's gone." She looked at him. "We both have sadness in our past, you and I."

Rowan reached out to balance her chin on his finger-tips. "And we both feel that hurt still."

"Should we?" She looked at him earnestly as a thought occurred to her, a feeling that she wanted to express to him. "Should we? They're nae ghosts to haunt us. All they've left us are memories, and many of those are good ones. Perhaps we're wrong to let them hurt us still. We should be the ones to decide if the past will hurt us." She felt the utter truth of what she said. She had clung to her grief for a long time, but now sensed a new emptiness, almost a peacefulness, where only loss and anger had existed before.

Rowan was silent, his brow furrowed slightly as he listened. Mhairi drew a breath and leaned forward, certain that she had realized something of importance in her life. "I have to let go of this, Rowan," she said. "I dinna want this pain in my life any longer."

His gaze contained a depth, a spark, like light through green glass. "And what do you want?" he asked softly.

She looked at him, feeling as if all the tender places in her heart had been exposed. And yet she felt safe.

"You," she whispered.

His thumb moved lightly over her chin, and his fingers glided over her cheek. "I tried to tell you, but I didna say it well." He drew a breath. "When I saw Heckie take you down—I've never been so frightened as then. Never. I only wanted you safe, Mhairi," he said. "Naught else mattered to me but that."

Tears stung her eyes, glimmering over her vision. She nodded, and a hot tear slid down her cheek. What welled in her now was a deeper joy than she had ever known. "If I hadna come after you, we wouldna be together now, here."

"Ah," he said. "Ah. Now that is true." He smiled, a little wan lift of the corner of his mouth where his beard began. "Mhairi, this talk o' sorrow, and fears, and feelings—" He hesitated, looking away, his black lashes sweeping low, rising again. "Just days ago, we were suspicious of one another, and angry, yet now—"

" 'Tis fast, this," she agreed in a whisper.

"Aye, fast, sudden. Strong." He paused. " 'Tisna easy for me, all this. I have always kept my thoughts to myself. And I am nae poet, to talk o' my heart, nor ever will be. But—" He stopped again, looking away, as if he searched for something.

She watched him, waiting, her breath quickening.

"But my heart's full, lass," he whispered. His hand slipped down to take hers. "I dinna know how, or why, or when, but 'tis muckle full."

"Oh, Rowan," she whispered, feeling the meaning of his words pour into her, filling her soul past the brim. "I know." She moved toward him, her heart thudding, her gaze caught in his.

He lowered his mouth over hers, and the warm touch of his lips surged like lightning through her body. She felt his fingers slide into her hair as he deepened the kiss and pulled her to him. Sighing against his lips, she splayed her hands on his chest and felt the soft, warmed cushion of hair there, sensed his deep pulse beneath the muscle. His mouth slanted over hers, and his tongue slipped out gently to touch her lips, opening her to him, asking, showing, sharing. His mouth tasted hotter and sweeter than any sherry, and she drank it in, inhaling, wrapping her arms around his neck.

The blankets slid away unheeded, and she sighed again as his hands slid around her rib cage, spreading on her bare back. His touch, hot and sure, slipped down to her buttocks, pressing her into the pillows as he lay beside her.

He shifted on his side and they sank into the soft, giving mattress, surrounded by crimson draperies, as if they were caught inside the heart of a fire. Her body fit fully to his, abdomens touching, the penetrating warmth of his body caressing her skin. She caught her breath when she sensed him, warm and bold, against her thighs, and a subtle, exciting shiver swept through her.

His lips touched hers again, his tongue deep, insistent,

exploring. The feeling plunged through her body like flame. She pressed closer, melding her body against his, shifting her hips sensuously against his hard, warm, silky length.

"Rowan," she murmured against his mouth. "Rowan—" His name on her breath held some elemental, mysterious magic, some protective charm, like the story he had told her about the rowan branch. She whispered his name again and the sound tapped the same inner core of passion and yearning that he had found before with his touch, his lips, his hands.

He answered her, she knew not what, a sound lost in a sigh. His mouth traced down her cheek and throat, his tongue wet and hot and delicate against her skin, sending surges of pleasure through her. His mouth slid lower, sipping at her, until she arched to offer him her breast. She gasped softly as his lips closed around the ruched nipple, gasped again, an intake of joy, when the feeling spiraled through her and touched off a blissful spark inside of her.

His mouth lifted from her breast and she felt his fingers there in its place, swirling over the center bud, finding its twin; she cried out and he silenced her sweetly, gently, with his mouth. Then his lips traced over to the delicate swirl of her ear, his breath swelling there like the echo of the sea.

"Mhairi," he whispered, as if he, too, felt some magic in uttering the word. "God have mercy, Mhairi—" His lips found hers, savored her, his tongue gentling over her lips, drawing back, taking her breath with him, returning his own to her.

She wrapped her arms around him and kissed him as deeply as he had her, caressing him, exploring his muscled body with her hands, her fingertips. When he lay full on his back, she shifted her body over his, pressing her breasts to his chest, sensing the intense thunder of his heart beneath her own. Leaning her head down, her hair brushed over his like a dark curtain of mingled silk.

With the silent eloquence of her lips and her body, she offered him what she had, her body, the air she breathed, her soul. Lifting up, she let out a quivering sigh as he touched his lips to her breast, his breath hot as his tongue pebbled the nipple, his fingers warm as he skimmed down to her abdomen, seeking lower, slipping inside of her. A spark quickened at his touch and flowed like liquid flame, and she cried out softly. She ran her hands down the smooth, firm expanse of his shoulders and torso to the strength and power of his hips and legs. She sighed against his mouth, drawing a deep moan from him.

He lifted her and she settled over him, gently pushing downward to sheathe him. His breath escaped into her mouth, so sweet and hot that she shivered and felt her inner core melt and run like poured honey.

The shared rhythm of breath and body created a shimmering power that burst through her, an instant of joy when his body and heartbeat merged with hers. She cried out as she felt release, and relinquished, in that moment, something she did not need, and accepted something far more precious in its place.

"I have never seen anything like it," Anna mused, turning the black stone in her hand. "You say you found it on that beach? This is what you were telling Jock and Sandie about last night?"

Rowan nodded. "Two scoundrels attacked me to get it." Mhairi listened as she stood near the window in the great hall, looking out at a remnant of blue sky that showed through the clouds. A cool breeze tickled her cheek, and she shivered, wrapping the woolen shawl closer around her; Anna had loaned her the gray shawl to wear over a borrowed gown of blue serge that belonged to Grace. Her own shirt and breeches, the only clothing she owned now that Iain's house had been burned, were still damp from a washing.

She glanced at Rowan and Anna, who sat near the hearth, and saw Anna peer into the stone. " 'Tis a mirror?" Anna asked Rowan. "Not much good, is it, with the stone all dark like that. Though it has a high polish. What could be the use of it, I wonder?"

Mhairi glanced at Rowan. He met her gaze, frowning, then looked again at Anna. "The stone has a strange power," he said hesitantly.

"What do you mean?" his grandmother asked.

" 'Tis a charm stone of some kind," Mhairi said. "Rowan and I have both seen images in its surfaces. I saw my brother in his prison cell—" She stopped then, unwilling to mention the other vision, when she had seen Rowan ride through a wild night storm.

"And you, lad?" Anna asked. "You saw something too?"

"I saw Mhairi's face," he said softly, "before I met her." He spoke to Anna but looked at Mhairi. The depth and sincerity in his green gaze caused her heartbeat to quicken.

Anna watched them both for a long moment. " 'Tis indeed a charm stone," she said. "Could these men be after it for that reason? It can have no other value. 'Tis not even a pretty thing."

"I wish I knew why they want it, Granna," Rowan said. "We can only assume 'tis because some who gaze in it see visions. There are many questions still unanswered in this matter."

Mhairi lowered her eyes quickly, knowing that Rowan wondered what she held back from him concerning those Spanish pages. Her thoughts were confirmed when he slid the folded letter out of his doublet and handed it to Anna.

"I know you dinna read Spanish, but you have French and Latin. Perhaps you could make some sense of what is written here," he said.

"Let me see." Anna set the mirror on the table to take the pages from Rowan's hand. "This is a letter of some kind, but there is no name. Oh, here it says 'roses.' I'm sure of that. And this phrase here would be 'given to'— oh, these words are very close to French and Latin. I think it must say something like, 'many roses both white and red are given—or will be given, perhaps—to the most excellent and beautiful lady.' Does that make sense?"

"Roses?" Rowan looked dismayed. "Beautiful lady?" He pushed his fingers through his hair.

"And here's *luna*—that has to be 'moon.' Is this a love letter?" Anna scrutinized the paper.

"Moon. Jesu. 'Tis some kind of code." Rowan shoved his hand through his hair again, a frustrated gesture. "Even if we got it translated, we canna understand it. 'Twill be useless in finding these spies unless I know what the code says."

"What will you do?" Anna asked.

"I dinna know," Rowan said, frowning.

Mhairi turned away, a heavy, sick feeling in her gut. She stared out at the sky and the hills, at a flock of sheep, at two men on horseback who wandered the crest of a hill, all tiny, meaningless figures in the landscape while her thoughts tumbled and fears rose inside of her.

The Spanish document, if written in code, was truly meant for an agent, then. She had never told Rowan that she had found those papers in Iain's loft. Folding her arms over her chest, she felt the breeze lift her hair from her forehead, and waited, dreading that, in spite of the code, Anna might find Iain's name somewhere among those foreign words.

Anna and Rowan continued to murmur near the hearth. After a while, Rowan got up and walked over to the window.

"Mhairi," he said quietly. "You must tell me where you got that letter. Dinna expect me to believe you took it from a king's messenger. That is secret correspondence, never meant to be seen by the crown."

She looked out the stone-framed window. "Believe what you will," she said stiffly. "Truce day is in two days. Do you think I will give you any cause to suspect Iain further?"

He sighed. "You didna take them from a messenger at all."

She said nothing, although she knew that in itself was an admission. Unable to lie to him, unable to tell him the truth, she was caught in silence.

"I promised you that I would try to help Iain," he said after a moment. She felt the heat from his body as he stood close behind her, felt her body soften in response to his nearness. Wanting to turn, she did not. She knew if she did, her resolve to protect Iain might melt. "But I canna if you willna tell me what you know," he said.

"I know naught," she said, keeping her back to him. "Find out what the pages say. If my brother's name isna mentioned there, then you canna use the papers as evidence against Iain."

"Mhairi, I have to know where the papers came from."

"I found them," she said woodenly. "I just found them."

"Where?"

"Somewhere. Nowhere," she whispered.

He sighed heavily. "Why are you so afraid to tell me?"

"You are the warden's deputy. You have an obligation to present this evidence if it concerns my brother in any way."

"So it does concern your brother. Did he give them to you?"

She shook her head. "I canna tell you. The council wants you to prove his guilt. Simon wants to prove his guilt."

"I gave you my word that I would help you," he said.

"You also gave your word to the council to find the spies. And you are nae truly convinced Iain is innocent."

He sighed. "I am trying to see it. God, I am trying," he said fiercely. "But you willna believe that of me, for all the faith you have in your brother, who has evidence clearly against him. You protect him nae matter what, and willna believe me when I say that I am doing all I can to help now."

She hunched her shoulders slightly, turned away from him, his words hurting, the truth hurting more. Rowan turned abruptly and walked away from her.

She bowed her head. Deep fear had engulfed her when he had handed those pages to Anna to decipher. She was not afraid to trust Rowan. But she was beginning to suspect that Iain might be guilty. And she was not certain she could face that.

As she looked out the window, she suddenly noticed something and straightened. The two horsemen had ridden closer, and she recognized Jock and Sandie, wearing steel bonnets and jacks as they rode up the hill toward Blackdrummond Tower.

Jock held a small bundle in his lap, a bundle with glossy black curls and small hands that lifted in excitement.

"Anna," Mhairi said, "did you know where Jock and Sandie went early this morn?"

Anna looked up from scrutinizing the Spanish pages. "Out to take a herd to the south hill, I think. Why?"

She turned. "Open the yett. Jamie's come home."

Anna gasped and tossed the letter aside as she ran toward the door.

Chapter Twenty-four

~

At Kershope-foot the tryst was set,
Kershope of the lily lee . . .

—"Hobie Noble"

Mist flowed along the ground, white and soft in the early light, wrapping around the horses as they moved forward. Mhairi sighed out a frosted breath and shivered, flexing her hands on the reins. The shiver did not come from the chill in the dawn air, but because she felt Iain's presence near.

Although the warden, his troopers, and the prisoner had not yet arrived at the site of the truce meeting, she had felt Iain close by for the past hour, once as if he touched her shoulder, another time as if he had whispered into her ear. She closed her eyes and sent him a thought of caring, and of hope.

She glanced at Rowan where he sat on Valentine, just beside her. They had waited here, a short distance from the foot of the Kershope burn, since well before dawn, having ridden from Blackdrummond in cold darkness. With the sunrise had come this pale, obscuring mist, adding to the tension.

She pulled her black cloak close and adjusted her skirts. Anna had insisted that she wear the borrowed blue gown to the truce meeting. "You will not want to look like a reiver this day, dearling," Anna had said, and Mhairi had agreed.

Jock was mounted on a tall black on her other side, and Sandie sat beside him. Near them sat Devil's Christie, along with others who had accompanied them to the truce meeting; Nebless Will Scott and his two sons Richie and

Andrew, and other Scotts and Armstrongs, all waited quietly in the mist.

More men gathered as the time passed, drifting over the large field near the Kershope burn, at the border between England and Scotland. Although she could barely see the others, she heard scraps of low conversation and the creaking of horse trappings through the fog. She had heard Rowan and Jock, not long ago, estimate that over a hundred Scotsmen already waited there, with many more to arrive by late morning.

"Simon comes, just there," Rowan said, his quiet voice carrying easily. Mhairi looked where he pointed. Fifty or more riders crossed the flat moor through swirling white mist.

As they came closer she saw that Simon Kerr led his troopers, a motley assortment of grim faces beneath brim helmets, wearing steel breastplates or leather jacks, and armed with swords, lances, pistols, and bows.

Mhairi watched them advance through the fog. Simon rode between his land sergeant, John Hepburn, and a tall blond man. She narrowed her eyes, but could not see Iain, although she felt him so strongly now that her hands and knees trembled. Beneath her, Peg, usually placid and steady, began to sidestep nervously.

Simon raised his hand and the troopers halted while the blond man rode forward and reined in his gray horse. "God's greeting, Blackdrummond," he said pleasantly, then smiled at Mhairi and touched his helmet brim. "Lady Mhairi." She blinked in surprise, not having heard the title said before now. "I'm Archibald Pringle, a deputy in the Middle March."

"Master Pringle," she murmured, and did not return his smile, although she thought his brown eyes looked kind.

"We've come, as I told Simon we would," Rowan said.

"And we may nae stay," Sandie said, from his position several feet away. "Wi' this weather, the English warden may decide to postpone the meeting, and we can all go home, and nae bills o' complaint read for anyone."

"The warden is eager to be rid of one prisoner, at least, and willna tolerate a cancellation," Archie replied.

"Where is Iain?" Rowan asked sharply.

Archie frowned, looking at Mhairi. "You havena seen

your brother since he was taken, I think," he said. She shook her head silently. "Follow me, then," he said. He turned his horse.

She glanced at Rowan. He nodded, and she spurred her horse across the field after Archie. Simon glared at both of them, but said nothing as Archie led her behind a row of troopers. Looking to one side, she gasped.

He sat a black hobbler between two mounted guards, his head bowed forward, his hair lank and dirty, hanging down in his face. His hands were tied in front of him, and someone had thrown a brown cloak over him in the cold. She drew in her breath and urged Peg forward, stretching out her arm.

"Iain," she said softly.

He looked up, gray eyes nearly the color of the fog. His slack bruised jaw and the dark circles under his eyes made him appear dull-witted and passive. But his eyes snapped with will and life. "Mhairi," he said.

"Iain," she breathed out again, laying her palm over his bound hands. Tears welled in her eyes and her throat tightened. She leaned over and wrapped her arms around him, pressing her cheek to his whiskered jaw. *"Ach, leth—"*

"Mhairi, *leth,*" he whispered. She pulled back, wiping at her eyes, and kept her hand over his cold, strong fingers. "I hoped you would come here," he said in Gaelic. "But Archie told me that you are also charged with a crime."

"I am," she answered in Gaelic. "We will both have trials this day."

"What is the complaint against you?"

She glanced at the nearest trooper, but was certain that whatever she said in Gaelic would be understood only by Iain. "I was afraid that the king's council would send a warrant to order your death. So I rode out, and took the papers from the king's messengers," she murmured. He raised his eyebrows in surprise. "But the warrant got through anyway. I'm sorry, Iain, I tried to help you—"

"Hush," he said softly. "You have only my thanks. Have you heard from our father?"

She shook her head. "I sent a letter to him at the Danish court months ago, but nothing has come back. I do not think he has received it yet." She squeezed his hand. "He will help us as soon as he learns of it. We will come out of this, both of us. Wait and see."

He nodded, frowning. "Mhairi—did Jennet come with you?"

"Nay. But she's well, and your son is strong and handsome." Her lip trembled as she smiled. "Rowan Scott came with me. We—we've been wed," she blurted. "The wedding was fast. We hardly had time to realize what was happening, and it was done."

"Fast or well thought out, you would only wed for love, girl. I have met this man. He has a sense of honor." He looked at her keenly. "And you love him, I think."

She looked down. "I am confused about so many things," she said softly. "*Ach*, Iain, I have believed all along in your innocence, but—"

"But there is so much against me," he finished for her. She nodded. He glanced away. "Simon does not want to consider my story. He only wants to hand me to the English warden and be done with the matter. He needs a spy, and he has found one, or so he thinks, and no evidence will convince him otherwise."

"I found a letter," she said quickly. "In Spanish."

He glanced at her sharply. "Where is it now?"

"Rowan has it," she said.

He frowned and shook his head. "Mhairi, that letter—"

"Hey, lass." A mounted trooper moved toward her and took hold of Peg's bridle. "The warden wants to see you. Come on."

Mhairi grasped Iain's hand. "I will be with you when they read the complaint against you," she said in hurried Gaelic. He nodded, and she let go of his hand as her horse was led away.

Simon turned in his saddle. "You'll stay under guard o' my troopers, since you're one o' the accused," he said, and motioned her guard to lead her horse away. Mhairi opened her mouth to protest, but stopped when she heard hoofbeats. She glanced over her shoulder to see Rowan rein in beside her.

"She stays wi' me," he said firmly, and reached out to take the bridle from the trooper's hand.

"She's one o' the accused," Simon snapped.

"Days o' truce and Scots law are based on trust," Rowan said. "Any accused man—or woman—is free to roam the truce field. When she's called, she'll come to her hearing."

"Then that means Iain can walk freely here, so long as he's on the field," Mhairi said quickly.

Rowan nodded. "She's right about that, Simon. As warden's deputy, I'll take responsibility for him."

Simon's face took on a dark, dangerous hue beneath his black-browed scowl. "As soon as this meeting commences, I'll see that she and her brother have their trials." A shout rose nearby, and Simon turned to look. "Ah! The English warden has arrived." He snapped his reins and cantered across the field with several troopers.

The mist had begun to thin, replaced by a cold drizzle. Mhairi watched through a translucent veil of rain and fog as Simon and his men rode the length of the field toward the swirling waters of the Kershope burn, its flat banks edged with clustered oak trees. Beyond that wide water lay English soil. Mhairi saw a mass of riders, easily two hundred and more, gathering on the opposite side of the stream. As Simon lifted his hand in greeting, a few men broke away from the English group to approach the water's edge.

The English warden clearly had other plans, Rowan thought later, as he walked Valentine and Peg across the crowded field. Mhairi and Iain were not to be tried first, but would wait their turn among a host of offenders, English and Scottish both.

He led the horses inside the ropes of a temporary enclosure set up beneath a stand of wide, old trees. As the horses bent their heads to nuzzle at bales of hay stacked along the ground, Rowan glanced toward the meadow, where hundreds of men now roamed the field. He could see the banners of England and Scotland flapping on poles near the tent that had been set up for the wardens' use.

He had been eager to get away from the bickering that had been going on between Simon and Henry Forster, the English warden, over the selection of the juries and the schedule of complaints to be read. And he had been glad to escape the flat glare of both wardens.

He knew the English warden well. As a prisoner of rank, Rowan had been confined in a chamber inside Henry Forster's manor house for nearly two years. Just seeing the man's pasty, aging face brought back bitter memories of that isolation. But Rowan and Forster had gained a reluctant respect for one another, and he knew that Forster would not cause undue trouble for him now.

He had been pleased to see Forster's deputy, Geordie Bell, whom he had last seen at an inn in the Middle March. They had exchanged a few words before Geordie had been called to listen to the bills being read out.

Fragrant smoke from cooking fires rose into the overcast sky as Rowan walked across the field. Inhaling the delicious odor of roasting meat, he grew thirsty for an ale and headed for a group of trestle tables that had been set up as a tavern.

Despite mist and bouts of rain, several merchants had arrived and had set up cook shops and tables at one side of the field. Crowds waited now to purchase cooked meats, cheese, bannocks, roasted apples, and ale, while others looked over ribbons and gewgaws for sweethearts, or clustered near the dice games already in progress. At the far end of the long meadow, near the burn, a football match had begun. Rowan heard cheers drifting up as he made his way across the field.

He ordered an ale, paid for it, and received a sloshing full wooden cup. Sipping it, he headed toward the wardens' tent, where the bills of complaint were being read. He made his way through the men packed inside the tent, and saw Mhairi and Iain near the wardens' table at the center, waiting their turn before the wardens. Setting down his cup, he went toward them. Earlier, at Rowan's insistence and with Archie Pringle's cooperation, Iain had been allowed, unbound but under guard, to walk the truce field with Mhairi, and he stood now beside her.

She glanced up as Rowan came near, her eyes wide and wary. He put his hand on her shoulder to reassure her, and nodded to Iain. They turned to listen to Simon, who was reading out a bill of complaint concerning a reiver who now stood before the table, in an area scattered with straw. The man wore no chains or ropes, and was fully armed, while his reiving comrades stood nearby. Archie Pringle took notes, dipping his quill into an inkpot and writing on a sheet of paper while Simon spoke.

"This complaint states that you, Richard Storey, an Englishman, rode onto the property of Mistress Beattie, a Scotswoman, in the middle o' the night," Simon said, his voice echoing beneath the canvas cover. "She claims that you stole four milk cows and sixteen sheep. And you entered her house and took her pots and her children's coats and the covers off their beds. How do you answer?"

"I did that, aye," the reiver said. "But ask Mistress Beattie where her husband was that night."

"There isna a complaint against him," Simon said.

"He was over in England, snatching my brother's cows—"

"Nevertheless, you're ordered to pay Mistress Beattie an amount equal to three times the value o' her beasts and goods." Simon looked at the English warden. "Agreed, Sir Henry?"

"Agreed," the warden answered gruffly. Simon slammed the flat of his hand on the table in a final gesture. Archie made a note on a page and presented it to Richard Storey, who crammed it inside his jack and walked away, through an opening in the crowd where gray light spilled into the tent.

"Hector Elliot, Clemson Elliot, Martin Elliot, and Thomas Storey called the Merchant," Simon read out. "Come forward and answer your accusers."

Rowan looked around, as did many others. When no one came forward, Simon repeated the names loudly, and then sent a trooper to walk outside the tent.

"Nae here," the trooper said when he returned. Someone laughed, and murmurs drifted through the gathering.

Henry Forster cleared his throat. "There are several bills of complaint against these men and others who ride with them, by both Scottish and English citizens," he said. "I say they are fouled for lack of answer. Guilty by default."

Simon shook his head. "The day is early. They may yet come. We'll call them again." He snapped open another paper.

"Thomas Armstrong, called the Priest. Come forward."

Rowan looked around, startled. Beside him, Mhairi took his arm. "Tammie!" she said. He nodded and scanned the crowd. A moment later, Tammie the Priest shouldered forward into the cleared space. His elfish grin was firmly in place. He saw Rowan and Mhairi, and winked.

"Hey hey, the Black Laird and his bonny bride," he said, and smiled broadly at them before turning to Simon. "Yer wardenship, sir. Bless ye."

Simon shot him a flat glare. "Thomas Armstrong," he said. "You were named an outlaw last month, and twice last year, for nae answering your summons. Now here's another bill for you."

"Aye, and I'm here. I wish to make redress for my sins," Tammie said blithely.

"And you will. This most recent complaint says"— Simon regarded the page, his lips moving silently before he spoke again—"that you stole eight head o' cattle and four sheep from John Heron in Tynedale in England, and the next night you returned to take his mother's goat."

"John Heron took my beasts. I went back to reclaim them," Tammie said. "I took only what was mine. Including the goat. And I give my own oath that I am clean, sir."

"You swear by heaven and hell, by Paradise and God himself, that you are innocent of art and part in this?" Simon asked. Archie scribbled earnestly while he spoke. "So help you God?"

"I do. And I have an avower." Tammie pointed.

Dickie the Mountain parted the crowd with ease to approach the wardens' table. "I'm Richard Armstrong, a kirk minister," he announced, his huge, thick voice filling the tent. "I swear by all that is holy and made by God himself that my brother Tammie didna take gear or beasts from John Heron that didna belong to him already."

Simon frowned and repeated the oath for Dickie, who swore to it. Then Simon muttered to Henry Forster. The English warden nodded and slapped his hand on the table.

"Cleared by your own assurance and by your avower's good faith, as the Border code allows," Forster said. "But we demand compensation for what you stole last Sep-

tember, when you did not answer your summons. Three
times the value of those goods."

"If I see your name on another bill, Tammie Armstrong, you will be imprisoned and fined," Simon said.
Tammie nodded, smiling, and took the paper that Archie
handed him before turning away into the crowd.

From outside the tent, Rowan heard raucous cheers
swelling up from the far end of the field, where the football match continued. A few men left the wardens' tent,
apparently meaning to watch the game.

"Mhairi Macrae," Simon called. "Come forward."

Rowan saw her tense and clutch at the cloak around her
shoulders, then lift her chin and move toward the table.
Simon handed the paper he held to Henry Forster, who
read it and raised his eyebrows. "This is a matter for the
Scottish crown," he said. "Assaulting king's messengers
is treason."

"I act as the Crown's representative in this," Simon
said. "Mhairi Macrae—"

"Lady Mhairi of Blackdrummond," Rowan interrupted
sharply. "My wife."

Simon snapped his brows together at the correction.
"Lady Mhairi, you are accused o' riding out on the Lincraig road to willfully assault and rob messengers at arms
sent by the Scottish council. You were seen on the night
o' October the twenty-first, attacking a man along that
road. Tell us who else rode wi' you to commit the other
highway crimes listed here." He read out the dates on
which the messengers—with the exception of Rowan—
had lost documents to the Lincraig riders. Then he sat
back.

"Do you have witnesses who saw me ride out on all
those dates?" Mhairi asked, her voice low, but without
tremor. Pride swelled within Rowan as he listened. Beside
him, Iain watched somberly. Christie came through the
crowd to stand with them, his blue eyes infinitely serious.

"Someone assaulted these men. You were the only one
seen riding on the Lincraig road in such a manner, clan-
destinely, at night, dressed in black gear. As warden o'
this March, I must accuse you o' taking down the council
messengers. Now tell me who else was wi' you. Arm-

strongs from Liddesdale?" He scowled. "Blackdrummond Scotts?"

Mhairi stood straight, her shoulders squared beneath her black cloak. She looked slight and demure, surrounded by burly reivers and officers. "You have nae assurance against me, or anyone else, in this matter," she said firmly.

"Others witnessed you, and have avowed this to me."

"I admit that I have ridden that road, as have most others in the upper Middle March." A ripple of laughter echoed through the crowd. "But I didna rob purses." Rowan knew that was true, if literal. "Are there messengers here who accuse me?"

Simon looked irritated. "We didna wait for them to be summoned from Edinburgh. You were seen the night Jennet Macrae's house was burned. A report made to me said that you attacked a man on that road."

Rowan saw the sudden tension in her posture. "Who made such a report?" she asked.

"There were many riding out on the moors that night. And I dinna need to reveal their names to you. They were out on private matters concerning the wardenry."

As far as Rowan knew, only he and Clem Elliot had seen her on the Lincraig road. If there were other witnesses, they must have been warden's troopers. But Mhairi had robbed and attacked no one that particular night. The witnessed crime that Simon emphasized was false. He had no proof whatsoever that she had taken down the council's messengers, although he obviously suspected her and seemed determined to name her guilty.

Simon scowled when Mhairi did not answer him. "Rowan Scott, come forward," he ordered. Mhairi glanced at Rowan, lightning quick, as he went to stand beside her. "You took this woman down on the Lincraig road and arrested her that night in October."

"I aided her when she was injured by Clem Elliot," Rowan said. "And I will avow for her for that night. She wasna riding to assault anyone. She meant to fetch help after Heckie Elliot had set fire to her brother's house. I swear this to be true."

Rowan watched as Geordie Bell, the English warden's deputy, leaned forward and murmured to Henry Forster, who nodded and looked at Simon. "Rowan Scott's avowal clears her o' that charge," Forster said. " 'Tis the Border code."

"He's her husband!" Simon sputtered.

"And your deputy. The Border code still applies," Forster said.

"Well, she's still suspected o' the other crimes," Simon insisted. "My witness saw her riding out there. No one else had a reason to attack the king's messengers."

"I am a council-appointed deputy, and my avowal clears her. You dinna have a witness against her for the rest," Rowan said.

"Then I will avow against her," Simon said. "I believe she meant to steal the council's warrant for her brother Iain Macrae, since the Lincraig riders only took down king's messengers. She was seen later on that road, in reiver's gear. Attempting to steal from a king's messenger is treason. And I want to know who else was wi' her. Speak, Mhairi."

Mhairi held her head high and said nothing, though Rowan saw the high pink flush that stained her pale cheeks in the dim light. Rain drummed on the canvas roof, and then, like a rushing, mumbling sea, speculative murmurs rose among the crowd of reivers. Rowan heard comments of admiration, rather than condemnation, for such a deed, proven or not. He remembered that Jock and Sandie had done the same when they had heard of Mhairi's reasons for riding out on the Lincraig road. Loyalty to kin was so highly valued among Bordermen that any deed, even murder, could be construed honorable in its name.

"I dinna take any papers that condemned Iain," Mhairi said carefully.

Rowan watched silently, his fear for her and his pride in her fortitude, and in her literal turn of mind, mounting equally. She had not taken a purse from any of the men she had attacked; she had sought only the warrant, and had never found it, since he had hidden it inside his pouch.

"Say what you were doing out on that road, Mhairi Macrae, and tell what you know about the Lincraig riders," Simon insisted. "Or by God, you will hang for treason wi' your brother. Both o' you know more than you will say about several matters."

"Warden," Christie said, stepping forward. Mhairi spun to look at him, and Rowan glanced over his shoulder in surprise. "I rode that highway, meaning to save Mhairi's brother. 'Twas a poor plan. Mhairi is innocent of all these charges."

"You?" Simon asked disdainfully. "Christie Armstrong, you're a pup. Be gone." A few of the reivers laughed.

Christie blushed to the roots of his blond hair. "I am the Lincraig rider," he insisted. "I took down the messengers—"

"He didna," Mhairi cut in. "He's a wee bit enamored of me, I think, and means to play at chivalry. He's likely never been on that road but in daylight."

Simon snorted a flat laugh. "I suggest you pin your heart elsewhere, Christie Armstrong. And when I see a bill o' complaint wi' your name on it for snatching cows, I'll believe it. You're a reiver's pup, after all. Now go on, so we can continue this case." Christie stood, staring at Simon. The warden waved him away impatiently. "Go, or I'll have you removed. Or worse, I'll accept your avowal, and you'll hang." He laughed coldly.

As Christie turned, Mhairi touched his sleeve, but he jerked his arm away. She looked at him, and Rowan saw genuine hurt on both their faces. Christie shoved between Iain and the troopers and walked toward Jock and Sandie, who had come through the crowd to stand behind Iain.

Simon leaned sideways to confer with Henry Forster. While they spoke, Mhairi looked down at the straw scattered around her feet. Watching her slender shoulders and her glossy, dark head, Rowan wanted to hold her and lend her his strength. But he knew that she did not need it. She could endure this on her own, and somehow he knew that she wanted to bear it alone. But he would stand beside her throughout, and make certain, no matter what, that no ill came to her.

He felt a certainty in his gut, like a bitter blade, that Simon was determined to condemn her regardless of her innocence or her motives. Rowan was equally determined to prevent it. Her deeds, he knew, sprang from loyalty and love for her brother.

Rowan had known the love of a brother, and betrayal as well. He would not let Mhairi suffer punishment for what she had done. Once he had disagreed with Jock when his grandfather had admired what Mhairi had done. Now Rowan understood.

He turned his steady gaze to the wardens. "I avow for this woman in all matters," he said. "I swear to her innocence. I will place my life in the balance for hers."

Beside him, Mhairi drew in a soft breath. He touched her arm to keep her silent.

Henry Forster looked at him, frowning, assessing him. He leaned over and murmured to Simon. As Rowan waited, he saw Geordie Bell, who stood behind the English warden, meet Rowan's gaze, deep concern in his eyes.

Finally Simon shook his head and looked up. "Mhairi Macrae, this bill hasna been proved foul or clear. I willna accept avowal in a treason case. I declare warden's honor, which means that I myself avow your guilt, on my own responsibility." He smacked his hand on the table. "Mark the bill fouled," he told Archie. "She will be held at Abermuir until the messengers can be brought to give witness against her. Send word to Edinburgh."

Murmurs rolled through the gathering. Rowan sensed Mhairi sway a little beside him. He took her arm. "Warden," he said, "you lack cause to make such a decision. I have avowed for her."

" 'Tisna enough," Simon growled.

"Then I will avow for her as well," a voice said from behind them. Rowan turned quickly. Jock Scott stepped toward the warden's table. "I swear that Mhairi is clean in this."

"I avow for her as well," Sandie said, striding forward.

"As do I," Christie added, behind them. "Though I'm a pup."

Simon came to his feet behind the table, his face darkening. Beside him, Henry Forster stood, and then Archie, watching with dumbfounded expressions.

"I will swear for her too," Dickie Armstrong said from within the crowd.

"I will also," Tammie said. "And we're men o' God."

"As will I," another man called out. Rowan saw Neb-less Will Scott raise his hand, and his sons spoke their avowals after him.

"I do too," echoed a deep, sure voice. Thinking that voice, too, sounded familiar, Rowan glanced around at the faces shadowed by helmets and hoods, but could not see the man.

Nor did he see each man who called out after that. So many avowals came forward, so many arms raised up inside the tent that it soon seemed that each man who watched the proceedings called out an avowal, whether or not he knew Mhairi Macrae.

"Och, see, ye'll have to let her go," Tammie said with a grin.

Rowan turned to Simon. "You've heard these men swear on behalf of her innocence," he said. He glanced at Archie and pointed. "Write that on the bill—cleared by avowal of all witnesses present."

"Wi' pleasure," Archie said, and picked up his quill.

Mhairi looked up at Rowan, her heartbeat quickening in a blend of relief and elation. "Why do they avow for me?" she asked. "Most of these men dinna even know me."

He leaned down. "They approve of loyalty to kin. And they willna let Simon declare your guilt on such poor evidence. If he was allowed to take such a liberty, they might all be in trouble one day at his hands."

She shook her head. "Their loyalty is to the Black Laird o' Blackdrummond. Your notorious reputation saved me just now."

" 'Tis your loyalty that touches them," he said.

Simon pounded his hand forcefully on the table, startling Mhairi. "This bill may be cleared," he shouted angrily over the swells of chatter and laughter still coming from the crowd. "But there is another matter to consider. Iain Macrae, come forward!"

A subdued silence drifted over the ranks of the reivers, filled only by the patter of rain on the tent's roof. Mhairi felt Rowan's hand tighten over her elbow, but she could not take her gaze from her brother. Iain stepped toward

the table and stood tall and quiet, gazing directly at
Simon.

"I have a signed warrant from the king's council,
marked by their seal," Simon said, picking up a folded
parchment sheet with a dangling red ribbon attached.

Mhairi felt suddenly sick inside. Simon held the document that she had repeatedly risked her life to capture, the
document that she would have taken from Rowan if she
had known he had hidden it. That page, fluttering in
Simon's large hand, marked that she had failed her
brother, and proclaimed Iain's death.

Her heart pounded and she fisted her hands, and
stepped away from Rowan. Regret and fresh anger and
resentment poured through her. She felt a dawning sense
of horror to find herself caught in this tightening web of
loyalties.

She had married the man who had made her brother's
death an imminent reality. No matter how deeply she
loved him—no matter how much she needed him in her
life—she was not certain that she could ever forgive him
for that one deed.

She watched Iain's back, straight and proud, and lifted
her chin. And though she felt Rowan at her back, she did
not turn to him, even though she wanted, desperately, to
do just that.

Chapter Twenty-five

~

"O has he robbd? Or has he stown?
Or has he killed ony?
Or what is the ill that he has done,
That he's gaun to be hangd sae shortly?"

— *"Geordie"*

Mhairi watched Simon hand the warrant to Forster. "I entrust this prisoner to you," he said. "The man has committed treasonous acts against your queen in league wi' Spain."

"Have you brought the proof of the matter? The Spanish gold?" Forster asked quickly. "I've been ordered to accept the care of that, as well as responsibility for the prisoner."

Simon nodded. " 'Tis there, guarded by my men." He gestured toward a small chest at the back of the tent. Henry nodded and signaled two English troopers, who took Iain by his arms.

Mhairi felt as if her heart would rend apart. "Iain—"

He looked at her, his grey eyes somber and wise. Then he turned away. Mhairi's heart hammered so strongly that she felt dizzy. Yet when Rowan's hand came around her waist, she stepped away from him and looked at Simon. A kind of wildness erupted inside of her, a fierce blend of anger and loyalty.

"This is wrong!" she insisted, facing Simon. "You dinna have proof that Iain has ever acted as an agent!"

"I have all the proof I need," Simon answered.

"You have nae witness to swear against him!"

"I will swear against him," he said emphatically.

Rowan stepped forward and looked at the English warden. "Where will you take Iain?" he asked, his voice calm.

"To Carlisle Castle, to be imprisoned," Forster answered.

Mhairi heard Rowan's breath hiss sharply. "Border code allows him to walk free and unbound on the truce field."

Forster shrugged. "Well enough, if he's under guard," he conceded. "I'll have my deputy see to it."

"What will happen to him at Carlisle?" Mhairi demanded.

"He will be tried according to English law for treason."

"He isna an Englishman!" she said, nearly shouting.

"Border code gives us the right to take him and try him by our laws," Forster answered.

Simon leaned forward. "Mhairi lass," he said, his voice soft, his eyes cold and dark, "I suspect you've known something of your brother and this spying ring all along. You have found men to avow for your freedom, but you canna do the same for your brother. He'll be tried in England. And hanged there."

Mhairi stared at him, her breath heaving in her chest. "I swear on my honor that he is innocent."

"Your honor," he sneered, "isna worth much wi' me." He turned away from her abruptly and raised his head to address the reivers gathered inside the tent. "We will hear the other bills o' complaint after our midday meal," he announced. "Any others accused o' crimes are expected to be present then. Spread that word to your comrades." He nodded to Forster, who stood with him. They turned to walk to the back of the tent.

"Simon—" Mhairi said. He ignored her, murmuring to Forster. She stepped forward, but Archie Pringle turned to face her, glancing from her to Rowan.

"I'll see that the English keep their word, and let Iain Macrae walk the truce field, as before," he said. "Come back here in a little while to meet him."

"Aye," Rowan said, and put his arm around Mhairi to lead her away. She jerked back, her anger and anxiety boiling like water in a cauldron. He took her arm firmly.

"Let go of me!" she snapped.

"Listen well to me," he murmured sternly as he led her

out of the tent. "You canna dispute certain matters here
without bringing suspicion back on yourself. The Border
has its own code of laws, which allows wardens to hand
over prisoners who have committed crimes against the
opposite country. Scots can be tried and sentenced according to English laws that way."

"They shouldna take him to Carlisle—they should try
him here. I will avow for him!"

"As if Simon would listen to that," he said brusquely as
they set off across the muddy, crowded field. The rain had
lessened again, though the air was chilly and damp. "Iain
is accused of a crime that is outside the jurisdiction of a
truce day meeting. Simon has a warrant from the king's
council—"

"Aye, because you brought it!" She glared up at him.
"And I wish I had taken it from you."

"That wild scheme wouldna have prevented this day,"
he said sharply. "Iain would have been brought here
anyway. Or worse, Simon might have decided to render
warden's justice, and Iain would have been hanged
already. Have patience. The day isna done yet. I mean to
help your brother, whether you will or willna believe it of
me." He kept a firm grip on her arm as they walked over
the wide field. Loud cheers from the crowds watching the
football match barely caught Mhairi's interest, although
she noticed groups of men heading that way.

"Are you hungry?" Rowan asked, as they passed the
cook shops, where savory smoke rose into the misty,
dismal air.

She shook her head and walked on. After a while, her
anger began to calm. "What can be done for Iain?" she
finally asked.

"The best means to help him is to find the truth."

Mhairi sighed, and fear shivered through her. The truth
might prove impossible to discover—yet Iain would die
unless the spies were found.

Rowan led her to the tavern area, sat her down at a
table under a tree, and walked off to purchase some food.
As she waited, a few reivers who sat at the other end of
the table grinned at her and touched their hands to their
helmets. She smiled faintly, recognizing them from the
wardens' tent.

Rowan returned a few minutes later with two flagons filled with ale, two joints of roast chicken, and a large oatcake.

"I'm nae hungry," she said wearily.

"Eat." Hearing his firm tone, she relented and picked at the hot food, which warmed her fingers and her stomach. Rowan sat across from her, and she noticed that he ate little.

"If Iain is innocent, there is proof of it somewhere," he said, keeping his voice low. "Once he's in Carlisle, we could still get him released if the spies have been found."

"If the English dinna find him guilty first, and—" Unable to say the rest, suddenly unable to eat, she set her food down.

He sighed. "There's a man here today who might be able to help. I still have that Spanish letter, remember."

"But 'tis in code."

"Then we'll have to get it deciphered," he said. "I've decided to go back to the Debatable Land, Mhairi. Alec knows more about this than most. Iain's chance at freedom lies with him." He looked down. "I'll find Alec and talk to him."

Mhairi knew what that decision had cost Rowan. She reached out to touch his arm gently, feeling a wash of gratitude that began to cleanse away some of her inner turmoil.

But when he glanced up, his eyes were a cool, severe green. "Tell me where you found that document," he said.

She sighed heavily, then sighed again. "In Iain's loft," she murmured. "Hidden away."

"Oh Jesu." He looked away, shaking his head.

"He isna guilty," she insisted. "I know it now. I asked him, and he told me he has done naught wrong."

Rowan emitted a scant, skeptical chuckle. "If Simon had learned of that letter, Iain would have been hanged already."

"He willna know, unless someone tells him," she said pointedly. Rowan cast her a wry look. "Perhaps you should tell him that you think Heckie and his gang are part of this. If Simon would capture those ruffians, this matter might be cleared up faster."

"I'll talk to Alec first," Rowan said. "And I doubt Simon is willing to hear much from me on any of this."

"Rowan Scott!" Hearing the shout, they both turned. Tammie the Priest came striding toward them, a leather flagon in his hand, ale sloshing out of it. "Here, this way! We need a bonny braw man such as yourself!" He grabbed Rowan's arm until he stood. Mhairi rose with him.

"For what?" Rowan asked.

"We need a good forward man," Tammie said. "Our best man's been injured." He pulled Rowan away from the table.

Mhairi hurried to catch up. "What are you talking about?"

"The football match," Tammie said. "Dickie's agreed to be the back man, and none can stop him, hey, on that back line. But our best forward man has just been taken down, see—" He pointed to a man who was carried past them by two others, groaning, his nose bleeding profusely, his clothing covered in mud and blood.

"Oh dear God," Mhairi said, gasping.

"Och, he'll be fine, but he tried to run wi' the ball. A man could be killed for that, or at least mauled. These reivers treat their football matches as serious as their cattle forays," he added. "Ye look like a man who could kick a ball far, hey."

"I dinna have time for ball matches, Tammie," Rowan said.

"Och, this one ye'll want to be in. I ken that well."

"And how do you know that?" Rowan asked. Mhairi ran with them, listening earnestly, holding her skirt out of the mud.

"I just ken it." Tammie grinned. "Hurry, they're waiting."

They reached the edge of the ball field, where two groups of men clustered in the middle of a muddied, trampled area. A few hundred men lined the sides, yelling and gesturing. Some threw scraps of food onto the field, followed by loud insults.

"The match began between reivers waiting for their complaints to be called," Tammie explained. "But now the crowd wants to see reivers against officers. Over fifty men are out there now, and more keep joining. One side are troopers, and the other side, reivers, English and Scots both." He looked at Rowan. "Though I hear ye're a deputy, the reivers are the ones who've asked that ye play on their side." He pointed. "See, there comes Kerr and Forster, to watch their men."

Mhairi saw both wardens walking toward the field, ale cups in hand, surrounded by troopers. Archie Pringle limped along with them. Behind him, two troopers escorted Iain, whose hands were unbound. Mhairi caught her breath, and wanted to cross the field to stand with her brother. But the sight of the fierce men roaming over the midground kept her where she stood.

"They say Archie Pringle was a fine forward for the officer's side last truce meeting," Tammie said. "But he was taken down by the enemy, and had his foot cracked."

"*Ach*," Mhairi said sympathetically. "He ran with the ball."

"Nah, he made it to the goal, but the other side didna like it much. Ye'll go in, Rowan Scott, and show 'em what the Black Laird can do wi' a ball, hey. Can ye kick it muckle high?"

"High enough, but later, Tammie—"

Tammie lifted off Rowan's steel helmet and handed it to Mhairi, then shoved him onto the field. "Go, man."

Rowan gave Mhairi a wry look as he undid his jack and doublet and handed them to her. Then he ran out on to the field in shirt, breeches, and boots, just as most of the players wore.

"Will they stop for the rain?" she asked Tammie. He only laughed in reply. Mhairi set Rowan's gear down and then pulled up her hood against the insistent drizzle. She watched Rowan join the men on the field, and saw Dickie the Mountain, a head above the rest, speaking to him. Some of the players were nearly as large as Dickie, most of the smaller ones looked utterly mean-tempered, and all of them were covered in mud.

"Ye just watch, lass, and ye'll be muckle entertained," Tammie said. "Now, those trees way over there mark the reivers' goal. The troopers must get the ball beyond them trees. And the burn is the goal for the troopers—"

"The reivers need to get the ball to the burn's edge?"

"Ye learn quick. Actually, they'll need to get the ball into the water, or the troopers will declare foul."

Mhairi nodded, watching as Rowan handled a large, round, leather-wrapped ball. He drop-kicked it toward the burn, and the men raced in pursuit. Rowan and another man reached it, each struggling to kick it again. Another reiver ran up and swiped it away with his hands, throwing it behind him.

"Why did he do that?" she asked Tammie.

"Few enough rules in this, but they did agree that the ball can only be kicked forward. But ye can throw it back to another comrade who can kick it."

She nodded, watching as several men caught up to the man about to kick the ball. All of them went down in a pile. Fists flew, she was certain, before one mud-coated man wriggled out and threw the ball toward his comrades. A trooper caught it and kicked it toward the reivers' goal under the trees.

Rowan and the others scrambled to their feet and ran in pursuit of the ball. Dickie Armstrong stomped forward from where he had been standing near the trees, and slammed into three troopers at once, taking them down in a jumble of arms and legs.

"Dickie!" Tammie yelled in delight. "Hey hey!"

Another trooper caught the ball and kicked it, sending it neatly between the trees. A crowd of men ran and fell over the ball, while the troopers shouted victory.

"Bah! Blessed Mother Mary could play better than that!" Tammie hollered. Another fistfight erupted under the trees, while a few of the reivers kicked and tossed the ball back toward the burn. Dickie still pinned the men he had taken down, though they pushed futilely at him.

Rowan caught the ball and kicked it, lifting it with such finesse that the leather sphere rolled cleanly through the air to land a few yards from the edge of the burn. Mhairi cheered, suddenly, grinning at Tammie as a roar went up from the crowd.

"Go!" Tammie screamed. "Run! Kick it into the water!"

The men rushed forward in a mass. One dived past the rest, pinning the ball to the ground. Then another reiver grabbed it from him and ran in the other direction.

"What is he doing?" Mhairi asked.

"Och, he's drunk," Tammie said in a disgusted tone.

Several reivers caught the man, took him down by the legs, and began to beat on him. The ball was tossed straight up and came down, to be caught by another man who was covered in mud.

This man, a tall, dark-haired reiver, kicked the ball as effortlessly as Rowan had. His comrades chased it as it sailed once again toward the burn, landing to roll along the edge, barely missing a fall into the water.

Wild shouts went up all around. Mhairi screamed almost as loudly as Tammie now, who jumped up and down as he bellowed. Rowan and the others ran toward the burn again, tumbling along its edge as a trooper managed to lay hands on the ball and drop-kick it back, away from the burn. Another trooper caught it.

"Tricksters!" Tammie yelled. "Lackwit troopers! Ye'll burn in hell do ye make another goal!"

Mhairi blinked at him, then turned back to watch the game.

Rowan saw nothing but the ball. He ran toward the man who held it, legs and arms pumping, and dove for his booted legs. The trooper went down beneath him, and others collapsed on top of Rowan, a frenzied pile of panting, determined men, coated with sweat and mud.

Scrambling with the rest for the ball, Rowan felt an elbow in his side. A knee thrust into his back, and someone fell over his head. He wriggled free and threw himself onto the pile again. The ball popped loose, and he reached for it.

Another man grabbed just as he did, and they collided, shoulders slamming together. Rowan saw a mass of long black hair and a muddied face, and recognized, vaguely, the reiver who had gracefully kicked the ball toward the burn. A man to be assisted, not taken down.

Rowan shoved at a burly trooper who lunged at the man, and discovered that he pushed at Geordie Bell, who grinned at him. The moment gave the dark-haired reiver time to stand and kick the ball. As it arced, Rowan spun to race toward the burn, the others following in a frantic pack. The ball landed precariously on the edge of the bank, and finally tipped into the water.

Plunging into the chilly, deep stream with the rest, Rowan turned in churning water as dozens of men searched for the ball. Bending again, hitting into legs and arms, he swirled rapidly and faced the man who had kicked the ball, now rinsed of his mud.

His heart seemed to stop. "Alec!" he gasped.

"Rowan." Alec grinned. "A fine kick, hey, brother?"

Rowan stared at him. "What—what are you doing here?" He shoved his hair out of his eyes, still stunned.

"I'm here to help a friend," Alec answered, then sucked in a breath and dove down, disappearing beneath the surface.

While men shouted and struggled all around him, Rowan spun in the cold water, searching for Alec, who had slipped away into the crowd. Geordie came up holding the ball and gave a triumphant whoop, then scrambled to the bank. The rest climbed out and chased after him.

Rowan left the water more slowly, glancing around. But he did not see Alec amid the players who ran and tumbled and lunged after the ball. Rowan ran loping down the field to catch up, water streaming from his breeches and squeaking inside his boots. His gaze flicked from side to side as he looked for his brother.

The crowd was a blur of faces and waving arms. He briefly noted Mhairi standing alone, saw Christie and Sandie and Jock nearby, shouting with the crowd, but he did not see Alec. He wiped his wet hand across his face and looked again. Spectators hollered at him, and he ran toward the players, who were already massed at the other end of the field.

They turned and ran back toward him, and someone rammed into him. As he went down, the ball was thrust into his hands. He struggled to his feet, then drop-kicked the ball toward the burn. He watched it sail upward. And then saw it snatched in midair.

A horseman galloped across the field, grabbed the ball, and tucked it under his arm, riding a black horse like a streak of dark lightning toward the burn.

Rowan was carried along on the tide of frantic players,

all of them yelling and pumping their legs in pursuit of the horseman, who turned in the stream and held the ball over his head. Tammie the Priest grinned and waved the ball in an invitation for the reivers and troopers to retrieve it from him. Then he surged out of the water on the English side of the burn.

Most of the spectators were running too, many bellowing with anger at the loss of the ball, others laughing heartily. The field swelled with chaos. Some of the men plunged into the stream to fetch the ball, and a few climbed out on the other side in pursuit of Tammie, yelling insults. Simon Kerr and Forster ran past Rowan, shouting, while Archie Pringle came more slowly, laughing to himself. He smiled at Rowan as he passed him.

"Did you ever see such a match, hey?" he called, and ran on.

Rowan, breathing hard, stopped at the back of the surging horde of men and turned to look for Mhairi. He glanced around the nearly empty field behind him, and narrowed his eyes.

Alec was mounted on a gray horse near the trees, and led a bay by the bridle. A moment later, he galloped to where Simon and Forster had stood with the troopers, deserted now but for one man.

Rowan began to run. He saw Alec ride toward Iain, saw Iain reach out a hand and grab the bay's reins, then swing up to mount. Both men turned their horses and galloped off the field, quickly disappearing over a swell in the moor.

Rowan stopped and stared after them through the cold drizzle, stunned. Then he ran to the side of the field where his helmet, doublet, and jack lay. Grabbing them up, he glanced around for Mhairi, but did not see her. He had no time to look for her, and assumed that she was still with the crowd down by the burn's edge, and would be safe with his grandfather and kin.

Only moments had passed since Tammie had galloped into the burn. The men who clustered on the bank still shouted after him, and some now chased him on foot over English soil. Rowan realized that the entire crowd had been distracted by Tammie's antic. No one seemed to have noticed that Alec and Iain were gone.

If he knew his brother, that had all been planned.

Shrugging on his doublet and sleeveless jack as he ran toward the horse enclosure, Rowan grabbed up Valentine's reins and took off after Alec and Iain.

The sky grew dark quickly as he rode, filling with heavy, threatening clouds. Through the dimness, he glimpsed Alec and Iain in the far distance, heading north. Leaning low, Rowan rode in pursuit, over moor and bog land, crossing shallow burns and climbing rocky hills. Rain spit down on him and thunder rumbled eerily above the whine of the cold wind.

He realized that they were not heading into the Debatable Land, as he had first thought, but followed a long, circuitous route—meant to confuse pursuers—that went north into the upper Middle March. Rowan halted Valentine on a slope and saw the two horses vanish between the hills far ahead. He took off again, wondering if Alec had enough nerve to ride to Blackdrummond.

But he knew that Alec had never lacked nerve.

He covered league after league while rain spattered his head and shoulders. He was so wet that it hardly mattered to him, though he knew that the horse would need to rest soon. The sky grew even darker and the cold, stinging wind whipped at him. He shivered and reined in again, narrowing his eyes to gaze ahead.

Unable to see clearly, he lost Alec and Iain in a downpour among a maze of rocky hills that formed a jagged path northward. Galloping to another high slope, Rowan looked out, but saw nothing. But he felt certain that they still followed their northern route, which would take them to the Lincraig road and Blackdrummond Tower.

He rode through thickening darkness and heavier rain and eventually approached the Lincraig road, a league ahead over the moorland. Hearing another growl of thunder above the keening wind, he looked up at the restless, shifting sky. Then he ducked his head against a new blast of rain and rode on.

By the time he neared the road, he had left the truce day field hours behind. He was stiff and cold, hungry and wet. But deep inside, he felt a kind of intense torture that drove him onward and would not let him rest. He had to find

Alec now. Not only because he thought that Alec knew the whole truth of this matter, but because he knew now that Alec was going home.

Rowan knew now that he hurtled with full awareness toward the moment when he would face Alec at last, and face the fearful, angry shadows that had haunted his thoughts for three years. Mhairi had said that the choice was his to feel hurt or betrayed. She had been right. And he had waited too long.

He wanted to help Iain, and this was the way. Perhaps it was the way to help himself as well, for he knew now that he loved Mhairi with the fullness of his whole being. He sensed a chance for happiness, and wanted it desperately.

But first he had to clear some lurking demons from his soul.

He halted Valentine at the edge of a stony outcrop that overlooked the Lincraig road. Twilight and rain and heavy clouds had nearly swallowed the light, but he saw the silhouette of the ruined castle on an opposite hill. He tucked his head down against the rain and watched the road and the moorland below. If Alec rode toward Blackdrummond and had not yet passed this way, Rowan would see him from here.

Thunder cracked overhead, and Valentine sidestepped and nickered. The horse's nervousness reminded Rowan of the dangers of the coming storm. He took off his helmet and hung it on the saddle, knowing he should find shelter. Rain gusted down over his face. Shielding his eyes, he watched the road.

Soon he saw a group of riders approach, fifty and more warden's men, their helmets and breastplates and lances glimmering. A few lanterns sputtered like small golden stars in the black rain. In a crack of lightning, the riders looked like a demon's army.

Rowan narrowed his eyes and saw Simon clearly enough in the lead, his swarthy, wide face grim under the light of a torch. The warden and his troopers were returning to Abermuir, Rowan realized. Either the weather or the uproar following Iain's escape had caused the wardens to cancel the truce meeting. They had reached this point by a far more direct route than he had taken by following Alec and Iain.

He wiped his face again to clear the rain from his vision. Thunder exploded among the clouds, and the wind battered him. Rain sluiced down, hard and cold, beating on his head and his shoulders, soaking his jack and breeches. He ignored it and watched the warden's escort, tiny figures lit by flickering golden light. They followed the fork in the road that led to Abermuir.

And then Rowan noticed that Simon rode beside the small, dark figure of a woman in a black cloak, on a black horse, hardly visible in the darkness and the rain. But he saw the pure oval curve of her face turn up in the darkness, and look toward the outcrop where he sat.

Mhairi. His heart pounded and his hands clenched the reins. Simon had her, and was taking her to Abermuir. She had either succeeded in becoming a pledge—or she had been forced into it.

He bellowed a wordless protest. The bay turned anxiously, rearing to his back feet, pawing the air. Mhairi appeared to be going docilely, willingly. But all of his instincts clutched and roiled in his gut. She was in great danger. Rowan knew it as surely as he felt the rain on his face.

"Mhairi!" he screamed. *"Nay!"*

Rain burst out of the clouds with tremendous strength. Thunder crashed, and lightning split the black sky like a glowing, delicate, deadly vein.

He swore, and spun Valentine, urging him down the slope toward the moor that led to the road. He felt a wild, desperate panic as he struck out across the moor.

Then he pulled back quickly as Valentine nickered, slowed, and balked. The moor was boggy from rain, saturated and treacherous. Rowan would have to ride cautiously to avoid the dangerous pits of muck hidden in the dark, or he would have to turn and take another, longer route.

Lightning broke white through the sky, illuminating the moor, the road, the old castle on its lonely hill. Rowan stopped to control the horse as the bay whinnied and rose up on his back legs. "Mhairi! Nay!" he yelled.

He saw Mhairi turn back, saw a flashing glimpse of her face, illuminated by flares and lightning. Then she vanished into darkness and glinting rain.

"Mhairi!" he bellowed. His throat was raw, his lungs burned. He urged the horse forward, and shouted again. The sound echoed, desperate and anguished, and was lost in thunder.

Mhairi looked back over her shoulder, while rain pounded on her hooded head and water slipped into her eyes and down her cheeks. She could hardly distinguish hot tears from cold rain.

Shivering violently, she pulled her sodden cloak around her and kept gazing behind her, though she could not see him any longer. But she thought his shouts still rose strong and desperate above the thunder and the thudding rhythms of rain and hoofbeats.

The vision that she had seen in the black stone, that Iain had seen in the calm surface of a puddle, had come into reality before her eyes. Moments ago, she had looked up to see Rowan silhouetted on a craggy hilltop in the midst of the furious storm. A white burst of lightning had illuminated his face, far off on that high perch.

And she had heard him shout her name with a fury and a desperation that had brought answering tears to her eyes, and had chilled her soul.

All she saw now was the glint of slanting rain in the darkness. She turned back, her hands trembling on Peg's reins.

"He willna come for you now," Simon growled beside her. "Nae across that bog, nor wi' all these men surrounding you. I'll send word to your Black Laird to inform him o' his orders from me. He's my deputy, after all. If he wants to gain you back, he'll bring me Iain Macrae and Alec Scott."

"Simon, let me go," she said. "Please."

He laughed. "You once asked if I would accept you as a pledge for Iain, lass. Well, here you are. When I took you from the truce day field, I told you that your time to act as a pledge had come. 'Tis what you wanted, after all. If Rowan Scott wants you, lass, he will fetch his brother and yours quick enough, and barter them for you."

She bowed her head and said nothing. The image of Rowan in the storm, lightning flashing around him, stayed in her mind. Iain had feared that the vision foreboded his own death. She knew, now, that he had been right. Rowan had set that in motion. And she had failed to stop it from happening.

She tucked her chin down and tightened her jaw against the fear that gathered strength within her. Iain had escaped, but the vision would complete itself now that it had begun. Iain would be captured, and that would lead to his execution.

Her brother had predicted that the man who rode through a ferocious storm to find her would bring danger to her and to Iain. And she had married that man. By committing her heart and her soul to him, she had brought the disaster closer.

She knew that Simon meant to offer Rowan a barter: Mhairi's freedom for the capture and custody of Iain and Alec. Mhairi had no doubt that Rowan would find both of them quickly.

But the choice that lay ahead of him was a bitter one.

Chapter Twenty-six

~

"Away, away, thou traytor strang!
Out of my sicht thou mayst sune be!
I grantit nevir a traytors lyfe,
And now I'll not begin with thee."

—*"Johnnie Armstrong"*

"Rowan! Hold!" Hearing the shout and the thud of hoofbeats behind him, Rowan spun around to see a group of riders coming toward him through the darkness and the rain. Recognizing Jock in the lead, he waited until they halted in front of him.

"Simon has Mhairi," he told Jock. His grandfather nodded as he reined in his horse. Rowan saw Sandie and Christie behind him, alongside Archie Pringle and Geordie Bell.

"Aye, we know," Jock answered. "And we know that Alec took Iain as well. Mhairi saw it happen, and saw you ride off after them. She came to find us, in the midst of the chaos after Tammie Armstrong took the football. The March wardens are furious. Simon is convinced that Tammie was in league wi' Alec in the escape, and he's named Tammie an outlaw again. And he sent his troopers in pursuit o' Alec and Iain, but lost them."

"I lost them too," Rowan said. "But I'm sure they came north toward Blackdrummond."

Jock nodded as if he was not surprised. "The wardens called off the rest o' the truce meeting just as we left. That was when Simon Kerr took Mhairi. None could stop him."

"I'll stop him," Rowan said grimly.

"He wouldna dare to hurt her," Jock said. "Every Scott

and Armstrong, aye, and every Kerr, in this March would have cause to feud wi' him if he did."

"He willna have a chance to harm her," Rowan said. "I will have her out of there this night. He willna take my wife for a prisoner." He gathered the reins.

"Rowan, hold." Jock paused. "Simon has taken Mhairi as a legal pledge in her brother's place. He intends to keep her in his custody, and he plans to escort her to the English warden to serve Iain's fate. He said that she offered to be a pledge. I doubt that, but—"

"Dinna doubt it," Rowan muttered. "What more did he say?"

Archie stepped his horse forward. "Simon sent me out to find you and give you your orders as deputy."

"Well?" Rowan snapped.

"You are to bring Alec and Iain to Abermuir, alive or laid out, Simon doesna care. Bring them by downing of the sun tomorrow, or he says your wife will be taken to Carlisle."

Rowan gripped the reins tightly, staring at Archie. Valentine nickered and shifted beneath him. "They're still riding," he said decisively. "I'll get her back now."

"Nay," Archie said. "She's guarded by fifty men and more on the road, and a hundred more at Abermuir. You willna win her free out here on the moorland, and in this blasted rain."

"Here and now is best as I see it," Rowan said coldly.

"Simon has a legal right to hold her as a pledge," Archie said. "If you take her, or attack him, you're on the wrong side o' the law, and he remains in the right. You'll be outlawed wi' your brother. Find Alec and Iain. Simon will let her go then."

Rowan stared at him, his heart pounding. "You are asking me to betray both my brother and hers," he growled low.

Archie looked at him evenly. "I know. I'm sorry for it."

"Rowan." Geordie came forward. "Simon has the right to keep Mhairi as a pledge as long as those men are not found. But Henry Forster likely will not accept her in Iain's place. Pledging is peculiar to Scots law."

"Are you saying that I should wait until Simon takes

her to Carlisle, and then take her back if Forster refuses her?"

Geordie shrugged. "You may have no choice."

"I have a choice. I'll take her back from Simon on my own terms—if I have to take Abermuir apart stone by stone to do it."

"By hell, lad," Jock said. "Your horse is weary. Have some sense. You need a hot meal and dry clothing."

"You sound like Anna," Rowan said. Jock mumbled something and rubbed his white-whiskered chin.

"Your grandsire is right," Sandie said. "Get dry first. Then perhaps we'll all go visit the warden, hey." He looked at Archie. "If you mean to go off and tell your warden that, by God, I'll make you a prisoner here and now. There must be someone who'd pay good ransom for you."

Archie smiled dryly. "None, I think. But I'll ride with the lot o' you." He looked at Rowan. "What Simon has done here isna right. I willna act as his deputy in this."

"I'll ride with you as well," Geordie said.

"My thanks." Rowan nodded to both men. "We'll go to Blackdrummond. Perhaps Alec and Iain have gone there."

"I doubt they'll be waiting by the hearth," Christie said.

"Where do you think they've gone?" Rowan asked.

Christie shrugged. "Iain has a wife and a new son to see, and Alec has wee Jamie. They'll seek out their kin, I think, but they'll do it wi' caution, after the wardens and the troopers have given up looking for them for the night and have gone home. They'll hide until then."

"He's right. But where?" Jock asked, frowning.

"After we're warm and fed, we'll think on it," Sandie said. "Come ahead, then."

Rowan sat thoughtfully while the others turned their horses toward the road. "You go on. I willna be long."

Jock looked at him, his gaze keen even through the darkness. "Be wary o' the phantoms that ride this road, lad."

"I will, sir." Rowan touched his fingers to his helmet brim. "If there are ghosts here, be sure I will find them."

Jock watched him, then nodded and rode away with the others. Rowan urged Valentine forward and headed for the Lincraig hill.

Dismounting quietly in the yard outside Lincraig's chapel, Rowan led his horse into the dark interior of the ruined building. He patted the glossy neck while the bay lowered his head to nibble at the grasses between the fallen stones.

Rowan looked around the chapel through shadows and rain, seeing only the vague black and pale shapes of the collapsed stones that littered the floor. He moved forward with cautious steps, his eyes adjusting to the thick darkness. When he reached the entrance to the small corridor at the back of the chapel, he stood by the doorway and listened.

He heard only the rain, pattering in delicate layers over stone and earth. Only rain, and profound silence.

No voices, no other noise. But he knew they were here. He felt it in his gut, like a rope pulled tight. He stepped toward the stairs that led to the crypt, and began to descend slowly.

As he neared the crypt, he smelled the faint odor of smoke, as if a flame had been recently extinguished. The silence here had a new depth, a vital quality, as if someone listened, or hid in the shadows.

"Alec"—he spoke in a low, easy tone—"I thought you didna like to come into the crypt."

There was a long moment of quiet. "Och, well, I've grown up, then," a deep, mellow voice replied. "Greetings, Rowan. Have you come to arrest us?"

"Perhaps," Rowan answered as he stepped down into the chamber. A spark flickered from a scraped flint, and he smelled fresh smoke as Alec lit a candle. Rowan ducked his head to allow for the curve of the low vaulted ceiling, and moved toward the stone tombs that filled the middle space.

Alec stood beside the center tomb sculpture, watching him warily. Iain stood beside him and set the lit candlestick on top of the tomb, near the feet. The faint golden light cast flickering shadows around the small chamber.

Rowan stepped forward. His heart thundered inside his chest, his mouth was dry, his hands trembled as he faced his brother over the stone effigy.

"Alec," he said softly.

"Rowan." Alec tipped his head in greeting, black hair sliding along his dark-whiskered cheek. "You saw our horses, then, inside the corner tower."

"I didna see them," Rowan said.

"Then how did you know we were here?" Iain asked.

Rowan kept his gaze directed at his brother. "I knew," he said simply. "I had a sense there were ghosts in this place."

Alec smiled, a wry pinch of his lips that Rowan knew well. His eyes crinkled, and the candlelight showed the brilliant color in his hazel eyes, deep green and brown ringed together. He had not shaved for days, and his beard stubble was dark and thick over the squared jaw and handsomely shaped chin. He shoved a hand through his unkempt black hair and smiled again, ruefully.

"Ghosts, aye," he said. "Say boo to my brother, Iain."

Iain nodded briefly and silently to Rowan. His gaze, silvery gray and keen, and so like Mhairi's, seemed to assess Rowan's intention.

Rowan looked steadily at Alec, giving no hint of the turmoil inside as his blood pounded in his head and his heart hammered. He fisted one hand to bring himself under control.

"What are your orders?" Alec asked. "I assume the warden has sent his deputies and most of his troopers out looking for us. Do you mean to bring us back to enjoy the warden's fine sense of justice?"

Rowan stared at him silently. Outside, thunder roared and he heard heavy rain pound against the upper stone wall, gusting through the cracks. He placed one hand slowly on the cool stone sculpture that separated them, and realized that the figure was Lady Isobel Scott. A cruel irony, he thought, to have the tomb of a dead woman between them now.

He glanced again at Alec, and then suddenly reached out, with force and speed, and grabbed his brother's loose shirt, pulling him forward over the tomb.

"We have matters to discuss," he said with fierce precision. "Then we will consider my orders."

Alec watched him, leaning over the tomb, breathing hard. But his expression showed no fear, and his hazel eyes never wavered. Behind him, Iain's gaze flickered from one man to the other, while he kept still and tense.

"Three years," Rowan said. "For three years I have thought about what you did to me. I wanted to come and find you, I've wanted to ask why you did such a thing. But I knew the answer—a coward's deed, to take my betrothed as you did, while I was helpless to win her back from you." He dragged Alec closer, his fist tightening on the shirt, his knuckles white, his breath hard and fast. "You betrayed me. And even when I was free to find you, I did naught. Naught. But I havena forgotten it. I canna forgive it."

"You stayed away from Blackdrummond when you were freed from prison," Alec said huskily. "You didna come to find me."

"I didna come back," Rowan said, "because I feared I would kill you."

The silence in the crypt grew heavy, saturated with unspoken thoughts, with anger, with resentment. With some other emotion that caused Rowan to suddenly release Alec's shirt, stepping back, tensing his opened hand in the air.

"I feared I would kill you," he repeated softly.

Alec straightened, staring at him beneath lowered brows, his eyes darkened, inward. "I regret that Maggie and I didna explain this to you," he said. "But I canna regret what we did."

"Maggie died, man," Rowan said in a hushed, tormented whisper. "She died. I never had the chance to see her again, to speak with her. And you—you have a son o' this. A bonny son."

His voice nearly broke on the last word. Grief and anger flooded through him, and he swallowed its bitterness again, as he had always done. He wanted to know more, and yet did not want to hear more. But if he did not clear this demon from him, he would never find peace.

"Maggie wanted it that way," Alec said softly. He touched the tomb sculpture with long, gentle fingers, resting his hand over the lady's folded, serene hands. "She asked me to keep all this from you. I didna agree, but finally I said her aye. She was a sweet lass, was Maggie," he added. "A man might do anything to see that smile."

Rowan stared at him. "Sweet, aye," he drawled skeptically. "What did she want to keep from me? That she didna love me, as she had promised, but loved you instead? That 'twas easier to wed the man who was there, than wait for the man who wasna? That she would rather wed an innocent man than a guilty one?"

"Nay. She knew you went to prison for me."

"And yet she wed you."

Alec looked at the effigy's cool, still face. "After your trial, Henry Forster sent word that you were to be executed as soon as the gallows were built. He sent your belongings home, but for what you wore, and told us to make arrangements to fetch the corpse. Maggie came to me then and asked me to marry her."

"You couldna wait until the body was returned and buried?" Rowan asked sarcastically. "Maggie and I were handfasted, after all. I would have expected loyalty from both of you."

Alec flickered a glance toward him, then away. "She pleaded wi' me. I—I couldna deny her. We were wed the next day."

"Why?" Rowan asked harshly.

Alec raised his gaze to Rowan. "To give your son a father."

Rowan felt as if Alec had landed a blow directly to his heart. He almost stepped back at the silent impact.

"Jamie?" he asked, nearly whispering.

Alec nodded. "She didna want you to know, after we heard you would live. She said, what would be the use o' that, and only hurting you more? She was so happy that you were alive, but she was deeply upset that we had hurt you without intention."

Rowan blew out a breath and shoved his fingers wildly through his hair, looking at the placid, beautiful stone face of the woman in the fluttering light, looking back at his brother.

"Without intention, Rowan," Alec repeated. "I'm sorry."

Rowan drew a deep breath. "Jamie is my son? You are sure?"

"Aye," Alec said gently. "Aye."

Rowan, still stunned, let out another long breath. "Do Anna and Jock know?"

Alec shook his head. "Maggie didna want anyone to know the mistake we had made. I wonder if Anna suspects it. But we let everyone believe that we—" He paused.

"That you were cold in the heart?" Rowan asked. Alec shrugged. "Oh God," Rowan said. He sighed. "Dear God. I owe you an apology, Alec. I thought, all this time . . ." He did not finish. What he thought was obvious. He saw the understanding in the faces of the two men who watched him.

"You were imprisoned for my crime, Rowan. 'Twas my obligation to watch over Maggie and your child." Alec held out his hand, and Rowan took it, wrapping his grip tightly around his brother's fingers. "We are brothers, Rowan. Kin. I would never betray you. Never."

Rowan nodded, hardly able to speak as he looked at his brother. Then he glanced at Iain, who watched them silently.

And he suddenly realized that the loyalty that Mhairi had always shown to Iain, the trust that he himself had lost when he thought Alec had betrayed him, still existed in his life, and had been there all along.

The feeling nearly overwhelmed him. He pulled in a deep, steadying breath and grasped Alec's hand over the stone tomb.

"Aye, kin," he said in a gruff, low voice.

"Aye." Alec smiled. "Aye. Now, brother, we do have urgent matters to discuss with you, about spies and gold." Iain nodded and murmured his agreement.

At this abrupt reminder of his other task, Rowan stepped back and leaned against the tomb behind him, folding his arms over his chest as if to protect his newly exposed feelings. He had so much to think about, so much to talk to Alec about, that his mind and emotions were whirling. But all that must wait. Mhairi's life was in danger. He had to act soon on his plan.

"I'll hear your tale," he said. "But first, know that Simon Kerr has ordered me to bring you back to his tower. He means to send you both to Carlisle and let the English deal with you." He looked evenly at them. "Simon is holding Mhairi as a pledge for your necks. When you are brought in to him, she will be freed."

"Jesu," Iain muttered. "He wants you to barter us for her."

"'Tis what he expects. But 'tisna what I have planned."

"What will you do?" Alec asked sharply.

"I canna say yet. I want some answers first. If you're guilty, either I will take you down, or someone else will," he said grimly. "But if you're innocent, then I want proof of it."

Alec and Iain exchanged rapid, wary glances.

"You can tell me now, privately, or you can tell all of us at Blackdrummond," Rowan said. "Simon's other deputy is there, as is an English deputy. You did me a kindness, brother, when I thought you had played me false." He looked evenly at Alec. "But I willna hesitate to take you down, here and now, if you have committed treason."

"Simon holds Mhairi pledge," Iain said. "That gives you a reason to capture us. But why do you care about the rest of it? You were notorious yourself, long before you were a deputy."

Rowan nodded to acknowledge a fair question. "I was sent here by the council to pursue Scottish spies who took some Spanish gold from a shipwreck. I know now that Heckie Elliot and his brother are among them. But there is more to it."

"We know about Heckie," Alec said. "We've been blamed for his crimes in some o' this."

"Mhairi believes that Iain, at least, is clean, and she thinks Alec may be clean as well." Rowan smiled, flat and brief. "For myself, I canna yet say. But I promised her that I would find the truth." He drew a breath and sighed it out. "But the English queen will ask for my head on a pikestaff if the gold isna found in full and the spies discovered. I am, after all, notorious in English eyes, and the brother of an accused spy." He raised an eyebrow and looked at Alec.

Alec glanced at Iain, and said nothing.

"So tell me, lads," Rowan said. "Where did you acquire that Spanish gold that Simon found?"

"We only had it in our hands less than an hour when Simon took it," Alec said. "Iain and I rode out together one night to follow some English reivers who had snatched Blackdrummond cattle. We did that, and were crossing the border into Scotland wi' our cattle when we met Heckie Elliot and his gang. They ambushed us, but we turned on them wi' guns, and the beasts panicked and chased them, and they ran. We captured Heckie's packhorse. There were two large sacks strapped on it."

"We saw the gold, and were muckle pleased, thinking we had taken Heckie's own horde," Iain continued. He laughed a little. "Though we knew Heckie would be back for it. But soon after that, Simon took me down wi' the gold. Alec got away. I learned later 'twas Spanish stuff."

"Two large sacks?" Rowan asked. "Two? What was in them?"

"We hardly saw, before Simon appeared and took it all."

"I wondered what Scottish reivers were doing wi' Spanish gold," Alec said. "I knew what 'twas when I saw it, though Iain didna. I went into hiding so that I could try to find out the truth o' the matter. See, there is more. We had found a letter in one o' the sacks, which I kept. 'Twas in Spanish."

Rowan drew his brows together. "Full o' nonsense?"

Alec shrugged. "I dinna know. 'Twas in Spanish. I couldna read it, but I went back to Iain's house and hid it in his loft, meaning to come back for it in a day or two. I never got the chance, for Simon had troopers searching for me everywhere."

"Mhairi told me that she had found the letter," Iain said.

"I have it now," Rowan replied. "Tell me this—why should I believe any of your tale? Found this, stumbled on that." He folded his arms and looked narrowly at his brother. "There is a muckle load of evidence against you both."

Alec blew out a heavy breath. "The council sent you out here to follow spies?" he asked. "As a deputy?"

Rowan nodded once. "They did."

"Last year, the council sent a man to offer me a barter. He said if I acted as the king's agent, they would guarantee your release. I agreed."

"That was why I was pardoned?" Rowan asked, astonished.

"Aye. And the privy council gave you that first post in the East March. I acted as a land sergeant to Simon

Kerr for a while," Alec went on. "I began to suspect that
Heckie and his brothers were linked to something un-
scrupulous, and I began to follow them. Archie Pringle
was helping me. He's a trustworthy man. He sent two letters to the council about the matter."

"And while I was in Abermuir, Archie did his best to
help me when he could," Iain said.

"A few months ago," Alec continued, "Simon dismissed me from my post. He would have dismissed
Archie too, but Archie's father is a powerful man."

"Around that time, Heckie began demanding rent from
Alec and me," Iain said. "Simon didna do much to stop
him."

"I've noticed that myself," Rowan said. "I've noticed
other things as well. Go on. Is there more?"

"We've told you what we know," Iain said. "We are the
last ones who would be spies against Scotland. I hope you
know that, Rowan Scott."

Rowan regarded them thoughtfully. "Perhaps the
raven's moon could tell us something about this matter."

They looked at him blankly. "Moon? 'Tis still raining, I
think," Alec said.

Rowan saw that neither of them had ever heard the
phrase. He smiled. "I think I owe you another apology,
Alec. And you, Iain. I suspected you both of treachery. I
was wrong," he added quietly. He offered his hand, and
each man gripped it in turn.

Alec looked around. "This is a cold place, full of ghosts
and memories. I never liked it here much as a lad." He
looked at Rowan. "Let's go home. I long for some hot
food—though I think we will all have to down some of
Anna's cream posset if we come back as wet and filthy as
we are."

Rowan chuckled softly in agreement, and blew out the
candle as Alec and Iain turned to climb the steps.

As he went up behind them, he stopped and looked
down into the shadowed crypt. He had always liked the
solace and peace that seemed to exist here. Now, the blend
of silence and rain formed a quiet, tranquil atmosphere.

He drew a breath, and took a little of that peace with
him as he ascended the steps.

Chapter Twenty-seven

~

Ay through time, ay through time,
Ay through time was he, lady,
Filled was wi' sweet revenge
On a' his enemys, lady.

—*"Rob Roy"*

"Scumfishing," Sandie said. "That's what we'll do."
He sat back with an air of finality, and looked at the others. Jock, Christie, and Geordie, seated at the trestle table in the great hall of Blackdrummond, stared at him. Alec, Archie, and Iain, who stood near the hearth, also turned to stare at him. Rowan, seated in a chair by the hearth, grimaced to himself.

"Scumfishing?" Jock repeated. "In the warden's tower? Are you daft?"

"Practical," Sandie pronounced. "We'll go to Abermuir now, while 'tis still dark, and send smoking torches into the windows, and smoke them scum out o' there. Scumfishing. 'Tis a fine Border custom. Jock and I did it many times, hey." He grinned.

"Och, we havena cleared a tower wi' smoke for years, man," Jock grumbled. "There are better ways now."

Archie shrugged. "None more direct than that, I'll admit. But I wouldna recommend it for a March warden's tower."

"And what o' Mhairi?" Christie asked. "She isna scum, but she's in there wi' the warden."

"True," Rowan said. "Mhairi is the reason we have agreed to breach Abermuir. Scumfishing flushes everyone out. We only want to remove Mhairi, without disturbing anyone's rest. Although I will stop to say a few words to Simon," he added.

"You willna bring him the prisoners he requested, then?" Archie asked.

"He willna have to. We'll be there," Iain said.

"Are you part o' this, Archie Pringle?" Rowan asked.

The other deputy nodded. "I am. Simon has pushed my good nature too far."

"And you, Geordie Bell?"

Geordie looked up from the page he was reading. "I've been a March deputy for three years. I'm a bit weary of all my fine, lawful behavior." He grinned.

Rowan nodded. "Then we're agreed. We'll fetch Mhairi from her duties as a pledge, and I'll have a wee talk with Simon."

"And then we'll find Heckie Elliot, and this matter o' spies should be over by tomorrow," Christie said.

"If we can find Heckie," Archie said.

Anna crossed the room from a corner table, where she had poured a cup of milk for Jamie. She held him now by the hand, and paused by the hearth. "And when will you sleep?" she asked. "'Tis barely past full dark. Rest for a few hours, all of you, and go out a couple of hours before dawn."

"She's right," Rowan said. "They'll be asleep at Abermuir by then." He smiled as Jamie toddled toward him. "Hey, lad," he said softly. He stared at the child, hardly able to drink in all of that wonder, his own son. He held out his hand.

Jamie walked past him and went toward Alec, whose eyes brightened. But Jamie toddled past him as well, and held up his arms. "Jock," he said. "Jock."

Jock chuckled and lifted the child to his lap. "Hey, laddie, you should be asleep."

"He'll not sleep with all this commotion," Anna grumbled. "Here, do not give him that dirty old thing, Jock," she said.

Jock looked up after handing Jamie the black mirror that had been lying on the table. "He just wants to see his face."

Rowan exchanged a glance with Anna, and then shrugged. The child would come to no harm by looking in the polished stone. He watched as Jamie stared into the stone for a few moments, then pressed his nose against it and gave it a smacking kiss. Rowan laughed softly and turned away.

Geordie looked over his shoulder. "Rowan. Come here and look at this."

Rowan went to the bench and sat beside Geordie, a little away from the others. "What have you found?" he asked.

"I've seen letters like this before. A few months ago, the queen's spymaster sent a man to meet with the English warden, an English agent who understood codes and ciphers well. He taught me some of the simple ones that the Spanish use."

"What does it say?"

"I have not worked all of it out yet, but enough to have a good idea. Roses are often a code for coin and bribes. Red roses mean gold, white means documents, passes, deeds, that sort of thing. The beautiful lady—I'm still working on that, but I think 'tis whoever is to receive the gold and the documents."

"And the moon that is mentioned there?" Rowan asked.

"The entire phrase is there more than once, and means 'raven's moon.' " Geordie looked up at him. "The letter says that the white rose will blossom in the raven's moon."

Rowan wrinkled his brow. "Sounds like utter nonsense. But the black stone must be this raven's moon."

"We have to assume that. Heckie wants something that you have quite badly, and that mirror is the only thing you have from the Spanish shipwreck. 'Tis black, and round, and might be described as a raven-black moon. A letter such as this would not refer to it as a round black stone mirror," Geordie said wryly. "This letter may have been intended to inform this Scotsman, whoever he is, that the raven's moon was going to arrive on the ship with the gold."

"We found no documents, if those are white roses," Rowan said. "But such things would easily be lost in a shipwreck."

"There is no writing on the thing, no inscription? No design?" Geordie asked. "Let's look at it again."

Rowan held out his hand toward Jamie. "Give it here, mie lad," he said. "Please."

"Na." Jamie hugged the mirror to his chest. "Mine."

Geordie rolled his eyes in amusement and went back to rusing the letter. "Hopefully I'll have time to decipher e rest before we go," he murmured.

"Let's set our plans, then," Rowan said to the others.

Anna lifted Jamie from Jock's lap. "Time for sleep, ee one," she said gently. Jamie shook his head vehe-ently and clung to Jock. Anna pried him loose and egan to carry him away. Jamie protested, kicking out, d the black stone mirror fell to the floor.

Rowan watched it hit, saw the frame splinter and crack. omething small and pale, folded several times, slipped t from inside the frame.

He leaned over and swiped it off the floor, turning it in s hand, thoughtfully, carefully, his fingers trembling.

"What is it?" Jock asked. Rowan was aware that all of em in the room—with the exception of Jamie, who cried r his mirror—stared at him in stunned silence.

Rowan unfolded the page and saw immediately the amped Spanish words there. "Ah," he said. "This is why ey wanted the raven's moon." He handed the page to eordie.

"That must be our white rose," Geordie said.

Mhairi sat on a stone seat beneath one of the windows at flanked the wide fireplace at Abermuir, and looked t at the night sky. The rain had finally ended, and a ight crescent moon now sailed high and clear over the udding remnants of the storm clouds.

An hour or more had passed since Simon had left her one in this huge room, posting a silent trooper outside e arched doorway. Only a sullen serving maid had come since then to give her a bowl of soup and pour out a agon of wine. The soup had been watery, but the wine d been quite good, dark red and vibrant, and Mhairi had pped at it until she had finished it. The warmth coursing rough her now was partly due to that heady wine, and rtly due to the fire in the hearth.

Weary but unable to rest, she looked out the window. ch time she closed her eyes the image of Rowan out on

the crag in the lightning and the rain still haunted he
thoughts. She did not think that Rowan would betray h
own brother, or hers, in spite of the past. She did n
know what would happen by the end of this night.

But she sensed it coming in the wind that pushed th
last dark scraps of the storm past the moon. She felt th
threat and the danger, and she shivered.

She was tired, and did not know if she would sleep in
bedchamber or in a dungeon this night. Some pledge
were confined hospitably for years; others were kept
wretched circumstances; still others, she knew, we
released on their own avowal. She simply did not kno
what Simon intended for her.

Bowing her head, she sighed. When she heard the do
open at the far end of the room, she turned to see Simo
enter. His booted feet thudded on the wooden floorboard
as he came toward her, and he paused to look out th
window. His steel breastplate took on a reddish glint fro
the fire, and she saw that he wore his helmet still, as if h
had just come inside, or intended to go out again.

She wondered if he planned to ride in pursuit of Rowa
and Alec and Iain, and she swallowed the surge of drea
that rose in her throat.

"The sky is clearing," Simon said. "There have bee
too many o' these demon storms lately. Thunder an
lightning this late in the year is unusual. Some say suc
storms are an omen."

"An omen of what?" Mhairi rose to her feet.

He looked at her, his dark eyes flat, his square ja
whiskered and swarthy. "The kirk ministers say thos
storms are Jehovah's wrath. We should all beware. Th
end o' the world is coming." His nostrils flared, and h
eyes shifted.

Mhairi took a step backward. "'Tis just poor weather.

"Disastrous weather. Storms, floods, fires, all com
when God decides to destroy the world." He reached pa
her and slammed the shutter. "We'll see more rain befor
dawn."

"'Tis late," she said. "I am tired. You havena shown m
to my room." She lifted her chin. "Or do you mean
keep me in your dungeon?" She had asked Rowan th
same question once, and caught her breath against th

memory; the yearning that followed the thought nearly brought tears to her eyes.

"Dungeon?" Simon chuckled as he poured himself a full flagon of the red wine. "Nay, I willna put a woman in a dungeon, particularly a cousin o' mine. I'm nae ogre, lass, though you may think it. Though you're nae the sweet lassie I thought you were, hey." He sipped the wine and regarded her thoughtfully. "But I'll keep you here as a guest."

"Guests may leave when they choose."

"Mm," he conceded, swallowing. "Well, then, you're here as an honored pledge. Though you dinna deserve honor," he added. "I've ordered the serving lass to prepare the second bedchamber, next to my own." He looked at her over the edge of his cup.

She felt sick inside. "How long will you keep me here?"

"Until I get Alec Scott and Iain Macrae. The council has charged me wi' finding the spies who took that Spanish gold."

"They're not the men you seek," she said quickly.

"Nay? Who is then?"

"Find Heckie Elliot," she said. "Then you'll have your spy. And he knows who else is involved."

He narrowed his eyes. "Heckie Elliot is a petty sneak-bait and a common reiver. A troublemaker, but nae spy."

"'Tis true," she insisted. "Heckie is in league with this spy ring. I'm surprised you dinna suspect him already."

He watched her intently. "I see your scheme. You want me to go after Heckie and leave your brother be."

"There is proof. Rowan will swear to it, and prove it."

"Damn Blackdrummond. D'you think I would trust his avowal? He's a notorious ruffian. No one would believe him."

"Many would," she said. "Most would. Simon, my brother had naught to do with this. He told me. And he tried to tell you."

"Lass, you're too soft on your kin." He set down his cup and walked toward her. "I took you as a pledge because I suspect those men, and I want them in my custody. The council expects me to turn over the gold and the spies to England. I never meant harm to you in this, lass.

But your criminal behavior leaves me nae choice but to take you in my custody as well. Your husband's reiving comrades prevented me from arresting you by their clever avowals. Very well. But I can keep you as a pledge, as long as I like. Though I willna harm you, lass," he said quietly, and laid his hand on her shoulder.

She tensed away from him. "I've given you the name of the man responsible. Once I thought you were a fair man, Simon."

"Hah," he said. "Once I thought you were a bonny sweet lassie. Good enough to wed my own nephew. But you're like many o' your kind, strong-willed as a man, and spiteful wi' it. But I'll get what I want, your brother and Alec Scott. And you."

She felt his heavy hand on the back of her hair now, felt his thick fingers on her neck. Her skin crawled. "Rowan willna betray his own brother and mine, even for his wife."

"He'll betray whom he likes. He comes from a riding family o' notorious outlaws and murderers. Sneakbait thieves, all."

"They're reivers," she said, and held up her head proudly. "There is a difference."

Simon grumbled a curse. "Rowan is my deputy," he said. "He has his orders. He will do what I have told him, if he wants you." His fingers stroked her neck and shoulders. Repulsive shivers ran through her. "Why did you wed him? What can he offer you? I'm the warden. You knew I would have helped you. But you had to go out on those foolish night rides, and you ruined all that I had in mind for you. And you had to follow that notorious reiver." He paused, his hand running the length of her arm. "I've been a widower a long time. I had my eye on you myself after Johnny died. But he'd be ashamed o' you now, lass."

"He would be proud." She stepped abruptly away from him. "And you never had it in mind to help me, only yourself."

He began to speak, but the door opened, and Hepburn beckoned to Simon. He went to the door, murmured with Hepburn, and returned.

"I have a wardenry to attend to," he said brusquely. "I

must meet wi' someone. You and I will talk later. Come
this way." He took her arm and led her toward the wide,
high hearth built in the end wall. Mhairi blinked in surprise when he led her around the side of the deep fireplace. In the shadows behind the fireplace was a small
door. Through there, built into the thickness of the wall, a
short stairway led upward.

"My bedchamber is up here," he explained, leading the
way. Mhairi climbed behind him in the dark, warm recess
of the enclosed staircase. As she went up, she noticed a
tiny window in the chimney wall, and wondered vaguely
why someone would design a window to look into a
chimney.

Simon opened the door at the top of the stairs and held
it wide. Mhairi passed him and entered a large, firelit bedchamber.

"You'll be comfortable here. I'll come up later, hey,"
he said, a smooth threat. Then he shut the door hastily.
She heard a key turn in the lock.

He had trapped her. Alarmed, she ran to the door and
pulled on the iron latch. The handle gave easily under the
pressure. Simon had been too hurried to make certain the
door was secured.

She opened the door slowly, wincing as she heard it
creak. Stepping out onto the top stair in the shadows, she
stood there for several moments, listening to the muffled
tones as Simon spoke to another man. The second voice
sounded familiar, and she frowned in concentration as she
crept down the staircase.

As she went, she noticed again the tiny grated window
in the chimney wall. A thin drift of smoke floated out, and
a little light. She lifted on her toes a little, smothering a
cough as she looked into the opening.

The inside of the chimney was visible, but Mhairi also
had a clear view of the great chamber beyond; an identical
opening was situated in the chimney wall opposite the
window. She had noticed it earlier, and thought it was a
decorative carving in the high stone hood that fronted the
fireplace.

Together the windows formed a spyhole. Mhairi had
heard of such things, but had never actually seen one. She
stood on her toes and peered through the grate.

Simon's back was to her. He faced a man who was cloaked and hooded; Mhairi could not see his face in the low light.

"I heard about what happened at the truce meeting," the man said. He laughed harshly. "A disaster, hey?"

"Aye," Simon barked. "And where were you? I expected you to deliver it to me. I paid you well. Where the devil is it?"

"You only paid me part o' what you promised. If you want that stone, then give me the rest o' my first payment."

Mhairi gasped as she recognized Heckie's voice. When he swept off his cloak and turned toward the table, sloshing wine into a cup, she saw him more clearly.

"I had to turn over some o' the gold to the English. Call it a tax," Simon said. "The rest is safe. You'll get paid."

"I want it now. I've done a muckle lot for you. I rode to Berwick and killed a man for that Spanish letter."

"Which you then lost," Simon barked. "The Spaniards had to send another messenger, and a risky thing that was, wi' that damned lass out on the road playing saint for her brother."

"I've collected black rent and cattle and sheep from those who were in disfavor wi' you, and I've given you a share in all that I snatched. Now I want what you owe me."

"You failed to do what I ordered. You lost that Spanish gold to those two rogues, along wi' that letter. I've had naught but trouble from that night. I should have hanged you."

"You need me. I took that gold off that beach for you, wi' deputies and wardens crawling nearby. And I've been to hell and back looking for that damned raven's moon."

"And I still lack the letter and the stone. Rowan Scott may well know by now that you and I are art and part in this, if he has found either." Simon cursed and turned toward the fire.

Mhairi listened, her heart thundering, her hands trembling against the wall. She had been a fool not to see that Simon was part of this. As often as he had threatened to go after Heckie, he had never caught him. And he had been far too eager to blame Iain and Alec on thin proof—

allowing them to be punished as a screen for him and Heckie. She watched in dread and fascination, and wondered if Rowan suspected any of this.

"I trusted a lackbrain reiver wi' a task that needed discretion," she heard Simon say next. "The council sent Rowan Scott to sniff out the truth. You've left him enough clues!"

"I'll get the stone," Heckie snapped. "And him."

"If you had come to the truce meeting, you could have taken him down then."

"Wi' all those Border officers there? Some o' them are honest, Simon, unlike you. I'd be taken down and hanged quick."

"I told you I would've made sure you were only fined. Now I'll have to tend to this myself. I have his wife here now. He'll come for her, and when he does, I'll kill him."

"If he has it wi' him," Heckie said.

"As long as I have his wife I will get what I want. I dinna need you any longer."

"Remember, I know what you've been up to, Sir Warden," Heckie sneered.

Simon still faced the fire. He quirked a brow. "Will you try to get black rent from me now, Heckie Elliot?" he asked smoothly. "I'll arrest you and hang you whenever I like."

"I'll send word to the council," Heckie said. "I'm a reiver, man. If I'm to hang, I'll hang. But you'll go wi' me."

Simon sipped the wine. "Very well. You've made your point. I'll give you something more for your trouble. But I want the black stone by tomorrow."

"Aye, then." Heckie turned to set his cup down. "How much?"

Simon watched the low fire, scowling. Mhairi drew in her breath, seeing the demonic glint in his eye, heightened by the red glow of the fire. She felt a heavy, awful spin of dread in her gut and sensed danger. She wanted to cry out, and did not dare.

Simon turned, flashing his dagger out of its sheath, raising his arm. He plunged the knife into Heckie's back from behind, and watched the man drop, writhing, to the floor.

Mhairi clapped her hand over her mouth in horror.

Simon kicked at the body, then threw Heckie's cloak over him. Mhairi stood on the steps, her heart pounding, her breath heaving as she stared through the little window.

Simon turned and looked directly up at the spyhole, and frowned. Then he came quickly toward the hidden staircase.

Mhairi spun on the step and raced up to Simon's bed-chamber, yanking open the door with trembling hands. She stumbled inside the room just as he thundered up the stairs.

She stood and faced him as he filled the doorway. "What did you see?" he demanded. "What did you hear?" He came toward her, his hands out, his face twisted with rage.

She ducked past him and ran out the door, flying so fast down the stairs that she nearly fell. Reaching the hall, she ran across its dim expanse, skirting around the dark form on the floor without looking at it.

Simon stomped after her. "Mhairi!" he roared. "Stop!"

She spun uncertainly in the middle of the room, remembering that Hepburn stood just outside the closed door. Seeing a small arched door in a far corner of the huge room, she raced toward it, her shoes thumping on the wood, her heart slamming in her chest. With no idea where the door led, she yanked on its handle, leaped over the threshold, and slammed the door behind her, heart pounding fiercely.

She was inside a narrow space, facing a set of dark, turning stairs that led upward. Faint moonlight lit the stairwell from a high window. She climbed upward rapidly, keeping a steadying hand on the walls that flanked the wheeling stairs.

Below, she heard Simon wrench open the door and come up the steps. Lighter and far quicker, she reached the top in moments, stepping out onto a wooden floor inside a small, bare stone room. Through two windows, moonlight spilled into the room.

She was in a watchtower. She remembered seeing Abermuir's round corner turrets, added on like after-thoughts to the angles of the tall, massive Border tower.

From up here, guards could see the countryside for miles around.

"Mhairi!" Simon's steps were heavy, louder, much closer.

She opened the small outside door and stepped out onto the roof.

Chapter Twenty-eight

~

She's turnd her right and roun about,
The tear was in her ee:
"How can I come to my true love,
Except I had wings to flee?"

—*"Johnie Scot"*

The wind pushed against her with unexpected force, billowing her skirt and tearing at her hair. Glancing around, she saw the pointed caps of the turrets, and the low parapet wall that surrounded the L-shaped plan of the roof. Hoping to slip back into the castle, she went toward another turret, but saw the gleam of a torch inside the half-open door. Guards were inside, but she feared they would listen to the warden and not to his pledge—or his prisoner. She turned away.

In the center of the flat roof floor, a pitched wooden roof thrust upward. The sloped sides glistened in the moonlight, damp from the earlier rain. Another structure had been added onto the ridge, a tiny house with its own identical roof, riding the larger one like a child on its parent's back. Mhairi guessed that this was a chimney house, built around the existing central chimney to provide shelter and warmth for watchmen.

Just as Simon shoved open the turret door, Mhairi ran toward the larger pitched roof, climbing the slant to reach the chimney house. The door gave easily, and she slipped inside, slamming it shut. Moonlight flowed in from two small windows, and she could see well enough to throw the door bar.

The room was only about six feet square, with a narrow wooden platform floor built around the peak of the larger roof, which jutted up inside. The wide chimney itself nearly filled the center space. Mhairi stepped backward and leaned against the warm chimney, breathing hard as she watched the door, waiting.

"Mhairi! Open up! I order you!"

The thumping beat of her heart measured every second until Simon pulled on the door handle, then pounded on the thick wood.

Mhairi stayed still, praying that the bar would hold, hoping he had no other way to get inside. She had gone into the chimney house without considering how or when she would get out. Now she watched the door through the dark, every heaving breath a new, wordless prayer for safety.

"Mhairi," Simon called through the door. "Come out, lassie. I willna hurt you. I only wanted to know if you saw that rascal Heckie attack me. I had to kill him to defend myself."

Mhairi gasped at the lie. Although she had always felt tense and uncomfortable around him, Simon was more selfish and grasping than she had ever realized. But she had given him her cautious trust because he was Johnny's uncle and her own distant kin, and because he had been appointed warden. She knew now that she had been wrong to ignore her instincts about him long ago.

Now she could only try to protect herself from him. She glanced around the cramped, dark house to look for a weapon.

A few lances stood upright in the corner, leaned against the wall. She ran there and hefted one in her hands, but its length was too difficult to manage in the awkward space.

Then she saw the pistol on the floor, glittering like newfound silver in the moonlight. She closed her hand around its heavy handle and realized that it was a wheellock, left by a guard who might return soon. Beside it on the slanted floor, she found a leather pouch that the same guard must have left behind. Inside were lead balls, gunpowder, and the tiny, essential key.

Although her hands trembled severely, she managed to load it and turn the metal key to wind the mechanism inside. Then she heard Simon slam against the door as if he meant to break it down. Sucking in an anxious breath, she lifted the gun in both hands and aimed it at the door.

Silence. The gun was heavy, and she could not hold it steady for long. She lowered it and jumped, startled, when Simon called her name from behind. She spun, and saw the glint of his steel bonnet and breastplate near the small window.

"Mhairi," he called, his voice too calm, too smooth. "If you willna come out, I can fish you out wi' smoke."

Mhairi aimed the pistol toward the window. The silence that followed was so thick and extended that she thought she would scream with frustration.

Then she realized that he had gone to fetch a smoking torch.

"Now that, my lads, is a reiving moon," Jock said. "The kind the Scotts have always liked best. White and clear, and nae too full to show all that we're doing out here."

Rowan glanced up. "Aye, for now. Those dark clouds in the distance will bring another storm before we are through here." He returned his gaze to the rugged, stark silhouette of Abermuir Tower. In one turret he saw the glimmer of torchlight.

"Then we'll hurry," Sandie said. "Scumfishing's quick."

"Nay," Rowan said firmly. "If we smoke them out, we will have a hundred troopers after us. And how would we find Mhairi?"

"She'd come running out wi' the rest," Sandie said.

"'Twould stir up more trouble than I'd like." He turned to Archie. "Where might he keep her?"

"I dinna think he'd put her in the dungeon," Archie said. "Perhaps in the bedchamber on the top floor beside his own."

Rowan nodded. "We'll go in wi' Archie, as we discussed, through the yett and up the steps. We have business wi' Simon, after all. But Archie and Geordie will gather the guards in the barnekin and distract them somehow."

"We'll set a fire if we have to," Archie said, nodding.

"Then we'll split up and search each floor until we find her," Rowan said. "Ready your pistols and weapons."

"Eh, scumfishing's the way," Sandie grumbled.

"I heard once o' reivers who took a tower by the roof," Christie said. "They cut down a tall pine tree and leaned it against the wall, and climbed up its branches. Then they took off the roof and went in." Sandie gave a soft, approving hoot.

Heavy clouds floated past the moon. Rowan glanced up again. "Another storm comes for certain. Let's go. Geordie, hand me the papers, and the mirror as well. I mean to tempt Simon."

"And well you should, after what we've discovered," Geordie answered, giving him the stone and the pages.

Rowan gathered his reins and led the way. The silence among the others was as determined and as grim as his own.

Thunder growled overhead as they rode toward the tower.

Smoke swirled into the tiny house, filling it quickly, obscuring the milky light. Mhairi covered her nose and mouth with her hand, and tried to breath shallowly. Simon had sealed the first window by leaning a board against it, then had thrown burning, pitch-soaked rags inside the second small window. Black smoke poured upward, choking the light and the breathable air.

Mhairi tried to stamp out the rags, but saw that they would burn themselves out quickly; the smoke was the greater threat. She could scarcely fill her lungs, and her eyes were tearing.

She would have to go out, though she knew Simon waited. But he did not know that she had the pistol. Gripping it tightly, aiming it straight ahead, she opened the door.

But as she eased out, Simon jumped at her from the side and grabbed her. The gun fell from her hand as he pinned her arms to her sides and lifted her from the ground. Although she kicked and struggled, screaming loudly, he did not relax his hold as he carried her across the roof.

She saw two guards inside one of the turrets. They looked out the door and clearly saw Simon dragging her away, but then turned back inside as if they had no intention of interfering.

"Are none of your men honest?" she cried breathlessly. "Are they all like you, traitors to Scotland, and agents of Spain?"

"You were looking in the spyhole after all," he said. "I thought so. Then you did see Heckie attack me."

"I saw you attack *him,*" she said through clenched teeth.

"You saw wrong," he said forcefully. "And you saw naught, if you value your life, and the lives o' your husband and kin."

"You canna barter my silence," she said.

"I wouldna want to kill you," he said. "But a fall from this tower might prove deadly. Or a fall down the watchtower steps." He set her on her feet, still holding her securely.

Thunder rumbled loudly overhead. Simon glanced up, and Mhairi stomped on his foot, then kicked backward and caught him hard in the knee. He grunted and faltered. An instant later, she let her weight drop, bending her knees and sliding downward out of his grip. She shoved him and ran. Simon stumbled and fell, then rose to his feet, cursing.

As she ran for the turret, he lunged toward her. Spinning, she pounded across the roof back toward the chimney house. She scooped up the pistol with both hands, swinging wildly around to point the gun at him.

"Stay there," she said. "I'll fire this. 'Tis loaded."

He took a step closer. "You wouldna hit me wi' that thing, Mhairi lass."

"I can," she insisted. "I will fire it."

"I willna harm you."

"I saw you backstab a man coldly," she said. "You wouldna stop at killing me."

He took another step forward. "'Tis a shame you saw Heckie and me, lass. I was hoping you and I would be better comrades than this, hey." He held out his hand. "Give me the pistol."

Behind him, in the darkness, she saw the turret door open. Shadowed figures crossed the roof. Mhairi flickered

her glance between the advancing men and Simon,
fearing that the guards would only help their warden.

He dove toward her, swatting his arm toward the gun
barrel. As Mhairi took a quick, instinctive step backward,
her foot hit the edge of the sloped roof. She stumbled, her
arm flew wide, and the pistol misfired, an explosion of
sound and flashing light. The recoil jarred her arm and
knocked her fully back. She dropped the gun as she fell.

Simon lunged then and grabbed her roughly, hauling
her to her feet, spinning her around to trap her in front of
him with one arm. She felt the tip of his dagger at her
throat and wrapped her hands around his arm, but could
not free herself.

"A loaded pistol canna be trusted," Simon growled.
"One poor shot, and 'tis useless. Now, lass, come wi'
me." He pushed her forward a little, then stopped
abruptly. Mhairi glanced up and gasped.

"She'll come wi' me, I think." Rowan's deep voice cut
like a keen, capable blade through the rising wind. Mhairi
widened her eyes as he stepped out of the shadows, a
pistol held steady in his hand.

Wind whipped his hair, and he stared unmoving at
Simon, like a dark, powerful angel of judgment.

"Blackdrummond, you blasted scoundrel," Simon
growled. Rowan saw how tightly the warden held Mhairi,
saw the stinging gleam of the dagger point as it pressed
the gentle undercurve of her jaw. He wondered what had
happened in the time she had been alone with Simon, and
he had an overwhelming urge to lunge for the man and
destroy him. But he only gripped his gun tighter, glancing
once at Mhairi and away.

"Simon," he said with a steady, disguising calm in his
voice and an icy contempt in his expression.

"What are you doing up here?" Simon demanded.

"We came to Abermuir to talk with you. And we found
Heckie's body in the hall." Mhairi sucked in her breath.
Rowan guessed that she had seen that awful sight, and he
turned an even colder gaze on Simon.

"The rascal jumped me," Simon said. "I had to kill
him."

Rowan had turned the body over, and had seen the

wound that had killed Heckie. "Did you?" he asked. "By stabbing him in the back? And he held only a wine cup, if I remember."

Simon glowered at him, his face shadowed beneath the rim of his helmet. Mhairi glanced quickly from Simon to Rowan.

"Simon and Heckie have been together in this spying ring—" she said breathlessly, then cried out as Simon pressed the dagger blade against her jaw.

Rowan took a step forward, his fingers tense on the pistol. But even if he shot Simon, the man could still slit Mhairi's throat. "Touch her again with that blade and you will have nae head on your shoulders," he said. "Tell me again, Mhairi," he said, without looking at her. He could not look, or lose his hard won control. "You said that Heckie and Simon are spies?"

"She tells lies to protect her brother," Simon said. "Though I suspected Heckie was in on it all along."

"Did you?" Rowan asked calmly. Thunder grumbled somewhere nearby. Rowan saw Simon glance upward, and saw how convulsively he squeezed Mhairi as he held her. The coming storm seemed to distract him. Mhairi had wrapped her hands around Simon's leather sleeved arm to relieve some of the pressure of his grip, but Rowan began to fear that Simon would choke her as he grew more anxious.

"Let go of her," Rowan said, low and fierce.

"Bring me the prisoners I want," Simon said.

"I've done that." He beckoned, and Alec and Iain stepped out of the shadows behind him. "Now let her go."

Mhairi gasped, clearly stunned. "Rowan, nay—"

"Dinna fret, my lass," he said gently. He had forgotten that Mhairi might think he had fulfilled Simon's orders. "I am loyal to my kin. And they to me. Lads!" he called softly.

Alec and Iain lifted pistols and pointed them at Simon.

"What is this?" Simon snapped viciously. "They should be arrested. Where are my guards?" He whipped his head around, keeping his constrictive hold on Mhairi.

"Archie and Geordie Bell and my grandfather are seeing to your guards," Rowan said. "We've started a small fire in the barnekin. Just enough to give your

watchmen a task," he added calmly. "And Sandie Scott
and Devil's Christie came up here with us. They are
tending to the watchmen in that turret."

"Archie wi' you! By hell! You'll both hang for this!
Deputies canna usurp their warden. I represent the king's
authority here. 'Tis an act o' treason."

"Is it?" Rowan asked. He reached into the unhooked
upper part of his leather jack and withdrew a folded
paper. "And what is this?" He held the paper out.

Simon jerked. "A warrant for your blasted arrest, I
hope!"

"'Tis a letter written in a Spanish code," Rowan
explained patiently. "The translation is quite poetic. A
lovely lady gathers red roses by the sea, it says, and
watches for the raven's moon, when the white rose will
blossom."

Simon snorted. "'Tis nonsense."

"Unless you understand what it signifies. And I do. I'll
barter with you, Simon. My wife for this—" He slid his
hand inside his jack again, and took out the black mirror.

Rowan saw Simon's shock in the tensing of his face
and posture. "I dinna know what that thing is," Simon
said disdainfully. "I am done wi' these games, Blackdrummond. You're my deputy. I'll give you a chance to
redeem yourself, or I will report this to the council and
the king myself. Now fetch my guards and have those two
scoundrels arrested for spying!"

Rowan held out the stone. "Take it," he said. "Go on."
He watched Simon evenly. The warden looked, for a
moment, tempted to snatch it and run. But he smiled flatly
at Rowan.

"Nonsense," he said curtly. "Why would I want that?"

"Just look at it, Simon," Mhairi said. Rowan nodded
approvingly, knowing that she tried to distract the warden
so that Rowan and the others could take him down.

He held it at an obliging angle so that Simon could see
the polished, smooth convex surface. A few splashes of
rain washed the slick skin of the stone to a glistening,
eerie, blackness.

Simon looked at it for a few seconds, then blinked and
grew pale beneath the shadow of his helmet. Thunder
crashed overhead and he glanced upward, squeezing

Mhairi to him. He looked anxiously toward the nearest turret door. Rowan saw that Simon was frightened. He wondered if he had seen something in the stone. Then he realized that the warden was deeply afraid of the approaching storm.

"We've got to get inside," Simon blurted. "Go ahead o' me."

"Soon," Rowan said, deliberately drawing out the moment. He too had no desire to be up on this roof in a fierce storm, but he would not give Simon the chance to get away so easily.

"If you dinna want the stone," he said, sliding it inside his jack, "perhaps you'll want what I found inside of it." He displayed the folded paper that he had tucked in his palm, flicking his fingers as if he had conjured it.

"What is that?" Simon barked. "Give it here."

Rowan smiled. "I'm sure you know well what 'tis. A writ from the Spanish government, signed by King Philip himself, promising the bearer payment in gold, and free passage on any Spanish trading ship. And it has your name written on it, Simon."

Simon watched him, his eyes narrowed. Mhairi clung to Simon's restraining arm, listening, her gaze fixed on Rowan. He glanced at her once, then away again, his heart pounding.

"This was why you wanted the raven's moon," Rowan went on smoothly. "'Twas supposed to be smuggled to you from that ship that wrecked."

Simon laughed. "Ridiculous. Why would I want that?"

Rowan heard the rising winds and the thunder that rolled closer, and wanted only to grab Mhairi and carry her to safety somewhere. But he nodded politely to Simon. "Why? My guess is that you made an agreement with the Spaniards, and planned to leave Scotland once you had gathered your fortune and completed your promise."

"Hah," Simon said. "Your brother and Mhairi's might have planned such a thing. I am a warden. A king's man."

"Are you for the king—or for yourself? What did you promise in exchange for tremendous wealth, and the chance to live out your days in a luxurious castle in a warmer climate, or even in the New World?"

"Paradise," Mhairi said suddenly. "You were looking for Paradise, weren't you, Simon?"

Rowan did not understand what she meant, but he saw a flicker of acknowledgment in Simon's shifting, haunted eyes.

"What did you promise them, Simon?" he asked. "Access to the Middle March, so that they could bring in troops and cross the border to invade England? You would have to be in league with agents in the East or West March for that. This ring of spies may be far larger than the privy council suspects."

Simon huffed a flat chuckle. "Pure fancy. You're trying to conceal your own involvement."

"We have your name," Rowan said softly, wiggling the folded paper. "I have already posted a report to the council by fast messenger." He had not yet, but he surely would. "Heckie is dead, but we will get Clem. I'm certain he knows all about this. And he willna be pleased that you've killed his brother. I dinna think you can look for loyalty from him."

Simon sucked in a sharp breath. "You canna prove anything." Thunder boomed, close and loud. Rowan saw Simon shift sideways toward the turret, dragging Mhairi along.

"Stop!" Iain called out as he and Alec stepped forward, their pistols aimed at Simon. Rowan held up a detaining hand.

"I said you canna prove any o' this!" Simon snapped. "You are all the criminals here. Guards!" he bellowed.

"We have proof, Simon," Rowan said.

"There is none!"

"Heckie took a gold medallion from me several weeks ago. I saw it again in that small box of gold that you claimed Iain had taken. But Iain and Alec say they took two large sacks o' gold from Heckie, rather than one small casket."

"Liars. Sneakbaits."

"Heckie didna take that medallion from me until after the gold had been stolen," Rowan said. "How did it get all the way into your tower and into that casket?"

Simon was silent, watchful, his breath heaving.

"Heckie must have given it to you later, after Iain was

taken," Rowan continued. He lifted his brows calmly. "That may be enough to prove the link between you two. You turned that casket over to the English warden, claiming that was all you had recovered. But two large sacks were taken from the shipwreck. Where is the rest, Simon?"

"You are all art and part in this together," Simon said stubbornly. A crackling stream of lightning flashed high overhead. "Go ahead of me down those steps if you want this lass to live. Go!" He motioned toward Rowan with his chin. "You hold a gun, but I hold your wife, and I'll cut her. Go!"

The wind sliced between them as he spoke, and the next blast of thunder seemed to shake the floor of the roof. Simon looked up as if in terror. Then he pushed Mhairi roughly, suddenly, into Rowan, with such force that they both went down together as Simon ran.

"Dinna fire!" Rowan shouted as Alec and Iain took off after Simon. He rolled to his feet, and lifted Mhairi away. She nodded to him that she was fine and stood up, silent and calm. Rowan moved across the roof toward the others.

Simon was already running toward the turret, with Alec and Iain behind him. The door opened, and Archie and Geordie stepped out, pistols held steady. Jock came behind them with several troopers at his back. Simon spun away, knocking heavily into Alec and Iain and running past them in a panic.

The sky seemed to split open as lightning illuminated the dark clouds from within and thunder roared overhead. A powerful blast of wind tore across the roof, and Rowan turned back to push Mhairi toward a small guardhouse on top of the pitched roof.

"Get inside!" he yelled, desperately wanting her safe. "Go!"

She scrambled toward the small house and pulled open the door, fighting the wind. Rowan turned to see Simon run toward another door. Sandie and Christie stepped out of that one and stared at him, weapons held ready.

Simon spun, turned, stopped, turned again, and then dashed toward the parapet. Rowan ran forward, but stopped, uncertain what Simon intended to do.

Thunder resounded again, so powerful that Rowan felt its reverberation throughout his body. The wind beat his clothes back and whirled through his hair. He looked up to see heavy clouds roll menacingly over the moon. Lightning flashed inside the clouds like lantern light.

He waved to Alec and Iain. "Get inside!" he shouted. They turned. Simon hesitated by the parapet edge, staring upward.

"Simon!" Rowan yelled. "Go there!" He gestured toward the nearest turret, where Sandie and Christie waved him toward them. Simon hesitated again, then moved in that direction.

Rowan spun and looked for shelter as well. Mhairi held the door of the guardhouse open for him. He ran there and turned just outside the doorway, one hand holding the door open.

Thunder cracked like a cannon. Out of the black sky, another stiff, silvery thread of lightning spooled down directly toward the roof.

Crossing the roof, Simon suddenly seemed to jerk and throw his arms upward. A glowing cage of light slid over his helmet and breastplate and enveloped him in its delicate, fatal web. He seemed to hover in the air for an eternal moment.

Rowan stepped forward, but then stopped, knowing he could do nothing. Beside him, Mhairi gasped and covered her face with her hands. He turned her gently inside the guardhouse and shut the door, then ran across the roof.

Curled on the floor of the chimney house, coughing from the lingering smoke inside, Mhairi slowly sat up and wiped a shaking hand over her face. She felt stunned and numb, hardly able or willing to think about what she had just seen. She got to her feet, but her knees trembled so much that she leaned against the wall for a moment.

Outside, she heard shouting, heard Rowan call out to the others to keep back. Thunder rumbled overhead, its power beginning to fade. She rested her head against the wall and wrapped her arms around herself until her shallow breaths slowed and her legs became more steady.

After a while, she heard no more voices. She imagined that they were probably moving Simon's body, but she

did not want to look out the window. Pushing back her
hair wearily, she stepped forward in the darkness, but her
foot caught one of the lances leaning against the wall, and
she stumbled to her knees.

As she put her hands down to get up again, her fingers
slipped inside a wide crack between two loose planks in
the wooden floor. She pushed down on the wobbling
board, but it would not fit into place, as if it was
obstructed from below.

She knelt there in the darkness, and smelled the residue
of the smoke, and suddenly remembered another house,
burned weeks ago, a house with a false wooden floor in
the loft.

She tugged on the board, then pulled harder. Lifting an
end of the plank, she shifted it to one side. The chimney
house had been constructed over the pitched roof of the
tower, and the wooden floor that surrounded the chimney
was a mere platform. Underneath the wooden planks lay
empty space. Mhairi reached into the blackness.

Not so empty, after all. Her hand closed on thick,
coarse cloth, and she felt, inside that, something bulky
and hard. She found a loose corner of the cloth and tugged
it aside.

Then she heard the door open, and looked up to see
Rowan step into the tiny room. Mhairi caught her breath
and stood, moving quickly toward him across the
planking. He held out his arms to her in the darkness, and
she went into that safe, strong circle, bowing her head
against his chest.

Rowan held her silently, his lips against her hair,
against her brow, his hands steady on her back. She tilted
her head and found his mouth, and wrapped her arms
around his neck.

Thunder rumbled again, and another flash of lightning
lit the room. Rowan looked down at her in its flickering
whiteness.

"Mhairi, Simon is—"

"I know," she whispered against his cheek. "I know.
Come here, Rowan." She took his hand and pulled him
toward the open section of the floor, and knelt. He bent
one knee and reached down, pulling the cloth aside.

"God have mercy," he said in a low voice. "This must

be all of it. There's another sack beneath this one." He dug his fingers down, and Mhairi heard a cool chinking sound.

Lightning poured an instant of brilliance into the room as Rowan spilled a fortune in shining gold out of his hand. Mhairi saw it shimmer, then watched as Rowan tucked the coins back inside the cloth sack.

"The English queen will get her Spanish gold after all," Rowan said, looking at Mhairi.

"Then this will clear you of any charges the English might lay against you," she whispered.

"Aye," he said. "Aye." He took her hands and pulled her toward him, then enveloped her in his embrace, resting his cheek on her head.

Thunder rolled again, quieter now, and rain began to patter on the roof of the chimney house, and Rowan held her. Mhairi listened to the rhythm of the rain, and to the beat of his heart, and felt contentment warm her in spite of all she had witnessed that night.

"Simon feared that these storms would bring the end of the world," she murmured after a while. "And the world ended for him in just the way he dreaded."

"Aye." Rowan brushed a tousled slip of hair from her brow, his fingers infinitely gentle. "But you and I, my lass," he whispered, "have found the beginning of our world."

Mhairi turned her face up to his, and felt his lips on her own, and knew that he was right.

Epilogue

~

"Be content, be content,
Be content wi me lady;
Now ye are my wedded wife
Until the day ye die, lady."

—*"Rob Roy"*

Rowan rested a hand on the cold, smooth, slender fingers of the old tomb sculpture, and looked at Isobel Scott's gracefully carved, serene face. Like this lady, Maggie, too, was gone, but he had never had the chance to take his farewell of her. He had come down here for a few moments to release her as best he could.

He thought of the night he had confronted Alec over this tomb. He had revealed his anger and his resentment that night, only to find that he had not, after all, been betrayed.

Rather, two people had loved him, and had loved his son, and had only tried to show it. He drew a deep breath, feeling humbled and honored, and knew that he was finally content to let go of what had haunted him for three years.

He turned, scanning the small, dark chamber, and saw glowing streams of sunlight slice through the cracks in the masonry. The crypt, with its broken walls and dark shadows, would soon be rebuilt, as would all of Lincraig Castle. He had already hired the workmen who would construct a fine new tower in the barnekin yard, using the old stones.

He had received word from the English queen, who had decided to reward him and Alec for finding the missing Spanish gold, and for uncovering, through interrogating

Clem Elliot, clues that led to a chain of Scottish spies who plotted with Spain against England. Elizabeth had sent a sum of gold that would be enough to rebuild Lincraig, and still keep the Blackdrummond Scotts comfortable for generations.

He walked toward the steps, turning again to glance back at the silent tombs of the Lincraig Scotts. He would honor their memory by repairing their crypt without changing its design.

Ascending the stairs, he moved out of the shadows and into the wide expanse of the chapel ruin, through translucent shafts of sunlight. He walked through the ruins and out into the yard, where the spring breeze ruffled his hair and shirtsleeves, and the gentle heat of the sun warmed his brow.

Mhairi waited there for him, holding his son's hand in hers. She turned and smiled softly, and came toward him. Jamie toddled past her, stopping to pick up a rock and put it down, then ran to choose another. But Mhairi looked only at Rowan.

She glided forward easily, gracefully, like the clouds that skimmed with the breeze overhead. Her gown blew softly around her, and she placed her hands on the gentle swell of her abdomen, where their child was nurtured within.

Rowan smiled and held out his hand to her, drinking in all of her as she came near. Her cheeks were whipped pink in the breeze, her dark, silken braid slid over one shoulder, and her eyes shone like new silver. And the soul that illuminated those eyes offered him more than he ever could have dreamed.

He would always feel this sense of wonder when he looked at her, always be aware of the privilege of loving her for as long as he lived, and longer.

"Jamie and I have been discussing the building plans while you were in the chapel," she said. "He has a fine eye for choosing stone, as you can see."

Jamie turned to show his newest rock, and Rowan admired it, then caught it deftly as it was flung toward him.

"While you were in the chapel, Iain and Alec came to bring me a letter," she said, pointing to where two other horses were tethered beside Valentine and Peg. "They've gone down into one of the towers to look at the foundations, since you asked for their opinion on the new tower."

"And your letter?" he asked. "Who is it from?"

"My parents are coming home from Denmark!" She smiled. "My father finally received my letter—along with the second one telling him that Iain is fine—and he and my mother will be arriving in Edinburgh early next month. I want to ride there to meet them, if we can. Iain and Jennet and Robin will come too."

He brushed back an errant drift of her rich brown hair, its reddish tint evident in the sun. "Of course we'll go," he said. "I will need to make another report to the council by then."

"Since you turned down the warden's post they offered, will they ask you to serve somewhere else?" she asked.

He shrugged. "For now, I'm content to be Archie Pringle's deputy in the Middle March. I've been gone from Blackdrummond for too long. I want to spend time with my family and rebuild Lincraig. Then I'll be ready for a warden's post."

She nodded. He put his arm around her and felt her arm come around his waist, and their steps fell into a gentle rhythm. He mused to himself that their bodies always seemed to fit together, whether they walked, or rested, or made love, as if they had been formed in harmony for each other.

Although he knew that they were both too strong-willed by nature to become docile and dull together, the conflict that had once existed between them had taught them a good deal about each other, and about themselves. Now they shared a deep bond of love and acceptance at the core of their marriage.

"Alec says he's decided to take the position in Liddesdale, as deputy to your cousin, the Keeper there," she said, stirring him out of his thoughts.

He nodded. "I know. He'll be leaving soon."

"Jamie will miss him," she said softly.

"Da, my da," Jamie said, and threw another stone.

"He wants Jamie to spend time living with us so that he'll become less devoted to Alec, I think," she said.

"Jamie will never lose his devotion to Alec," he said.

"Nor should he." They moved through the yard in silence for a few moments, while Jamie ran circles around them, looking for interesting stones. As they went, Rowan glanced through the ruined outer gate. The Lincraig hill was green now, and the strip of the road visible from here was a dry brown ribbon.

"I first saw you from that hill," Mhairi said, looking in the same direction. "Through a fierce storm. And I wondered then if you were the man my brother had seen in that vision."

He pulled her close, resting his cheek against her head. "And I first saw you inside the black stone," he said.

"Stone," Jamie echoed, and picked one up from the ground.

"What will you do with the black mirror?" she asked.

"Keep it where it is, wrapped and put away. We may never know where it came from, or why it has the power that it has."

"Iain thinks the Spaniards might have gotten it in the New World," she said. "He said he's heard of a similar kind of vision stone from our brother Conor, who sails the Spanish Main. But whoever used it to smuggle the document to Simon didna seem to know about its power. Only you and I discovered that, I think."

"Wherever it came from, lass," he said, "that stone led me to you. 'Tis all I need to know about it."

She smiled and wrapped her arms around his waist, and he buried his lips in the sweet silk of her hair. Jamie came over to them and held up his empty hand. "Roon!" he said.

Rowan smiled and took the tiny hand in his, and felt Jamie squeeze his fingers. He pulled Mhairi close with his other hand, caressing the gentle thickening at her waist.

He looked toward the dazzling sunlight that filled the spring sky, and knew that he held in his hands all that had ever been missing in his life, and his heart was full.

Author's Note

~

Writing historical fiction about the Scottish Border reivers is a little like writing a western. The two societies had much in common, from cattle theft to nests of outlaws to posses and lynchings. The Scottish Borderers were often bold, notorious, brash, violent, noble, and even comical. I have tried to convey some of that, and thoroughly enjoyed my foray into their territory. For information on reiving, truce days, Leges Marchiarum, and so on, I am indebted to many fine research sources, none more so than George MacDonald Fraser's fascinating study of the Borderers, *The Steel Bonnets: The Story of the Anglo-Scottish Border Reivers* (London, Harvill/Harper Collins 1971).

As in *The Raven's Wish* (Topaz Books, 1995), I have again used verses from old Scottish ballads to head each chapter and provide an echo for the action, or to highlight some aspect of the story. The most reliable source for this form of Scottish poetry is Francis James Child, *The English and Scottish Popular Ballads,* which was published in five volumes from 1882 to 1898, and can be found in a reprint edition from Dover Publications.

I hope you enjoyed *The Raven's Moon*. Please look for *Lady Miracle* from Topaz Books in late 1997. Set in fourteenth-century Scotland, it is the story of Michaelmas from *The Angel Knight*.

I love to hear from readers. Feel free to write to me (please include a self-addressed stamped envelope for a reply) at P.O. Box 356, Damascus, Maryland 20872.

If you enjoyed THE RAVEN'S MOON's
wonderful blend of deeply emotional,
heartfelt romance and the vivid Scottish
setting filled with mist, magic, and the
beauty of the Highlands, treat yourself to
Susan King's next magnificent novel,

LADY MIRACLE

Here is a special early preview.

LADY MIRACLE by Susan King will be
on sale this fall from Topaz Books

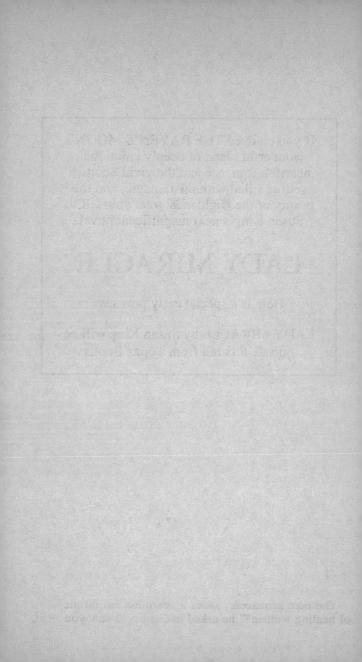

Prologue

~

Galloway, Scotland
Summer, 1311

She walked among the wounded like sunlight gliding through shadows. Mists floated over the field, obscuring the bodies of those who had fallen in that morning's battle, but Diarmid Campbell saw the girl clearly. He watched her, his fingers still as they gripped the scalpel, his attention captured for an instant.

Her pale gown and golden braids seemed to shimmer in the veiled light as she moved. Surrounded by mist and mud, she looked ethereal and graceful as she bent toward a wounded man and touched his forehead.

Like an angel come to find the dying souls, Diarmid thought. Then he shook his head to clear his battle-weary mind. No, not blessed vision on this cursed field, just a fair, slight girl carrying a basin of water and a handful of bandaging cloths. Obviously she had come with the local women to help in the aftermath of the battle between English and Scots.

Diarmid wiped the back of his hand, red with other men's blood as well as his own, over his sweaty brow. Then he bent to examine an arrow wound in a Highlandman's calf muscle.

The man grimaced, "Does a beardless lad do the work of healing women?" he asked in Gaelic. "I saw you fight, lad. That I know that you can do, and your brother with you."

"I have not yet reached my majority, that's true," Diarmid said mildly, "though I did study with the infirmarian at Mullinch Priory. And I have repaired hundreds of wounds more serious than yours."

"Ach," the man growled. "Then do the work and be quick."

Diarmid grasped the wooden shaft, set his jaw in determination, and swiftly yanked out the embedded iron tip. As the man gasped, Diarmid drenched the fresh wound with wine poured from a flask. Then he readied a silk thread and a steel needle, cleansed them and his fingers in a trickle of wine, and stitched the flesh together rapidly. Wrapping the leg in linen torn from the man's shirt, he looked up.

"Change the cloth often and pour wine or *uisge-beatha* over it when you can," he said. "And pour yourself a dram, too." The Highlander nodded his thanks.

Diarmid stood, swiping again at the blood that seeped from the cut near his left eye. He would have to ask Fionn to stitch it closed for him, though his brother had not a gentle hand for such work. For now, he would continue to ignore that as well as the aching gash on his left forearm.

He ignored, too, the lurking fear that he did not know enough about treating these wounded men, the fear that he could cause severe pain or even death through error or ignorance. He flexed his hands tightly as he walked across the field, and resisted the fatigue that made his steps drag.

He had not treated hundreds of battle wounds. He had told the Highlander that to reassure him. He had learned herbal lore and the ways of the body in illness and injury from a capable infirmarian, but the monk had had scant experience with battle wounds, and he had died before Diarmid had been able to learn all that he wanted to know about healing and the design of the body.

He knew far more now, most of it learned though experience, in grim circumstances outside the peaceful monastery infirmary. During the past year, while fighting beside fellow Highlanders for King Robert Bruce, Diarmid had routinely helped the wounded. Despite his youth he had earned a reputation as a capable surgeon. Necessity had proven a demanding teacher.

That morning his skills had been in constant demand. An English patrol had routed the small band of Highlandmen whom Diarmid had accompanied, and had left many of the Scots injured or dead on the damp ground. Some of the men were Diarmid's own Campbell kin, though he and his brother Fionn had been spared.

He had done his best to repair flesh and set broken bones swiftly and efficiently, but he had not been able to save every man who needed his skills. A quick hand, a keen eye, and a little training were not enough to stop the power of death. He shoved a hand through his tangled brown hair in mute frustration.

Glancing around, he saw the girl again. She glowed like a shaft of pale sunshine in the gray mist, a fragile thing, far too innocent and pure to be in such a sad, bloody place. As Diarmid watched, some of the wounded men called out to her or stared, as if she was a saint drifted down from heaven.

But Diarmid had no such illusions. The monks of Mullinch Priory had believed in miracles, but they had been sheltered men. At nineteen, Diarmid was well acquainted with the harshness of the temporal world. He had been educated by monks, but his father had trained him to be a warrior and a laird. He had seen death and devastating injury and had dealt them himself. Wielding a broadsword was as easy for him as using a scalpel.

Just now he wanted to use neither. He thought of Dunsheen Castle in the western Highlands, standing proud on its green isle, surrounded by water and mists and mountains. His new role as the laird there was challenge enough. His herds, his tenants, his widowed mother, and his wayward siblings all needed his attention in one way or another. But Dunsheen and its own would have to fend without him for a while longer.

Diarmid sighed as he walked across the field. Others moved through the wispy fog, too, injured men, whole men, the few women and a priest who had come to offer help and succor. The cries of the wounded echoed in the mist, chilling his soul.

He saw the girl kneel to cleanse a man's arm wound

and give him sips of water. She had a serene, assured manner, as if raw wounds and agony did not disturb her. He stopped and watched from a distance.

"If angels exist, they look like her," a voice murmured behind him.

"Ah, but angels are rare on battlefields, brother," Diarmid said, and turned.

Fionn Campbell nodded, his profile handsome and strong, framed by rich waves of brown hair. Diarmid knew, from images in still streams and polished steel mirrors, how much he and his younger brother resembled each other.

Fionn glanced at Diarmid, his gray eyes somber. "We have no time to contemplate the nature of the heavenly host. Come look at Iain Campbell over here. When one of the local wise women tried to repair his leg wound, it began to bleed heavily."

Diarmid followed Fionn's tall, spare form and knelt in the damp grass beside Iain Campbell, their distant cousin. The older man groaned and shifted as Diarmid examined the deep wound in his thigh, made from the wide sweep of an English broadsword. Wadding the cloth that Fionn handed him, Diarmid pressed it against the gushing wound for a few minutes. When there was little improvement, he sighed heavily and glanced at Fionn.

"Steady his leg," he directed. "I need to search the wound. If an artery is torn, I will have to close it before I can stitch this shut."

Fionn supported the thigh while Diarmid probed. "After this, you should tend to your own wounds," Fionn said. "The gash in your arm is bleeding through the bandage. And that cut over your eye is wide open again."

"My wounds will do for now. Later you can sew me shut."

"You will risk your life twice in one day, then," Fionn said. "Ask the angel to do it for you if you would survive."

Diarmid huffed a flat, humorless laugh and worked silently.

Fionn gazed over the field. "I've been watching her. She seems to know how to help these men. Perhaps she is an herb healer, or even a nun. Now, that would be a shame. She's truly fair, that one."

"She's too young to be a nun, or a skilled healer," Diarmid said as he bent over his task. He worked quickly and gently, but Iain Campbell passed out with a heavy sigh. Though that made Diarmid's work easier, it increased his concern.

"I mean to speak with her," Fionn said. "I wonder who she is. She has a sweet way about her. I will need a wife soon enough, you know. A fair one who could tend my battle wounds would be a blessing."

"Mm," Diarmid answered, distracted while he applied heavy pressure with the folded cloth. The cloth grew red far too quickly. He swore softly. "I need a strip of linen. Now!"

Fionn tore a long piece from the hem of his own shirt and handed it to him. Diarmid wrapped the cloth high on the leg, twisting it and holding it tight.

"If I cannot stop the flow—" he stopped, gazing at the unconscious man's pale face. The outcome was obvious.

"What did Brother Colum teach you in such cases?"

"Not enough before he died." Diarmid loosened the bandage, then tightened it again. "Pressure will do, or a tight band. Certain herbs will ease bleeding, but I have no simples or potions. I should have found a wise wife to beg a few herbs."

"None of us knew that an English patrol would attack us out here. We were assured that we could pass through his part of Galloway without threat. But then, we had the assurance of Englishmen," Fionn added. "Will the blood band work?"

"I will make it work," Diarmid said fiercely. After a moment he nodded. "It seems to be slowing some, thank God. I'll try to close it." He lifted the wineskin that hung at his belt, pulled the wax stopper free, and trickled wine over the wound. "Hold the leg," he said quietly.

As Fionn complied, Diarmid readied the needle with silk and dribbled wine, and began to pull together the deepest layer of muscle. He swore as blood pooled freely where he worked, making it difficult to see what he attempted to repair.

Leaning over his patient, he did not notice at first the

slight figure who knelt beside Fionn. When he glanced up, he saw the girl.

"Be gone," he said curtly.

"Let me help," she said. Her voice was young and soft, and she spoke in Gaelic, as he had, but he hardly noticed. A mix of voices floated over the field, Scots and northern English, Gaelic, the droning Latin of the priest. He understood them all.

"You can do nothing here," he said. He drew the needle in and out, in and out. Fionn and the girl watched.

Diarmid swore softly as the silk slid out of the needle, and swore again as the bleeding continued. He would have to find the opening in the artery or Iain Campbell would die soon. He rethreaded the needle and instructed Fionn to loosen and then tighten the blood band.

The girl leaned forward suddenly and laid her slender hands over the gaping, ugly slash. She drew in a deep breath.

"Girl!" Diarmid snapped. "Stop!"

"Hush." At the firm command he glanced at her in surprise. She was small and slight next to Fionn's muscular, plaid-draped physique, but she spoke like a queen. Eyes closed, back straight, she lifted her delicate golden head to the dreary, misted light.

She looked like a shining sword, beautifully shaped, hilted in gold and bladed in silver. Flawless and strong. Diarmid blinked in momentary astonishment, then stretched out his hand to remove her fingers from the wound.

Heat radiated from her hands. He paused in spite of the urgency, his fingers hovering over hers. She appeared to be praying, her hands cupped over the wound, her fingertips and palms stained deep red.

"Holy Mother of God," Fionn breathed after a moment.

The girl withdrew her reddened fingers, sliding them into her lap. Diarmid looked at the wound. The gushing flow had slowed considerably. He could see the tiny slice in the artery.

Diarmid repaired the tear, then closed the wound. He did not think about what he had seen as he worked. He simply could not address that yet. He focused on what he saw now, what he must do next, until he finished the task. Then he took the clean cloth that the girl handed him and wrapped it over the wound.

At last he looked up at the silent girl, who still knelt with her bloodstained hands in her lap. "He will live," he said quietly.

She nodded, a vulnerable little shake, as if her head were a trembling flower on a slender stem. She rose to her feet and wavered unsteadily.

Diarmid stood, too, reaching out to catch her arm and offer his support. "What was it you did?" he asked.

Her eyes were wide and round as she looked up, blue as a summer sky and fringed by gold-tipped lashes. Innocent, youthful eyes. Yet he saw wisdom in their depths, awareness, as if the soul that looked out at him had lived a long, long time.

"What is your name?" he asked softly. "I am Diarmid Campbell of Dunsheen."

"Michaelmas," she said. "Michaelmas Faulkener."

He frowned at the odd English name, but recognized that her surname belonged to an English knight who was now one of Robert Bruce's most loyal advisers. "Are you kin to Gavin Faulkener?"

She nodded. "He is my half brother. I came out here this morn with my mother and our priest to help. Kinglassie Castle is but a mile from this place. We heard the screams just after dawn," she added. "Oh! I must go. My mother is looking for me."

Diarmid did not let go of her arm, his long fingers rust red against her pale sleeve. Her bones felt fragile beneath his touch. "*Micheil,*" he said in Gaelic, unfamiliar with the sound of her strange English name. Michaelmas. He realized that she must be named for Saint Michael's Mass, a feast day, the twenty-ninth of September. "Your name is *Micheil?*"

She nodded at the Gaelic equivalent. "Michael will do."

"Tell me what you did, Michael. I have never seen the like."

"You're hurt." She reached up and touched the cut above his eye gently. He felt her fingertips tremble against his brow.

He looked down at the pale golden crown of her head, with its silky parting, and felt a distinct heat seep into his wound, like the warmth of sunlight or new wine. A moment later, he felt the heat throughout his body, as if he sat close to a fire.

As if this girl had fire in her touch.

She took her hand away. He lifted a finger to the cut and took it away, seeing only a thin line of blood on his fingertip. The stinging ache had diminished. He exchanged a quick glance with Fionn, who watched them intently.

"Sweet Mary," Diarmid breathed. "Girl, how do you come by such a gift?"

"My mother calls me," she said. He heard a voice sound from a far corner of the field. "I must go."

"Michael—" Diarmid reached out, but she stepped away.

"I must go," she said.

Diarmid looked up and saw the stocky priest walking toward them, accompanied by a slender, dark-haired woman who called out the girl's English name.

She glanced up at Diarmid. "You must never tell," she whispered. "My family knows, and our priest. But no one else. Promise me you will never speak of this."

Diarmid blinked in surprise. "You have the word of the laird of Dunsheen," he said.

"And his brother," Fionn added.

"Michael—" Diarmid began.

"God keep you, Dunsheen," she said. Then she spun away from them and ran lightly through the muddy field, lifting her skirts high, her thin legs nimble as she skimmed over rocks and tufted grasses.

"What in all this world and the next just happened?" Fionn asked after a moment. "I feel as if I've been struck by lightning."

Diarmid did, too. He watched silently as the girl greeted the slender woman and the priest and walked away with them.

"We've seen the making of a saint, brother," Fionn continued. "*Ach*, she will not wed me or any man. She'll become a nun, that one, and be beatified one day."

"She's better off in a convent, if what we saw is real."

"Real? For a lad taught by monks, you're a thorough skeptic. You should see the cut over your eye. I swear on my life and soul, it looks like it's been healing for days. We've seen a saint, man."

"Perhaps," Diarmid said. He touched the tender spot over his eye. "And if so, her family is wise to protect her. If others witness what she can do, or if the English ever discover her ability, she will be named a heretic."

"Pray, then, that her family keeps her well hidden." Fionn clapped his hand on Diarmid's shoulder. "But before she left, you should have asked her to tend to your arm. Now you have none but me to sew it for you."

Diarmid shot him a wry glance. "Let me find some strong wine first."

Fionn grinned.

Diarmid turned as someone called out for him. As he walked away, he glanced across the field once again. The girl had disappeared into the shifting mists, but he would not forget her.

She had shown him a golden miracle on this bloody field.

WE NEED YOUR HELP

To continue to bring you quality romance
that meets your personal expectations,
we at TOPAZ books want to hear from you.
Help us by filling out this questionnaire, and in exchange
we will give you a **free gift** as a token of our gratitude.

- Is this the first TOPAZ book you've purchased? (circle one)

      YES   NO

  The title and author of this book is: _____

  If this was not the first TOPAZ book you've purchased, how many have
  you bought in the past year?

      a: 0 - 5   b 6 - 10   c: more than 10   d: more than 20

- How many romances in total did you buy in the past year?

      a: 0 - 5   b: 6 - 10   c: more than 10   d: more than 20 _____

- How would you rate your overall satisfaction with this book?

      a: Excellent   b: Good   c: Fair   d: Poor

- What was the main reason you bought this book?

      a: It is a TOPAZ novel, and I know that TOPAZ stands
         for quality romance fiction
      b: I liked the cover
      c: The story-line intrigued me
      d: I love this author
      e: I really liked the setting
      f: I love the cover models
      g: Other: _____

- Where did you buy this TOPAZ novel?

      a: Bookstore   b: Airport   c: Warehouse Club
      d: Department Store   e: Supermarket   f: Drugstore
      g: Other: _____

- Did you pay the full cover price for this TOPAZ novel? (circle one)

      YES   NO

  If you did not, what price did you pay? _____

- Who are your favorite TOPAZ authors? (Please list)

- How did you first hear about TOPAZ books?

      a: I saw the books in a bookstore
      b: I saw the TOPAZ Man on TV or at a signing
      c: A friend told me about TOPAZ
      d: I saw an advertisement in_____magazine
      e: Other: _____

- What type of romance do you generally prefer?

      a: Historical   b: Contemporary
      c: Romantic Suspense   d: Paranormal (time travel,
         futuristic, vampires, ghosts, warlocks, etc.)
      d: Regency   e: Other: _____

- What historical settings do you prefer?

      a: England   b: Regency England   c: Scotland
      e: Ireland   f: America   g: Western Americana
      h: American Indian   i: Other: _____

- What type of story do you prefer?

  a: Very sexy
  b: Sweet, less explicit
  c: Light and humorous
  d: More emotionally intense
  e: Dealing with darker issues
  f: Other

- What kind of covers do you prefer?

  a: Illustrating both hero and heroine
  b: Hero alone
  c: No people (art only)
  d: Other_____

- What other genres do you like to read (circle all that apply)

  Mystery   Medical Thrillers   Science Fiction
  Suspense   Fantasy   Self-help
  Classics   General Fiction   Legal Thrillers
  Historical Fiction

- Who is your favorite author, and why?_____
  _____

- What magazines do you like to read? (circle all that apply)

  a: *People*   b: *Time/Newsweek*
  c: *Entertainment Weekly*   d: *Romantic Times*
  e: *Star*   f: *National Enquirer*
  g: *Cosmopolitan*   h: *Woman's Day*
  i: *Ladies' Home Journal*   j: *Redbook*
  k: Other:_____

- In which region of the United States do you reside?

  a: Northeast   b: Midatlantic   c: South
  d: Midwest   e: Mountain   f: Southwest
  g: Pacific Coast

- What is your age group/sex?   a: Female   b: Male

  a: under 18   b: 19-25   c: 26-30   d: 31-35   e: 36-40
  f: 41-45   g: 46-50   h: 51-55   i: 56-60   j: Over 60

- What is your marital status?

  a: Married   b: Single   c: No longer married

- What is your current level of education?

  a: High school   b: College Degree
  c: Graduate Degree   d: Other:_____

- Do you receive the TOPAZ *Romantic Liaisons* newsletter, a quarterly newsletter with the latest information on Topaz books and authors?

  YES   NO

  If not, would you like to?   YES   NO

  Fill in the address where you would like your free gift to be sent:

  Name:_____
  Address:_____
  City:_____ Zip Code:_____

  You should receive your free gift in 6 to 8 weeks.
  Please send the completed survey to:

Penguin USA•Mass Market
Dept. TS
375 Hudson St.
New York, NY 10014